KESHED

Stu Hennigan

ORTAC PRESS

We can regard our life as a uselessly disturbing
episode in the blissful repose of nothingness.

SCHOPENHAUER

N O

first retch

sunken zone coma state prepostlife bliss touch taste smell hear see

NO
THING

second

bile tongue savage burn brain ***sparks*** senses stir crack dark
fight light one birth too many one way dont remain thoughtless
thought slips away swims back

d

o

w

n

CONSCIOUS

rancid liquid squirting chin soggy torso peristaltic rush rapid breath spit reset deep slow in and out and in and out in and out got to keep it *down* guts crease pain stabs needles knives fetid bargain basement raw spirit choking gasping fighting sucking air like life itself convulsing waves eyes nose pouring tears snot hacking coughing puke spatters weakly wet cotton sticky chest hair halfawake fully drunk trapped gyroscopic blur unfixed centre ceaseless motion breathless sickness

going
going
one
more
heave
FUCK
d e e p b r e a t h
iiiiiiiiiiiiiiiiiiiiiiiiiiiiiiiin
and
gone

sinks back spent lumpy chair slept when time no more head pounding blood pumping tumescent mess brain tissue throbbing vein could pop just like *that* end whole sorry scene teeth chattering lips contorting parodic ecstatic gurning muscles wracked iceblood shivers pumice stone tongue mouth hot desert sand wasted arms fleshless ribs brief warmth sick shirt cooling clinging cloying chill spinning slowing living room wreck spinesnapped sofa dead tv fireplace mirror shattered object hurled fury lost unremembered blur indeterminate past curtains torn sunshine spewing double glazed glass splashing winewhite light stains floor whats that fucking *smell*

stale fags poison seeping gaping pores petrol reek white label something else rich organic ripe oh fuck not *again* clammy claggy wet denim bending double gagging dry elbows knees hands cupping head plastered arse tepid shit glint sun glass weightless vessel head back bottle tipped vain hope drops dregs fumes no *nothing* shakes it bone dry drained primal screech standing slowmo wobbling cushion sticking wet cloth peeling thoughts of scalded skin faecal stench lurching blindly up rests sink halfupright bearing scant weight trembling cold grimy bath grasping old pint tin ravaged facehole turbid moist relief semisolid soggy grainy boking scratching tongue desperate hands nails splintered bitten quick skin cracked sore cuticles rusty red spitting tab end misted flat foul ale climbing in turning tap arctic cold stealing breath shocked melting merging burning gelid cling clothes growing warm shuddering marionette full grand mal shower swilling rotten cavern tearing threads free running water stickman frame washing wiping sick sticky diarrhoetic shit fingers thin grey crows claws lifting rags jet scrubbing wanting craving needing

drink

drink

drink

drink

drink

drink

drink

tap back wet towel slick black tiles mildewed drying dead flesh skin stretched tight on bone only clothes horse dressing torn jeans black top shapeless holes damp loam mould shit sweat needing needing *needing* cupboards bare sick sick sick cant wont *must* leave need need fucking *need* loose carpet tripping broken rail sharp stab

bleeding palm down stairs shoes wallet keys together praise the
saints in fucking heaven key lock tumblers click rattle chain cold
brass handle cold white hand heart mouth horrors here horrors
there sunlight traffic noise people people all those *people* hinges
creak door ajar

no

yes

no no no no no no no **NO**

swallowing acidbilepuke deep clean hit morning air

NO

door wide

NO

head follows neck follows chest follows waist follows legs follows feet

NO

stepping

NO

From one world

NO

to the next

NO

and outside to face

TH

EN

1

Later he'd say he could never forget the night they met but the truth was he could barely remember a fucking thing. He knew the story off by heart, mind, all those years of spinning the same tired yarn, and he had a feel for the gist but he'd picked up the details second-hand; the memories belonged to someone else.

He'd had a shithouse morning, that was for sure. He'd caught his usual white-knuckle ride to the site in Billy the Scrote's death-trap Transit and rocked up at half seven, brain-fogged and head-fucked from a post-work pint last night that had collapsed into an eight-hour sesh round town with a cheeky gram scored from an old crony in Spoons to boot. He was hanging bad style till first brew, but a couple of menthol rollies and a coffee-with-four perked him up just about enough to remind Big Marl that he'd booked the afternoon off.

You what? The gaffer wheezed past his fag, red-eyed, jowls wobbling like a Basset Hound. He must've been a fit fella in his prime, but he was fit for nothing but the knacker's yard now, knocking sixty, swathed in so much lard from his ten-pints-of-Guinness-a-night diet that he couldn't move any part of his body without another bit rippling in sympathy. Ah never said you could finish early today. We've shit to do, lad.

Come off it, Marl, we sorted this last week. The fat fuck was trying it on, and they both knew it. Ah've mentioned it every day since. An I told you again last night before we knocked off. Ah know yer memory's shite cos of yer age an that but it's not *that* bad.

Well, you musta mentioned it quietly cos Ah never heard you.

Ah'm jacking at twelve, Marl, Ah don't give a fuck what you say.

You best get that brew down yer neck sharpish then, boyo. If yer fuckin off early we've whole day's work to get in afore you do.

Nightmare. He'd been planning an easy run-in, skulking through his hangover, taking his sweet time with tidying and shit-shovelling he could do in minutes if he had to, or hiding in the Portabog for half an hour at a stretch playing Snake on his Nokia burner if he was too rough to even manage that, unless some scruffy bastard had got in there and polluted it first. But Marl meant business and he was in no state to argue with the coke jitters in full swing, armpits pissing gin sweat. Before he'd finished his third fag the noise started.

Gerronwithitthen you fuckin lazy cunt. Yer havin t'afternoon off not whole bastard day. Shape yersen. There's plenty other lads wantin to work for us an Ah'd get more graft outta them an all. If you weren't yer father's son Ah'd've got shot of you ages ago.

And on, and on, and on.

And on.

A backbreaking morning, his muscles burning from humping bags of compo up the skeleton staircases into the second-floor attic of the new build they'd boarded out the day before; slopping gallons of water into the tub, dumping in the plaster, churning it up with a drill that was basically a kitchen blender the size of a small child. Mixing looked a piece of piss when someone else was doing it but it was fucking hard work on his arms and chest, the way the drill twisted and kicked against his hands like the recoil from a twelve bore. The hangover didn't help, like, but that was standard.

Few months labouring for Marl'll fill yer skinny frame out good an proper, his old man had said when he'd first swung him the job, but it felt like it'd kill him most days and often he wished it would. Anything to avoid carrying another twenty-five kilos up those fucking stairs.

The embryonic house, little more than a brick and wooden frame like the twenty others they still had to do on the new estate, was airless in the morning heat. Rank smell of fresh sweat, stale booze, dry compo and the soggy stench of Marl's eggy farts fought with the acrid pall from the Bensons the wittering old cunt chained while he blathered on the scratch coat, chuntering all the time about the fuckin braindead twats he had to put up wi' and how they'd never have lasted five minutes when he were learning t'trade and t'first thing they taught you were pride in t'job.

He was about to start on a fresh batch when he clocked the time. Quarter past twelve. Fuck's sake. That was an extra fifteen minutes he'd had weaselled out of him. He'd bet his last tenner Marl knew it was past midday and never said; he'd have to make sure to get that back next week, and a bit more on top. He couldn't have the boss thinking he could put one over on him that easily.

Right Marl, Ah'm away.

Yer can't go now. Ah need another mix.

Get someone else to do it. Or do it yersen. Ah'm done. See you Monday.

That'll give us summat ter look forward ter, won't it, like, eh? How—

But he was downstairs already, Marl's chelping drowned out by the lumpen dinosaur shite – Led Zeppelin or Deep Purple or some similarly bloated atrocity – blaring from the tinny transistor, half-petrified with decades of dust, that never left his side.

He was on the train by two, showered and changed and ready for action. It'd been a while since he'd had a sesh out of town. They'd not seen each other much since Rob moved away and the useless fucker never replied to texts anymore; the idea of picking up a phone and actually *talking* was so ridiculous it never even occurred. It was a forty-five-minute ride so he snuck in a few cans for starters, chugged them out of a plain white carrier stashed under the seat when no one was looking. The cheap cider tang fizzed the gypsum grains from the back of his throat, blunted the edge of the headache that was blinding him behind his shades.

He stuck his head on the cool glass as the train pulled away, looked on as the town was swallowed by a grassy blur of countryside. Cow fields, the greyblue snake of the Aire, the turbid, shitbrown run of the canal, the climbing slopes of the moorland pastures spotted with dirty sheep and tumbledown barns broken up by the graphite pencil lines of age-old drystone walls. A roll-call of mill towns sped by; Keighley, Bingley, Saltaire, places that boomed when the hills were alive with the shake rattle and roll of shuttles and weaves, shrouded in smog from the industrial big bang that ignited the global capitalist dawn, but had fallen as fast as they'd risen and could never even dream of reaching those heights again. A few surviving chimneys remained here and there but not like when he was a kid and he'd fed the ducks with his gran on the towpath near the old tin bridge, dodging the furred white dogshit festering in the penile shadows of these relics. With the antiquated barges lining the cutting, the smoke from the coal fires in the terraces built for the workers way back when, the lonely call of the rag and bone man echoing with the clop of his horse's hooves on the cobbled backstreets and his grandparents' tales of the crippling poverty they'd grown up in ringing in his ears, the old days were close enough to touch, like he'd been born way before his time and lived it all himself. Most of the mills had been turned into flats or offices and the chimneys demolished, the comfortable disease of progress reshaping and readapting them for the twenty first century, workers in flat caps and clogs replaced by a new wave of drones in high street smart-casuals, the textile din that deafened his forefathers wound down to a background hum of clacking keyboards, buzzing photocopiers, dial tones like flatlining heart monitors.

Subtly at first, the countryside receded into the past and the train slowed into the sprawling railyards of the main station, rusty redorange tracks branching out like spider's legs, the hills and mills traded for tower blocks and warehouses, then the glittering office spaces of the modern city centre rose into view, steel and glass Towers of Babel to glorify the gods of new finance. He'd just finished his fourth can when it stopped.

Sean, you fucker. Rob greeted him with a bear hug. It's good to see you, it's been ages. How've you been?

Not bad, you know. The usual. Work's shite. Ah'm getting by. Y'alright?

All the better for seeing you, man. I've got something in my bag to get us started. Come on, let's go to the park.

What's craic?

You'll see, fucker, you'll see.

Another of Rob's rib-cracker hugs, then they ploughed headlong into the insect hive of human life swarming in the roiling heat. Sean struggled with cities. The crowds freaked him out, for a start, gave him the horrors when they made him feel like he was penned in and couldn't see a clear path out. Too much sight and sound. Lights flashing, horns blaring, sirens screaming, voices coming in from every which way. The sensory overload scared him shitless when he had to do it alone; but he was safe in the protective circle cast by Rob's presence, so he focussed on putting one foot in front of the other, tried to block it out.

It wasn't far but it was uphill all the way. They passed somewhere near the corporate shithole that used to be the Town and Country Club, through Millennium Square past the Civic Hall, then up again for the last push by the university building with its ex-white façade and steep stone steps, the clock tower that never told the right time. It was a right mission. The cider had weakened his legs and the hangover had got a second wind, fighting the influx of fresh poison, reminding him he'd barely slept and had no fucking business getting back on it at this time of day. Sweat sheened his forehead, stuck his Ramones shirt to his back. He was too out of puff to talk, but Rob – who was hardly an Olympian – wasn't in much of a state for conversation either, until they stopped outside The Library and got their breath back.

You wouldn't have had to be Mother Shipton to predict that the park would be lively, the air thick with the scent of student central in late summer. Shit sausages cremating on disposable barbies from the Co-Op on Cardigan Road, the sweet leaf reek of Hyde Park skunk, fags, Red Stripe, the distant whiff of horseshit from the pile of manure by the allotments, diesel fumes from the buses on the main road. Boom boxes pumped out roots reggae and ambient dub, overlaid with a babble of chat, laughter and the frothing of opening cans. In the children's playground a group of women in black niqabs who must have been *boiling* were pushing their kids on the swings. The skate park next door was full of bare-chested stoners, sunbrown and buff, trucking up and down the ramps like they were too cool to care but skegging round on the downlow to make sure people were checking out their moves, stopping to toke on their hash pipes or quaff from king-sized bottles of Frosty Jack's when they needed to cool off. It was busy but not *too* busy, a nice buzz but plenty of space for everyone to spread out and do their own thing; the perfect place to put the afternoon to bed.

The something in Rob's bag was a bottle of Jim Beam Black; it had bitten the dust by teatime. Sean was stretched out on the grass, inflamed by the bourbon and the sun's UV, eyes half-shut behind the black tint. Man, he was done in, half a mind already on a pick-me-up and whether or not Rob knew a place they could score, as if that was even a fucking question, but all in good time. Rob kept moaning about the heat so he'd propped himself up in the shade of a grand old chestnut tree, tipping the last of the bottle into his mouth and licking his lips like the Big Bad Wolf. The silly twat was wearing his battered black leather jacket, insanity on a day like that, but in the couple or three years they'd been mates Sean had never seen him without it.

So what's next? He lit a fag, inhaled, wished it was full green like every fucker else's. Too early to stop now.

Fucker, you *know* we're only just getting started. What time is it, anyway?

Half five.

They laughed at the mischief to come, the time to be squandered, the day an empty vessel to fill with all manner of undetermined chaos, then settled into an easy silence as overlapping basslines rippled the heat haze and wasps leathered on the dregs of abandoned cider cans buzzed between them, gagging for a scrap. A dragonfly with a body the size of Sean's little finger slowly descended, settled on the toe end of his DM for a couple of seconds then lifted off again, vanished in a gossamer flash. He tried to track its flight but it was *rapid*, gone before it had arrived.

Is that an offie? Sean waved at the parade of shops across the road beyond the end of the park. A homeless man was sitting next to the door with his back to the graff-tagged bricks trying to collect money in a Starbucks take-out cup; but he was a ghost, invisible to the half-cut kids threading in and out without a downward glance.

Yeah.

That whiskey's made me fuckin thirsty, man. Let's go get some cold ones. Ah'm parched.

I told some people we'd meet them in the pub at seven. Why don't we grab a table there? There's someone I want you to meet, I think you'll like her.

Yeah right, Ah've heard that one before. Whatever though. As long as the beer's cold Ah don't give a fuck where we are.

They dusted themselves down, made a beeline for the boozer on the corner and swagged some seats under a parasol at the front looking out over the four-way stop and the side of the park. Sean was so pissed he sparked up while he was waiting to be served and got a gentle bollocking from the lass behind the bar, but her smile made it clear what *she* thought of the new ban on smoking inside.

After that things get murky. He pretends he recalls Rob's mates – a whole new crowd of them that he'd met since he moved – breezing in a few pints later, high on sunshine, passing round packs of smokes and tearing open bags of crisps for the table to share as names were traded and glasses clinked in salutation; but he's kidding himself. Forever after no one could agree on a definitive list of who was there, but in this version there was only one person that mattered.

He can hear Rob's voice say the words, but he's making them up.

Sean, this is Amanda. Mandy, this is my best mate, Sean Molloy. I think I've told you about him before?

In years to come it became a performance piece, delivered with the chemistry of seasoned stage actors who knew each other's lines backwards and didn't mind hamming it up for the folk in the cheap seats at the back.

Was it love at first sight? someone would ask.

I thought so. Sean always got in first.

He *definitely* had his beer googles on. A coquettish laugh, a pantomime eyeroll. I didn't know *what* to make of *him*. He was so wrecked he could barely remember his own name.

Never forgot yours though, did I?

He was pissed when I met him, and he hasn't changed a bit. Split-second timing, deliciously arch, one eyebrow raised like a switchblade, punctuated with a tousle of his spiky hair and they'd join in the laughter, which was often uproarious. The words never changed but later they were hissed through clenched teeth, a tight smile beneath a murderous side-eye while she blew out a sigh slow like a dying breath, heavy with the weariness of the world and every sad thing in it.

Legend had it that everyone, whoever they were, clocked something was going on from the off; that they only had eyes for each other, spoke to no one else; how he ended up sitting on her knee despite him being taller by the best part of a foot, whispering the lyrics to his favourite songs in her ear until the bar staff kicked them out sometime after last orders. It was definitely possible, but he could've been go-go dancing bollock naked on the table for all he knew.

The story went that Rob had his chivalrous head on and wouldn't let Amanda walk home alone, even though she lived five minutes away and insisted she did it perfectly safely every night of the week. She'd tell of the awkward moment when they reached the front door, their clumsy hug and her hesitant, mistimed peck on his cheek.

It was lovely to—

—definitely do it again sometime

Talking over each other in the rush of goodbye, flustered like schoolkids. Rob – and he couldn't *believe* he didn't remember this – was shitfaced as per and tripped over a loose flagstone, face-planted into a Hydrangea at the end of the front garden. Sean was halfway down the path to help him up when she called him back.

You know what. Why don't you stay here tonight? That was exactly what she said. He knew because she told it the same way every time. So did he.

She phoned a cab while he struggled to get Rob vertical and keep him there. He was away with it, off-keying *Jet Boy* at the top of his lungs as Sean shoved him into the back of the taxi. Before the door slammed shut he stopped singing just long enough to slur, See you in the morning, fucker. You know where the house is, right? Something along those lines, anyway. Then the car drove off and all was peace.

Privately they'd reminisce about what happened next. The laughter when he asked if there was anything else to drink and all she had to offer was a brew; how he thought she was as pissed as he was but she'd only had three all night; the way she lay on top of the covers fully-clothed, waiting for him to make the first move while he perched on the end of the bed like a sinner on a psalter, wondering what the fuck to do and hoping he'd not misread the signs. The raw power of the first kiss, the ferocity of what came next and when the fuck was one-night sex ever *that* good, then? The fact they were still at it at dawn when her housemate was banging around the kitchen making breakfast; how she'd never been late for work, ever, but was the next day as they lay in bed, entangled in the sweat-soaked sheets and each other.

How they knew, there and then, that their lives as individuals had ceased to exist.

TEZ

Eeeee, you are like yer uncle Terry, yer gran used to say.

Aye, yer mam would agree with a weary smile. A bit too much like him if you ask me. Ey mam, remember the time we had a row in t'kitchen? How old were we?

I'm not sure love but you were both in junior school. He might have been ten or eleven, so you'll've been about eight.

Can't even remember what it were about, can you?

No, or who started it.

Me neither.

Ah know who finished it though.

Aye, we all know that.

Broke a plate over me head, the silly sod. Ah didn't know whether to laugh or cry.

Wouldn't've been so bad if his dinner weren't on it. Faggots and mash all over me clean floor, and you there wi' me best onion gravy running all down you face. What a bloody carry on.

Me dad didn't half leather him.

Quite right an all. Kids these days are short of a bit of that.

Grandma.

Well, it never did you any harm, did it? Spare the rod, spoil the child. Says it in t'Bible.

But—

You only ever got a good hiding when you deserved it. Yer mam would always take her side. Ah marched you to you bedroom in t'attic once and you gorra clout on every bloody step on t'way up both flights of stairs Ah were that mad. You'll've only been about three.

Painter n decorator were in, Ah'll allus remember that. Think Ah put fear o' God in him cos he never said a word to us all day after.

Well, let's not fall out about it. We know you don't think like us normal folk, Sean. We couldn't afford to be wasting food in them days though, Ah'll tell you that for nowt. That's what you grandad were most cross about, really. Ah must've brought you mam up right cos she knew. What did she do? Wiped her face on t'dishcloth then scraped all t'mess off floor and took him it up on a fresh plate. If any of me brothers had done that to me Ah'd still not be talking to 'em now if they were here, God rest 'em.

Ah knew he'd be hungry. He were allus hungry, weren't he, mam? Found him with his kecks an his strides round his ankles an his arse red raw, bent over rubbin dubbin on his footie boots.

You bloody soft, you are. Always were. And Ah bet he didn't say sorry neither.

Course not, but he didn't need to. Ah knew he was.

You'd heard it enough that the memory had become as real as one of yer own, but you'd laugh like it was the first time while the pair of them smiled with watery eyes like they were talking about something that happened yesterday.

■

Tez was a local legend, a working-class hero, or anti-hero, maybe, it was hard to say. Everyone knew the stories, didn't matter who was doing the telling; it could've been yer grandma, yer mam and dad, family friends or a load of folk down the pub, but whoever they were, they knew the script verbatim.

He were a great footballer, your Tez. Proper good laiker.

He coulda gone places with that if he'd kept his head screwed on. Bugger all chance of that though, eh? He never were one to know when to stop. He could play like Georgie Best, that lad.

Aye. But he drank like him an all.

Had trials and everythin. Who were it for?

Man United, weren't it?

Man United bollocks. Bradford City, it were, them an Huddersfield Town.

That's it. Scout from City saw him score seven in a match, an all of 'em in t'second half. Allus played better after half time cos he'd usually sobered up by then. He were amazing that day, they said he'd have the world at his feet.

Town offered him a contract as soon as they clocked him dribble, but they changed their mind pretty sharpish, didn't they?

Aye, cos he turned up to training one day that pissed from t'night afore he couldn't lace his boots.

He'd turned down City, but he went back wi' his tail between his legs to see if offer still stood. But word gets around, like. So that were the end of that, and none of t'other clubs'd touch him wi' a bargepole.

Silly bugger could've had it all. And look where he ended up, eh?

■

Hated school, didn't he?

Didn't we all. All them bloody books, no good to man nor beast. Young lads need a trade. You can't learn one of them sat at a friggin desk.

Only class he ever went to were woodwork. Rest o' time he were round back of t'bikesheds havin a fag an chattin up lasses. No wonder he ended up bein a chippie when t'footy went belly up.

Never mind chipping, he should've been a carpenter. He were marvellous wi' his hands. Could make owt he wanted out of a bit of wood, it were marvellous, really.

Couldn't stay out the pub though. So he got stuck doin

t'day-to-day instead, and it were right enough for him, like. But he were too good to be doin that.

He weren't bothered though, were he? As long as he could pay for his fags and ale. Work hard, play hard. That were Tez all over.

He were never stuck for brass weren't Terry. Ah don't know where it all came from. Even when he stopped workin wi' his chest an that, he'd have a roll that'd choke a bacon pig.

You'd clocked this yourself. He'd come round to see yer mam and pull it out of his bin, casual as you like, a wad of twenties an inch and a half across with a laggy band holding it together and peel a few off to cover whatever she'd sorted for him, stuff out the Littlewoods catalogue usually. Sometimes he'd chuck you a few sheets too.

You mam tells us you skint again, he'd say around the rollie that never left his lips and pass you a ton like it was nothing. You'd crumple it without looking and shove it in yer backburner, trying to reckon it meant as little to you as it did to him, a negative of the Queen's face seared onto yer arse cheeks as it burned a hole through yer pocket.

Don't be taking it to t'pub though, eh? We don't want you ending up like me. His eyes would flare and for a split second his face, which wasn't one to slip, would crack into a devilish smirk as he foresaw the day's end – you, pissed out of yer head under the table somewhere in town, as pitiful and penniless as you were when you got up. Takes one to know one, and he knew alright.

Thought he might've settled when he met you Aunty Nance, but he were havin none of it. She were even feistier back then than she is now and we thought she could've made him toe t'line, like, but there were no tyin him down.

She were as ratarsed as he were half the time – it's a wonder they could ever get outta bed of a morning to go to work. You've never seen a lass sup like that, I'll tell you that for nowt. She couldn't keep up wi' him though—

What bugger could?

—until they had Hayley, anyroad, an then she packed it in right enough.

He didn't though, did he? Sat in t'Fleece from openin to last bell callin for drinks all round. Talk about wettin t'babby's head – he bloody well drowned it.

Aye, no one who were there'll forget that in a hurry. He went on such a bender that Nance had been on her own wi' that kid for a fortnight afore he even set eyes on her.

He called you mam from a payphone in Southend and begged her for t'brass to get t'bus home. Christ knows what he were doin down there—

Christ might've known, but Tez hadn't a clue.

Loved that kid though, didn't he?

He did that. An he tried his best, bless him.

He were daft though, eh? Remember when Nance come home from work an found him in bed wi' that lass from – which pub were it?

Cock n Bottle.

Cock n bottle, that's it, aye. Sonya, think her name was. She heard 'em goin at it from downstairs, ran into t'bedroom wi' a carvin knife and threatened to chop his tackle off on t'spot.

Big lass, Nance. Couldn't get through t'door wi' her blockin t'frame.

So off he went out the window and t'barmaid an all, not a stitch on either of em. As Ah live an breathe that must've been a sight to see.

Tried to catch her, Tez did, so Nance said after, but she landed on top of him, broke a couple of ribs—

His not hers—

That's right. She scarpered sharpish in a tarp she fished from t'skip in t'garden an there was he, rollin round stark bollock naked wi' all t'wind knocked out of him and Nance chuckin his clothes out t'window, tellin him to piss off out of it an never come back.

They'd had their ups and downs, but that were the end of it. She took him back for a bit, like, for Hayley's sake, but he'd lost the plot by then an she booted him out for good a couple of years after.

■

He were knackered at thirty, so he was. All caught up wi' him in t'end.

Aye, couple of close calls, he had, and that were him done.

Loved his motors. You could tell t'story of his life wi' his cars.

Allus playin t'flash bugger, weren't he?

Remember that Capri? Flame red, it were. Went like shite off a shovel. Asked him to take us for a ride in it once an Ah damn near filled me crackers. Thought we were gonna take off. Asked if Ah could have a drive mesen, like, but he wouldn't have it. Dunno why. Ah'd've been a lot more careful wi' it than that ruddy pillock were.

Had a Cosworth an all. Not for long though. Allus after t'next 'un.

Then he got a taste for t'sports cars, and it were Porsches all the way. How many did he have, two, three on t'trot?

Summat like. He had that yellow nine eleven last, but he totalled it drivin home gantered when it'd've been quicker to walk. He pranged it into a lamppost down by t'cop shop an, bang, that were it – banned. What were he, six times over t'limit?

An the rest. Ah can't mind it now, but it were enough to put most fellas six foot under.

An that were when he got badly.

Aye. He were lost wi'out his wheels so he hit it even harder, till he keeled over outside t'Red Lion one Friday night. Everyone reckoned he were messin about an told t'silly apeth to get up, but his pancreas had gone an t'party were finished then. Blue light to intensive care, an no more boozin fer Tez.

Poor bugger. Apart from Hayley it were all he had.

Aye.

Aye.

■

That was the Tez you knew, the sober one.

Before he dried out he wasn't around much. Once in a blue moon he'd call on a Sunday morning, sweating and shaking and reeking of ale, but he'd only stay long enough to have a brew and a fag and be away in time to be first in the queue when the pub opened. But after he came out of hospital he came every week, and you got to know him more then. He didn't talk much but you liked to listen to him and yer old man's quiet reminiscences about the days of thunder when they were thick as thieves; then they'd turn to cars, the one thing that bonded them aside from boozing and the fact they both loved yer mam to bits, and you zoned out of it then.

No one knew how he'd get on without it. He hadn't notched up half his three score years and ten when he had to stop; even yer mam doubted he could do it, but the docs who'd given him the Scarborough warning said a dish of sherry trifle could kill him so it wasn't like he had a choice. He kept on with the fags though, even though he'd had asthma from being a kid. It turned into full-on emphysema later and that's what stopped him working, still in his thirties but washed up to fuck.

He'd not lost his love for footie and you enjoyed talking to him about that. He never mentioned his playing days but he always had a natter about the leagues and who was doing what, always up on the ins and outs across all four divisions. He had a season ticket at Burnley and sometimes when you were in yer early teens you used to go and watch them together. That was back when the Premier League was new, before Murdoch's filthy money had properly settled in and ripped the heart out of the game. Memories of Hillsborough were still red raw in the North and the big grounds had been made all-seater, but Burnley played down the ladder so you could still stand up at Turf Moor.

It was proper football, none of this seventy-five notes a ticket and fifteen quid for a sarnie with fucking prawns in it bollocks. Like that mid-week match against Liverpool in the Coca Cola Cup. You were on the open terrace in the Bee Hole End behind the goal on a hideous October night, eating soggy chips in the lashing rain amid a howling gale as the Scousers put the Clarets to the sword. You heard the fourth go in from the car park as you left early to get the bus, trudging head down through the vicious Lancastrian squall, soaked to yer skids with hands so cold they felt like they weren't yours while the hardcore stayed till the bitter end, cheering as if they'd won. It was brilliant.

One time you stood on the Longside for the derby against Blackburn, the tackles flying in on the pitch nothing compared to the carnage happening off it. The fans were segregated and there was Old Bill everywhere but some of the Rovers lot had infiltrated the main stand and there was loads of scrapping. Before the game had even kicked off you watched some poor cunt get booted from the top of the steps to the bottom; he must've been rock hard cos somehow he got up, wobbling like Bambi on Buckfast while he tried to work out where the fuck he was, but then from out of the seething mass someone found enough room to swing a massive haymaker and stuck it right on the end of his chin. He got stretchered out not long after and the Longside celebrated louder than if they'd scored. You can't remember the result but you've never forgotten the violence of that day, the visceral, tribal hate, no nay never, no nay never no more will we play the Bastard Rovers, no never no more, the pure, unadulterated fucking bile of it, the officials getting escorted off by the pigs at half time in a hailstorm of pie crust and bottled piss.

He was bored with the quiet life but he soon found his feet, set himself up a side-line making trips to Turkey to pick up knock-off designer gear he flogged to his old drinking buddies round town. He made a pretty penny an all; the roll in his back sack got so big it looked like it was near to busting the stitching. If he fell in a bucket of shit he'd come up smellin of roses, yer old man once said. There was no getting away from the pride on yer mam's face as she nodded her agreement.

What happened with Hayley flattened him. It was bound to. But to cap it all he was the last person to see her alive.

He'd run into her on the high street on his way back from one of his clothes-selling missions and stopped for a natter. She was off to get some fags, she said, she'd call on him for a brew the next day, but she never did. He said, months after, when he could stand to speak about it, that she'd looked fine, seemed happier than she had for ages. God only knows what must've been running though her mind.

Even yer mam wasn't brave enough to try to stop him drinking at the funeral.

He held himself together long enough to at least look like he was sober in the chapel but after that all bets were off. He'd been dry for a decade but that didn't stop him going at it hammer and tongs, back in the game, big time. Yer old man was with him for the first day and half but even he couldn't stick the pace and came home defeated to an almighty bollocking from yer mam.

Someone had to try for Christ's sake, he said, when he'd crawled out of the plane crash of his hangover a couple of days after. Have to be a better man than me though. The way that bugger were goin, he'd've put Alex Higgins in a body bag.

He hospitalised himself again but pulled through, like everyone said he would when they heard he was in. The fella was indestructible. The whole town admired his spirit, but he was never the same bloke again.

He outlived Hales by ten years, and it was the fags that did him in the end. He coughed and rattled his way out over a torturous week while his lungs flooded with blood from internal lesions caused by the cancer that had been chewing them up for fun. Yer old man sat with him for the duration, talking him through it even though the poor fucker couldn't talk back, and he was with him right at the end when the light left his eyes and he went off to meet back up with Hayley, wherever she was.

His was a funeral you did make it to. You'd grown up a lot by then and hated yourself for missing hers. You never talked about it and no one ever said, but you'd let the family down proper style and knew it. The chapel was fucking rammed, so many distant family members you didn't know the half of them, plus every gangster, wide-boy, pisshead and fighting man in town. Waterloo Sunset piped through the speakers as the casket was fed to the flames and you bit yer thumb so hard it bled all day then seeped pus for a fortnight, but you shed no tears, and it got you through.

It was a right do after. Even the Brentwood lot, yer mam and Tez's cousins, came. They'd done the Auf Wiedersehen Pet job with him in the early Eighties, working on sites and raising all kinds of hell in Germany and they'd come for one last blow-out to help him on his way. It was always an event when those boys showed up. Big Ted, in his sixties, swaggering round in an open neck shirt, his chest tattooed with a golden eagle and clattering with bling, was going strong even after cancer of his own had left him with only half a working lung, still on his Old Holborn rollies like it were the fags themselves keeping the reaper at bay. He smashed a bottle of White and Mackay for breakfast and no one saw hide nor hair of him after the service. Dave and Tom, his brothers, put up a good show, bought you and the big man Cubans and cognac, arguing over whose knuckles were more busted out of shape from all the brawling they used to do, and sometimes still did, but they shot their bolt early doors and were flagging by teatime. They fucked off back to the B&B and said they'd meet you later when they'd had a kip, but they never resurfaced either.

With the Southerners out of commission yer old man needed watching so you took one for the team knowing no one else was up to the task. You matched him shot for shot for shot until sight and speech and sense were gone, then staggered home in shitfaced silence when none of the taxis would have you. You did the job a good man should, like he'd tried to with Tez after Hayley's, and he was grateful in his way, not that he ever said. Yer mam, pole-axed with grief, not yet sixty but looking as old as time itself, tried to thank you for looking after him, but words had failed her too.

Everyone marvelled at yer gran, eternal stoic that she was. In her mid-eighties then, she'd outlived two husbands, nine brothers and sisters, most of her friends, one of her grandchildren, and now her first-born child; but she was never anything other than calm in the face of death and accepted it without complaint. If there was any rage at the injustice of a life spent living with loss upon loss upon loss, she kept it to herself.

He allus did what he wanted, our Terry, and there's nowt any of us could've altered, was all she'd say. He were his own man, Sean, just like you are, for better or worse. I allus said you two were alike.

2

Sean, I *really* have to go now. She was laughing as he grabbed her arm, tried to pull her back into bed. I *mean* it. I should've been at work an hour ago. She yanked herself free.

Fuck it. Phone in sick.

That might be how things work where you come from, young man, but I've never pulled a sickie in my life. She was indignant, fighting it but couldn't stop smiling.

What, *never*?

No, not once. Ever. She swatted his hand away as he tried to pinch her arse then darted out of reach, giggling. And I'm not about to start now.

They shared an easy intimacy from the off. Sean wasn't the type to go chasing one-nighters but he'd had his share since uni and the aftermath did his nut in. He couldn't stick the awkwardness, the lurching sickness of the hangover slash comedown, the iced-water-to-the-face shock on waking when he clocked he was naked, half-fucked in surroundings unknown, that there was someone else next to him and she was naked too and oh for fuck's sake not *this* again. The desperate scramble for details, groping blindly for memories that were never there, where the night had started, who he'd gone out with, where they ended up, and who the fuck is this girl, anyway? The instant knowledge that the chemical connection he'd been conned into feeling was gone, a deeper shame than if someone had walked in on him wanking. Worse was the thick-tongued small-talk, the guilt of the unremembered unknown cutting like a blowtorch through the brainfuzz.

Hey, how are you feeling?

Fuck, last night was *mental*.

Did you get much kip?

Plastic smiles, wondering if her mind was as mashed as his, avoiding eye-contact while trying to scan her face on the sly for anything that might give him a clue; his pathetic attempts to play it cool while fighting the shrieking urge to leap out of bed, grab his clothes and get the everloving fuck *right* out of there. Once or twice he'd done a bunk while they were asleep and felt a right cunt after, shovelling more guilt onto the pile. But it was miles better than the alternative.

This time there was none of that.

Amanda's – fuck, he remembered her name and everything – housemate had gone out by the time they surfaced so once they'd disentangled themselves they walked unclothed to the bathroom, pissed in front of each other like a married couple long-since bored with the sight of spousal flesh, shared her toothbrush to scrub away the night's residue. It was so normal it was fucking unnerving.

Where d'you work, anyway? He was sitting on the bog with the seat down, watching her shower like it was something they did every day. He was useless around women, most people, actually, when he was sober, never knew what to say, but it all came easily that day. He was probably still pissed; he'd drunk enough to be.

The extractor fan was borked, the air wet and steamy. The scent of the soap she was lathering herself with was sickly and strong but it covered the shared-bathroom-in-rented-house aroma of piss and damp at least. For years after the faintest whiff of vanilla essence would catapult him straight back there.

A coffee shop up the road. She finished wiping her face with a flannel, bent down to rinse some stray suds from her legs. You can come with me if you want, I'll sort you out a freebie when no one's looking. We can walk it in fifteen minutes.

Ta. Ah think maybe Ah should get going though, like. Ah promised Rob—

Wait a minute. She was coy again. Her forehead was frowning but the shape of her mouth suggested something else. If you think I'm one of those girls you can just screw and then leave you've got another thing coming. I'm not letting you out of here until I've got your mobile number, mister, so don't even try it.

You welcome to it. I've got nowhere to be but I said I'd go see how Rob's doing. What time do you knock off? I'll come meet you then if you want. Christ, hark at him talking like a normal person; it was like listening to someone else. He cringed as he realised he was trying to soften his accent for her.

Oh. Okay then. A trace of surprise, like she'd been expecting resistance and was disappointed not to get it. The fake frown broke into a girlish grin that turned his legs to butter as she wrapped herself in a huge white towel and they padded back to her room. The shop shuts at four. I'm meant to finish at five but I might have to stay back after to make up for this morning. I'll see what the others say.

No worries. Why don't you text us when you're ready?

Sure.

Right then.

Great. My phone's over there on the desk. Be a love and put your number in for me while I find some clean knickers. I need to get dressed now, I'm late enough as it is.

They parted on the doorstep with a fully committed hug, although the kiss didn't live up to the billing. Dry lips, tentative tongues, like they weren't quite sure how far they should go with it. It was awkward but in a nice way, the last time it would feel anything but right.

Keep your eyes on your phone. I'll message you later.

Have a good one. He waved over his shoulder as he set off up the street, didn't look back in case he'd imagined her and found himself looking at a pillar of salt.

An indecisive morning walked the tightrope between summer's end and the first chill of autumn. The sky was cloudless and bright but the breeze had some teeth. He knew the city pretty well; he'd misspent the arse end of his teens getting hammered at punk gigs upstairs at the Packhorse and the Duchess in town, and he'd been to Rob's new place before so he knew he'd find it alright.

It wasn't far, along the side of the park, past the offie then down towards the old picture house, somewhere round there anyway, but he had the address in his phone if he got stuck. He liked it round there; there were tons of student houses but at the same time it was a magnet for writers, artists, musicians, pill heads, weed farmers – anyone who needed cheap digs and didn't mind dealing with shady landlords or give too much of a fuck about little things like rats, subsidence, black mould and dry rot. It was down at heel and looked like shit, but the vibe was interesting. Intense, sketchy but never threatening in the way Manchester could be when he was at uni.

It was a twilight zone, a temporal void where normal rules didn't apply. Dazed lads and lasses haunted the streets with pupils vast and dark or else shrunken to pissholes in the snow, so he couldn't tell if they were freshly resurrected from their pits and getting on one for the day or they'd been up all night and were trying to find their way home. Most of them looked like they didn't know either, and he could dig it.

Music, twenty-four seven. The skronk and screech of distorted guitars blasting up to street level through basement air grates as bands rehearsed their sets, the mattress and eggbox soundproofing visible through the filthy windows doing fuck all to keep the noise in. Banging techno blared at mind-boggling BPMs where ravers were giving it large in their living rooms; flattening dub rattled sash windows in rotten frames at stoner houses whose super-skunk signature could get you mashed from the opposite end of the street. Strands of psychedelia floated on wisps of patchouli incense; dealers' cars blasted swaggering hip-hop, once the music of those without power now somehow warped into the apex of capitalist aspiration, so loud it's a wonder it didn't shake the engines apart. Punk, metal, chiming indie pop; it was all there, and more.

Urban bunting junked the place. Discarded trainers hung from telephone wires; translucent candy-striped carriers dangled like used johnnies from wherever the wind had blown them; occasional pairs of lacy knickers or shit-stained grundies decorated the lampposts. There was litter all around, upended wheelie bins, broken glass, red brick walls shimmering with damp, covered in spray-painted tags and slogans.

ACAB.

MOOSE

STAB YOUR FAMILY. KIDS ARE SHIT. BOOM.

TALK MORE.

CHANT DOWN BABYLON.

COCK PISS WANKSHAFT CUNT.

BECOME THE DATA.

Rob's gaff was buried in a warren of two-up, two-down back to backs, Victorian slums that had escaped the demolition man and decided to fall to bits themselves while the bastard landlords were still coining it in. Identikit streets with identikit names – Harold

Grove, Harold Terrace, Harold Place – in a dense potato waffle lattice, wrought iron grills barring the windows and doors of every house. The rusty security gate at Rob's was open, thank fuck; without the portcullis to dodge it was easier to hammer on the knackered timber.

No answer.

He tried again, waited, then pounded with his fist.

Fuck's *sake*.

He made a quick rollie and drew deep, sweet lady nicotine stirring up yesterday's booze as she fizzed through his blood. Still pissed, no two ways about it. He jabbed at the keypad on his phone, put it to his ear; heard it ring a couple of times before it clicked onto voicemail. He hung up, flicked his tab end into the gutter with a thousand others.

Rob! Rob! He booted the door a couple of times. Shit, did he hear something crack? Maybe that was too hard. Wake up, you fuckin useless cunt.

If there was an answer it was lost beneath the hi-hats and snares of the house tunes coming from an open window next door but one, synth melodies shimmering like sunshine on rolling surf. His phone said it was barely eleven. It was gonna be a long day with nowhere to go.

The morning had warmed up alright, so he mooched back to the park and kaffled in the sun. He wasn't far from the offie so he missioned over every now and again to pick up a tinny or two and supped them slowly while he watched the skaters practicing their ollies and kickflips on the ramps.

He kept rerunning memories of yesterday, or trying to, but there was a lot of blank space. He remembered meeting Rob at the station and walking to the park, the thrum of traffic and noise, the dense tides of people drifting in allelomimetic waves. His tongue remembered the bourbon despite being brushed till it hurt before he left the house; the red skin on his face recalled the burn of the afternoon sun. He conjured a hazy picture of going to the pub and the barmaid pushing an empty bottle at him – quick, have another puff then chuck it in here, love, or you'll have me bloody shot – then a blur of faces without features or names, a drink that never ran out. There wasn't much to go at after that. What had they even been talking about? He could be silent around strangers till he'd sussed them out, but drinking loosed his tongue and that could be dangerous with his auto-filter off. He could have been twattering on about *anything*. Fuck, he wished he could remember but the more he tried, the less he got.

He managed a sketchy recollection of walking her home when he thought properly hard about it, something about Rob singing, maybe, someone calling a cab. He remembered the sex but not the details. How it started, who did what to who and in what order, there wasn't a trace of that; but it didn't matter. He usually spent the day after a hook-up trying to forget the whole thing, so *something* had happened for definite cos he couldn't get this girl out of his head. He was convinced they'd properly clicked, not the hot and horny why the fuck not it's Friday night kinda thing, but it was hard to be sure. He was probably bullshitting himself. He'd always wondered what having a steady girlfriend would be like but never come close, unless he counted the couple of mates he'd slept with more than once. But the less said about those lasses the better.

The day passed quickly once he'd started. He called Rob again but got the same automated message every time and decided to sack it off; he'd have to catch up with him later. Early in the afternoon a gnawing pain reminded him he'd not eaten since – what, Wednesday? – so he went back to the pub for a student meal deal, cheeseburger and chips and a pint for a five spot. A quarter pound slab of solid fat and gristle topped with a liquid puke of sweaty-sock grease, chips that conspired to be burnt to fuck and completely raw at the same time, but the barmaid – who reminded him with a wink not to light up while he was ordering and asked with a cancerous laugh if he'd come in for some hair of the dog – pulled a mean Guinness and that settled his guts right down. After that, he did a slow circuit round the park then went back to watching the skaters.

By three he'd lost count. He was getting a thirst on so he thought he'd best make the one he was drinking his last. It wasn't having another that was a bad idea – it was the ten that would follow that were the problem. He couldn't be doing that with Amanda to meet and risk fucking it up before he'd started. Drinking would have to wait for once.

She texted him bang on four.

Hey. Quiet day so locked up early and finishing now. Where are you, mister? :)

His heart stuttered, butterflies tickled his stomach as he realised he hadn't actually thought she'd text, that he'd've been gutted if she hadn't.

His thumb flashed over the keys. In the park, near the skaters. Shall I come and meet you?

Wait outside the shop. I'll be ten minutes.

Ok. See you then.

He smoked while he waited, slipped some shrapnel and a plug of baccy to the imaginary homeless man no one else could see, ducked inside for a pack of spearmint Extra. He was glad he'd stopped when he did; he could feel it, but not in a way anyone would notice, and he hoped to Christ Amanda wouldn't. Fuck he was nervous, fiddling in his pockets with his keys, his change, his lighter, anything that rattled or jingled or shook, left foot tapping out a staccato rhythm on the pavement as he looked around like a smackhead waiting for El Hombre.

The burning red of her dyed hair glowed like a beacon in the sunshine as she rounded the corner. Even from there he could see her smile. She waved with both hands above her head as she started half-walking, half-running towards him. Shit, the way she was moving it was almost like she was excited to see him. This was a new one and it flipped his lid.

what the fuck are you gonna say cunt what the fuck are you meant to do give her a hug maybe thatd be weird you hugged this morning didnt you that was different though morning after the night before an that what did you call her Amanda or Mandy did she prefer one or the other what the fuck was it did she say did you ask an what does it matter cos you cant fuckin remember anyway and fuck you must stink your clothes are minging youve been sweating out yesterdays booze as fast as youve been suppin todays fuckin gross you smell worse than after a day on the site shell whiff you from half a mile away an fuck straight off rather than come near youve just had a fag an all great move genius but she was smoking yesterday too wasnt or was she fuck youre such a cunt why do you get like this so fuckin spun over every bastard thing but you cant help it its not your fault youre pissed anyway tongues too big hope you dont slur your words you need to sort it sort it sort it cunt cos shes coming closer youre gonna have to start thinking about what youre gonna say an actually deal with it shit shit shit fuck shes nearly here youre running out of

Heeeeeeey. She threw herself into him, locked her arms around his neck and planted a kiss wet with fresh lipstick bang in the middle of mouth. So you're still here, then?

Ah wasn't. Ah mean ah…

she mustve thought you werent gonna stick around cunt is that what kinda guy she thinks you are got you bang to rights already fuck did you say something last night that let on youve a bit of previous on that score you

were really fuckin smashed you could've said anything thatd be the fuckin
worst just like you runnin off your stupid fuckin mouth youve always been
a gobshite like your old man says he might be a moaning bastard but he
aint wrong about that

Where's Rob?

Oh. *Rob*. Ah dunno. Ah've not been able to get hold of him all day.

Poor thing, he was sozzled last night. What had you naughty
boys been doing before we arrived?! He's probably in bed. And
poor *you*. Have you been here all day on your own? You must've
been lonely without me if he stood you up. Come on, you can tell
me all about it on the way home.

She grasped his hand and led him away, chattering about her
day at work, how lucky it was the manager wasn't there to see her
rock up two hours late; how the girls pretended to be annoyed but
were secretly pleased because they were late *all* the time and she
was the only one who never was but now she had been so they were
all in it together; how they couldn't *wait* to hear about what had
happened when she told them she'd gone for a drink after work
and the night had taken a completely unexpected turn, that they
knew she'd been up to something from the look on her face when
she came in and wouldn't stop pestering her about it until she said
what had happened, but she hadn't told them *everything*, no way,
she wasn't the kiss and tell type, well, she might have told them
about the kiss but *definitely* no more than that no matter how hard
they tried...

They crashed together as soon as they got over the threshold
and kind of fell up the stairs, a mess of lips and limbs bouncing
from wall to wooden banister and back again and the bedroom
door shook as she slammed it, a wriggle of hips sent her black work
skirt sliding to the floor as she tore off her top and went for his belt
buckle, their tongues entwined probing soft wet, his clumsy hands

struggled to roll the knot of tights and knickers past her thighs and she yanked them down herself, got her feet caught trying to kick them away, pulled them both off-balance and they tumbled half-laughing into the unmade bed, racing reaching grasping flesh and skin, the desperate rush to reconnect, instant sweat, the heat of two bodies as one melting the day's remains into the shivering throes of the musky dark.

3

Sunday.

The curtains stayed closed; the clock laid-off.

Four walls. The mattress, the duvet, the unchanged sheets.

Urgent whispers, laughter, groaning, gasping. Muffled squeals.

Fuck. Chat. Fuck. Sleep.

Repeat.

A pheromone rush stronger than all the drugs he'd had put together. They didn't bother to eat.

Mandy had Monday off so Sean belled Marl while she was catching some Z's to say he wouldn't be in tomorrow. The raucous background laughter told him Marl was down the pub, probably sat with his gut out in the beer garden round the back of the Black Horse with the lads while his missus was home cooking his Sunday roast. He wittered on in between slurps of ale and puffs on his gasper about Sean tekkin t'piss and needin to get his fuckin act together cos labourers are ten a penny round here, right, you fuckin workshy shite, but the job was cash in hand so there wasn't much he could do about it, and Sean didn't give a toss if there was. He wasn't going anywhere, and if Big Marl didn't like it, he could fucking do one.

They lost most of the day in the park, hand in hand, aimlessly walking from nowhere to nowhere, stopping now and then to sit on a bench and share a smoke or a lingering kiss, baccy and spearmint, the greased cherry sweetness of Mandy's lip balm. At dinnertime she took him to a fancy caff where she laughed when he asked, what's a panini? and he was so embarrassed he had a job on not getting up and legging it out the door. It was nothing but a posh word for a sarnie, it turned out, so they ordered those, chorizo and mozzarella with crisp green leaves that tasted like sweat – rocket, she said they called it – sharp red onions and heavily salted home-made crisps, frosted bottles of Peroni to wash it all down. He didn't eat much of his, but she finished it for him and he bought her a thick slice of raspberry cheesecake to cap it off. Just for luck, he treated himself to a double shot of brandy to chase the espresso he'd got for pudding.

She was sleepy after, so they went back to the park and lay in a patch of dappled shade, his arm around her shoulders and her head on his chest, lulled by the white noise hiss of the traffic crawling up and down Otley Road. He was too caffeinated to snooze but he closed his eyes and let it all sink in, the soft press of her body like it had been custom-moulded to fit his; the gentle warmth of her breath snuffling on his throat, the smell of her hair oil and subtle perfume unspeakably perfect until it met the fumes of fags and ale from his own poisoned gob. He was bone tired, hadn't stepped off the rollercoaster of work work work drink drugs crash that he'd been riding since Christ knew when, coming back from uni, probably, and that was, what, five years ago? It was bliss to do nothing, all the better for having someone to do it with. If he'd had a beer in his hand he'd never have wanted to move again.

you might think youre happy now but theres no way its gonna last best enjoy it while you can cos youll do something stupid or say something ridiculous and shell clock you for the knobhead you are youll be back to square one then and if you dont spanner it yourself something else will no point being so fuckin smug about it as soon as she susses what youre really like its game over cunt dont think Im gonna let you forget it cos I—

The shadows were lengthening when she stirred, kohlblack eyes struggling to open for a couple of minutes before she was back in the land of the living. He gave her a squeeze to let her know he was there, picked at the threads of hair that had covered her face while she slept. She lifted her head and stretched, yawned like a baby as she sat up and brushed a few tufts of grass from the back of her dress, smoothed it down where it had scrunched a bit north of the knee.

Mmmmmmm. God, I needed that. You tired me out this weekend, mister.

You too. He sat up alongside her.

It's getting chilly, isn't it? Let's go home and get a coffee.

He took off his flannel shirt and draped it round her shoulders. She kept stopping on the way to stroke the neighbourhood cats, scratching their necks, tickling their chins, cooing at them in a voice that made him think of bed and all the things they were going to do to each other as soon as they got back in it.

Mand? Babe, is that you? A voice called as the door closed.

Yeah, it's me, you alright?

Where've you *been*? The voice was coming from what must've been the kitchen, although he hadn't ventured in there yet. All he'd seen of the house outside Mandy's room and the bog was the hallway and he'd even not taken much notice of that. He looked around; emulsion yellow walls, a mirror in an ornate metal frame next to the door, a few postcard-sized charcoal drawings in wooden frames going up the stairs, an A3 print of a vibrant café scene and a star-scattered sky that he recognised but couldn't name. Brightly lit, warm, welcoming. Proper nice.

bit too *nice for a shitkicker like you cunt dont you think good look fitting in in a gaff like this youve got—*

The owner of the voice slunk in. She was barefoot and slight, blonde hair streaked with bubblegum pink, rocking an unfastened

51

white kimono over a cut-off vest and some lacy shorts that looked like a cross between French knickers and a pair of his boxers. She had a leather thong around her neck spangled with coloured wooden beads that clacked like his mam's knitting needles, bracelets on both arms, a silver one around her ankle with a charm in the shape of a teardrop.

I'm glad you're home. You never answered my texts. I've not seen you all weekend, I've been so – Oh, *hi*. She looked him up and down with slow deliberation. He clocked straight off that Mandy's cheeks were scarlet, felt his own start to burn.

Sorry, Pops. I've been—

Busy, yeah, I can see that. A knowing laugh, an upward tilt of the chin that tossed her hair just so. Well? Aren't you going to introduce me to your *friend*?

Poppy, this is Sean. Sean, this is my best friend Pops. We live together.

Nice to meet you. He spoke to his boots, not knowing where else to look. He'd been so caught up with Mandy that he'd forgotten she shared the house with someone else. He was nervous around new people, hated it when meeting them was sprung on him without warning, blagged to fuck that this lass looked like she wasn't long out of the bath and hadn't finished getting dressed, but she didn't seem bothered and Mandy hadn't batted an eyelid.

Charmed, I'm sure. She took his limp hand, stroked the back of it with her thumb, the slightest of squeezes as she pulled away. No *wonder* Mandy's been hiding all weekend. I was just going to get a bottle of wine out of the fridge. Come on through, we might as well share it. You're not going to let me drink it all on my own, are you?

I've got work tomorrow. One glass won't hurt though. Sean?

Sure. He was ready for a top-up.

He followed them into a smallish kitchen that opened out into a dining-cum-living area with a round pine table and chairs and a plump purple sofa. It was a tidy spot, imitation wooden flooring, light oak, a couple of Chinese cookbooks on a shelf above the kettle, a white marble pestle and mortar on a faux-marble counter dotted with scraps of ginger husk and garlic peel, bits of lime zest; a bouquet of incense sticks smouldered on a bookshelf near the sofa; some kind of ambient new age stuff was playing at low volume but he couldn't see a stereo or speakers. It was very grown-up, or middle-class twentysomething anyway. He thought of the environmental disaster zones that passed for cooking spaces back home, strewn with dog ends and filters, crystalline dandruff leftovers of the weekend's lines hiding between empties and crockery thick with the calcified residue of unidentifiable culinary fubars.

Have a seat. Poppy was bustling round, the kimono swishing like a cape. You guys have the sofa, I'll be alright at the table once I've got this wine sorted out. She made a show of looking for glasses, twisted off the screw cap, poured it out.

christ alive shes posh ah mean bloody hell mandys plummy to be sure but check that fucking accent sounds like one of them with that much brass they dont even know what money is what the fuck are you going to have to say to her best start thinking and try not to sound so fucking rough they think lads who talk like you are only good to be the hired help unless theyre doleheads they avoid folk like you in the street in case you rob them least shes got some wi—

He sat down, sank so low his arse nearly touched the floor. No wonder she didn't want to sit on it. The springs were fucked to hell, the cushions worn thinner than he'd thought; from a distance it looked fairly sturdy but up close it was standard shite from Ikea, and bottom end at that. He straightened his back and crossed his long legs, tried to look comfy.

So, Pops, how's your weekend been? Mandy leaned into him, pressed her knees together as she took the glass Poppy offered and had a tiny sip.

Oh, you know, business as usual. Things to see, people to do, didn't spend much time in bed. Not *sleeping*, anyway. *You* know how it is. Never mind that though. I want to hear *all* about *yours*.

It's been okay, I suppose. She sounded indifferent but the blush hadn't quite faded, the cutest dimples pitting her cheeks as she tried to keep her face straight. He couldn't tell if she was properly embarrassed or this was a game they were playing without him and they were stringing each other along.

I bet it has. How about you, Sean? It *is* Sean, isn't it? How's *your* weekend been? I bet you've been having *loads* of fun with my luscious baby girl, hmmmm?

Man, she was so forward, oozed the kind of confidence he could only dream about. If it *was* a game, he'd been pushed in the deep end. He was back to his normal dumbass self, not so much lost for words as forgetting what words were. He filled his trap with wine, rolled it around to buy some time, untie his tongue. It wasn't bad, hints of acid and sulphites but plenty cold enough to be quaffable. They were both looking, waiting for him to speak.

Well. He swallowed, had another one while he thought what to say, how to dial in his accent a bit. Let's just say it's been full of surprises.

Right on cue, the lasses' eyes locked at last and they scream-laughed like pre-teens in the playground. Even he, Mister fucking Serious, had to crack a smile. The ice, if it was ever there, was broken.

With three of them drinking it the first bottle didn't last long. Poppy had a second to match but they made short work of that as well. Mandy kept resting her hand over the top of her glass, but whenever she went to the bathroom Poppy was swift to top her up, putting a finger to her lips and shushing at him like a littl'un who knows she's getting up to no good but isn't going to let something silly like that get in the way of her mischief.

Late afternoon glugged into evening and he started to relax. Pops was a born talker and led the conversation while she flirted with them both, playing with her hair, rolling her eyes, leaning over to pat legs and nudge arms when she wanted to reinforce a point or a punchline. He chipped in when he needed to – he even managed to make eye contact once he clocked she wasn't gonna fasten her robe and he started to feel rude for talking to her glossy purple toenails – but mostly he was content to be swallowed by the sofa and soak it up.

When the second bottle ran dry he offered to walk to the shop, but Mandy was adamant. I've had more than enough for today. And so have you. Now come on, mister, it's time for you to say goodnight to my darling Pops and take me to bed.

Man, what a downer. It was barely nine thirty; another bottle would have settled the night, but he didn't want to argue. It crossed his mind he could take her upstairs then go to the offie when she'd gone to sleep, but he pushed the thought away with a firmness he didn't know existed. He wasn't gonna blow it for the sake of a couple more glasses, however much his body begged for it.

Come on then. He helped her up. It was nice to meet you, Pops. Ta for the wine. My shout next time, yeah?

You're *always* welcome. We should make a *real* night of it if we're doing it again. I think it might be fun, don't you? She drained her glass, eyes sparkling over the rim. See you tomorrow?

Probably.

I'll look forward to it. Missy, give us a cuddle, babes. I won't keep you from your man any longer. Though I can't blame you for wanting to keep *him* all to yourself. Even half-pissed the wink she shot over Mandy's shoulder as they shared a wobbly hug set his face on fire. He loitered by the door watching a triple air-kiss, mwah, mwah, MWAH, love you, freaking over what to do if Poppy wanted to hug him too. She seemed like the type but he hadn't drunk anywhere *near* enough for that, especially when she was barely dressed, but she didn't try in the end, thank fuck.

Pops is my soul sister. Mandy sounded sloshed, gushing praise as he helped her totter up the stairs. Isn't she gorgeous? I'm glad you got to meet her today. I knew you two were going to love each other, *knew* it. Can you help me with my dress? Bloody arseing thing. I can't reach the zip. She gave up fumbling, slumped against him.

He unzipped it but even with that done she couldn't get it off herself, tittered as it got stuck round her head. He finished the job and poured her into bed, puzzled that she seemed as drunk as she did. She was tired, maybe that was it, or maybe she just couldn't take a lot, some people were weird like that. The lasses back home could sup a couple of bottles apiece and walk in a straight line to the pub for the main event, or the ones he knew, anyway. It was funny to think of someone getting bombed off a couple of glasses, and she was so ditzy with it, it turned him all to mush.

you gettin soft cunt what the fuck let yer guard down good and proper this time usually so careful with it something's rotten in denmark no messing yer settin youself up for the biggest fall you should know better too fuckin late now cunt

She set off snoring as soon as her head hit the pillow, a soft sort of snort-and-whistle like something on an old cartoon. The duvet was pulled up around her ears, her face hidden under a mop of scarlet curls. He chucked his clothes on the floor and slid in next to her, snuggled up close and buried his face in her hair. He'd only told Marl that he'd be off today, so he'd be in for some earache when he didn't show up again tomorrow, but he'd deal with that mardy cunt in the morning.

4

He was dead to the world when the alarm went off. Christ it was fucking awful, one of those cheesy muzak ringtones ascending a bog-standard scale, getting louder with each note before it peaked and started again.

The digital clock said 6 a.m. What kind of fuckery was this?

He pulled her to him, imagined himself snatching up the phone and launching the bastard out the window but he must have been zonked because he went right back off and that was the last he heard of it.

Next time he opened his eyes she was standing over him in her work togs, a shortish black skirt, navy tights, a purple skinny t-shirt with a unicorn and a rainbow on the front, cut off just above her pierced belly button with its dark blue jewel, nails and lips painted the colour of a ripe plum. Even dressed for the caff she looked great; she could've made a binbag look like a ballgown.

Hey mister sleepyhead. Are you coming with me? You can get a fry up or something.

Sean was in no mood to face the world. Unless he was surfacing to eat Mandy for breakfast, he wasn't moving. He grunted a negative and tried to hide under the covers but she was all charm, cajoling and coddling like she did with the scratty old moggies on the street, nibbling his ears with promises of more to come later if he'd only get out of bed and walk up the road with her. The chemimint blast of Aquafresh on her breath slapped him wide awake so he gave in, chucked on the clothes he'd been wearing

58

since Friday and tried to get his head together while she hustled him along.

The sweetness of the early morning air was tainted by the smog of the standstill traffic on Otley Road. Engines rumbled, horns honked, beepers beeped as platoons of green men on a parade ground of traffic lights signalled that it was safe to cross. It made his brain hurt, circuits jammed, ready to crash like a fucked laptop. But on he went, a couple of steps behind her like a lazy old mutt being taken for a drag.

Painfully, reluctantly, the city cracked its knuckles and creaked back to life. The sun wasn't long out of bed itself and the streets were filled with folk who looked like they'd just been dug up. Lost souls with bleary eyes milled around shoving pasties and breakfast baps into yawning maws, drinking brews out of Styrofoam cups as if some bone-dry pastry and a half-pint of boiling arsewater from Gregg's was gonna cure the Tuesday blues. A few straight-up lunatics were pounding the pavement on a morning run; but surely whatever good the exercise was doing would be cancelled by the fumes farted out by the automotive crocodile that went beyond the vanishing point in both directions? The silly bastards wanted their heads checking.

As they were leaving he'd texted to say he wouldn't be at work again, then switched to silent mode and waited for the screen light up as Marl, the stupid predictable knacker, rang straight back.

Fuck's sake yer boilin me piss bone-dry now, boyo. If yer not here at crack o'dawn tomorra Ah'll have yer nutsack round me rear-view where me furry dice are meant to be, right? The voicemail hollered when he played it back, but he wasn't arsed. He didn't give a fuck if he never worked another day for Marl again, but Mandy was at the caff most of the week and she had plans for a couple of the evenings that she'd sorted out in the before time, that far-away place where their worlds had yet to collide, so they'd agreed he might as well head home, get a proper shower and grab some fresh clothes. It wouldn't hurt to do some work and lay his hands on some cash either, although he wasn't looking forward to facing Jabba the Cunt and listening to his lardy arse mithering on all day.

Mandy said she'd sneak him a breakfast box to go if he came in and bought a coffee and he was sorely tempted. Outside of yesterday's lunch, which was mostly liquid, and the shit cheeseburger on Saturday he'd barely eaten for a week. Some sausage and beans and a greasy fried egg dripping HP sauce down his stubbly chin would have really hit the spot now he was out and about; but when they rocked up two of her workmates were peeping through the window, trying not to look conspicuous as they craned their necks to peer at him from behind the counter. They had their mouths covered with their hands but he could see enough of their faces to know they were laughing. Their eyes darted sideways when they realised he'd clocked them noseying, and they creased up good and proper then, stopped bothering trying to hide it.

Fuck it. It wasn't even seven. He couldn't face introductions and small talk at this shithouse hour, however nice a breakfast bap might've sounded. He'd forget about food soon enough, mastered that game years back.

You know what, I think I'm gonna skip it today.

Don't be shy, mister. It's only Cheryl and Tash. They're dead nice, I'm sure they'd love to meet you. They won't bite. Not like *me*.

Next time, eh? I'm done in. I could do with getting some kip in my own bed. We've not had much in yours.

Well, alright. They can wait. But you've got to *promise* to come next time. She looked peevish.

Sure.

I won't let you forget.

I bet.

It was a wrench saying goodbye. A mournful kiss and frantic promises to text later, as if they were being separated by war. He was surprised how sad he was when they untied their tongues and she went inside to the delighted squeals of Cheryl and Tash, who'd been scoping them all the while. The noise set his teeth right on edge, made him want to tear off strips of his own skin. Thank fuck he'd decided to leave it.

It was a couple of miles to the station, along the main road and past the Uni, maybe half an hour of a job to walk so he sparked a fag and got his head down, chucked some tunes on his buds to keep him going and stave off the panic, watched his cherry reds and nothing else. The station was rammed with worker bees clocking in for the daily grind, all polished shoes and ironed clothes and those stupid fucking suitcases that people had started trailing around behind them instead of carrying a bag. There had to be more to life than that. But was he any better?

Eeeee, imagine one of ours getting a cap and gown, eh? Never thought Ah'd see the day. You'll never have to struggle like we did, kidder. That was his mam when he became the first person in his family to graduate from university, having also been the first to stay at school post-sixteen; there were plenty of fellas on both sides, his old man included, who hadn't even managed that. Half a decade on here he was, breaking his back for some other cunt's benefit like all the ones who came before him, his degree no more use than an empty bogroll tube to a man with the riving shites. He'd just missed a train and had nearly an hour to wait for the next so he stood opposite the taxi rank chaining rollies, watching the drones pass in their thousands, sunglassed eyes staring with smouldering anger.

How he hated them.

Himself too.

He dozed on the train, came to as the brakes skreeeeed it to a halt. The shakes said they were ready for an eye-opener so he sat on a bench by the canal basin to kill the ten minutes until opening, watched the ducks and swans flap and squawk as they fought over crusts tossed into the murky water by pensioners and their grandkids.

Aeons ago he'd done the same with Granny Molloy, after his mam went back to work and he was still too young for school. See that building there, she'd say, pointing at a hulking edifice that was derelict then and stayed that way for decades, but had recently been gentrified into collection of luxury apartments no one local could afford to buy. That were the old mill, that. Ah used to work there before Ah got married, and a few years after an all, till I started cleaning at t'hospital. Yer grandad Pat, he were only your age when they came here from Ireland and they used to live behind there, down in Union Square. Then little Sean would listen, rapt, as she told of eleven brothers and sisters in three tiny rooms with wooden shoes on their feet and no clothes but the ones they stood up in, hungry bellies filled with cabbage and spuds that were all wind and water, and not much else to speak of unless the butcher took pity on yer great granny and gave her a sheep's head to chuck in the pot. He loved that bit, pulled faces of mock disgust while revelling in the thought of his grandad and his kin fighting over who got to eat the eyes when the broth was done.

He'd sat on the same bench drinking a bag of cans one Sunday teatime last year, utterly keshed, doing corner kicks off a credit card with one of his wreckhead drug buddies and literally laughed till he puked when the guy stripped to his skids and dived in headfirst, too coked-up to do anything but doggy paddle in the stagnant wash while the tourists in the restaurant round the back of the bougie chippy stared open-mouthed through the windows and choked on their fish suppers, a couple of them pointing and taking photos with their phones.

wouldnt be so fuckin funny if yer new ladyfriend found out about it though would it dickhead seems pretty obvious shit like that doesnt go down in her neck of the woods can you imagine what shed say if she knew about the shit youve got up to for all these years you and your loopy mates shed drop you like a sack of hot shite if she ever got a sniff of that and the rest shes way too good for you anyway its only a matter of time cunt

He was in the Crown at eleven, thinking to sink a couple of slow ones then fuck off back to his bench with a chip butty. The pub was empty, aside from a brace of pickled old coffin dodgers who were as much part of the place as the broken jukebox and the pool table with its ragged red baize and cues that doubled up as weapons if things got tasty on a Saturday night, which they usually did. He could never go in during the day without seeing them, slurping pints of mild and blethering about the cricket. He looked over from the bar, raised his glass in salutation once it had settled; they nodded once apiece to show they'd seen, and went back to their chat.

He'd just sat at his favourite table by the back door when his phone vibrated.

Hey. Work is crazy today. Where have all these people come from?! Missing you already :(

A couple of gulps took care of most of his Guinness before he replied. Nightmare. Are you ok?

Just having a break. I thought I was okay earlier but I'm REALLY hungover now. I'll kill Poppy, she's always doing this to me XD I wish I was back home in bed with you :(

Drink lots of water, you'll start feeling better soon x x x

When she didn't reply it dawned that he was missing her too.

He missed her smile, the smell of her hair, the hands she couldn't keep to herself, the laugh that melted him like ice cream in the sun, the way every time she called him mister in that reckoning-to-be-a-cross-little-girl voice it went straight to his groin. He never had to think about what to say to her either; she was so bubbly she rarely paused for breath, but when she did and he was called upon to speak, the words flowed in a way that seemed inconceivable even as he heard himself saying them. He couldn't fettle it. Without her the world was as grey and lifeless as it had been before they'd met, and had it really only been five days? Impossible.

He wiped his mouth, gave his loaf a shake, opened his throat and poured the rest of his pint down. He nodded at Tess for another, gave her the signal to stick a brandy in the top but she was already on her way to the optics. Thoughts of the chippie were fading faster than his washed-out jeans. He was lost, like he'd forgotten how to fill the time when he was alone; but he was a creature of habit so his animal brain knew what to do.

He was half-gone by the time she messaged again. Ping. Ping. Ping.

Made it through the day, thank God 8-D Poppy's making pasta to say sorry for feeding me all that wine. She knows I'm no good at drinking! XD

Then: I'm snuggled up in bed while she's cooking it. I'm SO tired! I like this bed much better when you're here to share it! ;-) ;-*

And: How are you, mister? Are you getting lonely yet? 8-D

Christ, what time was it? Nearly six. No wonder he was feeling fuzzy. Ah well, forget it. He read her texts again. All that wine. She can't have had two full glasses. He thought of her face, dimples and all, and it mushed him up like the sappiest cunt in the world. What the fuck was happening to him?

I'm okay. Pretty boring day. Not looking forward to work tomorrow.

The messages flew back and forth, hers scattered with exclamation marks and emoticons, his more strait-laced. They drove him spare, those stupid fucking smiley faces, as if humans hadn't been able to communicate for millennia before they were invented, but her texts wouldn't have been the same without them. Everything she did was adorable. She was perfect. God, he wished she was here. Or better, that he was there, so he could wake up with her hair in his mouth and his arm round her waist instead of having to clock Billy the Scrote's ugly mug first thing and spend the day trying to avoid looking at fat Marl's hairy builders arse crack.

He was struggling to focus. He'd never got his head around text messages, struggled to gauge the tone, and the way most folk wrote them meant anything! that! didn't! have! an! exclamation! mark! sounded! terse! but he did what he thought was right and hoped he was sending the right signals.

I can't wait to see you again.

Me too. When can you come back?

Let me talk to that knobhead at work and I'll see what I can do.

You've GOT to come this weekend!! Meet me after work on Saturday and we'll go STRAIGHT to bed I promise!!!! 8-D 8-D 8-D

Sounds good.

I WON'T take NO for an answer mister!! XD XD XD

He paid for one more pint with the last of his shrapnel, then picked up a six pack on his card from the offie where Rob used to work. He called in there for a few cans on the way home if he was proper parched, which was more days that not, and one day a few years back Rob had appeared behind the counter, a balding hulk with a face like Captain Spaulding. He said something about Sean's Nirvana shirt and they got to chatting about bands so they arranged to meet when Rob clocked off at 7. Long story short, they drank themselves under the table in Spoons then went back to Rob's with a bottle of Jack and a gram of coke each, stayed up all night and most of the next day spinning vinyls. They'd been solid mates ever since.

There'd been a few new Robs since he'd gone; tonight's specimen was a kid barely old enough to shave, pustulant, zitty, enough grease on his forehead to fry a brickie's breakfast. No way this lad could be old enough to sell booze, but here he was. He looked wary when Sean dropped his cider on the counter and asked for twenty Marlboros with a voice so slurred he struggled to understand it himself. His folks must have gone out cos he didn't remember seeing them when he got in, didn't remember much at all to be perfectly fucking honest, until his alarm shattered his skull and he had to drag his carcass up the road to wait for Billy's fag-fumed ratter.

Hope you've fetched some earplugs. The Scrote blew a lungful of Lambert smoke right in his phizzog. Marl's got t'right fuckin arse on with you, fella.

Well, what's fuckin new? Ah'd be more worried if the fat bastard said summat nice to us. Now giz one of them fags before Ah spew. And call at t'garage on t'way, will you? If Ah don't get some Lucozade down Ah'll be fuckin dead by nine.

■

For a couple of months they matched their hours; he stayed with folks and busted his hump for Marl when Mandy was in the caff and spent the rest of his time at hers when she wasn't. They were in her room a lot, the arthouse films they played on the decrepit VHS an excuse to lay in bed and fuck, or kiss and cuddle in between. It was in these pillow talks where he started getting to know her.

She was from Surrey, some gaff where it sounded like three trips abroad a year were a given, every kid got straight-As and life was all china teacups, summer fetes and cake sales; houses with more bathrooms than his folks' place had bedrooms, motors that cost as much as a mortgage back home, rosebushes, golf clubs, shadow-mowed lawns. The kind of place where lads like him got shopped to the pigs on spec if they stopped on a streetcorner for too long, and no one wore hand-me-down clothes three sizes too big, or bought their trainers out of a holdall off a bloke on the doorstep, or had beans on toast for tea because it was Wednesday night and there was too much week left at the end of the wage again. It was the stuff of nightmares, proper middle-class, middle England, *Daily Heil* shite, but it was *her* world and to hear her speak of it was morbidly alluring.

Her dad was an interior designer and her mam was head of art at a grammar school for girls so she was always going to veer towards doing something creative, she said. She'd come Up North to do her degree and met Poppy when she was living in halls in the first year. They'd fallen in love with the city and stayed on after they finished, but their arty qualifications hadn't been much help finding work in a market saturated with graduates, so she'd got the job at the caff as a stopgap, found she liked it and never left. Her family couldn't have been short of a few bob with jobs like that and he reckoned they must've topped up what she earned at the caff, especially considering how high the rent must've been at their place but he never said.

doesnt she remind you of those kids at uni all those well to do bastards whod have nothing to do with you you can pretend all you want that shes different but youre kidding yourself what the actual fuck do you think a nice girl like that is doing with a shitkicking cunt like you probably a bit of rough with some local colour to shock her mam and dad with and show off to her posh mates when they come to visit but shell get bored of all that soon enough cash you in for a proper luxury model from somewhere closer to home one of them silver spoon cunts with the hair and the clothes and the manners and a proper job who talks like her and a family thats never scrabbling round for coppers and having to stretch every quid so thin you can see right through it its bound to happen and you fuckin well know it the novelty cant last forever youre a loser from the inside out always losing always have been always will no fuckin use to no one especially not a lass like that imagine meeting her parents jesus fuckin christ what will they think shell be embarrassed to take you home and you cant blame for her that can you shes way out of your league and your fuckin price range an all

In the evenings the three of them would hang out when Poppy wasn't off partying somewhere. They'd sit as before on the sofa – which should've been given the last rites and hoofed down the tip – while Mandy drank pots of fresh mint tea with acacia honey and Sean shared Poppy's apparently limitless supply of cheap white wine as the incense burned and the time dissolved into yesterday.

He found Pops hard going at the start. She was fucking full-on, every word that came out of her mouth overflowing with innuendo, stories full of gory details about people she was sleeping with, or had been, or was planning to shag at the first chance she got. She was tactile too, invaded his space with fingers quick to stroke, poke and prod when she was close enough to touch, blew ironic kisses and wicked smiles across the room when she wasn't. When she clocked how uncomfortable it made him she thought it was hysterical, and it only made her worse.

Don't mind her, Mandy told him one night after she'd stupefied him with some spiel about a guy whose Prince Albert had got caught on her necklace, the hilarious carnage of separating them. If you stranded her in the middle of the desert, she'd find a cactus to flirt with. It's just how she is. She'll get bored and stop if you ignore her. I don't think she had enough attention when she was little and she's trying to make up for it now.

You don't say.

Her folks are old-money bohemian types, I think, one of her great grandmas was a writer or something, hung around on the edges of the Bloomsbury set. She spent a lot of her childhood in one of those back to nature communes where clothes aren't exactly *de rigueur* if you know what I mean, that's why she dresses how she does. I forgot to tip her off the first time my parents came to see us, so you can imagine how it went down when we'd just started lunch and in walked Pops wearing nothing but her skimpies and a towel on her head.

Scenes.

You could say that. I thought my dad was going to choke on his Earl Grey. He'd *seen* a lot more than he bargained for, if you ask me. His mouth was open so wide you could've driven a train through it.

Sean could relate. She was a lot of fun if he was in the right mood though, and it was obvious her and Mand – Missy, as she called her – adored each other. After a couple of drinks she'd be dialled up to eleven, but the same pair of openers loosened him up enough that he could deal with her a bit better. A few weeks in he was easy enough to stay up a while if Mandy was after an early night and they'd put away another bottle, sometimes two. Turned out she was a proper mad one, had as many crazy stories as he did; once they got to swapping those, they found their common language and he really grew to like her, although he made her promise not to share any of his with Mandy.

I *love* a wild boy myself, she pouted. And Missy's not as prim and proper as you might think, you know. She's been around me for long enough to have seen a thing or two, even if she doesn't want to join in the fun herself. But if you don't want my darling girl to know what a naughty thing you are, I can keep a secret.

You'll have to make it up to me one day though, in *any* way I choose. Deal?

She took his hand in both of hers and explained what a pinkie promise was while he tried to look solemn, blagging her head he'd never heard of one. He was used to her touching him by then and it didn't bother him anywhere near as much as it once did; and anyway, he was pissed enough not to care.

■

When they felt like getting out they'd go to the park or pay a couple of quid to catch a bus into town if they couldn't be arsed to walk. Mandy loved shopping, and though being kettled in the crowds made him want to scream till his teeth fell out, he endured it. He'd traipse after her, in and out of Zara, Top Shop, Debenhams, the vapid, all-treble Europop blasting from the speakers enough to drive him demented while he sat on uncomfortable chairs outside the fitting rooms, taking a great interest in his bootlaces to avoid the eyes of other poor bastards in the same predicament who were desperate for him to return their looks of blokey solidarity. He soon sussed how he was supposed to react when she came out to model, when to be enthusiastic, when to hold off. He concentrated as hard as he could on engaging brain before gob, never a strong point, tried to behave how he thought a good boyfriend should.

dont be getting too complacent fucker you know full bastard well yer winging it and sure youve done well so far but its more luck than judgement she seems to be liking it though so keep it up as long as you can you never know what might happen yeah but itll be all the funnier when you die on your arse with it cunt dont think you wont cos you fuckin well will

When it all got too much he'd mime that he was stepping out and stand by the front doors smoking his head off, not feeling as edgy when he had his back against the wall. If it had been a long afternoon he could usually talk her into a trip to the Packhorse on the way back, so he kept his eyes on the prize, the pub his reward for the afternoon's nightmare.

The first time they went in he got careless after sneaking a couple of double Jaegers at the bar while she was in the bog and let slip one about a gig he went to upstairs there in the late-Nineties, some American hardcore band that were passing through. He'd had a few too many sherbets and afterwards one of the bar staff caught him in the act as he leaned over – glass in one hand, pump in the other – to pull his own pint after last orders. He got kicked out – literally. Hoisted off the ground by collar and belt, with a foot up the jacksie to launch him through the door.

Catch you tryin that shit again an Ah'll break yer fuckin arms you skinny little cunt, the fella had shouted, swilling him with the suds of his half-pulled Heineken as he sprawled dazed on the pavement, flinching to avoid the empty glass that was launched at his head.

Oh my God, she said when he'd finished, you could have been really hurt. That's assault. Didn't you call the police? Hand over mouth, horrified eyes.

youve fucked it now dickhead she doesnt look right pleased with that it you were always gonna make a bollocks of it sooner or later but youve not wasted any time here have you

Did I balls. I was bang out of order. If I was him I'd've kicked me up the arse an all.

He was sick to the stomach, waited a couple of centuries for her to process it; but she broke into a grin and laughed till her face went red.

You're one of the funniest guys I've ever met. And you don't even try. Have you got any more stories like that?

A crack about bear shit and forestry nearly slipped through, but he bit it back. I might have one or two. Why don't we get another round and I'll see if I can think of some?

■

The Indian summer that year was glorious, driving Mandy's mark two Fiesta – an old-school rust bucket the colour of custard powder – to market towns and seaside villages far and wide while the russets, ambers and coppers of the trees flamed numinously around them. In the rush of romance they lived in a world of their own, a quaint realm of tea shops and penny arcades, the scratch of sand and shale on sockless soles, cold foam frothing over numb toes as they paddled in the icy edges of the north sea while gulls screeched and wheeled above; the silhouette of Whitby Abbey stentorian atop the cliff behind St Mary's and its garden of weathered headstones as the sunset exploded in a blaze of blood and gold; the diabetic hit of a bucket of candyfloss shared in the sprawling ruins of Scarborough Castle; the twin churches of Heptonstall an eerie sight after Mandy's pilgrimage to see Sylvia Plath in the Arcadian cemetery next door, fly agarics and liberty caps sprouting between the grave curbs with shrooming season in full swing.

Flashbacks then to eating mushies out of the ground up Chapel Hill, behind the castle at the top of town, losing whole days to trips that were darker, speedier, more intense than anything he'd had before or since but could bring on giggling fits that slayed him for hours. After the night in the Packhorse it turned out she didn't mind his debauched confessions after all, so he told her about the time in sixth form when he'd had a hot Ribena brew with a couple of hundred in and Luke Stoppard's ancient black and orange tortie cat morphed into a tarantula then leapt on him, purring and slobbering all over the crotch of his jeans.

Nearly had a fucking heart attack. He was smirking, but he wasn't joking. I've been shit-scared of spiders ever since an all.

She howled at that one.

I'm serious. Say no to drugs, kids. They can really fuck you up.

And then she howled some more.

■

A day for the ages in the South Lakes. They'd pottered round the crafts shops in Bowness and had a cracking chippy dinner, crossed the glossy iron mirror of Windermere on a pleasure boat where they'd sat on a bench at the prow and never stopped kissing the whole return trip. They were so wrapped up in it the crew had to tell them when the boat stopped and it was time to get off, half-dizzy from lack of breath. It was at least a couple of hours drive back and time was knocking on but they couldn't accept the day was over so they hung around until nightfall, sitting on a jetty smoking roll-ups in the most comfortable silence as the dark water eddied with petroleum rainbows turned their bare feet blue and the starry sky spun madly above, the great fells a circle of elders around them, timeless in their silent wisdom.

■

They were house hunting by the end of the year. Things were moving fast but it was the only thing that made sense. He was spending far more time at Mandy's than he was at home, so much so that the lads had started calling him the Scarlet Pimpernel, hollered his theme tune whenever they saw him approach—

They seek him here, they seek him there, they seek Marl's labourer everywhere—

73

which went down like a sack of shit with the gaffer, whose patience snapped at the end of a week when Sean turned up at dinnertime on Wednesday, late.

Three days late.

Say bye bye to yer bollocks, kid, counselled the Scrote when Sean arrived on foot from the station, not even dressed for work. Yer not gonna be Marl's best boy today.

But Marl was silent. It wasn't like him to miss a chance to chew someone's arse out so he should have known something was up, but his bonce was cluttered with estate agents and houses and wondering where the fuck he was gonna find the money for a deposit, so it went right over his head. Friday teatime, Marl handed him his envelope, sparked up, hawked a gob of brown phlegm at his feet.

There's an extra twenty quid in there for you.

What's that for?

Partin gift. Let's just say Ah'm payin you to not come back, eh? Ah've had enough o' you slackin off, you lazy little twat, treating us like some cunt you can ride roughshod over, swannin in an out whenever you fuckin feel like it. Who'da thought a lad of Jack Molloy's'd turn out to be such a bone-idle shithouse? yer grandad'd tan yer arse from here to hell and back again if he were livin. Now fuck off out me sight. And if you ever run into us down pub don't be comin over expectin a warm welcome. He shook his head, popped his knuckles. Ah might not be as friendly as Ah'm being now, boyo. And if mah skin's full enough, which it will be, and mah fists are in t'mood, Ah won't be givin a tuppeny fuck who yer old man might happen to be. Alright?

This wasn't exactly a shock; it was more of a mystery how it had taken so long. What a fucking relief to know he'd mixed his last tub; he never wanted to see another bag of plaster again. Part of him wanted to thank the fat twat for sacking him; but there was no way he could be on the end of that kind of aggro without having a dig back, and he never could hold his tongue when his blood was up. One of them had to have the last word, and it sure as shite wasn't gonna be the wanker in the string vest.

Marl's eyes lasered him as he scored open the envelope with a black thumbnail, flicked out a purple one and tossed it in a puddle in front of him.

Here. You can keep yer fuckin twenty. Ah wouldn't wipe me arse wi' it. Get yersen down t'pie shop, you fat cunt. Be a cryin shame if you starved to death.

The big man bellowed like a bull with its bollocks caught on a barbed wire fence and swung a right hook that would have taken his head clean off if it had connected, but he was out of shape and slow as fuck. Sean clocked it from miles off and ducked out the way, flicked the vickies at the sad old fucker and ran like fuck, laughing his tits off. It looked for a minute like Marl was gonna chase after him, but he'd never have caught up. When he looked over his shoulder he could see him standing there still, waving his arms about and hurling abuse he was too far gone to hear. Hopefully he'd be so radged he'd have a stroke or something, fall down dead on the spot.

With no more job and no more fucking Marl to deal with he had no reason to stay in that shithole a minute longer. With a rare smile and his wages snug in his rocket, he kicked up his feet and legged it to the station, dead set on getting back to the real world as fast as the train would take him.

THE SHY RETIRER

Spangled to high heaven, you floated around a lampshade caked with years of cobwebbed dust and the shells of dead flies, watching yourself as you rolled around on the living room floor in your mate's flat with, what was she called, Corrina, Kayleigh, something like that. The carpet was minging, couldn't have been cleaned in months. Baccy and scrunched up skins all over it, bits of grit and crumbs of stale pizza crust, shrapnel, shards of plastic from lighters that had been stepped on, blims of resin like tiny blobs of rabbit shit. You were knocking over cans, tipping ashtrays, cracking your legs on a knackered glass coffee table that had a fair whack of gear left out on it. You'd definitely be having some more of that before you were done. Even from up there you could feel the wet heat on your palm between her legs where she'd planted it with a firm hand of her own, the wriggling slug of her tongue so far in the back of your mouth it was hard to breathe. She wasn't so much kissing you as trying to eat you alive. You saw yourself trying to move your hand out from under the six-inch strip of denim that was doing a piss-poor impersonation of a skirt but she kept catching hold and putting it back. A couple of times you had a go at pulling away from her completely but even though she was a good bit shorter than you she was heavier, stronger, and dragged you back in, arms imprisoning you like a wrestling hold as you tumbled onto your sides and her tongue went round and round like a cement mixer.

It's not that you weren't into it. She was a nice lass an that and under any other circumstances you'd not given it a thought; it was just that you were worried about her boyfriend, who was sparked on his back across the fag-burned sofa with raspberry ripple trickles of blood and bugle dribbling from his hooter. He was fucking out of it and didn't look much like moving but it'd have taken some explaining if he'd come to his senses and clocked what you were up to.

What a fucking mess.

Another one.

After Hayley, two months walked straight past you into a drab and dark December where you battered your way through the saddest Christmas you've ever known. It was normally a good do at your mam's, a right ale-fest from the first of December all through to January the second and sometimes after if there was any leftover booze that wanted finishing. She's a cracking cook, your mam, made a roast so good even you'd scoff it in the days when you were eating fuck all else, and her festive fodder was famous. Everyone would be trolleyed by the time dinner was served at half one and it'd carry on from there, a proper balls-out, gluttonous piss-up, not a bit like the airbrushed, middle-class, pass-the-buttered-asparagus bollocks on the telly ads.

But not that year.

Both sets of grandparents were there as usual, Tez too. Poor cunt had nowhere else to be and there was no way your mam was gonna let him spend it on his jack. Shame he couldn't have a drink but that ship had sailed and sunk and he'd not long since come out of hospital after what happened at the funeral. It still had all the trappings; a turkey the size of a fucking sheep, more spuds than a paddy's picnic, enough hooch on the table to sink a war fleet, but everyone was subdued. Sure, they talked, threw a few lines around about how good the grub was and thank god your mam was the cook she was cos no one else could make a spread like that, standard shite, but their hearts weren't in it. There was a collective intake of breath when you sat down to eat and everyone clocked she'd set an extra place at the table, but you never knew whether it was deliberate or not because either way it was devastating and you were too shit-scared to ask.

Your mam spent the day buzzing about keeping busy, playing her favourite role of hostess with the mostest, but she'd not look anyone in the eye and a couple of times you caught her in the kitchen bawling. You put your hand on her shoulder once to let her know you got it, that you were feeling it too. Mam, you said, but she shrugged you away, didn't turn round. Don't worry about me, love. I'm alright. It's been a hard morning, that's all. I'm fine. I'm fine. Like if she said it enough times it'd make it true.

Tez went home as soon as dinner was done, looking like he'd risen from the grave to show his face and couldn't get back to his coffin quick enough. The old folk stayed a while longer for your mam's sake but you could tell they were itching to get off an all and it wasn't long before someone asked you to bell them a taxi to share. So then there were three, and no more need to pretend. You sat in the living room with your stupid fucking paper hats on, too fragile to point your eyes anywhere but down, no one saying a word, while you mechanically, methodically, drank yourselves senseless. If anything else of note happened, you're fucked if you can remember.

Spin forward to the thirty first, the loneliest night of the year. You spent it in the company of the litre of Jack your Aunty Jean bought you for Christmas, got stuck in as soon as your folks went out at six. You'd done the lot by ten, your lifeless frame Horace – as in, Horace Ontal, a favourite one of Hayley's – on your bedroom floor till dinnertime. There was no one in when the urgent need to shit woke you up so you pebble-dashed the bog, spewed in the sink then sank a couple of bottles of wine from your mam's Christmas stash for breakfast, nothing on the agenda but falling back into the bottomless chasm you'd just climbed out of.

Happy new year.

A dreary January smudged into a February thick with snow, the air so cold it felt like it could crack the windows. You hid in your room and your folks left you to it, busy fighting their own private wars in the aftermath of Hayley and the hand grenade her death had lobbed into their lives.

One Friday night you couldn't stand your room or yourself anymore so you took the bit of Christmas money you'd not already blown into town for a pint and ended up smoking a joint outside the Rose and Crown with a guy whose face you thought you knew but couldn't think why. Drinks were bought, shit was shot, and you ended up back at his place snorting mingled lines of coke and ket off the kitchen table with him and his mates until you didn't know who you were or where you were or which fucking way was up, which was the only place you needed to be.

They called him the Captain, he said, cos when he was around you never knew where you were gonna end up but you were guaranteed to be flying. His ragbag posse all had nicknames too, like they were living a small-town Yorkshire version of an Eighties frat boy film. There was Jonny Skins, who never left the house without any; Pacman, a top-ranking space cadet and gold star madhead who couldn't get enough of shoving little white pills in his gob and could put away more of everything than anyone until you came along; one guy went by Pikachu. Fuck knows why they called him it, but that cunt was crazy. He got stopped by the coppers one night when they clocked him on his phone while he was driving and he'd done so much K that when they opened the door he fell out into the road, laughing his nuts off at them. He got a night in the cells and a three-year ban, but it did fuck all to slow him down.

If anything not having to worry about driving made him worse. Then there was Pace – cos I'm a quick mover, boy, he'd say, leering in the direction of any lasses unlucky enough to be near the filthy twat – and his comedy sidekick Sid, who was fucking vicious when he ran out of sniff. They were mental, fucking radged, exactly the right kind of crazy bastards you needed to help you in your quest to lose it big time and kill yourself while you were at it.

You bonded with these lunatics over tramlines and twenties, furtive fingers dipped in baggies in the bogs of High Street pubs, E's necked in those viscous, timeless hours when the world glows like a pearl in the pink velvet light of the ambient dawn. They were comp kids you'd have given a proper wide berth ten years ago cos they'd batter any cunt in a grammar school blazer for fun, but they were sound enough now when the gear was being passed round, especially when they were paying.

Friday to Sunday you'd cane so much it'd be Wednesday before you started coming down, and Thursday night was nearly the weekend, wasn't it, so a few of you would go out for a pint to get in the mood. But Pace'd get lairy and buy a gram; Sid would get jealous and buy an eighth; The Captain would get greedy and buy a quarter, then next thing you knew it'd be Saturday night again, post-pub, in a trashed house wondering where the fuck two days and the fat end of half an ounce had gone, with every other cunt in the room making wired calls to score some more, or some ket, or pills, acid, even, if there was any about; whatever they could lay their hands on, just to keep it going. And you could bet your arse at least one connection would come through.

You took drugs every other day of the week and drank twenty-four seven even when you were working. There was so much different shit going round that you'd swallow a handful of something without bothering to ask what it was and deal with the effects when they came. No one could keep up and they didn't mind subbing you cos your consumption made them feel better about their own atrocious habits. You never knew when you'd had enough, and you never said no. You knew your body wouldn't be able to sustain it. At twenty-two it was wrecked from years of not eating, drinking too much, all the other horrible shit you'd done to it. One night you were bound to mix too many of the wrong things and it'd give up the ghost, or you'd get so fucked you'd fall in the canal and drown or something stupid like that. Whatever. The pain would be over, the problem of your life solved by its end. But until that happened, it was party time.

You managed to get out of the flat that night without having to fuck Catrina or Claire or whatever the hell she was called, but it was touch-and-go. She was proper getting going, had you sort of pinned down on your back with her knees on your shoulders while she tried to get her top off when her fella started grunting like he was after waking up and she jumped off you like you were made of fire, sat next to him stroking his face like she'd been doing that all along. It was definitely time to do one so you chopped what was left on the table, a couple of grams at least, into two finger-length lines, smashed them both and fucked off out of it without so much as a thank you and goodnight.

When you met them in Spoons mid-week you and Chloe acted like nothing had happened and had a good giggle like you generally did when she wasn't throwing herself at you and trying to shove your hand in her knickers. Pikachu stood you pints all night so he was none-the-wiser and you thought that was the end of it, but then on the Saturday her best mate, Sasha, Samantha, Sarah, collared you when you were having a fag outside the Shepherd waiting for everyone to finish having a piss so you could move on to whatever pub was next on the crawl. She got straight down to it.

Did you get off with Caz at Pikachu's last week after everyone else had gone?

You played dumb.

You're a fucking liar. You got a slap round the chops for your troubles but she'd need to hit harder than that for you to feel it with your pain threshold and you didn't move a millimetre never mind flinch. You tuned out while her non-stop gob said that Chloe had told her everything, then rattled on about what a bastard you were for taking advantage of a girl in that state and what kind of man blah blah blah. It was all bullshit though. Even fucked off your mash you were too uptight to make a move; things kept sort of happening somehow, but you never kicked it off. You didn't know how. The way you remember it, you'd wanted to get some air so you'd gone to sit on the back step and skinned up a twiff to blaze while you cooled off. Ciara came with and you were jawing away, loved up to fuck cos of the E's you'd eaten in the pub an that, so you had your arms around each other's shoulders like you do in that state and that was when she started kissing you, all skin-tingles and giggles. You kinda went with it cos you were mates and you really liked her, plus she was a pretty good kisser at the start and the E was pulling the strings so it's not like you had much of a say, but it didn't last long and you thought it was just one of them spur of the moment things that'd be forgotten by the time you'd gone back in and hoofed some more gear. But when Pikachu landed on his arse she was on you like a shot and everything went a bit sideways then.

It took fucking ages for everyone to come out the boozer and Sophie was tearing strips off you the whole time; she buttoned it sharpish as soon as the door opened but she carried on glaring at you and it was doing your head in by the time you got to the next pub.

You were forgiven at the all-back-to-mine when everyone was rinsed on an unholy amount of pure MDMA the Captain had ferreted out from somewhere. She found you in the kitchen chatting shit with a load of randoms, saucer-eyed and shaking over a spliff you'd been failing to roll since the first syllable of recorded time, whispered that she wanted to talk. You snuck upstairs and ended up locked in a bombsite of a bedroom that made your student gigs at uni look like the fucking Ritz, where she spent an eternity apologising in between racking up on the turntable lid, said she didn't mean those things she'd said outside the pub, she'd been mates with Kelly since primary school and knew what a slag she could be when she was on one, she knew you were the quiet sensitive type, it was obvious from the first time she'd seen you and you were such a nice change from those other loudmouth fuckers taking the piss out of everything and everyone all the time, couldn't they see how fucking stupid they looked, and sounded, trying to outdo each other with their silly little boy jokes, so fucking immature, they should take a leaf out of your book, she was amazed how clever you were, like that time someone asked some mind-melting shit like, why is the sky blue, and while everyone was going, wow, mental, heads blown just thinking about it, you said it was because of the light bending through space, was that what you said, she'd never forgotten how surprised everyone was when you first started coming out with shit like that, like it was the most obvious fucking thing in the world, but they were used to it now and they all talked about you when you weren't there, you know, couldn't decide if you were a madman or a genius, but she knew, she knew, you know, and she was so so sorry for slapping you, did it hurt, my poor baby, did it leave a mark, come here, can I see it, and on and on with this shit while you boshed another line and you'd've brought some weed up if you'd known this was where it was heading, not that you'd've been able to skin up if the abortion you'd left in the kitchen was anything to go by, and she was still gabbling on when she got up from doing hers and took her vest and leggings off without any kind of warning or preamble or anything and stood there in this thong that was so fucking small she might as well not have bothered wearing it and said, I don't know whose bed this is but it's ours now, don't just sit there staring at my tits, get over here and fuck me, genius boy, so you did, what else were you gonna do, but christ that girl could yap for England and she talked and talked the whole fucking time, only stopped when she sank her teeth into your shoulder when she came, lifetimes later, shivering and stiff like her veins had frozen solid, and then she started up again, I've not come like that for ages, professor, we should do it again sometime, definitely, yeah, I've been wanting to ride you for ages but fucking you it's like fucking a bag of coathangers, you know, you need a girl to take good care of you, feed you up, get some meat on them beautiful bones of yours, and she walked naked and spectral to the turntable to chop out another brace apiece while you watched coloured fractals spin in the darkness like graphics on that 48k Spectrum you had as a kid, the one everyone took the piss out of cos your family were so poor you had a computer that loaded using tapes instead of disks, and the shittest version at that, because the tape player wasn't even built-in and you had to plug it into an external one of your old man's, and wondered if the wetness you could feel where her mouth had been was blood or just spit on your shirt.

There's nothing wrong with a shag between friends, Sadie said when she'd got dressed and you were missioning back downstairs, and that pretty much summed it up. You moved in a wide circle of chemical cronies where everyone ended up with everyone at one time or another and thought less than nothing of it. If you'd got a

84

piece paper with the lads' names in one column and the lasses' in another and tried to draw neat arrows showing who'd had who and when, you might as well have scribbled all over the cunt and it'd've made no less sense than plotting what had actually happened. You were every bit as bad as the rest of them, but you never found the connection you were after and despaired of it ever happening.

■

Time passed, unnoticed.

Weeks, months. Years.

You were supposed to be dead; your body was tougher than you thought.

Jobs came and went.

Your boredom outshone a hundred suns.

You worked in a petrol station, briefly, until the gaffer caught you nicking fags by the hundred and that was the end of that. You tried your hand at valeting cars, but that went tits-up when you rolled in with a rough on and puked in the footwell of a brand-new Merc. You even had a go a dry-stone walling, but one day someone came to see how you were getting on and found you cabbaged on the hillside, snoring, the dog end of a joint burning on the grass next to the bottle of Gordons you'd just finished for a mid-morning snack. In-between you signed-on and did cash-in hand work, odd jobs gardening for your gran's mates an that, robbed booze from the supermarkets to keep yourself lubricated if times got too hard, but with the Captain and Co leading the merry dance it wasn't often you had to dip your hand in your bin.

■

Not long after you started working for Marl your mam made you go to the quacks.

Ah've booked you an appointment with Doctor Sumnall in the morning, she told you the night before when you came home from work, dusty and weary and dying to die.

What fo'? You opened the fridge and shoved your Scrumpy inside; seven for the shelf, one to wet your whistle. It burped and frothed as you cracked it and necked the lot. It was proper nasty, warm cos the cooler at the shop was bust but it'd've taken ages to chill and you were never gonna wait.

You know what for. You've not been right for ages.

Ah dunno what you on about.

Come off it, Sean. You think Ah don't know? Ah'm you mam.

You crumpled the can and reached for another.

Ah'm fine.

You fine? Right. So fine you need to drink eight cans o' that stuff every night instead of having yer tea, an spending all yer weekends out of yer bloody head on Christ knows what. Fine enough that you've started doing those things to youself again like you used to. Don't think Ah've not noticed, Sean, yer mam's not daft, whatever you might think.

Under your work shirt your bicep burned; three fag burn blisters the size of pennies, one on top of the other like traffic lights. You'd tried so hard to be good but you could never manage it for long.

Just go see what he says. You never know, he might be able to help. There's pills an things they can give you now.

Take more'n that to sort me out.

That's as maybe but you'll never know till you ask.

You stood and drank.

Please, Sean. Remember how bad it was before? Yer like Our Hayley and Tez rolled into one when yer like that and no bugger can deal wi' you then. Her voice wobbled with the 'H' word. Ah can't cope wi' that again. Do you not want to get better?

God, she was so fucking reasonable. It was maddening. The list of people you'd happily tell to go fuck themselves was without end, but you could never refuse your mam. Your nod would have gone unnoticed by anyone else, but she clocked it as soon as the first muscle moved.

■

For a medical practitioner, Doctor Sumnall was a shocking specimen, a porcine, flatulent old fucker who looked like he'd been giving the pies way too much stick. Blotchy face, shaving rash, bottle bottom specs surfing an ebb tide of sweat down his scarlet conk.

Depressed?! What's a fit young lad like you got to be depressed about?

He was so dismissive it was all you could do not to jump over the desk and deck the doddering old cunt. Only the fact you were hungover to fuck and didn't trust your legs enough to land on saved his nose from being splattered all over his mush. It was a short appointment. You had no words to describe how you'd been feeling since you hit the wall in your early teens; he was more interested in drumming his chipolata fingers on the desk and inspecting his watch than he was in helping you find them. You left with a prescription for a two-week course of pills – flupentixol – that he said might take the edge off, and a raging thirst you quenched in the Club straight after.

You need to go tell him if yer no better, your mam pleaded when you'd finished the meds. Mebbe they can give you summat else?

He can shove his pills up his arse, the geriatric bastard.

Six months later you were back. She'd phoned again after she found you catatonic in the garden one morning in nothing but your boxers, your blue-tinged skeleton not far off hypothermic in the cold October sun. Fuck knows how you'd got there.

This new doctor was younger, a lot more sympathetic. He managed to get you under the care of a consultant psychiatrist and you thought there may be light at the end of the tunnel when you heard that. Maybe if you could see someone who knew how to get you to talk you might be able to start making some kind of sense of the fucking mess that had been decaying your mind for so long. But that wasn't his job; all the shrink had to offer was pills, pills and more pills, and you had quite enough of those of your own to be taking, ta very much. You tried to behave and had what he gave you but there was so much shite in your system they were never gonna work. Maybe if you kept mixing them with everything else it'd hasten the end though, so you ate them like Tic Tacs and carried on as normal. After six months you said that nothing had changed and he more or less told you that if none of the drugs worked he was shit out of ideas.

So much for talking therapy.

You were discharged.

5

The place was bare. Bright clean rectangles of unfaded paint shone on the walls where art prints and posters had been taken down, a few stubborn rocks of Blu Tack stuck like barnacles that even a knife couldn't shift. The knick-knacks and ornaments had been suffocated in bubble wrap and packed away, drawers and cupboards emptied, surfaces washed, floors swept and mopped. Stacks of cardboard boxes nicked from Morrisons stood watch, sealed with parcel tape, black sharpie scrawls saying whose was what and which room they'd come from. Devoid of clutter it was a non-place: the husk of a redbrick rent without a soul.

They had a Chinese straight from the cartons with whatever odds and sods of cutlery they could find, nothing much to say, like a bunch of strangers thrown together over a meal on a crap reality show who couldn't wait for the cameras to stop rolling so they could fuck off home. When they got bored of pretending to eat they cleared the table, cutlery and all, into a garden rubbish sack and shifted the chairs outside for their last night as a threesome. It was after eight but hellish hot, Mandy and Pops wearing bikinis and Sean in nothing but shorts, sweating like a fatboy in a bakery. He was slamming some Becks he'd been chilling in the freezer, Poppy her usual plonk. Mand said it was a busy day coming up, so she didn't want anything stronger than a jug of iced water with a couple of wedges of lime.

They were mostly quiet. Every now and again someone would say something and it looked like a conversation might break out, but they couldn't keep anything up for long. Even Pops, the Duracell Bunny of idle chat, was struggling, but she came to the rescue once her wine did its thing.

I can't believe this is it, babe. She was laid on a sun lounger in between them, reached out to pat Mandy's thigh, let her hand stay there.

Me too.

We've had some times here, haven't we? How long's it been, three years? She emptied her glass, poured another, drank half straight down. Remember the housewarming party? When those guys who used to live across the street turned up with all that amazing coke? That was *crazy*. I didn't sleep for two days. I wonder what ever happened to them?

You know very well I didn't touch that coke, and I know why *you* didn't sleep. Mandy's eyes were sad, but the rest of her face smiled. You couldn't keep your hands off – what was that fair-haired one called again? Said he played guitar in some band or other, but *I'd* never heard of them. Looked a bit like you, Sean, come to think of it.

Oh, I can't remember that *now*. Chris or something? Why should I remember his *name*? I remember his muscles though. Did I ever tell you—

Yes, you did. And you don't need to tell me again.

You're quiet tonight, blondie. It was Sean's turn now. What's up with you, cat got your tongue? She poked hers out at him.

Never much chance for anyone else to talk with you holding court, is there? She could still make him squirm at will if she was feeling mean but after nine months he had her pegged and gave as good as he got.

I know what's up with you. You're sitting there thinking, I don't know *what* I'm going to do without Pops feeding me wine and keeping me up talking at night when poor Missy's in dreamland upstairs and I should be joining her in bed. She was wearing shades, but he could feel her eyes twinkle behind them.

It's been great living with you two. He dropped his fag end into the dregs of his beer. Seriously.

I *knew* you were a charmer from the moment I set eyes on you. She shoved his arm, gave him a sly pinch that he felt with his whole body. I said to Missy as soon as I got her on her own, you're gonna have to watch that one, babes. I bet he could talk the birds out of the trees if he wasn't so shy. And he's fucking *fit* too. She paused for the comeback but he wasn't biting.

I mean it. Truly. I've always been an uptight fucker but I never realised how bad it was until I started living with you. I'm so relaxed here. Not like at home where I've got to keep switching personality depending on who I'm talking to. Here I'm just me. I've never had that anywhere else. It was the most unguarded he'd been with anyone, and mostly it was true. The bits they didn't know – Mandy especially – wouldn't hurt them.

Give it up, blondie. Mand, have you popped an E in his Becks?

And where do you think I'd get one of those? Apart from that box you keep next to your bed, I mean. Anyway, you *know* I never go near the stuff, so why are you asking me that?

Miss, chill. I'm kidding.

I'm sorry. I know. It's just – I'm going to miss you too. With that the floodgates opened.

Come here. Pops took her hand, pulled her over, sat her on her knee. Let's not be sad. She stroked her face. Tomorrow's the most exciting day of your life. You're moving in with a fucking *dream-*boat any sane girl would be ga-ga over. What's to cry about? Now come on, turn the waterworks off and drink some wine. You've been hiding from the bottle all night. Sean, there's a couple more in the fridge and Little Miss Mandy here is sharing them with me whether she wants to or not. Be a sweetheart and go get one for us, will you? I'll make it worth your while. This is supposed to be a happy time and I'll not stand for any more tears.

But he swore he saw a couple trickle down from behind her Oakleys.

■

Moving day was brutal. Punishing work, merciless heat, nothing but a hired van and Sean's shit-shifting skills to get them through. Mandy had shared a bottle with Pops to keep the peace, although Sean spied her tipping a glass into the flowerpot next to her when she thought no one was looking – then gone straight to bed. She was up at dawn, pottering around with a feather duster and panicking about bits of cleaning he wouldn't have dreamt of in a million years. Him and Pops had drunk the sun down and most of the way back up. Neither of them had an off switch once they got started and they ended up finishing every bit of leftover booze in the house, castled with a couple of jumbo lines each from an old baggie she said she'd found when she was packing.

Don't tell Mand or I'll be in some right shit. I've not done any of this since we met, and I don't reckon she'd be happy.

She lifted her head and sniffed, eyes wired and wild. As if I would. She blew a kiss, handed him a plastic tube that might have been a tampon applicator in a previous life. Your turn, blonde boy. Dunno how long I've had it but it's pretty shit hot. Fuck, I can't feel my face. I can't feel my face. Then she turned her gaze skywards, dropped to her knees and howled at the moon like a wolf.

When he said he was gonna miss her, he meant it.

■

His hangover didn't figure high on the scale – a five out of ten at best – but he was parched from the MSG in the bit of Chinese he'd actually eaten, his head banging from too many fags. A gallon of water would see to that though; he'd sweat the rest out later. Pops hadn't been so lucky. Mid-morning she was at the table, head in hands, ill enough to say she was never drinking again.

Blondie you *utter* twat. How could you let me end up like this when we've got so much to do today? She was projecting the every-day Pops but she sounded muntered and looked rough as sin. Inside her open robe, still in last night's bikini, he could see her whole body quivering.

Remind us who bought so much wine?

We were *all* meant to drink it.

And we did. But some of us drank a lot more of it than others, didn't we? He yoinked the duster from Mandy's hand and tickled Poppy's nose with it. Now get your arse in gear and put some clothes on. There's shit to shift and you're no help to me dressed like that.

Give me ten more minutes. *Pleeeeeeeease*? She lifted her shades, flashed her baby blues as wide as she could manage.

Two.

Five.

Done.

It took most of the morning to empty the gaff. Sean lugged the boxes and some smaller bits of furniture into the Luton on his tod, cursing like he was back under Big Marl's cosh while Mand finished tidying and going through the estate agent's checklist of final tasks. Pops didn't have much more than a few bags of clothes so he packed them into the back of her Mini as a parting gift. Even that looked like it would have been too much for her to handle. He thought he'd heard her puking earlier, but Mandy would have gone mental if she knew so he kept it to himself; he'd have to send a text taking the piss later. She was still languishing in her pit when they set off.

You think she'll be alright? Mandy sounded concerned as he gunned the engine and the van pulled away.

She'll be fine. She looks broken now, but you know what she's like. Once she gets up she'll sweet-talk the girls at the new place into unloading the car for her and be on the pull round town while we're still unpacking. They call themselves artists but it sounds like they spend most of their time caning sniff on tick and going out clubbing. They'll see her right.

God, it's gonna be strange living without her though, isn't it? It is.

A pause as they weighed what it meant.

Anyway, are you feeling strong? We're not halfway there yet. I might need some help at the other end.

There was barely a couple of miles between the houses but with every fucking student in town moving the roads were gridlocked so it took well over an hour door to door. He could've walked there and back in half the time for fuck's sake. He was flagging when they finally made it; he'd been sweating out water faster than he could drink it and the shakes were starting to insist that he was more hungover than he thought. It had to be done though, so he gritted his teeth, pushed through it.

Dusk was settling when he locked the van for the last time. He stood on the back step smoking, sweat pooling at his feet as his muscles remembered the shithouse feeling after a hard one on the site, but at least today the work had been worth it.

Hey, mister. Mandy tapped his shoulder, offered him an open bottle of Becks. I hid some of these for you. You've earned it.

His eyes lit up. He handed her his fag, took the beer and necked it.

Fucking hell, I needed that. Where…

In the freezer. I'll grab you one. You must be shattered.

Might as well make it two. They won't touch the sides.

He polished off the six-pack in about ten minutes before they went in. Mandy had thrown all the windows and doors open as soon as they got there but the heat of the day was trapped in the bricks so it hadn't done much good. He lay down on the fake leather sofa, closed his eyes. He could do with a few more ales for his dry mouth but there was no fucking way he'd make to the shop. It wasn't far but he was so beat it might as well have been on the moon. He was nodding when Mandy sat on his legs.

You poor thing. I've never seen you look so tired. Can I get you anything?

Not unless you've got some more Becks.

Sorry mister. You'll have to drink some water instead.

His eyes drooped again.

Oooh, wait! There's one last thing we've got to do.

This wasn't welcome news; she might as well ask him to free-climb Big Ben as stand up again.

Whassat?

Well, she guided his hand up her dress. We need to go christen the bed, don't we? She bent down, brushed his lips with hers. I'm going to pop upstairs so I can have a quick wash and get these dirty clothes off, and I won't be putting *anything* else on afterwards. You can follow me in ten minutes and I *don't* want to be kept waiting…

Christ, for a second she sounded like Pops. His fingers traced a line down the inside of her thigh as she got up, the lace trim of her dress tickling the back of his hand as she sashayed away. Christening the bed would have to wait though; and so would sleeping in it.

She woke him in the morning, every bit as naked as she'd promised to be, his drowsy brain barely awake enough to understand the words as she whispered, alright mister, have it your way – we'll christen the sofa first.

REALITY BITES

The first time she saw you properly hammered you'd not been in the new place long.

It was a Saturday in mid-July, maybe a couple of weeks after you'd moved in. You were woken early by the sun streaming through the diaphanous gauze of the curtains but Mandy was fast asleep so you rolled over and dozed off again, knowing you had nothing to do and all day long to do it. You were stirred sometime after by a warm wetness under your chin, teeth nipping your throat, hands rubbing your chest, hot breath tingling in your ear.

Hey mister, it's time to wake up.

Soft kisses with stale mouths, sex, soporific and slow, then a leisurely shower in the cubicle that was only just big enough for both of you. You soaped each other down with knowing hands and stroked another orgasm apiece into the bargain, then had coffee and cigarettes at the chipped wooden table in the kitchen as birdsong fluted in through the open door on the slightest of summer breezes. The sun was cracking the flags.

The garden was small, but perfect. The fractured stones of a lumpy patio splintered onto a messy lawn bordered on three sides by a ramshackle fence, tall trees and hedges making it way more private than the one in the house you'd shared with Pops. The lawn was a mess, scorched and brown, spotted with coloured daisies, ragwort, red clover and dandelions, but it was yours, so you loved it. One sultry night you'd Christened that too, sticky and sultry in the pristine moonlight, clothes scattered like weeds all around. The sun started to climb over the tops of the trees on one side in the middle of the morning and baked the garden for most of the day, dipping behind the ones on the opposite side after tea; it was a proper sun trap and a killer place to unwind.

What's the plan today, then, mister? Mandy docked her fag in the ashtray, blew smoke through the door.

I fancy a couple of cans in the sun. What do you reckon?

Bit early for me yet. It's not even lunchtime. Don't let me stop you though, I'm happy reading. I can't be bothered doing anything else today.

Might as well have a walk to the shop then. You coming?

It's okay, you go. I'm not exactly dressed for it. She gestured at herself, barefoot and bare legged in a lacy bra and thong with one of your flannel shirts unbuttoned over the top. She loved wearing your clothes and looked better than you in them, no matter how much they swamped her. I'll get myself sorted out while you're gone.

Sure. You want anything?

What are you getting?

Cider. It's all I want when the sun's out like this.

Get a couple extra then and I might have one later.

Cool beans. See y'in a bit.

A kiss and a cuddle and off you went, topless, camo shorts and Converse, rattling in anticipation.

By midday the thermometer on the outside wall was north of thirty. You were sitting on the grass chugging Olde English, a few down but no one was counting. A dead soldier nearby was filling with the remnants of your rollies as you chilled out to a seriously deep dub techno mix humming from the iPod hooked up to a docking station in the kitchen. Mandy was laying on a rusty sunbed she'd found in the clapped-out shed, lumps of foam poking out from the multitude of holes in the moth-eaten fabric, a Seventies mess of lime green and orange with big yellow flowers for added cringe. She smelled of heat and flesh and sun cream like Malibu that you'd rubbed all over her when you came back from the shop. When you pressed your hands on her stomach and thighs she'd wanted to go straight back to bed, come on, mister, the sun can wait, but you shushed her, cracked your first can and rolled her over, brushed away her curls so you could massage her shoulders, back and neck, slipped your hand inside her bikini for a quick squeeze before going down the backs of her legs and even the soles of her feet. Earlier she'd been engrossed in a novel, but the heat had made her tired and now she was dozing with the book covering her face, pale skin turning a lightish pink in the sun despite the factor fifty.

She didn't move until the treetops shrouded the sun and shadows began to creep up the side of the lawn. She hadn't noticed when you covered her with a couple of towels and replaced the book on her face with her straw sun hat.

Hey, mister. The hat tumbled to the ground as she sat up. What time is it? God, I must have been totally out of it.

Dunno. Maybe about five?

Five? Shit, have I been asleep all afternoon?

Yeah, you must've been.

You should have woken me up.

What for? It's not like we were doing anything.

True. She stretched, yawned, languid and luxuriant like the idle rich. Did you save me some cider?

I'll go have a look. You drained your can and went in, buzzing with the fuzz you loved, the calming, leaden drag of your limbs as if you were walking through water. There was plenty of food in the fridge but no cider, and there was none in the chest freezer either. Fuck, that hadn't taken long.

Looks like it's all gone.

You drank all of it? How much did you buy?

You knew exactly how many but didn't want to say; you'd already crushed most of the empties into a Tesco bag and shoved them in the top of the recycling bin on the drive down the side of the house.

Just a few. It doesn't matter, anyway. Come on, let's go buy some more.

Oh, it's no biggie. I'm not fussed.

You were though. You'd had twelve already, your legs were misbehaving and your thoughts were turning soupy but you needed more more more more more more.

Might as well. It's still early.

Are you slurring your words, mister?

Nah, I'm alright. Shall I roll you a tab for the road, or do you wanna stay here while I go?

No, don't go without me. I could do with a walk; it might wake me up a bit. Give me five minutes while I get dressed.

You went in, locked the back door and sat down, flicked the dial on the iPod until you found some reggae, Nah Nah Jah Jah No Children No Cry, decided to leave it playing while you were out so you'd have something righteous to listen to when you came back. When Mandy came down she was wearing a polka dotted summer dress and sandals, creaming something into her arms and the top of her chest.

What's that?

Aloe vera. Thanks for covering me up. I'd've been burned to a crisp.

You know I'll always look after you. You took her hand with a daft grin as you left through the door at the side of the house, sparked the fag and put it between her lips. There was a corner shop a few streets away, one of those that sold everything from Diamond White and Spesh to tampons, Super Noodles, Sellotape and tinfoil. The lad who worked there most days was a crusty looking twenty-something with arse length dreads and a face full of piercings. You'd got talking to him the first time you went in and chatted enough since to be on first name terms.

Hey Sean-o, how's it going dude?

What's up, Gandhi? It can't have been his real name, but he'd told you it with a straight face and it suited him in a Trustafarian kinda way.

Fuck work today, man, seriously. Fuck it. All this sunshine and everybody coming in for beer. Look at the fridges, man, they've pretty much cleaned us out. Too busy for me. I'm ready for offski.

Any Olde English left? This is Mandy, by the way – I don't think you guys have met. You were gregarious when you drank; life was so much easier that way.

Hey, Mandy, nice to meet you. He stuck out a hand for a fist bump; she looked puzzled for a sec, then realised what he was after and reciprocated. Yeah man, there's always plenty of OE. There's only you drinks that shit – if it wasn't for you I don't think Rafiq would order it in. What you up to later? I'm off to a squat party in Holbeck if you wanna come. Should be sick.

Ah cool, that sounds—

Not tonight, mister. Mandy killed it dead at the source as you took a couple of four packs from the cooler. I've not seen you all day – you're spending the evening with me.

This was a real drag. A squat party meant drugs, and drugs meant the kind of weekend that had become a thing of the past; you were well up for it now you'd had an early start, all the old instincts firing. You could picture the scene. A dangerously over-crowded room, thick with smoke; drum n bass or savage techno at jet engine volume, passing round bongs and spliffs, chatting shit with strangers who became best friends you'd never see again, scoring whatever chemical cocktails came your way, the synchronicitous chaos magic that would follow, the whole universe of endless possibility that come with being fantastically, irredeemably fucked out of your tree, way beyond the laws of any kind of accepted objective reality. Once of a day you'd have got the address and been there before Ghandi had even clocked off work, but not now.

Maybe next time then? he smiled as you put the cans on the counter. This everything?

Let me go grab a bottle of wine. You were gutted about the party and trying not to show it. It was her fucking fault she'd been asleep, so why should you have to miss out on the fun? Might as well finish the job at home instead, although it wouldn't be the same and you were gonna be bummed out about it all night.

Sean, are you sure? We don't need that. I'll only have one of these ciders, two at the most.

Nice cold glass of wine will be lovely in the sun. You were definitely slurring, could hear it yourself.

There's not going to be much sun when we get back.

It's hot though. I feel like sitting outside all night.

She didn't reply, hung around by the magazines while you paid.

See you round, dude.

Sure. Enjoy the party. Have something for me, yeah? You could have fucking murdered a couple of E's on the spot, and that was just for kick-off.

You knows it bro. You bumped fists again before you hefted the bags.

She was quiet on the walk back; when you squeezed her hand she didn't squeeze back. You'd been together for nearly a year and it had mainly been plain sailing, but something was definitely up.

What's wrong, grumpy? You hoped you could make light of it.

Nothing. Nothing. It's just – you're not going to drink all that, are you?

Are you kidding? You properly meant it. An eight pack and a bottle of wine would have done you for the day, never mind sticking it on top of what you'd put down earlier. I'll have a couple of cans with you and we can share the wine.

You seem like you're drunk, I'm not sure you need to have anything else. I'm not fussed for wine. I might have a tiny bit but you know I can't drink a lot.

I'm fine.

Well, okay. I guess I just want you to look after yourself is all.

■

You struggled back to consciousness through the pain of a cerebral blitzkrieg as you fought like Dracula to drag yourself out of a patch of blinding sunlight on what you eventually recognised as the living room floor. As your vision cleared Mandy's face swam into view; she looked fucking radged.

What time is it? You tried to get upright against the sofa but toppled over, fought hard not to retch. The vom was halfway up; one gip and you'd toss your cookies all over the carpet.

It's one o'clock.

I—

What the hell were you playing at yesterday? Do you remember what you did last night? You absolute dickhead. I couldn't believe it.

You tried as hard as you could but there was nothing there.

You can't, can you? Shall I tell you?

You didn't want to know but she filled you in anyway. You'd started drinking the cider like crazy as soon as you got back, can after can after can, she'd never seen anyone drink so much so fast, she said. She'd had one – just a single one – while you guzzled the rest and then started on the wine, straight out of the bottle like an alky or something, Sean, is that normal where you come from cos it bloody well isn't for me. Most people I know only have wine when there's food. I mean, it's fine for you to have a drink, but it's like you were a completely different person. You were talking so much crap I couldn't keep up so I left you to it and went to bed. Then the neighbours came round at midnight cos you'd cranked the stereo full blast and woken them up, and you were being really rude to them until I came down and smoothed things over.

Mand, listen—

No. You listen. After they'd gone I said you should probably call it a night, but no, you insisted on finishing that wine, then you woke me up again later clattering about all over the place, and when I came down you were peeing in the kitchen sink. The bloody sink, Sean. We wash our plates in there. I mean – what the hell? It's gross. I was awake all night waiting for you, but you couldn't even get up the stairs. Must have been lovely for you, sleeping down there on the floor like that. I was worried you'd be sick and choke.

You sat in shamefaced silence while she shouted herself hoarse, tears streaking black mascara all down her face, cheeks the colour of a rotting beetroot. In truth it was a minor miracle something like that hadn't happened before; she was bound to find out sooner or later and there was never gonna be a good time, but you'd hidden it well and it must have been a hell of a shock for her.

I'm going to Poppy's and I won't be back till late. You've left a right mess in the kitchen. There's cans and fag ends everywhere. What happened to not smoking in the house? And the sink absolutely stinks. It'd better be sorted by the time I get back.

Say hi to Pop—

Poppy won't believe it when I tell her about this and she certainly won't want to hear from you. For Christ's sake. This is the first and last time, Sean. I'm not having this again, do you understand?

You nodded.

You'd been doing it all your life so the lie came easily, second nature.

The side door slammed and she was gone, leaving you alone with your pain.

6

After the first rush of excitement, reality hit. Hard.

The landlord was a parasite and made them pay two month's rent – thirteen hundred quid, fucking astronomical for the size of the place – up front. Sean was a wage-to-wage, spend-it-if-you-got-it kind of guy; whatever he'd had that might have passed for savings had been frittered away since Marl gave him the bullet, so Mandy had to stump up for all of it. She said she didn't mind and he knew her folks had helped her out because he'd overheard her talking to her mam about it on the blower, but still he burned with shame. As the man of the house, shit like that should've been on him.

He'd had a nightmare with the DWP after Uni. Once those bastards get their claws in they never get off your fuckin case, he told her when she suggested making an appointment; but she said he had to have some money coming in from *somewhere* so he signed on at the job centre down the bottom of Eastgate, a grim and toxic hellhole that radged him up every time he thought about it, never mind when he had to set foot in the poxy place. The fifty quid a week the dole paid was the fat end of fuck all but it was better than nothing; and at least when they moved in together, with his name on the contract, he'd qualify for housing benefit.

So he thought.

Ah told you they're a bunch of fuckin cunts. He was raging, waving his fag like a knife looking for someone to stab. He'd never lost his shit in front of Mand, but he was off on one now. Absolute shite, they talk. How the fuck are *you* meant to be responsible for *me*? We're not even married. We've only been t'gether for a year for fuck's sake.

Sean, calm down. You know I don't like the c word. Could you just—

Calm? Ah'll give you fuckin calm. Swear to fuckin Christ Ah'm never goin near that bastard place again, an if Ah do it's gonna be with the sole intention of burning it to the fuckin ground. An another—

Just tell me what they said?

Ah'll tell you what they fuckin said. They said if we're cohabiting as a couple an *you're* in employment, *you're* responsible for looking after me an *you* have to pay the rent. All of it.

What?! But—

Yeah, Ah fuckin know, right? You think Ah didn't argue? Ah were about ready to chin the know-it-all little twat, shithouse fuckin desk jockey reading his rules an regulations. But that's it, black an white. You can't appeal it. So we're fucked.

He was knocked back for jobs as fast as he applied for them. Back home his degree counted for shit; there wasn't much call for graduate skills in a market town with a tourist-centred economy, so he was rejected as over-qualified wherever he tried. It was only his old man calling in a favour that had landed him the job with Marl, but he'd assumed his uni certificate would guarantee he'd walk into a job in the city.

No dice.

Even shitty entry-level admin jobs, which he didn't fucking want anyway, said they'd prefer someone with more experience. What kind of experience did you need to put some files in a drawer and answer the phone for fuck's sake? He tried going through some agencies and they swung him an interview for something at the HSBC office behind the Merrion, but that went sideways too. He was doing fine until they asked him about the recent gap in his employment history and why he left his previous role. His gob was too fast for his filter when Marl's ugly mug popped up, and he spat that he packed it in because his old boss was a cantankerous, slave-driving shitehawk and if he ever saw him again, he hoped the fat cunt would be stone cold in a pine box.

End of interview.

He wound up working as a van driver for Morrisons, a soul-destroying mix of stupidly early starts and unsociably late finishes. He'd said he didn't want to do shift work but they told him to take it or leave it; even a no-mark offer like that was one he couldn't refuse when the wolf was drooling on the doorstep, and anything was better than having to deal with the cunts down the dole office. The hours aside it was a piece of piss, pootling round with crates of stuff that needed taking from store to store but he was bored rigid and hated the fact that if he was working a two-ten shift Mandy would nearly always be in bed when he got home; with both of them doing regular weekends, they went from being constant companions to ships in the night.

He stuck it out for a couple of months, longer than he thought he'd manage. He stumbled in one day at six a.m. in no state to be dealing with the early shift, and one of the lads grassed him to the management when his morning breath nearly knocked him over. He got a right bollocking there and then, in the middle of the yard.

What the bloody hell d'you think yer playing at, Sean?! Of all the things you can't do in this job, surely you've enough oil in yer can to know this is it? You meant to be a smart lad. They told us you had a degree. Maybe you should take a degree in common sense, eh?

Christ alive, he was Marl Mark Two.

Ah should sack you on t'spot but you've done well so far and yer only new yet. Bugger off home an sober up. Ah'll put you down as sick today, but Ah'm docking yer pay. And if it happens again, yer out on yer arse, right?

He could feel it building all the time the supervisor, Tim, was bawling him out. The heat of the blood rising to his face, fingers tightening into fists, ready to shut this guy's cakehole if he didn't stop yapping sharpish. Even at school he couldn't take a roasting without wanting to smack some fucker.

Sean? Sean! Christ, yer not even listening, lad. You can go now. But think on what Ah've said.

Why don't you just fuck off? Ah'd enough of this shit at me old job, Ah'm not gonna stand here takin it from a tit like you. Blow it out yer arse, you fuckin cock-end. An the rest of youse can get to fuck an all. Standin there gawpin like a load of fuckin nonces outside a nursery.

Half-cut from the Scrumpy he'd been drinking till well after midnight, he chucked his hi-vis vest in Tim's face and pissed off to the Spoons over the road to drown his sorrows or dampen his rage, whichever came first before his money was gone.

Staff cuts, he told Mandy when she came home at teatime. He'd sobered up enough to pass for tired but he had a minging same day hangover and felt like shit. Last in, first out. Them's the rules.

It felt like one step forward, two steps back; do not pass Go, do *not* collect two hundred pounds. Square fucking one. Again.

The house was worth the stress though. It was a two-bed semi in an area with grass verges and trees bordering the pavements instead of dog shit and broken bottles, their neighbours upgraded from students to the academics who taught them. If there was any noise in the night it was a baby crying through an open window or the chirp of a faulty car alarm. No more police sirens or showers of drunken wankers bellowing *Hey Jude* as soulfully as they could at four a.m., as if na na na na na na na was profound just cos the fucking boring bastard Beatles wrote it. There were only two rooms downstairs, the living room and a kitchen with enough space for a small table and a couple of chairs, with a cubbyhole pantry at the side housing a fridge and a small chest freezer, a couple of wonky DIY shelves that were super-useful for storing jars and spices. He kept twatting his head on them when he went in though, and it drove him spare.

Upstairs there was a smallish bathroom and two bedrooms, the main one big enough to have a full-length cupboard so big Mandy could get inside it. She told Pops it was a walk-in wardrobe, much to her delight, and insisted on taking her for a torchlit tour the first time she came around.

It was rough around the edges and could have done with a lick of paint, but it was bob-on otherwise. Mandy spruced it up, hid plaster cracks behind posters or gig flyers, splashed around colours to brighten up the drabness of the neutral décor. No flat surface was safe from her trinkets and baubles and kitschy bits of spangly tat. It was scruffy but cosy, a proper first home.

She used the boxroom as a studio and spent hours in there drawing, painting, fiddling about with clay, cloth, whatever. There'd been no space to do it in the shared house and she'd missed it, she said. She was never happier than when she was creating. He once found her dabbing a canvas with an abstract smudge of reds, purples and pinks that reminded him of the sunsets over the moors back home where the sky would blaze like Judgement Day as the sun melted behind the Dales across the valley.

Mand, that's fucking amazing.

What, this? I'm just playing with these colours. I probably won't finish it.

No way, seriously? You've got to. Do it for me, promise you will.

If you say so. But it's honestly nothing special.

He loved the finished piece so much that she had it mounted and framed for his birthday. He hung it in pride of place on the living room wall and could never pass by without admiring it, showed it off to everyone who came round while Mandy blushed in abashed silence. He'd never been encouraged to do anything creative as a kid, failed every art exam he ever had to take at school. He was dazzled by her talent and told her so, often.

You make it look so *easy*.

I like to fiddle around, you know, see what happens.

The fact that she was so modest boggled him all the more. Fuck, if he could do the things she could he'd've wanted to scream it from the top of Pen-Y-Ghent.

A few weeks after the driving job went south, Rob invited him out on the promise that the night was on him. Bloody good job. Sean didn't have a pot to piss in and things were getting so tight he wouldn't have a window to throw it out of either if he wasn't careful. He'd missed paying his share of last month's rent and Mandy had to borrow the money from her folks; he made her promise not to say why she needed it, but it was more salt rubbed into the festering wound where his pride had been ripped out.

They met in town after Rob finished his shift at Borders and hid in one of the old men's pubs in the bowels of town. The regulars, brimming with the piss and vinegar of those with too much time on their hands and Sam Smith's ale for blood, were ranting about the financial crash and what a fuckin mess those bastard bankers had made, and how it was the working man that'd have to carry the can like he did every bloody time. No fucker ever bailed them out when they got behind on their payments; if they'd borrowed if off the doorsteppers they'd get their fuckin fingers broke if they couldn't cough up, and that'd only be a friendly reminder, like. Why should they shell out so these cunts could do it all over again? Dark times were coming, no mistake. They knew the signs.

So how've you been, fucker? They touched glasses and drank deep.

Been better, you know.

How's the house? I can't believe you've not had me round yet.

Sorry man, it's been hectic. I'm snowed under looking for work at the minute. I told you I packed in the driving?

Yeah. What happened?

Fuck that, I'll save it for another time. But if Mandy mentions it they were cutting staff and the new boy had to go first, right?

Say no more. You know, I've a mate who works at the housing office on Great George Street. They're always looking. Do you want me to have a word?

What's the craic?

Oh, I dunno. Sorting council houses and stuff, I suppose. Think the money's alright. And if it's shit you could do it until something better comes along? Might be good to get in now before the apocalypse Mystic Mug and his mates over there are on about hits.

Yeah, go on then. Thanks dude. Working for The Man was the fucking last thing he wanted to do, but the shit was chin deep and rising. Desperate times an that.

I'll drop him a text tomorrow and see what he says.

I owe you one.

Normal service resumed after that. Talk of films and books and bands and binges of bygone days, a bottle of gutrot gin on a bench beneath the sad sad stars for afters. He felt like reheated shite in the morning, but the night out had done him good. The upshot was that a couple of weeks later, after an uncomfortable interview, feeling like a prized prick in a charity shop suit that smelled like a cat had shat in the pockets, he got the job.

Mandy was thrilled.

Hey, mister, that's amazing news! You're so clever, I *knew* you'd do it. She clapped her hands and danced a little jig. What a great thing to do too, helping people with their houses. It's properly worthwhile.

Sean, standing at the back door, imagined he'd spend most of his time doing the polar opposite. They'd probably want him to be like that cocky little wanker at the DWP, reading off a sheet, telling folk he'd *love* to be able to help but article such and such, paragraph two lines three to six said…

He chucked his fag, shrugged. Yeah. We'll see. He lit another fag and smoked.

There was nothing else to say.

NO

BEEEEEEEEEEEEEEEEEEEEEEEEEEEEEEEEEEEEEEE
EEEEEEEEEEP get out of the road you fucking madman snap
back blare blur van blue breeze gusts past

where am ah

left right left right left right left traffic lanes speeding white
line high wire dont look down no gap ahead behind spinning top
fairground childhood waltzer ride falling down oooopsie daisy no
not that anything but that dont say the name shit no ship steadied
upright stumbles on got to go hulk looms red right hand side too
late cant stop too fast

backstep too slow

OHFUCKHEREITCOMES

braced waits end begins halfspeed watches waits how fuckin long
welcome sweet relief greet kiss death over almost over holy mary
mother of god pray for us sinners be it done unto me according to

screeeeeeeeeeeeeech

swerve missing inches rattling bones runsrunsruns-
runsrunsruns kerb trips concrete scuffing shredded jeans grazes
knees raw bounces back safe gulps air thick like water news&-
booze redbluewhite muscle memory shambling day of the dead
feet trodden path worn paving stones thin golden goal oblivious
stares folk bus stop waiting see them no not there no figments
phantoms fevered brain dreams distance closing one step two
step three step four pushes weak metal door shut locked fuck
now what shoulder shoves gives a little bit then a little bit more
aaaaaaaaaaaaaaaaaaaaaand

IN

falls through frame bell chimes up she looks knew her once her
fucking name safeiah samayiah shushmita postwork rage raging
thirst hi usual is it cider crisps baccy skins wine sometimes hard day
at the office something like that cold eyes now blank face hard smile
like shes seen a ghost counter props him up she steps back wary

s   t   a   r   i   n   g
    s   t   a   r   i   n   g
        s   t   a   r   i   n   g

must speak words search dredges deep mouth moves mute fish
flopping on dry land click penny dropping lightbulb yes

two of those please

so much effort four small words pointing

no need she knows one each hand clink clink spit floods guts
spin cycle churn flee run run run done almost what else what else
what else what else

pack of those and one of those seven words marathon run
please one more extra mile knows those too amber leaf marlboro
drops them in anything else

looks down cant face her cant face him shakes head bleep bleep
how much tunes out focus shaking wallet card shoves it fucking
number what number memory fails fingers know thank christ
till clanks whirs receipt dentist drill sound hurts teeth thanks
mumbled sour breath thank you bye barely whispered wants him
gone so does he away from here from life barrels out bumps guy
wedged open door

watch where yer goin pal you some sorta fuckin nutcase or
summat

no fight not now fire pissed out cold embers drink drink drink
drink drink drink drink dead lead walk no legs can run weight bags
knuckles white bag clutched chest clinging dear life focus focus
drink drink drink eyes blind jet cars rush rockets warp speed fuck it

GOGOGO

heart offbeat near miss bike now words lost ploughs straight autopilot hillclimb high lactic sting muscles gone nothing there drags fights near victory drink drink drink drink stop no not soooooooooooooo close cant cant cant keep going pushing stop wont start

a

few

s   t   e   p   s   m   o   r   e

and   here   he   is

unsafe   unwell

leaving one hell for the next key lock tumblers click cold brass handle cold white hand back in to face

T H

EN

7

Sean, I think we need to talk.

Mandy was hovering wraith-like in the living room doorway of their new home, looking pensive, lips pursed. Her voice was like the one his mam used to use when she'd caught him bunking off school or forging her signature on fake sicknotes, or the morning after the time he came home tripping his tits off on acid while his old man was scoffing his dinner, and she broke a metal spatula over his head. The tone that said she didn't *want* an argument but if it came down to it she was fucking well ready for one.

He was slumped on the sofa scrolling the net on his new smartphone, skimming Wikipedia articles about Nineties punk bands, tapping an infinite chain of links that went nowhere; anything to distract from the twin horrors of the office and the news.

The first hung parliament in nearly forty years; that dickhead Clegg had torpedoed the Lib Dem's support base – decades in the making – overnight, his snout all the way up Cameron's arse till it led him to the trough he couldn't wait to shove it in. A coalition in name only, bloody blue blood bastards back in charge after twelve years out. Fuck's sake. In his sunlit grave in St Stephen's church-yard back home, he imagined the Old Red bones of Grandad Paddy spinning, spinning, spinning.

Back to the Eighties, Sean had said over his breakfast fag the day after the election. You just wait and see what happens with this cunt in charge. We're all fucked now.

■

The old house had turned out to be an environmental health hazard. The wooden doors at the back and side had gaps around them that were nearly as thick as Sean's finger; in the autumn the wind made merry whistling through, carrying in leaves and gravel and rain and anything else it could pick up on the way. They also let in fuck-off spiders with bodies the size of grapes that paralysed him with mortal terror and made Mandy shriek as she hoovered them up with the hose.

The single-glazed windows had timber frames he could've ripped out with his hands if he put a pair of gauntlets on, the boiler's last legs ready for amputation; the pipes creaked and groaned and pissed out mucky water near the radiator valves but precious little else. Obvious things in hindsight, but they'd never thought to look when they'd fallen in love with the place on sight and raced off to sign the contracts in case the agents followed through with their threat to show another three couples round in the afternoon.

The first winter they spent there was one of the coldest for years. Heavy snowfall in November packed down and solidified into permafrost inches deep that hung around well into March; the subzero temperatures overnight often running to double digits. Every morning they dressed with chattering teeth and scraped ice off the inside of the windows with white, rheumatic fingers, like on Jean and Harry's farm when he was a boy. In the evenings they came home from work and did it again. They left the heating banging away twenty-four seven but it barely took off the chill, so they bought electric radiators, convectors, a halogen heater. All they got in return was an N-Power bill with four figures before the decimal point that took three years to fully pay off. For the money it cost and the good it did they might as well have cashed in their wages and burned twenty quid notes in the empty fireplace to warm themselves.

The landlord was a cunt typical of his kind and refused to do anything about it. The estate agents, with their tidy commission, had no interest in helping either. The boiler passed its safety inspection and therefore fulfilled its legal requirements, they wrote in response to Sean's furious email. Never mind that it was thirty years old and the engineer said it would have only been sixty percent fuel efficient when it was brand new. He tried to find out through work if there was anything they could do, but as far as he could fettle, tenants' rights were non-existent. Meanwhile their damp clothes rotted in the wardrobe while black mould shroomed across the walls.

After tea they'd shiver in front of the telly, cuddled up under piles of blankets with a hot water bottle apiece, tell each other that one day they'd look back on it and laugh. But with Mandy's six-month bout of flu and the bronchial cough that Sean couldn't shift the comedy wasn't much evident, especially when the next winter was almost as bad and the reasons they'd used to convince themselves to stay after the first were about as appealing as dog shit on toast. When Mandy landed a tidy inheritance after her gran died and her house was sold, buying their own place was the only thing to do.

The new gaff was a 1930s two-bed-and-one-box-room semi in a postcode that was gentrifying to fuck after the Co-Op on the main road was bulldozed and replaced by a Waitrose shortly after they moved in, which added thirty grand to the value of the place overnight and it kept climbing from there. If it had had gone on the market a couple of months later, they'd never have been able to afford it. It was a beautiful spot, a twenty-minute walk from their old place, in full-on leafy suburbia. It was nice, *too* nice sometimes, a hotbed of middle-class hippies who'd outgrown Hyde Park having community apple picks, knitting their own yoghurt, riding pushbikes with wicker baskets and carrying on like they were in the fucking *Good Life* or something, but it could've been a lot worse. If he'd ever been told that one day he'd live somewhere like that he'd've laughed his bollocks off; the folks back home would've done the same, then asked which bookies he'd stuck up to get the money.

Mand lost her job when the caff became an early victim of the financial crash, but she'd landed a sweet gig in the city art gallery after Sean saw it advertised on the council vacancies bulletin, and she loved it to bits. She still worked alternate weekends but for far more coin as a flat rate, plus time and a half for Saturdays, which was a bonus she never had at the old job. Sean got promoted as soon as he finished his six months' probation at the housing office, then again soon after, more by default than anything. Housing had the biggest turnover of all the council departments because the amount of shit the staff had to put up with from pissed off punters far outweighed their poxy pay packets and not many folk could stick it for long. He wasn't keen himself; once of a day he wouldn't've lasted a week before he told them to shove it where the sun don't shine, but times they were a-changing.

He'd hated the job from off but once he'd got his feet under the table it was hard to leave with the sky-high rent to cover and then the mortgage to pay. He was languishing in the lower depths of middle management – a particular kind of hell encompassing the worst of all possible worlds – copping nothing but grief from staff below because of the shit he was forever being made to dump on their heads by the Management above. It was lose/lose, every time. The irony of being paid to tell other people what to do when his own first reaction to being given any kind of instruction was either, no, or, fuck *right* off, wasn't lost on him; but the money was pretty good once he'd moved up and much as he hated to admit it, that was important now. His biggest headache was his fascist manager Denise, the kind of arsehole who'd tell the cleaners to disinfect the shitters then complain about the smell of bleach, who did his scone in with her nit-picking pedantry and daily reminders that while no one in the office would *ever* be able to meet her high standards, it shouldn't stop them breaking their backs to try.

On the face of it, life was good. They cooked together in the evenings and were slayed to find that for a guy who hadn't known one end of pan from the other, Sean was a kitchen demon. His pasta sauces and curries were to die for, Mandy said, and the stodgy Yorkshire fare he copied from his mam wasn't bad either. They used ingredients from the herbs Mandy grew in tubs in the garden. Sage, thyme, rosemary. Unbelievably aromatic and exotic to Sean's tastebuds, long used to living on crisps, fags, coffee, ale. Even *he'd* started to enjoy eating; for the first time in his adult life, his frame filled out. Stuffed and sleepy, they'd cosy up to watch DVDs they got through the post from LoveFilm, make cheese on toast pizzas with tomato puree, oregano and Cholula if their bellies bullshitted them they weren't full enough after tea, brews and Hobnobs after if even that didn't suffice.

Mandy was big into poetry. She'd read to him for hours if he asked her and he'd drink it in, spellbound. He'd dabbled with it in his early teens after being captivated by someone on the radio reading a Dylan Thomas poem that reminded him of the farm, but he'd never gone further than buying a couple of anthologies. The words didn't click on the page like they did in his ears, somehow, like it was written in a foreign language he half-understood but didn't know how to read. He couldn't make it sound in his head like it had on the recording; everyone said poems were for poofs, so there was no one he could ask about it without getting a kicking and he lost interest. Mand got it though, nailed it every time, the rhythms and rhymes, the ebb and flow, the feelings locked away in the words, buried in the gaps between them. He loved those nights, especially in winter in with the curtains drawn and the central heating, which actually fucking *worked*, melting the chocolate on the biscuits Mandy ate every night before bed.

They'd go to the pictures, or out to eat if they couldn't be arsed to cook, sometimes both. She couldn't get enough Italian and there was a place nearby they must've spent a bastard fortune in if they'd added it all up. There were gigs, nights out with Pops and Rob on a weekend when they were in the mood, snuggly Sundays where they'd waste the morning sleeping if they fancied, or fuck till early afternoon if they were horny and had nothing better to do. Shit, they'd even been abroad. Yet somehow there was money left at the end of the month, an outrageous curiosity that never ceased to confound him. He was as close to happy as he was ever going to get.

check you out mister sellout with yer mortgage and yer polo and yer respectable job all nine to five keep yer nose clean and pay the bills on time shit council pension fucking passport thinking yer a big shot cos you flew on a plane savings accounts bank cards werent you meant to hate this shit said youd rather die than get stuck in this kind of rut swore to yer mam youd never do it but its suckered you in just the same you might think it feels good maybe it does surely its better than losing yer shit every weekend and taking all week to get straight definitely fucking boring though tv and tea shops what would you have said ten years ago even five or two if someone told you this would be yer life youdve been fucking disgusted so much for live fast die young stay pretty fuck thirty yeah right such a cunt despising

everyone who chases it out of one side of yer mouth and whoring yer sorry
arse out the other to get exactly the same thing youve even lost yer accent
only one thing worse than a hypocrite thats a fucking hypocrite and guess
whos a gold star one of th—

Sean? *Sean.* Did you hear me?

What's up? He knocked back a glass of Primitivo, refilled it, started to roll a smoke,

Heavy silence, waiting for the storm to blow in. He watched her watching him, fidgeting with her fingers like she didn't know what to do with her hands and was trying to work out what to say.

Want one? He licked the Rizla and stashed the fag behind his ear.

No, not right now. You know I'm trying to cut down. You should—

Ah shit, Mand, not this again?

I just worry about your health, that's all. She came over, sat down next to him. You don't look well. You've been so quiet recently. Is there something wrong?

I'm fine. What do you wanna talk about? As if he didn't know. He gulped his wine.

It's… well… you don't seem like yourself at the moment.

You know how it is. I've a lot on.

I know, Sean, I know. How was work today?

Fuckin Denise giving it the usual. You shouldn't send me an email without a subject heading, Sean. How am I supposed to know what it's about? It's very unprofessional and I run a tight ship here as you should know by now. His teeth ground like he'd had half a gram. Work's a bag o' shite. Do you really need to ask? Pause for breath; bristling.

Is that your second bottle tonight?

What?

The wine. How much have you had?

Who's counting?

It's Monday night. Do you *need* to have two bottles of wine on a Monday night?

Nothing wrong with having a drink, is there? Bang on the defensive, truculent like a naughty kid. He'd never changed.

I never said there was. But you were drinking all weekend, again. You were plastered on Saturday night; I thought you were going to get thrown out of the bar.

Poppy was pissed too. So were you.

You two are a bad influence on each other but it wasn't Pop's fault, and I had four drinks all night, that's all, *four*. We were there for hours, and they were all singles. You had more than that before we went out. I had to wake you up when the taxi came to take us home, and when the driver saw the state of you I didn't think he was going to let you get in.

Course he was, I were fine.

No you weren't, Sean. You *weren't*. You could barely stand up. You were sick when we got in and you spent all Sunday morning in the bathroom throwing your guts up. Or have you forgotten that bit?

I were alright, I'd not had a lot to eat, that's all. It happens, I don't know why it's gotta be such a big deal. Back home, puking was an occupational hazard. There wasn't a weekend went by without some poor cunt hurling; it was part of the entertainment.

You didn't sound alright. You sounded like you were dying. Then Rob called at lunchtime and you went out again. A quiet couple of pints and a catch-up, you said, I won't be back late. And what happened? You rolled in blootered at half past ten. We were supposed to be having a steak and watching a DVD. I'm surprised you can look at a drink today.

Look, I'm sorry, alright? We'd not seen each other for ages and we got carried away. You know what Rob's like.

Don't you dare blame Rob. I *do* know what he's like, but you're *always* getting carried away. You don't need any encouragement from him. She looked like she was going to say something else but checked herself.

Can we just get to the point?

When was the last time you came home from work and didn't have a drink?

Come on, Mand, I do it all the time.

When?

How about Wednesday?

That's one night out of the week. And anyway, you'd been to the pub on your way home again, hadn't you?

That's—

Don't lie to me, Sean, I could smell it on you as soon as you walked in. I think you think I'm stupid sometimes. You reckon you can cover the smell of Guinness and whiskey with chewing gum? Credit me with a bit of intelligence, will you.

I'm going for a smoke. Are you coming?

She shook her head. Sean, please. All I want is for you to be happy and you don't seem it. You never used to be like this.

It's fine. I mean, I'm *fine*. Seriously.

Promise me you'll have a night off tomorrow.

Okay, okay. Whatever.

And the next night?

Christ, Mand, I'm stressed to fuck at work. If you had to deal with the shit that I do all day, you'd want a drink when you came home an all.

I don't think it's healthy is all.

I'm just going through a bad patch. It'll pass.

I hope so.

He grabbed the wine and took his fag through the patio doors, sat in a plastic chair looking out over the lawn that backed onto a patch of woodland separating their house from the park. The sun was setting behind the trees, bats and swallows flitting silhouetted against the crepuscular sky. Being so close to the woods they got foxes in the garden sometimes. Once, not long after they moved in, he noticed something moving from an upstairs window and saw a mother with three cubs cavorting on the grass in the light of a skullwhite moon. He saw more of them there than he ever did when he lived in the country and they never failed to raise a childish thrill, even if their shit was fucking rank when he buzzed over it with the lawnmower. He smoked the rollie in four immense pulls, went to make another, realised he'd left the makings on the coffee table.

Fuck's sake.

He didn't want to go back in and face her yet. He'd got through the chat without a row, just about, and he didn't want to risk starting anything now. At least he'd brought the bottle with him. He put his empty glass down and started swigging from the neck. Instant calm. Easy to think about not drinking later with wine in the bottle tonight. Fuck it. He'd deal with tomorrow in the morning.

Mandy came out after a while and sat on the other chair beside him, handed him the baccy. Could you roll me one?

I thought you were stopping?

Don't push it, mister. They must be friends again if she was calling him that; a hint of dimpling in her cheeks softened him like cookie dough.

It's a lovely night.

Mmmmmmmm.

You know I love you, don't you? It was easier to say it then, especially with a bellyful.

I do. You too.

I just get like this sometimes, you know? I always have. You've not seen it much, but it's always been there.

I know. You think I don't, but I do. I just wish you'd talk to me about it.

There's not much to say. I wish I could explain it but I can't.

You could try?

The tension roared back; he choked down an angry reply as his defences flared. He took a deep breath, spoke as softly as he could. Not tonight, eh? It's been a hard enough day as it is without getting into all that.

Maybe you should see a doctor?

Pfffft. Been there, done that. All they do is give you pills, and they're about as much use as a chocolate teapot. I'm not wasting my time with any of that again. It was the first time he'd spoken to her about it explicitly, but he was double-dealing, giving it a nod and batting it away at the same time. She'd asked him once in the early days about the mess of scars that patterned his arms, and a few other places. These? Nothing for you to worry about. Ah got into a few scrapes in the olden days when Ah was fighting the rock n roll wars, that's all. Subject closed.

Okay. But promise me you'll think about everything we've said?

Sure.

Good. She squeezed his knee. I'm going to bed now. You coming?

Soon. I'll have another glass and then I'll be up.

Do you – Never mind. I'll see you in a bit.

Night.

A quick kiss – dry lipped, tongueless – then she went inside and slid the door shut behind her. It was a good job he'd put the bottle down before she came out; there'd've been fucking hell on if she'd seen him supping out of it. He picked it up and went back in once he was sure she was in bed. There was about half of it left; more than enough to finish the job.

MY PERFECT COUSIN

You'll never forget the day Hayley died.

A bright September sky, the early autumn sun reddening your bare shoulders as you watered your old man's front lawn in the slumbering warmth of a lazy Sunday morning. The spray from the hose threw rainbows all around, icy drops misting on your face, spattering over your chest. You were twenty-one, fresh out of uni with your whole life to look forward to, or so everyone said. Fuck knows what that was supposed to mean. You hadn't found a job and weren't much interested in looking, but money was thin on the ground and you were gonna have to bite the bullet and start applying for things sooner rather than later. It wasn't a day for thinking about that though.

Your mam and dad were out looking for Hayley. She'd been gone for a week and people were starting to worry. It had happened a couple of times before when she'd disappeared without warning, but it had only ever been a day or two, three at the most, before she turned up, calling her mam from a payphone somewhere, hungover and helpless or high as a kite with no fucking clue where she was. Then they'd pick her up and take her home to sit mute in bed mute while they tried to feed her soup and sweet tea and told her how much they'd worried, how they wished she'd stop this silliness and start trying to settle down, she was a grown woman, damn it, what did she think she was doing acting out and running away like a stupid teenager?

Everyone knew it was serious this time, although no one was brave enough to say as much. You'd heard your mam on the phone to your uncle Tez in the first few days. Don't worry, she'll be back soon enough, it's only a matter of time. She always surfaces in the end. You know what she's like. The same reassurances she gave your grandma, Aunty Nance and anyone else who'd listen. They were trying to convince themselves as much as anything, but it was getting tired. You'd almost finished with the lawn when the phone rang.

Hales was your childhood idol. She was four or five years older than you and she spent a lot of time round yours when her mam and dad split up. She loved Uncle Tez but he was too pissed to live with then, and she hated her mam's new fella's guts so when he moved in she pretty much moved out, kipped at her mates' houses when she could, dossed down in the spare room at your mam's when she needed a proper bed and some peace or she'd run out of sofas to crash on. She was more like a stepsister than a cousin; you loved her more than anyone in the world.

She was probably about fourteen when Tez and Nance split up for good, so you'll have been nineish. Even then she was chaotic, had these moods that swung from mania to paralysis and back again, sometimes in a day, but no one knew why, and they never bothered to ask.

She's a bit flighty, that one, is all your mam would say. Bad with her nerves.

Bloody moody's what Ah call it. This was your old man's carefully considered assessment. Ah love her t'bits though, so what can you do? Ah just wish the lass could settle down. She's nearly bloody thirty for Christ's sake.

She could be so much fun when she was up. She'd take you to the playground to kick a ball around, climb trees or have races on the swings to see who could go the highest. She always won. You'd watch in amazement as she soared almost parallel to the ground and leapt off right at the apex, flying like Supergirl. Sometimes she'd land on her feet, spin around to face you with a huge smile and a wobbly curtsey, touching the hem of her dress like a dancer at a curtain call. Other times she'd take a proper spill, but she never let on that she was hurt even when her grazes were bleeding, and before you knew it she'd be back on the swing challenging you to race again. She was fearless, bulletproof, invincible; you were awestruck by her powers.

One day after tea when you were ten or something like that, you'd taken your bike to the playground on your own. It was a couple of streets away, only a quick ride. It wasn't much of thing – a mess of half-dead, dogshit covered grass that separated the two sides of the estate, the one you lived on and the side you were warned to steer clear of, although you never knew why because your old man was born and raised there and your grandparents had lived at the far end of it since it was built after the War. There was a wooden climbing frame, green with mould and moss, a couple of creaky swings with chains rusted dayglo orange, and a concrete tunnel under a hillock of grass that you loved to crawl through playing armies until one day you dragged yourself out, damp and dirty from the stagnant water collected in the bottom, waving the treasure you'd collected.

Mam, mam, Ah've found a little sword.

Oh my god Sean, put that down!

But—

Now!

You dropped the syringe, watched as your mam picked it up with her fingertips, wrapped it in the tissues she kept tucked under her bra strap and dropped it into the top of a litter bin. Next time you went back, the tunnel was impassable, blocked up with hard, grey cement.

It was a nice evening but you were at a loose end, circling round on your bike, wondering if any of your mates would turn up. You were at that age where your childhood games had started to seem lame and whenever you met your friends it was awkward with the unspoken fear that anything anyone suggested playing was totally uncool so you usually ended up doing nothing, but at least if you were bored you were bored together. After a while a couple of kids jumped over the wall at the opposite end and started walking towards you. You didn't recognise them but you could tell from their trackies and trainers which bit of the estate they were from. All the kids over there dressed like that, like their mams and dads. When they got closer, you saw one of them was carrying a football.

Can Ah play?

Play what?

Football.

We're not playing football.

What's that then?

This? The lad with the ball goggled at it. Nothing. Can Ah have a ride on yer bike?

You knew then that something was up. There was a cast in his eyes, a hint of a sneer, an edge to his voice that said he wouldn't take no for an answer.

Me mam says not to let anyone else on it.

Well, yer mam's not here, is she? S'give him t'fuckin bike.

Instantly the mood changed and they stepped up, crowding you. They looked to be a year or two older, high school kids. You were scared but trying not to show it, moved to back away but you were straddling the bike so your feet got stuck.

You can't have it. Anyway, Ah've got to go. Ah'm going now, actually. Bye.

As you started to walk the bike around the first lad dropped the ball and caught hold of your shirt, bunched it in his fist and pulled you towards him, his nose nearly touching yours. If you don't gimme the bike Ah'm gonna take it anyway and Ah'll fuckin bray you shitless for keeping us waiting, right? His breath smelled of tobacco and baked beans.

Before you had time to answer he let go of your shirt and shoved you with his other hand. You wobbled but stayed on your feet and it was game on then. You weren't much cop at fighting, but only soft lads didn't stick up for themselves and you never backed down if it came down to it, even if it meant getting leathered.

Piss off, you told him to buy a bit of time, heart pounding as you tried to plan your next move, but there was no way you could take two older lads on your own; you'd just have to tough it out and hope for the best.

Y'ear that? The lad looked at his mate. This little bender just told me to piss off. D'you know what we do to shitstabbers who tell us to piss off? He shoved you in the chest again and you lost it then, swung at him as hard as you could. He wasn't expecting it and you caught him on the side of the head, but it was a glancing blow and he barely flinched before knocking you over with a punch so fast you were on your arse before you saw it. You lay staring at them through a mist of tears, your bike clanging sideways onto its pedal next to you, the reflectors on the spokes gleaming in the light of the setting sun.

Looks like yer in for it now, you little twat. He kicked the top of your thigh, hard.

Hope yer not too attached to yer teeth, cunt. You gonna lose em all in a minute.

You'd started to curl up into a ball when you heard heavy footsteps pounding up the path. Through your blurred vision you saw

Hayley steaming towards you at full pelt, her school skirt flipping up and down as she ran. She crossed the playground in no time and without breaking stride she kicked the lad who'd hit you so hard in the nuts with her patent DM that both his feet came off the ground before he crumpled to the turf, making this disgusting retching noise like he was choking to death. The other one looked on, mouth agape, until she caught his eye and feinted like she was gonna smack him, then he turned and ran like fuck, left his mate bawling his eyes out on the deck.

If Ah catch you little bastards anywhere near me cousin again Ah won't be kickin y'in t'bollocks, Ah'll be ripping em off an fuckin feedin em to you, right? She booted the ball into his face with such venom that the sound of it made you jump. The kid said nothing, lay there whimpering with one hand cupping his groin, the other groping feebly at the mess of snot, tears and blood swimming over his face. Even at that age you could see his nose was broken.

She helped you to your feet. Come on, kiddo, let's get you home.

You were sniffing, wiping your sneck on your sleeve.

Y'alright? She picked up your bike and held it for you to climb on.

You nodded as bravely as you could. You were shaking, partly from the shock of being punched, partly with excitement. There were fights all the time at school but it was primary playground stuff – blood was rare, and you'd never seen anyone go down like he did when Hayley's boot connected. You wished you could have done that.

She produced a fag from somewhere and sparked it. Most of your family smoked and you hated the smell, but you'd never seen Hayley do it before and she looked so cool as she exhaled a plume from the corner of her mouth then carried on chomping her bubblegum that you decided on the spot to start yourself as soon as you could.

Don't worry about him. She cast a scornful look back at the kid, who hadn't moved. Ah know his brother. He's in the year above me an he's another right, proper wanker. We were lining up once to go into class and Ah felt this thing on the back of me leg, and when Ah turned round it was him, trying to put his hand up me skirt. He wound up bleedin on his arse an all. Fuckin knobhead.

She'd never sworn in front of you either, although the rest of your family did, and something changed in you that day. As you ambled home in the lengthening shadows, you'd been shown a glimpse of another world, a secret place that had been hidden before. You were mortified that she'd seen you cry but you'd put a brave face on it, and all of a sudden you felt very grown-up, as if by smoking and swearing she was inviting you leave your childhood behind, join the grown-up cool kids with their fags and fights and kicks in the nuts. You wanted to marry her.

When she was down she'd fester in the spare room for days with the lights turned off and her rock music playing but she always had time for you, even when she wouldn't speak to anyone else. Come and sit on t'bed with me, kiddo, tell us what's happened at school, she'd say, and you'd talk about your day, or show her the picture you'd just drawn, or see if she could figure out how to make your new Transformer turn from a truck into a robot. Later, when you'd grown up and had problems of your own, you realised how depressed she was, how lonely, how hard it would've been to have to deal with a buoyant little lad and his boundless enthusiasm for life; but she never let it show and in your memories that made you love her all the more.

141

When you answered the phone it was Jim.

Sean, love, it's grandad. Is yer mam there?

Hiya grandad. She's not in. Her an the big man've gone down to see Uncle Tez. They're out looking for Hales again.

That's what I'm calling about, love. They've found her.

Where—

I'm sorry, but Aunty Nance found her in the woods. She's cut her wrists, Sean.

The words were like a lead cosh to the head. Your legs buckled and you sat on the stairs, staring at the phone cord, shaking so hard your teeth rattled.

Is she—

She is, love. Sean, I'm sorry. I've got to go see to your gran; she's in bits. Look after your mam. Tell her to give me a ring. I'll talk to you later. And look after yourself an all love, right?

You hung up without replying, went back out, lit a Marlboro Light and picked up the hose. You must've been in shock because you don't remember feeling anything, just a heavy kind of numbness. You caned the fag without touching it, squeezing the hose with both hands in a rigor mortis grip until you realised you were smoking the filter and opened your gob just enough for the charred cork to drop into the flowerbed, an ugly blot amidst the yellow and purple of your dad's pansies.

Morning, Mr Molloy.

It took aeons to lift your head and turn around. Waving across the street was Mr Taylor, one of your old teachers, out for a walk with his fat Dalmatian. In high school they refused to call kids by their first names, and he'd never got out of the habit. Back then you were sworn enemies, him putting you in detention every time he caught you smoking on the way home, which was often, and generally getting on your case about all sorts of minor shite like

142

the petty, pedantic bastard he was. His chemistry lessons were dull as fuck and you never paid attention, acted out and did everything you could to make his life as miserable as he made yours. One day he lost his rag and threw a blackboard rubber that bounced off the desk and hit you lamely in the chest. The rest of the class thought it was hilarious, but that was nothing compared to the uproar when quick as a flash you launched it straight back and bullseyed him in the middle of his stupid, bald, head. You got a month of Friday night detentions, but it was worth it. For a few years you'd've happily seen the cunt under a bus.

He lived around the corner so you ran into him a lot whenever you were back from uni, and you'd long-since made your peace, chatted about your schooldays like a couple of old soldiers swapping war stories. His presence that day was a distraction, so you were strangely pleased to see him.

Hey, Mr T, How's it going? You were amazed by the sound of your voice, so natural on a day that had nothing natural about it.

I'm alright. I've been off sick with stress though. I'm hoping to retire soon with a bit of luck.

What've you got to be stressed about? Ah left Steadman's years ago.

He laughed. You might not believe it but some of the little buggers they send us these days make you look like a perfect pupil. Still smoking, I see?

You were surprised to find another fag in your mouth; you couldn't recall getting it out of the pack, or lighting it.

Looks like it.

Bad habit, that. Stunts your growth. An old line. He paused, waiting for a laugh that never came. Well. I best get on, anyway. Dog wants feeding. You might wanna point that hose somewhere else though. You're watering your feet.

And with that he was gone, leaving you gawping at the puddle of water spreading around your tatty Converse. Just then the car pulled up and your folks got out.

Alright? Your old man nodded. Ta for doin that. Looks like you cut t'grass an all.

Where've you been?

We've come from yer Uncle Terry's.

Are y'alright?

Yeah, sound. Yer mam's gonna make a brew, you havin one?

Aye, go on. Then the world flipped upside down and the shakes came back, big time, as the unfathomable horror materialised; they didn't know.

Big man, you called after him as he followed your mam in, grandad Jim just phoned. Ah think you'd better ring him back.

Alright love, Ah'll tell yer ma.

Two minutes later there was a piercing scream. You rushed inside to find your mam on the floor, your old man trying to pour a glass of brandy down her throat. Come on love, get this down you, it's alright, he kept saying. His trembling hands slopped the liquor over the rim and onto the floor. He looked up as you came in. You'd never seen him cry, ever, but there were tears in his eyes that day, although he was determined not to give in to them. Not a single one escaped onto his face.

Hayley. Hayley. Choking on her name.

Fuck, Ah thought you knew.

He shook his head, rubbed your mam's shoulders and tried to get her to sit up while you stood there like a wean, helpless. She was making these fucking awful noises, kind of crying, kind of moaning, but mostly sounding like a pig in a slaughterhouse that's just smelled blood and knows the game is up.

Brandy. Brandy. Now. The big man's voice was shaking.

144

You found the bottle in the kitchen, had a long belt then filled a coffee mug to the brim, took it back into the hall; he snatched it from you without even looking, tossed it down.

More. You filled it up and he drained it again, then body relaxed and his eyes glazed over, sealing the tears inside. He exhaled through his nose, long and hard, rolled his neck and shoulders like a boxer waiting for the first bell.

Right, come on. Let's get yer mam upstairs t'bed. Have some o' that brandy if you want but don't you fuckin dare be getting pissed, lad. Ah need you help today.

■

In the days after, the three of you tiptoed round the house trying to keep out of each other's way, like you'd had a massive falling-out and couldn't bring yourselves to make friends again. When you met in the hall it was deathly.

Alright?

Yeah. You?

Fine. How's me mam?

Same.

Right.

Tears and tissues, gallons of tea for the wreck of your mam, sympathetic phone calls from family friends who meant well but had nothing to say. You stayed in your room as much as you could, blank and deathly calm, refusing food and coming out only to smoke on the back steps. Hundreds of butts littered the floor where the pathway at the bottom met the lawn. Usually the old fella went mad if he found a stray tab in the garden, but now you chucked them without a thought, and so did he every time he cadged one, till you complained he was smoking more of them than you were and he came home with two hundred Regal he'd bought off a bloke at work, left them in the kitchen for you all to share.

There was a post-mortem, but you couldn't see the point. Poor Aunty Nance had found her in some thick undergrowth in the heart of the woods that bordered the top end of town before they're truncated by the road that led up the Dales. She'd done it on her left side, down then across; the carving knife she'd used was so sharp her hand was hanging half off. When the verdict arrived it was death by suicide, a masterclass in stating the fucking obvious. There were no traces of drugs or alcohol in her system, and she hadn't left a note. She'd slashed her wrist and bled to death. End of.

The numbness never went. No tears, then or since, the habit of a lifetime unbreakable. You sat and sat and sat in stupefied silence for the longest weeks of your life, nicking the big man's booze and smoking like it was the fags keeping you alive. There was nothing else to do.

When the time came for the body to be laid out in the chapel of rest, everyone said you should go. She'll just look like she's asleep, they said, you can remember her like that, but you shook your head. Why would you want to remember her in a coffin, a waxen face, a shell where life no longer lived, knowing that underneath the clothes she'd been cut up and stitched back together like a carcass gutted in a butcher's? Fuck that.

You didn't go to the funeral.

Later you tried to justify it to yourself a hundred different ways. You'd grown apart in the last few years; she'd moved out of town and back again more times than you could count, and with you at uni you barely saw each other. As a teenager you withdrew from everyone, even her, painfully embarrassed when she came into your room to say hi.

Ah know you having a hard time, kiddo, believe me. Ah know all about it.

Part of you loved that she was paying you attention, but you've never known how to respond to kindness or talk about how you feel, so you'd shrug your shoulders, lay there on your bed with your fringe hiding your eyes, and mutter into your chest that you were fine; she'd never push it. If you say so, she'd say. But you can talk to us any time, right?

In your head you were strangers. The person that had died wasn't Hayley at all. She was someone who looked like her, a poor, fucked up woman to be sure, and it was tragic how she'd ended up, but she wasn't Hayley and if she was you didn't know her. Your Hayley would be fifteen forever, the girl with the ripped fishnets, purple lipstick, dyed black hair and Misfits t-shirts who snuck you sweets when your mam said you couldn't have them, the girl who kicked that bully in the balls and smashed fuck out of his face out of sheer love for you; the big sister you never had.

The girl who held up the fucking moon.

Everyone else could weep at the crem and watch the casket as it slid through the curtains into the flames that would burn her to dust, but not you. Your Hayley lived on in the summer playgrounds of your childhood memories, so there was no need to say goodbye, and never would be.

Deep down you knew the real reason you didn't go, but it was so shameful you'd never admit it to anyone and didn't want to face it yourself. You were scared to go because if you went, you'd cry, and you couldn't have that. At twenty one you couldn't remember the last time you had, probably not since the first year in high school when Michael Dawson from a couple of years above nicked your lunch money and shoved your face into a blocked, overflowing bog. You're still gutted to think you let the mask slip, beefing in

147

front of a circle of baying lads who pointed and laughed and called you pissface and shithead as if it was the funniest thing they'd ever seen while you stood there retching, dripping mucky bog water all over the floor. You'd held it in for so long you were an icicle inside, disgusted by feelings, proud to have mastered them. There was no way you could let that out in public, not even for Hayley. The sight of other people crying made you feel sick; the idea of anyone seeing you do it was unthinkable, and so, you chickened out.

When you told your mam she was silent for a minute, then just asked, are you sure? One day you might regret it. But you said yeah, you were sure, and not another word was spoken on the subject. On that grey October morning waiting for the taxi to your grandma's house where they were meeting the cortege, you dismissed your mam with a shake of the head when she asked if you wouldn't change your mind.

Ah hope it goes okay, you managed to say as she hugged you, your throat so tight you barely got the words out.

You waved them off, then took four bottles of wine to somewhere near where you thought she'd been found. Scattered flowers, a couple of stuffed toys ragged with cold and autumn rain, a few cards with scribbled handwritten notes, but you didn't read them. You couldn't.

You sat on a rock and drank until your guts overflowed and back it came, harsh like acid, dark red like old blood. Then you drank some more. And that's how you killed the day, alone, drinking and puking and puking and drinking until the sun dimmed and died and the teddy bears stiffened with frost. And when all the wine was gone, you wiped the spew off your face with the front of your shirt and groped blindly through the darkened woods until you reached the lights of town, stumbling numbly in the direction of any pub with barstaff daft enough to serve you.

8

The first time it came up he thought he'd misheard.

They were in their favourite restaurant sipping espressos at the end of a top-notch meal – antipasti for two, veal cutlets for him and seafood ravioli for her, tangy lemon sorbet dusted with sugar for pudding. He'd had a couple of beers when they got there and a bottle of Chianti with the meat; now he was sweetening the coffee's bitter edge with a double cognac on the side.

Sorry, what? He nipped his brandy. He was nicely on the way, hoped the snifter would take him over the edge.

I said, I've been thinking, wouldn't it be nice to have a baby?

shitting hell she did *say it what the fuck are you gonna do now imagine a useless cunt like you trying to look after a baby you couldnt even look after your old mans houseplants when they went away for a week got the right fucking radge on when he came back and they were all dead this is proper hardcore now told you it wouldnt last shes not gonna like it when you tell her youd rather cut you own dick off with a rusty breadknife than bring a child into this fucking mess and have the poor little bastard grow up with all your baggage christ you dont deserve to live yourself shouldve been fucking dead long since never mind spawning a replica with your poisoned genes*

Wow, Mand. I can't say as I've ever thought about it.

I've been thinking about it a lot.

You never said.

Well, I wasn't sure what you'd say. Pops was talking to our friend Sarah the other week, I can't remember if I've told you about her. It doesn't matter anyway, I've not seen her for years. She's a girl we went to uni with and she's back in Bristol now, I think, but Pops goes for a drink with her if she ever comes up. Anyway, she found out she was pregnant a while ago, and when she told her boyfriend he disappeared. Wouldn't answer her calls or anything.

Shit. Is he—

Yeah, he came back after a week or so. He'd been living on his mate's sofa, apparently. What a twat though. Can you imagine?

He could well imagine, actually, wondered how he'd react if he found himself in the same boat. Shit himself and do the same, probably. He couldn't blame the poor cunt for losing it, but he wasn't about to say so.

What are they gonna do?

What do you mean, what are they gonna do? They're gonna have a baby. She's four months gone now.

Right.

So, what do you think?

Well, good luck to them. They'll fucking need it, he almost said, but caught it just in time.

I mean about us.

I dunno. I kinda wasn't expecting to have this conversation tonight, y'know?

I think you'd be a great dad. You've got so much to give.

Do you honestly think *I* could look after a child? Seriously? I can barely look after myself. Come on, Mand, you must've lived with me long enough to see that?

You've always been amazing at looking after me though. Maybe it'd settle you down. You might be happier if you had a bit more of a focus instead of life revolving around work and getting smashed every weekend. Do you really want to spend the rest of your life drinking a gutful of wine every other night just because you've got nothing better to do?

He tossed back the brandy, longed for the days when you could smoke inside. He tried to catch the waiter's eye but he was polishing glasses and turning off lights, reckoning not to notice. By the time they'd finished their coffees and settled up, the conversation had moved elsewhere.

Talk about a wake-up call.

Even though they'd been together for a few years and got a mortgage, he didn't feel like he'd properly grown-up and that suited him fine. This was next level shit and it haunted him, a shadow future he could barely conceive. The responsibility of it put the fear of god in him. A *baby* for fuck's sake – a completely dependent living, breathing, sentient *thing* that would die without constant care and attention. He didn't have a Scooby how to look after a child and didn't want to learn. Leave that to – who? Every fucker else, that's who. Anyone but him. The loss of independence didn't compute either. He only stuck it out in housing because of the money, but if it got to a point where he really couldn't stand it, he could walk, tell them to keep their fucking job and find something else. It wouldn't be the first time. But there'd be no danger of that with a kid to support and the job market on its arse now Austerity was starting to bite on top of the crash.

Mandy had been moved up at work. She'd got a decent pay rise and things were pretty swish. They could travel more, weekend breaks at fancy spas in the lake district or the Scottish borders, more trips abroad. They'd spent time in Berlin, Paris, Amsterdam, five days checking out the piazzas and galleries of Florence and drinking the best coffee he'd ever had; a fortnight in the forty-degree heat of mid-summer Cyprus where they did nothing but flop on the beach. He was in heaven, caning Luckies at three quid a pack and keeping hydrated with super-chilled Keo while Mandy hid her pale skin under a parasol and a layer of factor 50, splashing around in the cobalt wash of the eastern Med when the heat got too much for her. It was the life of fucking Riley to be fair; hard to imagine trading it in when he'd only just got there.

She didn't mention it for a while, and there was no way he was gonna bring it up. He had a lot of thinking to do; but he was like a loopy Labrador chasing its tail, never any closer to grasping it. A couple of months later she asked again. They were at home this time, watching a long, slow Japanese film that was boring them stupid but they'd invested too much time in to turn off.

Have you had any more thoughts about that thing we talked about, mister?

What thing was that?

You know. About having a *baby*. She whispered it in his ear behind a cupped hand, like they'd just been introduced at a party and she was flirting.

Oh fuck. He thought she'd forgotten. Panic as he tried to formulate a quick reply that didn't start with the word no.

Well…

Well what?

It's an interesting idea.

An interesting idea?

Yeah.

Meaning what, exactly? A good idea, a bad one, what?

need yer top game now boyo she wants to properly *talk about it this time dont reckon the usual bullshits gonna fly lets see you try to dig your way out of this one*

I suppose we could maybe start thinking about it in another year or two?

I don't see why we'd need to wait. We've got our own house, we're okay for money. What's going to change in that time, other than that we'll both be two years older. Now would be perfect. I can't see why you don't think it's a good idea?

I just never imagined myself having kids, that's all. I've never wanted to, to be honest.

not the smartest thing to say dickhead too late now though cant imagine thats gonna go down well the way this chats heading

You've never said that to me before.

You've never asked.

Well I'm asking now.

Shit, Mand, don't be like this. I just don't think I'm cut out for it. And look around you. The planet's dying. Everything's fucked. What kind of world is this to be bringing kids into? There'll be nothing left by the time they're our age.

so you can *be honest maybe thats the best way whod want to bring a kid into this the yanks have got bin laden but theres plenty more where that mad cunt came from that psychopathic fucker in syria whod rather drop nerve gas on his own people than stand down those pictures on the news screaming orphans blood body parts smoke flame buildings bombed rubble dying shrieks rich men fighting over a planet thats terminal micro-wave atmosphere the one percent death cult capitalism one last heist before the earth cashes in her chips and scourges herself of people what a fucking relief youll be dead by then but this kid shes on about will live to see it why land anyone with that the whole fucking bleak disaster of it has twisted yer little mind all the way up since you were no no no no no surely shes got to see its mental*

There's always been problems, but people still have children. I know what you mean about the future looking dark sometimes, but that's not a reason not to do it. If anything it's an incentive to give some love while we're here.

What about the next load of cuts? You must've heard it mentioned at work. People have been protesting in the streets. We'll be on strike before the year's out, I'm telling you. Union's balloting soon. Housing'll be alright. They'll need more of us if anything, but you might be on shaky ground at the gallery the way it's shaping up. We'd be fucked with a kid and one wage.

I don't think we can worry about what *might* happen. If people lived like that no one would ever do anything.

Maybe if we just—

I had a text from Tash the other day – she's pregnant, and so's Ali at work. There's nothing stopping other people, so there's nothing to stop us. You've got to understand this, Sean. I *want* a baby, and I want one *soon*. Not in a couple of years, or a couple of years after that, or when you've had time to think about it so you can tell me you've still not made up your mind. My body is telling me that I need to have one now. I thought you were the man I was going to do it with, and I hope that you are, because I love you to pieces and I think you'll be a brilliant father for my children, but listen to me – if I don't have one with you, I *will* have one with someone else. Is that clear enough for you?

curtains cunt this is one even you cant win shes already decided you can go with it or not are you willing to chuck away everything youve got with her because youre scared of having a kid what life are you gonna go back to drink and drugs and sticking your dick in random lasses when youre so bollocksed you can barely see who it is your shagging great yeah cos you had a brilliant time doing that happy as larry in that poxy town dreaming about dying just to get away but christ a baby a baby a fucking baby you cant say no but yer life is fucking over an if you thought things have been bad its little biscuits compared to this still you never know maybe the booze has fucked up yer balls it takes a long time to get pregnant it can do then theres nine months to grow the fucking thing could be a couple of years left

154

yet maybe youll come round by then people have kids all the time maybe it wont be as bad as you think keep em crossed hope for the best might be plenty of time to get used to the idea at least but jesus suffering fuck wow this is the end of the line cant change your mind once its done youre going to be tied down foreverandeverandeverandeverandever the heaviest cross to carry till the day you—

9

He sat on the edge of the bed like a man in a confessional laying out a litany of the kind of sins no mere priest could shrieve, eyes locked on the carpet's topcoat of dust motes and strands of black sock cotton that the vacuum never picked up. Fuck he was nervous.

Mand? You alright in there?

I won't be long. Her voice was muddied by the door.

Can I do anything?

Just wait there and stop worrying. I'm being as quick as I can.

Once he'd said yes she'd been keen to crack on. He hadn't finished nodding his assent – yeah, yeah, alright then. Let's do it – when she'd launched herself at him and straddled him on the sofa with her dress bunched up around her waist, in so much of a rush she didn't bother to take her knickers off or close the curtains. Never mind that she'd had her pill that morning – she said they needed all the practice they could get.

She was delighted to come off it. She said it made her headache and her boobs sore, and it played havoc with her mood just before her period was due. She was right about that part. There were times she'd get tense and snappy, fly off the handle for nothing or erupt into fits of weeping without warning and he'd know it was on its way. Time for chocolate blocks and herbal teas, hot water bottles, kid gloves and backrubs; eggshells underfoot, the filter on his gob set to maximum lookout.

She stopped smoking just like that, packed in drinking too, not that she did a lot of it. She ordered stacks of books about ways to increase fertility, obsessed over superfoods that were meant to help, avocados ahoy whenever it was her turn to cook. Good job he didn't mind them, another weird thing she'd got him into eating, like spinach and chickpeas. He'd never even seen one before they'd started going out. She talked incessantly about cycles and ovulation, blocked off calendar dates that were prime times to get busy, but she needn't have bothered. After a couple of months of full-on Betty Blue banging, she was late, and there was Sean, feeling like a fella waiting to be shot at dawn, while she sat on the crapper and pissed on a plastic stick.

It was barely morning. He was dying for a smoke, gagging for a drink, but he'd been told that he *had* to abstain because fags and booze were known sperm-killers; it was best not to argue. He smoked at work, snuck in a couple of pints at lunchtime, and sometimes on the way home if she wasn't going to be in when he got back, but otherwise he was the cleanest he'd been since primary school. He was miserable, tense, irritable as all fuck but determined to do it for Mandy's sake.

I can see something! It's working, it's working!

What does it say?

But he didn't need telling.

Her cycle was clockwork. She hadn't said when her period didn't come but he generally had an idea when it was due even if her mood was okay, and once it had gone past three or four days it was odds-on. He kept schtum. If he didn't say it, it wasn't real. But that day she'd woken him up at six, the rays of a dazzling daybreak lancing his eyes like blisters.

I've got something I need to tell you, mister. She looked liked she'd been up all night but her eyes were sparkling.

Mmmmmmm. He rolled over.

Oh no you don't. She prodded him with a slender finger, the

point of her nail jabbing in between two ribs. Open your eyes. You know what I'm going to say, don't you?

He wiped crystals of sleep away with the back of his hand, winced at the stink of his breath, morning gob, garlic and the spices from last night's Karahi chicken takeaway.

My period's late.

Is it?

Course it is and you bloody well know it, so don't give me any of that. You know what it means, don't you?

What?

Oh, you're impossible. I bought a test yesterday. I've not slept for thinking about it. I was going to do it in the night but I thought it'd be better to wait until morning so we could see together. I'm going for a wee, and you'd better be up by the time I'm done.

you never thought itd happen so fast did you so much for having time to get used to the idea have you talked yourself round yet have you fuck as like gone even further the other way if anything too late now feel that in yer chest thats panic you might well fucking panic cos yer life is fucking over when she comes out of there with that test that twisting in yer bowels you can tell youself its delhi belly but its a fucking lie youre gonna shit yourself like you nearly did that time riding the pepsi max with a cock knocking hangover looking two hundred and thirty feet down from the top of that fucking hill in the front car seventeen pints of yesterdays Guinness and fuck knows what else swishing round you were fucking freaking out then that was nothing on this nothing clench yer hole youll look a right twat if she comes in and youve shat your pants or had a heart attack you know whats coming its been nailed on all week theres no point flipping out about it now what else is there to do got to play the game play it cool for her she cant know this is a fucking disaster waiting to happen you only said yes because you couldnt say no if you let on now youll curse the fucking kid before its even—

The sound of the door bursting open startled him.

Two lines! Sean, look there are two lines! She waved the test in his face and there they were: twin train tracks, the end of the line.

fuuuuuuuuuuuuuuuuuuuuuuuuuuuuuuuuuuuuuuuuuuuuuuuuuuuuu uuuuuuuuuuuuuuck

Can you see it? Look, one line here, and another here. See? I'm pregnant, Sean, I'm pregnant. I don't believe it. She burst into tears, arms all around him as she snuffled into his neck.

Wow, Mand. I mean, are you sure?

get a grip get a grip get a grip all these colours flashing room spinning brain ready to burst out yer fucking ears like poppers without the petrol smell or the giggles and its not fucking funny this breathe breathe breathe throats tight as fuck cant get the air in never mind poppers this is what it must feel like to get hanged by the neck until—

Course I'm bloody sure. Look! But he'd seen it once, and that was enough. Congratulations, mister. You're going to be a daddy.

Tears welled, but whether they sprung from joy or something else, he couldn't say. He swallowed the lump in his throat and hugged her back, kissed the top of her head.

I can't fucking believe it, Mand.

I know. I *know*. We're going to have a *baby*.

■

A doctor's appointment the following week banged in the final nail; the baby was due in the middle of May. Mandy was dying to tell everyone but sulkily accepted she couldn't, at least for a while. They told their folks, of course, and she *had* to tell Pops, who was so happy she sobbed for half an hour on Mandy's shoulder; when she'd blown her nose and finished dabbing her eyes she sat on Sean's knee and cried for even longer.

His head was blagged. It was like that quantum cat in the physics books, there and not there at the same time. He'd forget about it, amnesiac bliss, then the thought would pop back at random – oh fuck, she's pregnant – but it was beyond real. When they came home from the twelve-week scan with a monochrome polaroid of the black-eyed, fish-tailed bean growing inside her, he still couldn't fathom it, this mythical creature from someone else's life in a future light years away.

He told Rob in the pub. Where else?

It was an old-school come-on-in-and-drink-yourself-to-death joint full of grifters, grafters and dealers, like the Craven back home where you could buy anything you wanted and usually on the cheap as long as you weren't bothered where it came from, as if anyone who came to do their shopping in an alehouse like that would give an iota of a fuck. Clothes, tellys, shoes, car parts, drugs; he once heard two fellas agree a price for an industrial lathe. You'll have to give us a couple of weeks while I find one, like, one of them said as a folded deposit slid from palm to palm. You had to be careful though, know which scally to ask for what and which code words to use because violence seeped from the walls, hung in the air like the fag smoke it still hummed of even though it was a few years since the ban went through. One wrong move could have your teeth knocked so far down your throat you'd be chewing with your arsehole for weeks. They were a few pints in before he mentioned it.

There's something I need to tell you.

Rob looked like he was braced for a kick in the nuts from a horse.

Mandy's. Well. Yeah. You know.

Pregnant? Shit, that's amazing. With the look on your face I thought you were gonna tell me she'd finally kicked you out or something. Drink up, fucker, we've got some celebrating to do.

They chased pints with shots of Jäger till closing and spoke of everything but Sean's news while the regulars cracked wise with the landlady and she shooed them away with the boundless patience of a teacher in charge of a class of tearaways she couldn't help but love. They had to leave early, skirting a couple of scraps-in-the-pipeline before it kicked off big time; a vengeful scream of, that's the fuckin last time you say summat like that to me, cunto, and the sound of glass smashing following them out the door as they decamped to Rob's for the after-show.

He'd told Mandy not to expect him home. Good job too, when Rob's insistence on celebrating wiped out most of the weekend. He rolled home at teatime on Sunday, a contrite, devastated mess.

You fucking *stink*, mister. You're not coming anywhere near me. She held up a hand like a stop sign when he tumbled trembling through the door in the same clothes he'd gone out in. He tried to apologise but she waved him away.

You're a pillock, but I love you. I know it's been hard for you the last couple of months and you deserve to let off a bit of steam, but you've got it out of your system now so don't be thinking about doing it again, right? Get those clothes in the washer while I go run you a bath. Did you silly buggers get anything to eat?

Monday morning he phoned in sick.

On Tuesday, to Denise's obvious disgust and disbelief, he did it again. He had tougher shit than her to worry about though, and the snarky cow could chunter all she liked. Fuck her.

■

With pregnancy, Mandy bloomed. She'd never worn a lot of make-up but she stopped using it altogether and her skin was so clear and smooth it shone. She gave up dyeing her hair too, didn't want the chemicals to get inside her body and risk harming the baby. He'd never known her to be anything but a flaming redhead, watched in fascination as it faded like an autumn leaf. The red fell back to the same Candyfloss pink that Pops still used before it gave way to a silvery grey, then settled to a shade of burnt oak somewhere in between caramel blonde and chocolate brown.

In the early days when he'd asked her about her natural colour, she'd do a Mona Lisa smile and say, there are some things a girl likes to keep to herself, mister. He kept probing but didn't really want to know; truth be told, he enjoyed the mystery. He loved the red and was sad to see it go, but he soon got used to the natural look and she became more beautiful to him than ever.

She was in a nesting frenzy. She piled up junk for him to drive to the tip, spent hours of an evening poring over catalogues and websites looking at cots and mobiles, prams and highchairs, choosing colour schemes to turn her studio into the perfect nursery, moved her art stuff to the box room. The prospect of motherhood transformed her. He still couldn't imagine being a dad but he was happy for her and let her sweep him along, joined in the window-shopping, nodded in approval at whatever passing fancy she was excited about. It was like falling in love all over again, the endorphin rush that comes with a new relationship when the future is tremulous with fresh possibilities.

Now the deed was done his old habits crept back, but he was careful. She complained if he sat next to her after smoking, said the carbon monoxide lingering on his clothes was bad for the baby, and although she frowned if he came home with a six pack or a bottle of wine she never made too much of a big deal about it.

You might as well enjoy it while you can, mister. You're not going to have time for any of that when the baby's born. And you *have* to give up smoking. You know I don't like telling you what to do, but that's one thing I'm going to be absolutely strict about – there's no way you're holding our baby and having them breathing that.

It was probably a good idea. His chest had been getting tight and he often started the day hawking solid lumps of tarbrown lung-butter into his stinking stream of morning piss, so knocking it on the head wouldn't be a bad thing. It wasn't as hard as he thought. He stopped smoking at home, unless he was having a drink, but he'd only have a couple instead of the steady chain that had him standing by the back door every ten or fifteen minutes, whatever the weather. He didn't feel any better but it kept Mandy on side and he wanted to do the right thing for the baby.

At first the bump was invisible, but some people guessed from the way she carried herself with her hand laid unconsciously across her tummy as if to protect the precious thing inside. It expanded rapidly, swelled like a beach ball inflated with a tyre hose. She was so slight that from the back she looked the same, but side-on there was no hiding it. He kept getting flashbacks to primary school, when the girls would shove their jumpers up the front of their shirts at playtime, reckoning at grown-ups without a clue what a seismic thing they were faking.

The weeks vanished in the rush of spending and planning. His mood swings were wild. Elation, panic, profound horror, bland acceptance, bleakest despair one after another after another. The bairn was still a fantasy, but one day it would leap into stone-cold reality like the dead girl climbing out of the telly in *Ring*. The calendar mocked him daily from the kitchen wall until one day, without warning, there was no time left.

NEW DAWN FADES

Another wretched morning, or maybe it was an afternoon. How the fuck would you have known with the blind on the skylight closed? Faint shafts of sunlight crept through the cracks around the edges, dust floating like dandruff in the halo. You were kneeling on the floor in your room at Whitworth Park halls of residence, your fingers, no more than bones, hooked around the sink the only thing keeping you vertical, pummelled by waves of nausea so fierce they fucking hurt.

The tap was running full pelt. The tepid water, treacle-thick with so much chlorine you couldn't drink it, stank as it splashed back onto your face, but you were sweating so hard and your eyes were leaking so much saline that you barely noticed.

Another dry heave, and another, then out it came. A squirt of bitter bile flecked with blood jizzed down the sides of the yellowed enamel. It tasted so vile you spasmed again, spat more red than green. Your brain blagged your gut it was empty then; with that came relief and you relaxed your grip, watched hollow-eyed as the water swished the putrid mess away.

You craved Antarctic air to numb your ruined throat and clear your filthy lungs but the room was sweltering from the cast iron radiator with the fucked stat you couldn't turn off, forever stale with the smog from the Marlboros you chain-smoked when you drank, which was every night, and most days too. It was like you'd forgotten how to breathe, heart ready to burst out of your chest Alien-style. You knew you were dying and were glad of it. You let go of the sink and slid onto your side, foetal, the circle about to close.

So, this was what the end felt like; you'd had worse. You shut your eyes and waited for the void to open, willed it to get a fucking move on.

Manchester, around the turn of the millennium. When you left home you couldn't wait to see the back of the fucking place. There wasn't much to miss. The stultifying boredom, the suffocating insularity of life in a bell jar where everyone knew everyone else's name and everyone else's business and you couldn't sneeze or scratch your arse or puke in the gutter without it getting back to your folks. The small-town, small c conservatism, the way people talked about nig-nogs and coons and poofters like it was nineteen seventy five. Those bastards hated anything and anyone that wasn't like them; for young lads, if they weren't into football, Golf GTIs, designer gear and dance music, forget about it. With your knackered jeans, band t-shirts and Kurt Cobain barnet you sure as shit didn't fit the local buzz-cut Kappa and Kangol profile, but you didn't want anything to do with those cunts anyway and they wanted even less to do with you. You've got a scar on your nose from when one of the CK1 ladsmag crew nutted you in the queue for the cashpoint because only a fucking arse bandit would dye their hair blue and paint their nails to match. It wasn't a one-off; there were plenty of other close and not-so-close shaves with twats of the same breed that left you with chipped teeth, cracked ribs, a few more stray scars lost amongst the hundreds you etched onto yourself.

You weren't aware of a single queer person growing up; if there were any at school they were so far in the closet they must've landed in Narnia and if they'd ever peeped out, the poor fuckers would have been bullied to suicide. There was a small Asian community, mostly stallholders and taxi drivers and a few Bangladeshis that ran the takeaways, but they kept to themselves in an estate on the outskirts, next to the main road out. No fucking wonder with the poisonous shit people used to say about them, that they wiped their arses with their hands and ate with them too, or the chef at the Balti House in the bus station would spunk in your Vindaloo if you complained about the delivery charge. If a Black family had moved in, it'd've been headline news. You despised it all and knew whose side you were on. Uni was meant to be your great escape.

There was no reason to pick Manchester. The destination wasn't important; it was what you were leaving behind that mattered. A couple of lads from school who you'd got on with okay enough to meet in the pub sometimes were going so you thought, that'll do. You wanted to stay in the north but not too close to home, and it looked like a good fit. There was a great live music scene, and the modern history course looked alright so you decided to go with it and didn't bother applying anywhere else. You scraped in, just, despite turning up pissed to one of your A-level exams and answering a question about something you hadn't studied, but you were smart enough to blag it and still came away with the grades you needed. Your final hometown summer was a twelve week blowout of cheap cider, a nine bar of Z-grade resin that smelled more like benzine than hash, and carrier bags of class A's, capped off with a weekend at Leeds where you took more drugs in four days than most wreckheads get through in a year and lost your cherry, in full public view, in an open field near the car park, to a goth girl from Newcastle who was five years older and swore if she came to visit you at uni she'd never let you leave the bed. You exchanged a couple of letters after but she never made it down and you mourned her for years, drove yourself crazy imagining the kisses and cuddles that should have been yours being lavished on some other lucky cunt.

Funereal silence in the car on the drive over as you crossed into Lancashire and picked up the motorway near Burnley, your old man's knackered Orion dragging its way up to the summit under grey September skies through the miserable bastard drizzle the M62 wears like an overcoat. The motor ate up the miles westward, past the bleak bracken hills of Saddleworth, keepers of the darkest secrets and the moors for which the murders were named, then down again towards the fringes of the post-industrial sprawl. The cityscape stark against the gunmetal sky looked like a Joy Division song.

Your mam was unravelling in the front, chewing her nails and trying to look like nothing was wrong, so worked up she couldn't distract herself with mindless blether like she usually did when she was upset. Your old man with his customary undertaker's mug on made a big deal out of concentrating on the road so he wouldn't have to speak either, not that he ever said much anyway. In the back with Iggy and the Stooges in your headphones you were the third mute. There should've been so much to say yet no one was willing to try, scared that a misplaced word would make it kick off and spoil everything, although it wasn't as if there was a happy mood to piss on. It should have been a red letter day; you were coming of age, flying the coop, off to meet the world on your own. That's probably what she was worried about.

The M62 turned into the M60 and snaked towards the city flanked by the sooty red bricks of the outer suburbs, corner shops with barred windows, a few tower blocks. At one point you passed a police station that had metal shutters on all the windows; above the Raw Power racket you heard your mam gasp, clocked the twitch as she physically baulked at the sight of it. You passed sidelocked Jews, Jamaicans with mighty dreads, Asian couples in thobes and saris with hordes of kids trailing after them. For a woman who'd lived her forty-three years in a town of twelve thousand white working class and would have died rather than leave, cities were hellmouths. By the time you pulled into the car park she could barely contain herself.

There was some fannying about while you sussed the logistics, where to go for your keys, which of the buildings your flat was in, stuff like that, so that kept her going for a while. She was at her best when she was busy organising, taking charge. Doing that must've made her feel like she was in control, that you were still her little boy, still needed her to do mam things even though you'd be nineteen before the first term was done.

Once that was sorted you found your room on the ground floor of a building not far from where the car was parked. You hadn't brought that much stuff. Some clothes, a portable stereo, a box of CDs and a few mixtapes, the cumbersome load of your second-hand, bottom-end 486 PC to do your assignments on. Your mam had wanted you to fetch some food but you said you weren't bothered, you'd better see what the room was like first and figure everything else out later. It was tiny, maybe ten feet long and eight feet wide, a metal bed frame with a foam mattress that looked like it had been chewed by a dog, a desk and a wardrobe; nothing else. Blank walls, once white, now like the inside of a miner's lung. Your home for the next nine months. The three of you stood on the threshold like a bunch of spare pricks at a wedding until your mam made a titanic effort to smile and said, well, we'd better get you unpacked, hadn't we? That took care of another quarter of an hour.

The goodbyes were brief. Your mam was trying to be brave but it was obvious the poor lass was gonna have a nervous breakdown on the way back and your old man wouldn't meet your eye. You kissed your mam on the cheek, endured her iron embraces, patted your old man's arm and said, well, Ah'll see you in a few weeks.

Look after yourself, son, was all the big man said, and he didn't look at you again.

Ah'll call you when we get back.

Alright mam, sure. You knew that was the right answer; she'd not twigged there wasn't a phone in your room, or anywhere else in the flat that you'd seen.

When they'd gone you locked the door, closed the curtains. There was a window behind the desk which let in a lot of light, but because you were on the ground floor there were streams of people walking past and you couldn't be dealing with that. A friend of your mam's had given you a bottle of red wine as a going away present, so you opened it, laid on the bed and smoked a few of the awful tabs someone had brought you back from a summer trip to Prague, Trumpf Lights or summat weird like that, they were called. You were pissed by the time one of your new flatmates knocked on the door, and that was how you stayed for the next three years.

You were stuck with nine other boys, fully paid-up members of the Nineties Ladbunch, all football, fit birds and Fatboy Slim, posters of Cameron Diaz and Kate Moss in bikinis ripped out of Nuts and FHM plastered over the walls of the living room you never set foot in. Apart from their Southern accents and mobile phones, the flash new toy which everyone but you had, they were no different to the cunts at home.

They made an effort at first, invited you along when they were going on the piss but you never went, so they stopped bothering. You were such an awkward bastard you put everyone else on edge, so it was better if you kept out of the way. You were a ghost, only left your room when you were sure no one else was around, grunted and nodded if you mistimed a sortie to the shared bathroom and actually had to speak to someone before vanishing back into your cell, an anchorite devoted to your personal god of self-annihilation.

If you were alone in the flat, your course was no different.

You were desperate to connect with people like you, working class kids making a break for it who'd understand where you came from and what growing up in a place like that does to you, but you were shit out of luck. Everyone came from money and none of them, even the Northerners, had what you'd call a proper accent, like all the rough edges had been polished out. They talked in that fucking irritating way? Where everything sounded like a question? About, you know, what they'd done in the summer? Inter-railing round Europe, Greek island-hopping, trekking in Tibet, road trips around the South of France, shit like that? You'd never even had a passport. They reckoned to be casually dressed but it was fancy gear and proper swish on the quiet. Brands, labels, fragrances for men. You sensed eyes swivelling in your direction when they clocked your grungey get-up, especially the red and black stripy jumper you asked your gran to knit that you never took off and your only pair of jeans, fake 501's from Tez, which were so fucked yer arse hung out of the back. You couldn't see yourself anywhere. For protection you wore permashades, indoors and out and sometimes at night, with your hood pulled up to hide as much of your face as you could. When you bothered to go to class, you sat down as it was about to start and were halfway out the door the instant it was over, Walkman headphones maxed out so everyone could hear that you were deaf to the world and communication was futile.

Each day began with a cataclysmic hangover, your tongue a volcanic rock blackened by the Spanish wine you bought from Booze Buster on the parade round the front. At a fiver for three bottles it made the stuff the centurions fed Christ on the cross seem like high class hooch, but it was a companion and it knocked you out, which was all you were after. In the morning you'd wash away the taste with a can of warm lager – usually Harp or Henninger or whatever other muck was on special offer – from the case under the bed, choke your way down a fag and go out to brave the day, all the time keeping your eyes on the main objective – to get to the end of lectures unscathed, then throw what little coin you had over the counter at the offie so you could get back to the flat and make your communion.

The city was overwhelming. The crowds of students wending their way up and down Oxford Road in a viscous human river, the fucking cyclists on the pavement who kept nearly running into you, the people getting in your face to hand out flyers or try to blag you into donating to some bastard charity or other when all you wanted was to be left in peace. You'd never seen so much traffic; the towering double-deckers that dwarfed the couple of Pennine ones that served the whole town back home, the black cabs straight out of TV shows that crawled alongside, so many fucking cars. Where were they all coming from, or going to, and what about the people inside, what was their story? You couldn't process it. The dissonant blast of horns penetrated even the high-gain fuzz of the punk rock you mainlined through your in-ears, jangled your nerves until they were stretched beyond snapping.

By dinner you'd be ready for a drink. The student union was off-limits – way too busy – so you'd go to the Phoenix, a shady as fuck hovel under the brutalist overpass near Blackwells, or the Thirsty Scholar by Oxford Road station, it didn't matter as long as you were alone with your Guinness. It was the closest thing to food that passed your lips, aside from salt and vinegar Walkers and the odd tray of chips from Geminis, the takeaway on the corner. A couple of pints would steel you for the afternoon campaign of classes where your vow of silence would remain unbroken.

171

Sometimes you'd go out with Mike and Dean, the two lads from high school who lived in the same complex, and that would be okay for a while. Their familiar faces and accents were a comfort but once they'd put a few down in The Grovel or Big Hands they'd want to move on to some club or other and you'd get dragged along. The drum and bass nights they were so keen on would have been alright if you'd had a couple of Es but they weren't interested in any of that; when you did it without them, it fucked the vibe and no one had a good time.

Every now and then you'd get stir crazy and go out alone. Jilly's Rockworld was as much fun as it got if you'd drunk enough and were in the mood. It was a dark and dingy local institution that pulled in punks, grungies, goths, metalheads and various other species of moshers who were out on the batter. Fridays it stayed open all night so most of them were fucked on whizz or pills, which were easy enough to buy or blag once you knew which corners to look in. You might not've been a people person but you had a sniffer dog's instinct for that. Your favourite ever night from uni was the time you sat till the small hours, wrecked on snakebite and black and a wrap of disgusting Chickentown speed in the corner of The Fishbowl room, copping off with a lass who looked like an extra from a Jack Off Jill video who was over from Preston celebrating her eighteenth birthday. You were hoping to take her back to the flat but before you could suggest it she was abducted from you by the mates she'd come with who dragged your dark princess unwillingly away to get the last train while Type O Negative hammered your eardrums with their tune about loving the dead.

Later on you lost your shirt, a tie-dyed thing with Jim Morrison's face blurred into it like a Magic Eye picture, another one for the fuck-knows-what-happened-there files. At closing time with a nose that tasted like washing powder, having failed to cop off with anyone else but succeeded manfully at drinking yourself senseless, you stumbled down Oxford Road alone, the memento mori of your torso frost white in the Baltic dawn. When you clocked yourself in the mirror at the flat your chest was covered in these dark purple marks and you wondered what the fuck you'd done to yourself this time until you focussed enough to see your goth Cinderella had scrawled her name and number on it in lipstick, something else you couldn't remember, which was fully fucking gutting because it was, and remained, the coolest thing that ever happened to you. You struggled to read it backwards but once it clicked you learned her name was Lorna. You tried to call her a couple of times from the shared phone in the hallway, and once you spoke to her baffled old man who asked in blunt Lancashire tones who the fuck you were and what you wanted with his daughter when she had to go to college in the morning, shortly before threatening to track you down and brain you if you ever dared phone his house again. He wouldn't take a message.

You didn't shower for days. The sticky scribble kept your connection to the night – to her – alive, but even when the lipstick faded the memory never did. You wasted far too many nights lost in drunken wanking as you thought about her cherry red DMs, the white band of her thighs in the gap between her green and black knee-socks, striped like your jumper, and the rah-rah skirt which flared so hypnotically when she first came over and beckoned you to dance. You tried to feel her tongue in your mouth, the delicate frills on the thong that separated her perfect arse cheeks, the warm flesh and bra lace under her Nine Inch Nails top, the rake of her nails down your back as she slipped her free hand down the front of your jeans; it was fun while it lasted, but you were still alone at the end of it.

The first time you went home to get some washing done you were so relieved to be back you didn't want to leave. Your mam gave you an appraising look as you walked in and said, well, you don't look as bad as I thought you would, boy. She was well into a bottle of Jacob's Creek and trying her damnedest, bless her, but she was an abysmal liar.

Luke and a couple of other semi-mates from school were back the same weekend so you'd arranged to meet up for a few at the Oak, but it was a grim reunion. After a tooth-pulling hour of stilted conversation and silences so vast even booze couldn't fill them you made your excuses and left them to it, most of them looking like they wished they'd had the balls to stand up and bail out first. It was a savage night, mid-November. You'd left the pub early enough to call at the Wine Rack so you swagged a thirty five CL bottle of Bells to nip on as you walked through the rainwashed streets, cut in half by the razor-blade cold of a roof-ripping gale, then drank the rest in your room, comforted by the song of the wind howling down from the moors and the machine gun rattle of hail on the windowpanes.

When you left, you'd thought there was nothing you'd miss about home.

You were wrong.

At the end of the first year everyone buddied up, moved into shared houses and flats. You did some half-hearted fishing with Mike and Dean to see if they had room at their new place, but they'd swagged a five-bed down Daisy Bank Road with some lads from their halls, and their apologetic shrugs of refusal didn't seem too sincere. You ended up staying where you were, although you were moved into a bigger room in an upstairs flat. Other than the slight increase in size the place was much the same, although the addition of a sink was a huge bonus cos you could piss and puke in it and that sidelined two of the main reasons for having to leave your room. You kept bottles of bleach and disinfectant under the bed in case the smell got too bad, but if it did you never noticed, and no one ever came in to tell you.

Booze Buster had stopped stocking Escudero so you moved onto Royal Czar. It was six ninety nine for a seventy five cl bottle and it wasted you so completely you wondered why you hadn't thought to drink it before. You'd swig it neat from the bottle until your eyes went blind, but it magnified your sadness until all you wanted to do was cry. You didn't, of course, so it was cold steel on white flesh, just like before, as if you'd ever stopped. Smashed and hungover were a two-headed coin, life reduced to sickness, or the absence of it. In between was the blissful state of not-being which usually came on towards the end of the bottle, but its solace was short-lived. So you'd wake, puke, chug down your breakfast beer and the whole shitshow would start again.

The year passed slowly; but it passed.

And the next.

Your folks were fit to bust when you graduated, talked about your 2:1 like you were on a par with Einstein. You didn't want to go, but your mam made you.

Aw, look at you in yer robes, Sean. You look like you belong in those.

Mam, we hired them. We're giving them back after.

Shut you head you silly bugger. You know worra mean. This is a proud day for me, and none of you moaning's gonna spoil it.

Even the big man was smiling. Great day for t'family, our lad. We'll have a Jameson's when we get back, eh? Been saving a bottle Paddy brought us from his last trip home.

You didn't give a fuck about any of that. You were just glad you'd got through it. That day you overheard so many other kids talking about what they were doing next. Gap years, travelling, maybe taking some time out at home to figure things out, you know, try to make sense of where they were at? All that sort of shite. The luxury of kids whose folks had paid them through the last three years and stuck their student loan in a high interest account so they'd have a tidy bit of cash to get them started in their bound-to-be-successful lives. And you? With no mates, no plans, no ideas, and not a penny to your name, there was only one option.

Home.

10

There's no fucking way he should be driving but he's not got a choice.

Half-cut at stupid o'clock, fuck knows what time it is, speeding through the frost-bitten streets, slinging the car round corners like it's powersliding on Mario Kart. Mandy's horrorstruck in the passenger seat, losing it. The hospital said not to worry but she needs to get down there as soon as she can so they can check her out. It's unlikely that she'll be in labour this early on, but these things can happen, and it's better to be safe than sorry.

The nightmare kicked off less than an hour ago.

Sean. *Sean*. You've got to wake up.

He'd had a bitch of a day and was feeling vicious after jacking time. For the first time in forever he'd dropped into the King's Arms by the bus stop for a quick one, more like four or five, then smashed a bottle of wine after tea and a few cans for good measure. He was deep in the black land, no wish to return.

Wake *up*. A fist in his shoulder slammed him awake.

What the fuck, Mand?

I think I'm in labour.

What?

I think the baby's coming.

Don't be daft. It's not due for three months. How could it be?

I don't know, but it is. I've got these pains that keep coming and going and I've been timing them. I've been awake for ages reading about them online, they're definitely labour pains. I'm sure of it.

Probably just tummy ache. You'll be right in the morning.

I'm going to ring the hospital. Don't go back to sleep, this might be serious.

Sure. His eyes were half-closed. He snatched a few more minutes before she tore back in and shook him to his senses, breathless, tears well on the way to hysterical. He was up and dressed in seconds.

Don't worry, Mand. He's crunching the gears, revving the engine so hard it makes the whole car shake. I'm sure everything'll be fine. We'll see what they have to say, and we'll be back home in bed before we know it, okay?

She's nodding but she's ashen, holding onto her bump for dear life.

They screech into the car park, skid across two bays, nearly shunt the white Beamer parked next door, stop maybe half a foot short.

Rushes her inside. Practically running.

Reception are expecting them.

They're hustled to the Early Pregnancy Unit.

What happens next is hard to follow.

She's given a bed and a hospital gown; a curtain's thrown around them, a parade of staff mill in and out like clockwork soldiers. The squeak of rubber soles on disinfected floors, the rattle of the curtain being pulled back and forth, a burr of soft voices pitched to soothe, settle, calm.

We just need to take your blood pressure, love, alright? Could you make a fist for me. That's it, well done.

Quick blood test, okay? Are you alright with needles? Yeah? Right, let's just tie this on here. Squeeze a couple of times for me? Brilliant. Alright, sharp scratch coming now…

Do you think you could wee into this for us? There's a loo at the end of the corridor, or you can do it here if you prefer. Shall we come back in five minutes? There's a jug of juice here if you need a bit of help.

This is going to keep track of your heart rate? Nothing to worry about, it's just to help us see what's going on. I'm going to put this here. It might feel cold at first but don't worry, it'll soon warm up. Ready? Good girl.

Then another voice, shrill with full-fuck over-the-edge panic. I'm sorry, nurse, I think I've wet myself. Shit, shit, it's blood, it's blood. It's fucking *blood*.

Cut.

■

A square room, too much of the operating theatre about it, snapped to sobriety, convinced he's gonna puke, more faces but their words are less warm, smiles look drawn on. She's hooked up to all sorts of machines, it's been explained but he can't remember what they do, one for her heart rate, definitely, and he knows a drip when he sees one, the thing on the end of her finger, is that for measuring the oxygen in her blood? Something like that, fuck knows how you can measure it from there though. She's on her back, knees in the air, legs wide, not crying now, not doing much at all, just staring, staring, staring, biting her bottom lip like she wants to chew it off. They keep coming in and sticking a mirror up her gown, measuring something, it's getting bigger, whatever it is, and it's not good news.

Shit.

Shit.

Shit.

Shit.

Shit.

The nurse, or is she a midwife, is talking, he's got to tune in, sounds fucking important but he's shit at concentrating, worse when he's stressed.

Mandy, can you hear me? Just nod sweetheart. Yeah? Okay, you both need to listen carefully to what I'm going to say.

focus focus focus focus focus focus fuck fuck focus focus fuck fuck fuck fuck

Sitting on a chair next to the bed squeezing her hand so hard he's worried he'll crush it, trying to look her in the eye, he's here, she's not going to have to do it on her own, he's gonna scream if he's not careful, won't cry though, not even now. She's not looking back, facing the nurse, or midwife, whatever, her name's Lauren, he thinks, not that it matters.

Is the baby okay? Is it okay? Keeps saying it over and over. Please tell me it's going to be okay. Like a kid in the night who's scared of the dark and needs telling again that the monsters are all in her mind.

It's fine for now. But you guys need to understand that this baby is definitely coming out tonight, and there's nothing we can do to stop it.

Why – he's startled by his voice. Does he usually sound like this? Like he's got a speech impediment or his mouth is full of marbles or he's talking underwater or all fucking three.

We don't know at this stage, and right now it doesn't matter. We can worry about that later. The good news is that babies born at this point in the gestation period have a very high rate of survival, as long as there are no complications. Mandy, you need to stay calm and you'll give the baby every chance. Keep doing what you're doing, let us worry take care of the rest, and hopefully it will be over soon. I have to see another patient but the consultant's on his way.

what the fuck does she mean chance of survival oh christ does that mean
fuck that don't go there fucking dont

In he comes. An older guy, tall and grey, kind face, bald on top, harsh lights bouncing off his dome making his pink skin look as white as the walls and floor, talks and talks but it's all static, calm though, sounds wise even if none of it makes sense.

More people, one in, one out, spouting job titles, what they do, or might have to do, or are going to, but none of that sticks either, he's pure fixed on Mand, won't turn away for the hint of a thought of a second so if she looks she'll see him. She's wincing, must be the contractions, feels it himself, wants to take it away, he'd take every bit of pain in the history of the whole fucking cunting bastard world if it could stop her suffering and get this over with.

A single instant without end, twin sets of machines now, double bubble, more noise, something about monitoring the baby's heart, wishes to all fuck he could retain what they're saying but can't, just can't, mind works too fast to keep up day to day, this is a whole different kind of fuckery, he's got no chance.

what if the baby dont what if the dont you what if dont you fucking
what dont you fucking dare

Her breathing's ragged, pain must be getting worse because she's yelping, he's staggered by her bravery, looks so fucking determined, furious, possessed, how can she be doing that, here, now, in the face of this, he's all over the bastard place just watching. They give her gas and air, then morphine, could do with some himself, she's relaxed, conscious enough to do what she needs to but she's not winced since she had the jab, gasps have stopped, hand's hanging limply by the bed, can't squeeze his anymore, strokes her fingers instead, tries to ignore the bruise where the tube's sticking out the big vein.

Midwives come and go.

Biros scratch on clipboards, how can he hear that above the beep beep beep of the fucking machines, hates the sound, they tell her she's doing well, coo coo coo like fucking pigeons, can she hear them with the morphine, the smell, hospital bleach, his own disgusting sweat, the sharp metal tang of the blood that hasn't stopped oozing out of her since they got here soaking through the thick cotton pads they keep stuffing under her arse, between her thighs, helps change them, does as he's told, pulls them away while the nurse eases her up enough to slide them out, they're putrid sodden dripping like straw from a shambles, lambing time on Harry's farm, big fucking stains on the sheets, shoves them in the bin marked HAZARDOUS WASTE, hands slick, never seen it this colour, sort of purple, more the darkest maroon trickling out so stickythick it looks like engine oil.

Wash your hands in that sink love, gentle touch taps his shoulder pointing the way, scrubbing with white foam from the dispenser looking over his shoulder, water and pink froth splashing from the shallow bowl on his jeans like he's pissed himself, you're doing a great job here for your wife, love, strange she assumes they're married but no use in correcting her, she's only being nice, you can come back here and help me any time, you'll be an expert at this by the time you're done, he's been waiting for her to say it, this pathetic childish need for reassurance breaks him, entirely, in half, he's heading for the floor, the tears are coming, too late to stop, had to happen one day, no, straightens, what the fuck is he thinking, if he falls he'll never get up, if he cries he'll not stop.

you fucking sad useless little boy youve been wanting her to say that all night dont bother pretending you havent chin up chest out get the fuck on with it youre meant to be a man arent you fucking well prove it time to man the fuck up boy if youre up to it which youre obviously not why else

would you be wanting the midwife to pat you on the head like a fucking
puppy you spineless cunt

She's telling him to go get a coffee, shakes his head, won't leave her, can't, no way, when the pulsing sound goes up and up and up until it's one continuous unbroken beeeeeeeeeeeeeeeeeeeeeeeeeee eeeeeeeeeeeeeeeeeeeeeeeeeeeeeeeeeeeeeeeeeeeeeeeeeeeeeeeeeeeeeee eeeeeeeeeeeeeeeeeeeeeeeeeeeeeeeeeeeeeeeeeeeeeeeeeeeeeeeeeeeeeee eeeeeeep and this is it, the fucking shit's hit the fan, he's invisible, back on the chair, pandemonium, fucking awful racket, can't hear the machines, just Mandy, the world's loudest fire alarm played through the world's biggest PA, even above that fucking row she's screaming, properly, properly fucking screaming like she's fighting for her life or someone else's, where did all these people come from, no one's smiling now, can see it in their eyes behind the masks, latex gloves, blue gowns scrubs is it they call them, who the fuck cares, there's a trolley at the bottom of the bed

oh my fucking god is that a coffin is it fuck fuck fuck cant see it right
past all the bodies what if the baby what if the what if what what what
what what if oh fuck oh fuck oh fuck oh fuck oh

room empties like when you pull the plug out of the bath, whoosh, gone, trolley, box, every other fucking thing too, thank Christ that noise has stopped, still ringing in his ears, it's just him now, the midwife, down on her haunches patting Mandy's arm, looks like she wants to give her a cuddle, talking to her pushing her hair off her face, he tunes in, telling her she's done it, you've done it darling, the hard bit's over, everyone's so proud of you, Mandy couldn't care less, looks half-

no not that word never well she looks fucked then fucked to cunting
ruination hows that for you then

head squashed into the pillow, hair so sweaty it's fucking dreaded, skin so white it's yellow, piss wet through, legs stuck

183

up in the air, black blood all over, sweet fucking jesus weeping on his cross what a fucking mess down there, gown's torn to shreds, falling off, she's not moving, glass eyes like a stuffed cat, he loves her so so so much, overpowering all-encompassing so fucking overwhelming it makes him want to—

11

Mandy was wiped out, half-fucked from the morphine, too woozy to speak. She'd found enough strength to lift her arm so they could hold hands loosely at least, but her opiate eyes said she might not have known he was there. He was wracked with tremors, though not for the usual reasons. The heat was oppressive but he was perished, had to clamp his teeth together to stop the chattering; when enamel met enamel he started grinding them instead. Christ he wanted a fucking smoke but there was nowhere to go even if he had any and he couldn't leave her on her own if he did. The midwife said she'd be back later when Mandy had come round a bit to get her something to eat, but when was that? He couldn't remember what fucking day it was, never mind the time.

Beep.

Beep.

Beep.

Beep.

Beep.

He tried to count the seconds between the beats of the ECG but the numbers didn't make sense, like saying a word over and over until it turns to gibberish. Cold turkey sweat, skin like glass. One wrong glance and he'd shatter.

I'm sorry to have kept you waiting. The voice cut through the snowstorm where his thoughts should have been. It's been a very busy day here so it's taken me longer than I would have liked but I've got some good news for you.

The kindly man from earlier was standing next to him. When did he get here? Sean thought he was the consultant but couldn't remember through the fog. He looked mild, composed, not like someone bringing bad news.

dont let him fool you its just a front to put you at ease best get ready for the big one lets see you try to get through this wiout bawling you reckon you that fuckin tough time to show

Do you want to see a picture of your baby?

Is it… I mean… Mandy was instantly alert, like she'd been woken from a trance with a snap of the hypnotist's fingers. She tried to sit up, failed. A short, sharp intake of breath.

Settle down, Mandy. Your baby is fine. You'll be able to see her soon, but this'll have to do for the time being.

He showed them a polaroid, the strip lights reflected in the sheen like the moon on water. There was so much in the image that it was hard to make out at first. Once he homed in past the glare, Sean could see the outline of the plastic box, definitely *not* what he'd thought it was. In the middle of the shot was a tangle of wires, a red and purple carcass like a skinned rabbit, a roundish shape topped with the world's smallest beanie.

Congratulations. You've got a beautiful baby girl. Does she have a—

Daisy. Look, Sean, it's baby Daisy.

They'd spent hours kicking around names and hadn't been able to agree on one – or even a shortlist – for a boy, but Mandy had suggested Daisy for a girl from the word go and they were so in love with it they'd never considered anything else. He brushed the paper square with the tips of his fingers, a lump in his throat the size of a watermelon.

A beautiful name. Now, before I go, there are a few things you need to know. It was like listening to a meditation tape. He could have been telling them the city was about to be nuked and made it sound like he was inviting them to a picnic.

The good news is that Daisy is fine. It took us five or six minutes to get her started—

What—

It's alright, Sean. Sometimes when babies arrive this early it means they need a little bit of extra help when they come out, but it's all completely normal. Maybe we can talk about that later, but it's nothing to worry about at this point in time. So, for now, Daisy is doing well.

What do you mean—

I mean, she's fine *at the moment*. The emphasis was gentle. The first seventy-two hours are crucial, and I can't make any promises—

Oh god. Mandy, distraught.

But – and it's a *big* but – if there are no complications, which there don't *appear* to be at this stage, most babies born at this gestation are perfectly alright in the long run. We need to keep a close eye on her at first, then if everything goes as it should in the next few days, we might be able to start looking a little bit further ahead, alright? Now, I've got a nurse bringing you some tea and toast, then she'll show you where you can have a bath. Once you're all cleaned up, you can come and see Daisy. Congratulations to you both, and Mandy – well done. You've had quite a day, but you were brilliant.

■

Accessing the Intensive Care Unit was like getting into prison. Hermetic security, heavy doors that opened with electronic key cards, staff monitoring the ins and outs like ShowSec without the shades. Signs everywhere warned that hands should be washed frequently then sterilised with a gel from dispensers above the immaculate sinks because of the high risk of infection. The sanitiser was a warmish gloop that reeked of Czar and stung his hands when he rubbed it in.

The nurse who met them said her name was Samara. She was young, so fresh-faced she looked like she'd come straight from high school. She led them through to another room with strong operating theatre vibes, the air acrid with disinfectant and alcohol. In the corners, diagonally opposite each other, were two plastic boxes, each next to an array of machines on an upright stand. The lights were low – to keep the babies calm and protect their eyes, Samara said – but he could see now that the boxes were incubators. How could he been so blind to have missed that? Through the sides they could see Daisy laid out on a soft mat with a towel in a U-shaped curved under her feet and up the sides of her legs, her tiny frame swaddled in a mess of tubes and wires plugged into the monitors. She was wearing a nappy the size of a single sheet of arsewipe, and it still looked massive on her.

How could anything be so fragile and live? Her shinbone was the exact length and breadth as his bird-flipping finger. And holy shit, he couldn't see through her skin, could he? No fucking way. The purple splodges blurring through it couldn't possibly have been internal organs; but they most definitely were. The butterfly flutter of her heart shook her chest with every beat.

Mandy fell on his shoulder, beside herself. The nurses had said she should come up in a wheelchair but she was having none of that. There's no way I'm meeting my baby for the first time sitting in one of those things, she'd croaked in a voice that refused contradiction.

He hugged her, the smell of medicated shampoo strikingly unfamiliar amidst the blood and bleach stink that wouldn't shift from his nose. He couldn't take his eyes off the baby. The bond was instant. How could that be? As soon as he saw her he was filled with a love of the kind he wouldn't have been able to describe for all the riches on earth. So *this* was what his mam had been trying to get across when she talked about the wonders of parenthood. And he'd thought she was bullshitting him because she wanted a grandchild.

Hello, little lady. He leaned in, pressed his face up to the side. How're you doing? I'm so happy to see you. Aren't you beautiful? He spoke in a tone of voice he didn't know he had.

Oh Sean, isn't she lovely? The sobbing started again.

Hey, I hope they're happy tears, Samara broke in. Daisy's doing great. We'll see how she goes tonight, but if everything's alright you'll be able to give her a cuddle tomorrow.

What? Can I? Mandy sounded thrilled, hopeful but expecting to be disappointed. I mean, she's so *small.*

She is. But she's strong. She wouldn't be breathing on her own like that if she wasn't. She didn't even need a ventilator once we'd got her stable, that's impressive for a twenty-nine weeker. Tonight's a big night for her, but things are looking promising at the mo. I'll leave you alone with her for a few minutes, but I'll be right outside that door. She gestured with her head. If you need me, you call and I'll be straight in, okay?

What's she doing with her mouth? Why's it opening and closing like that?

Their skin's quite sensitive when they come out so early so they get a bit of pain but they're too small to cry so you won't hear her. Don't worry though, we're giving her something for that. I'll be there if you want me.

Look, Sean. She was whispering. I can't believe it. There she is. Isn't she gorgeous? She looks just like you.

Does she?

She's got your nose. There. Can't you see it?

Maybe. He tried to laugh but it sounded horrible.

I can't believe how small she is.

Me neither.

A pause, then: Sean, do you think she's going to be okay?

what if the baby no no no no no argue all you want theres no way something that small can survive no matter what they tell you you need to get ready for the worst cos you can bet its fuckin coming what happened with hales will have fuckin nothing on this nothing

Well, they don't seem *too* worried; and I think they'd tell us if they were.

I think so too.

We need to take it a day at a time and see what happens. What else can we do? He was fake firm, playing the rock, floundering in panic. Visions of funerals, flower arrangements shaped like teddies, a coffin the size of a shoe box, his mam keening like a banshee in a church as cold and dead as the freezing moon while the vicar mumbled prayers to an imaginary god.

Hmmmmmm.

They didn't speak, entranced by the life they'd created.

He was longing to pick her up, tell her that she'd had a hard start to life but she was so clever and strong, that'd he'd be there to look after her forever. He'd give up his own life in a heartbeat if it meant saving this child-in-waiting – *his* child, his daughter, Daisy – that was barely fully-formed.

Mandy started feeling faint not long after and called for Samara.

No wonder you're dizzy. You've been in the wars today. I'll call for a wheelchair and get someone to take you downstairs. Sean, normally I'd ask you to push but you look like you've just about had it too. I'll be two ticks.

■

They gave her a private room away from the noise of the general ward. She was lucky they had one, they said, but she'd been through the mill and she'd be much better if she could recover in peace and quiet. There was hot food, spuds and veg, grey cubes of unspecified meat slopped in gravy topped with globs of white fat; she inhaled it all without chewing. There was a large chair by the bed with a proper foam seat and a high padded back, much easier on the arse than the school assembly chairs in the delivery room.

Sean was drifting. He was fucked.

You should probably think about getting yourself home, a nurse told him when he came to clear the plates away. You can come back in the morning.

Can't I stay here, bud? I'm fine in the chair.

I'm afraid not. Visiting finishes at eight on the ward and it's quarter to now.

But what about Mand? She needs me here.

Mandy was drowsing, eyes barely open with the duvet pulled up to her chin. I'm okay, she murmured. You need to look after yourself. Make sure you eat.

You heard her. The nurse smiled. She'll be fine with us. You can come back from 10 tomorrow. By the way, is there anyone you need to call?

Christ, I've not told me folks. Oh *fuck*. Mand, what about your folks, aren't they in Portugal?

Don't tell them. They're due home in a couple of days.

You sure?

Mmhmmm. They'll only try to rush back, and they can't do much from three hundred miles away.

I'd better call mine. I can't believe I'd not thought of it. Me mam'll kill me.

Well, you get yourself off then, the nurse told him. I won't be here in the morning but I'll be about later on so I'll probably see you then. Get yourself fed, have a shower and take yourself straight to bed. You've two people to be looking after now.

She was too weak to sit up and hug him, so he lifted the duvet and showered kisses on her forehead, telling his tears to fuck right off. She was stronger and braver than he could ever be; she said she'd be fine, and he believed her, but she looked so small sunk into the bedcovers like that, almost as fragile as the baby in her incubator upstairs. He tore himself away, found his way down, and out. He couldn't even remember where he'd left the motor, but he couldn't miss it when he went out; the windscreen was plastered in bright yellow parking tickets. He ripped them from behind the wipers, tossed them aside, ground them into the tarmac with the heel of his boot. Thieving set of cunts could get to all fuck.

It was the strangest phone call he'd ever made.

Mam. Yeah, mam, it's me. Listen. The baby's come. Yeah, Ah know. Yeah, that's what Ah said. But she's here. Yeah, a baby girl. Daisy. What? Ah said Daisy, she's called Daisy. Daisy Louise. How much what? Ah can't remember. Two pound something, Ah don't fuckin know. Mandy's fine, yeah, she'll probably be asleep now. Look, Ah need to get off, Ah've no idea how long Ah've been here but they've told me to go home, Ah don't fuckin want to but they won't let me stay. Ah can come back in the morning, yeah. Ah'm fine, Ah just need a shower and Ah should probably try to get some kip. No, you don't need to come over. Mam, it's *fine*. Ah mean, come if you want, but there's nowt you can do. What? No, Ah'm not hungry. Mebbe some fags though. Yeah, Luckies. Marlboros if not. Whatever. Alright. Thanks mam. You sure you want to come? Yeah. Sound. Tell the big man to take it steady. Can't have him crashing the Honda and landing you two in here an all. Yeah, alright. See you in a bit. Yeah. You too. See you. Bye. Bye.

AFTERMATH

Fuck knows how you got the car home.

It must have been properly dark because it was Valentine's Day and it'll have been well after eight by the time you got off the phone, not that you remember any of that. You were out of your mind, no fit state at all, but in the old days you'd driven off your tits on speckled doves and Purple Oms and fuck knows what else so you can't have thought anything of it.

Your mam and dad came later.

You were in the living room with a bottle of Maker's, a birthday present from Rob you'd been saving for a special occasion, so spaced out you didn't notice when they let themselves in. Your mam was being brave, knew that if she set off bawling she'd be neither use nor ornament to anyone. She'd already have cried tears enough to fill an ocean and she'd fill a couple more before she was done, but she wouldn't do it in front of you, not that night; but she looked shocking, ravaged with the effort. The big man wasn't in great shape either, haggard and grey way beyond his fifty eight years, wearing a look you hadn't seen since he got in the car to go to Hayley's funeral.

You stood in the garden with him and smoked. You'd not said a word to each other so far. You finished one Lucky, drank off a full mug of Maker's and lit another. The whiskey was warm, sweet and soothing. Mother's milk. You couldn't have got drunk if you tried and didn't want to either but Christ alive you were glad to have it.

Your mam was doing her tried and tested. Here y'are, have a bite of this. She shoved a Ginsters steak slice at you but you shook your head, puffed on your tab.

You need to eat, love. She was right, but if you put that thing in your mouth you'd choke. Have you got a bag ready for Mandy? She'll be needing some things tomorrow.

You hadn't given it a thought. This is why you needed her here, if only to make sure you got it right for Mand. You were useless, no idea what the fuck you were meant to do.

What things?

You know, clothes, fresh knickers, toothbrush, that sort of thing. She'll want some sanitary towels an all, where will they be? Never mind, Ah'll go have a look. Is there a bag somewhere Ah can use?

As if you'd know.

It was typical of her. Always practical when the shit hit the fan. Even with Hayley she'd got herself together enough to make the necessaries when Nance was traumatised finding her and poor Tez so destroyed he didn't know his arse from his elbow. And now here she was again, keeping it tight for everyone else even though she was in bits. She bustled off while you went and sat in the living room with your old man. You offered him the bottle but he shook his head.

Won't do me any good tonight, lad, and anyway, Ah'm driving, aren't ah? You shouldn't have no more neither. How much've you had – were that full?

You passed on that one but you didn't argue when he poured you a final mug – a big one – and took the bottle away.

That'll suffice. This can come wi' me. Help send us off when Ah get back, like. You need to be in your right head and you're not gonna be if Ah leave this here with you, eh? He wasn't much of

194

a smiler – that's where you got your deadpan boat from – but he had a go; he looked like a cross between an old duffer in a gurning contest and mugshot from a line-up of murder suspects.

You weren't always close. He was a hero to you as a kid, but your teens put a stop to that. He was so proud you'd gone to the grammar but he didn't know how to say it so he took the piss instead, called you Brains Of Britain and Smart Arse so often you thought he'd forgotten your name. He'd always teased you like that when you were a boy but it was affectionate then. Come on, Mister Clever Clogs, he'd say, ruffling your hair with a look of wonder that this slip of a thing knew the answer to every question on Blockbusters, got more right than the kids on telly who were twice his age. But as you got older there was an edge – was he bitter, or just a buttoned-up Yorkshireman who couldn't express himself? You'd know all about that – and it hurt.

Hark at bloody Einstein over there, he's learned a new word, you remember him sneering once when you were having your tea and you said something was surreal. For days after he used the word like a bully's fist; persistent, remorseless, without pity.

Hey, look at that car, lad, that's surreal. Did you hear what your grandad said? That were surreal an all, weren't it, like, eh?

You constructed a shell around yourself, crawled inside.

Withdrew into silence.

You thought he was a museum piece, everything that was wrong with the town you wanted to wipe off the fucking map. The way he measured a man by how much ale his guts could hold, the homophobia and casual racism that caused screaming rows when you called him out on it. Once when you were seventeen you came home from Luke's cunted on Stella and threatened to stick one on him when he said something about the fucking Pakis on the stalls in town making the High Street stink of curry and why didn't they all piss off back to whatever raghead hellhole they came from.

It wouldn't have been much of a fight. He was six foot two in his socks and seventeen stone, built like a brick shithouse from three nights a week down the gym. You weren't much shorter but you'd given up on food as well as speech and his legs alone probably weighed more than you did. There was a right kerfuffle then as you swung at the three of him swimming in front of you and missed them all while he held you at arm's length with a hand in the middle of your chest like you were a toddler having a strop. He'd never seen you radged up like that, and even though he was cursing you seven ways from Sunday you'd've sworn the fucker was smiling.

Mebbe there's hope for you yet, boy, he said in the morning as you shoved your pukesoaked sheets into the washer. Ah didn't ken there were any vinegar in all that piss o' yours. It's not healthy for a lad your age to be so bloody quiet all t'time. It's good to know there's a cock hair o' life in there somewhere. But if you ever raise a hand to me again, I'm putting you through that fuckin wall, right?

You made your peace, of a fashion, before you left.

I'm sick of all this bad blood, your mam said one night. Get yourselves down to t'Club for a couple of pints and sort yourselves out. It's like having two bloody kids in here. If I were tall enough to reach I'd bang your frigging heads together.

Neither of you wanted to, but nor could you stand her weary disapproval, so it was a done deal. You began the night worse than strangers, sighing into your beers, taking way more interest in ashing your fags than you needed to. After a couple or four looseners the chat started. Some small talk about the weather, family jokes about Paddy and his prodigious gut, the time he came round for Sunday dinner and got so bladdered he put custard on his Vienetta. You moaned about school; the big man moaned about work and the boss he was itching to lamp.

Fuckin smarmy little scrote, I'd love to clock him one right on the end of his hooter. That'd shut the cunt up right enough.

It wasn't much but it was a start. You matched him pint for pint without much effort, and though he never said, you could tell he was impressed.

Thursdays at the Club became a regular thing. A swift six or eight scoops after he'd had his tea – ten or twelve if you had a thirst on – a few quid in the bandit and a fish butty for the big lad on the way home. He was a funny fella when you got talking, and home life was better once you realised you could sit down and chat without wanting to commit murder on each other. You'd always have your moments – like when you went to the Rocky Horror Show dressed as a schoolgirl with shaved legs, drag queen make-up and granny smith tits in a charity shop bra. You properly feared for your life when he clocked you and he didn't talk to you for a month – but for the most part you were mates, and your mam was like a pig in shit.

You were slayed with gratitude that night. The simple fact of his presence made you feel safe like it did when you were a boy and knew that this giant of a man could take out any burglar or monster or werewolf that came after you without breaking sweat. Nothing could hurt you with your own personal He-Man around. You wanted to thank him for being there, for sitting with you while you lost it, sanity fucked all the way off, reckoning that everything was normal because there was nothing else to do; to thank him for being himself, perfect in his many imperfections, to say you loved everything about him, even the bits you still couldn't fucking stand, that you never wanted to be without him, your one and only real life fucking dad, the one name you never called him by and hadn't since those years when you couldn't abide the sight of each other. But you didn't know how. Words like that came no easier to you than they did to him. To attempt it would have been hideous so you opted for silence and left it hanging like a corpse in a barn instead. But both of you knew it was there.

They offered to stay over but you said no. They'd be better at home and they could come back tomorrow; they had a key and could come whenever, didn't matter if you were out. Your mam tried to argue the toss, but you wouldn't have it and the big man told her not to push it. With the whiskey out of sight she put the kettle on, another failsafe; there was no disaster a cup of tea couldn't solve. You didn't want a fucking brew unless it was ninety percent Makers but she made you have one anyway, and she wouldn't go home until you'd eaten that bloody pasty so you scarfed it down with as much relish as you could fake. Your stomach said you were hungry but the rest of you didn't care if you never ate again, used to going without from all those years rotting to the bones to starve away your pain. As soon as they'd gone you legged it upstairs and got rid, undigested chunks of beef sticking in your craw as the Makers scorched its way back, gipping as the water from the bog splashed up in your face, lukewarm and fishy with your old fella's unflushed piss.

You didn't bother to shower. You crawled across the landing, literally fucking dragged yourself on your hands and knees you were that tired, pulled yourself into bed and blanked out for a few hours although it was nothing that anyone could call sleep.

You opened your eyes at six, straight back to the real-life nightmare that made your usual dreamland terrors look like Mickey cunting Mouse.

Your inbox was full of new texts, one from your mam and a few from Mandy.

198

Hi love back home safe and sound hope youre in bed getting some kip I cant believe youre a dad and Im a granny haha see you tomorrow love you night night ring me when you can x x x x

Hey mister. I hope you got some sleep and some food down you. Daisy is fine. I was worried and couldn't sleep but they said they'd call if anything happened and I drifted off in the end.

Later: I'm awake again. Everything ok. I woke up starving and the nurse brought me some more toast. I've been expressing milk with a pump and they're feeding it straight to Daisy. I went up to see her a couple more times after you left. I can't believe how small she is.

And again: I hope this doesn't wake you. Did you call your folks? I'll ring you when I wake up. If you don't hear from me don't worry, I'll be asleep. Visiting starts at ten so come as soon as you can, but I'll talk to you before then anyway. I love you xxxxxx

Finally: I can't believe we have a little baby girl. See you soon. Love XOXOXOXOX

There was no chance of you getting back off but you were too blasted to move so you lay ticking away seconds one at a time until you thought she'd be up and it'd be safe to call without waking her. Just as you were zoning out and ready to go under a spider as big as the palm of your hand scuttled across the duvet, right beneath your nose; your scream as you launched the cover was loud enough to wake the dead, long enough to make your throat hoarse for days. You couldn't stay in the room knowing that fucking thing was there so you sleepwalked into the bathroom and got in the shower, only remembered to take off your clothes when it was too late and you realised they were piss wet through.

You stood there under the jet, shaking, gasping, heaving. Everything but the tears.

You bit your cheek till you tasted blood and spat it down the plughole, stuck your tongue in the mess and zoomed in on the pain until a pack of blades from Mand's LadyShave caught your eye. You felt the pressure on your bicep, the sweet rush of tearing skin and flesh, saw the blood and water rushing down the plughole in a diluted scarlet flood, washing the tension away with it.

You really thought you were gonna do it, but you strangled that urge too.

You had a child to think about now.

NO

OW

shuts door bony arse bag down gently gently dont break worlds
end touches floor steadies bag upright good dont wobble fine
its fine first bottle hands weak barely fucking grasp earthquake
tremor top to toe screw cap drops fuck that crouching hands knees
floor smell hits killer cure lifts two hands choke cold neck one
above one below up up up sacrament eucharist smooth glass dry
lips dont drop dont dont no yes yes now done warm sweet squints
tears poisoned chalice glugglugglugglugglug thats better, room
slops in out focus settles here safe as houses bricks and mortar
four walls hearth and home is where the heart is empty lies dead
dreams dying dreams dead mutinous stomach chucks upwards
no swallows back doesnt budge needs another go and another
and another squatting no need grabs fags baccy tears pack sparks
straight should roll one shaking best not dont spill needs to sit
down calm down hauls sorry carcass living room used to be stinks
of shit goes to sit wet brown stain broken chair fucks sake who
when what how time never still moving further from **no no no**
cant forget remembers what no gin can drown another one down
another wipes hand shit wont last long good job theres two maybe
not enough cant go again skirts shitty chair anything else sofa
thats fucked too been attacked assaulted vandalised trashed whole
room same some fucking sanctuary this the fucking state of it guts
clench gurgle food whats that fuck that nourish what no only needs
one thing right here another seal it fucks it off sits on floor so dirty
it feels damp maybe it is doesnt care ease of pain shaken the shakes
thank god fogs lifting and he can think a little and maybe thats not
so great, who needs it, thinking is dangerous too many thoughts
lead one way two things lost never found never will be neither so

he sits and drinks and drinks and sits, pathetic specimen, sees it, knew he was no good, bad from the off, could never do right for doing wrong god knows he tried, nothing but harm, destined for this, all roads lead to rome hes the proof in the pudding the prophecy fulfilled, here to claim his birthright, years of guilty guilt not knowing why, flagellated, no better when the penny dropped, fucking history wrecked his blood, old man knew the score couldnt run fast enough but Paddy all them before him, poor bastards, hellfire damnation, wretched snivelling scum pissed off god with the hubris of birth, offending his sight, what kind of fucking solace is that, his mams lot on the other side, his mam when he was a kid, after her old fella died, she went to church every week, he had to go too, theyd cut a deal, proper shitstorm, what do you mean shes not one of ours, could only marry outside the faith if kids were brought up in gods sight so she dragged him along, frozen solid, it was never about him, or keeping the inlaws happy, she went to find her dad, talk to him, his gran the same while he sat bored fucking stupid in Sunday school in his blue parka with the bright orange lining waiting till it was time to go, got it later why they did it when she went back after hayley, his gran an all, hopes they found her or whatever they wanted, does she go back now and pray for them, for him, hes still here but might as well not be, wishes he wasnt, does she properly feel it or is it just hope, the comfort in believing it, your loved ones waiting in the clouds, sweet naivety play blind faith making sense of the senseless, more of a pull than being damned from fucking birth, no wonder it does in so many, thanks christ, him again, never had it to warp his mind like it did his old mans but got him just the same, in him, cant change that any more than the wafer can change into what the daft fuckers say, is that what it was all those years, decades on decades of it, accumulated, centuries, way back to the old country, forgive me father for I have sinned my god I am sorry for my sins with all my heart in choosing to do wrong and failing to do good I have sinned against you whom I should love above all things I firmly intend to do penance, word for fucking word he knows it, never even been in a confessional what does that say, doing penance all his life, scourged inside and out, the big man drove the old folk going to midnight mass every christmas eve, picture of the holy father on the wall he thought was his grandad, paddy looked just like him, was it heading here all along, like somehow he knew, had to be more to it, preordained, never had a choice, way too much to weigh one soul down, not now, the big one, the greatest guilt of all, no sin greater, he cant think about it, wont think about it, cant think about anything else so down goes some more, maybe hell roll one up now his hands are steady, takes a fucking age, doesnt bother with the filter, welcomes the cancer, come get me you cunt youre no more than I deserve, lets get hitched run away together, a match made in heaven heading for hell, maybe hes there, maybe this is it, who defines hell, devils, pitchforks, the flames the flames the flames, medieval stuff, no hell before dante, a fucked off Florentines wank fantasy to torture his enemies, set in stone since, to each their own hell, hed take dantes over this, freeze me at the bottom, feed me to the beast headfirst like judas, ahm more guilty than him, he was there to tune gods golden boy into his destiny if it was already written like the big book says, fuck it, take me, chucks the fag, sparks a straight, hopes it chokes him and its coming back looming like the great flood the day hell came to him or he came to hell, cant get it down quick enough but cant stop it now, the day they went away the depthlessness of the dark he was woken from by

TH

EN

12

Shivering outside the double doors of the Clarendon Wing in the biting cold, drinking Costa coffee and smoking his third since arriving. Visiting didn't start for ten more minutes and he'd been there half an hour already, clock-watching, reading and rereading Mandy's messages, checking for hidden meanings revealing everything wasn't as well as she said.

He flicked the fag, went to light up again then thought better of it. He couldn't go in stinking of smoke, so he drained the rest of his brew and shoved a couple of bits of chuddy in to clear the worst of the smell. It'd be right by the time he got up there. He chewed for a couple of minutes like Fergie on speed, went inside, palmed the gum, binned it. He was pale as death, bloated with fear and the handful of codeine he had for breakfast

Mandy was in bed. Her texts said she'd been up and down all night but she looked like she hadn't moved. It was a strange reunion, as if one of them had been away for a weekend and yesterday's drama hadn't happened. Kisses, hugs, smiles and hey, how are *you*, how'd you sleep? When can we go see Daisy? Me mam got me a Ginsters, yeah. Didn't get much kip, like, and there was a fucking spider in the bed this morning. Nearly shit myself. It was *massive*, you'd've been out of there like a shot. Daisy's fine, yeah. She's still breathing on her own and they've been feeding her my milk so she's getting all the colostrum, it's so important for their immune system. She's so brave and strong and clever.

Trite stuff, sub-soap acting. The unspeakable stayed unspoken, lurking behind every word.

The ICU was quiet bar the monitors, the dim lights a balm to his aching eyes. He'd caught sight of himself in the mirror in the bogs when he went for a slash in the lobby before, black bags both sides like he'd been sucker-punched by Lennox Lewis.

By the incubator opposite, a woman in a sari was wringing her hands, mouthing what looked like prayers. Beside her, what must've been her husband inspected his fingernails, shaking his head in slow-motion. Sean greeted the mam with his eyes, tried to look sympathetic; she half-smiled but her face was concave, hammered in, defeated.

Samara was there again. Had she even been home? Her job must've been so tough but she looked box fresh, carefree, reported that Daisy'd had a lovely night and this morning they could have a cuddle if they wanted. Skin to skin contact was super-important for bonding, she said, especially with mum if she wanted to breast-feed when Daisy was strong enough. It was best to start as soon as they could.

But she's so *little*. I mean, I can't wait to hold her but can she actually come out of there?

She can come for a little bit, no problem. We'll wrap her up all cosy-comfy and strap her to your chest. She'll be snug as a bug down there. And I'm telling you, she'd rather be with mum than where she is now.

shes safe in there as safe as shes going to get anyway why are you letting them get your baby out anything could happen what if one of yous carrying an infection without knowing and pass it on youve read the signs youre in a fucking hospital full of sick people clean your hands all you want theres got to be fucking bugs all over the joint look at those wires shes hidden under what if one of those comes unclipped what if its something important what if she cant do without it theyre all important dickhead why would they be there otherwise they know what theyre doing wouldnt say it was safe if it wasnt but shes got to be better where she is shielded from the fucking evil world shes gate-crashed well before her time they cant do it dont let them dont let them dont let them dont—

A scream was bursting to get out, no, leave her, but Samara had already started. The side of the incubator was hinged at the bottom and she'd flipped it open, slid her hands in, the lizard eye opacity of her latex gloves stark against Daisy's angry skin. She eased her up like she was a bomb that could go off at any moment, lay her against Mandy's bare chest as she sat in a high-backed padded chair. Her boobs were swollen and tight as drumskins; as soon as Daisy touched her, her nipples wept thick yellow milk. The nurse wrapped a blanket around her to keep the bundle in place, then fastened her dressing gown around it so all they could see of the child was the beanie poking out from a gap in the top.

It was amazing to see her without the distortive filter of the Perspex; his guts dropped through the floor when he registered that her head about as big as half his clenched fist. Mandy's cheeks shone with tears but she was as serene as a painted Madonna. Just once she looked at him with enough silent words to fill every book in the British Library. Only her lips moved as she whispered in Daisy's ear; he couldn't make out a syllable, but he understood it all.

Without warning there came a sudden change in sound.

Fuck what was that?

From the corner of his eye he saw red, clocked straight away the numbers on one of the monitors were flashing scarlet, bleeping shrill and strident as the pulses grew faster, faster, fasterfasterfasterfasterfasterfasterfaster beeeeeeeeeeeeeeeeeeeeeeeeeeeeeeeeeeeeeeep *fuckfuckfuck they should never have taken her out of there you fucking knew it isnt this exactly what you expected to happen fucking bad idea to get her out she should still be in mand for another three months for fucks sake what were they thinking saying she should come out all the world about to shatter and shit your hearts beating so hard its gonna blow good job youve been preparing how the fuck do you prepare for this you thought yesterday was bad and this is gonna be—*

Samara? Mandy half-whispered it, as if she was afraid to disturb the peace but her voice was terror distilled. Samara?!

where the fucks the nurse she said shed be right here listen to the fucking thing surely someone can hear it its so fucking loud you could hear it down

Hey, it's fine. Samara trotted over. She put her face next to Daisy's head and she must have said a magic word or something because right away the pulses slowed, the numbers rolled back up and were green again in no time. How could she be fucking smiling? He pictured himself on the floor clutching his chest, a rictus grin gashing his black face, purple tongue swollen like a rotting aubergine as a cardiac arrest took him out of the game for good.

What—

Don't worry, everything's fine. She was irritatingly calm. She's probably ready to go back though. They always let us know when they are. Mandy was chewing her lip again, still talking to Daisy, her mouth in silent motion mirroring the prayers of the mother by the other cot.

Let's get her back in there and I'll explain. But please don't panic. All this is totally normal, okay?

Once Daisy was settled, Samara said that one of the wires attached to her finger was a SATS monitor, which measured the oxygen levels in her blood. Mandy was wearing one yesterday too, someone would have explained it at some point but she didn't blame either of them for forgetting.

214

It rang a bell, now she mentioned it.

When babies were this tiny they get so tired that sometimes they forget to breathe and that's why the numbers went down. It could be pretty scary if you didn't know what was happening, she said. We're trained to think that red means danger, but on that monitor it's just a flag to let us know more than anything. Usually they realise and sort it out themselves, but it's best to give a helping hand when they're fresh out of the oven. She laughed. You'd better get used to it because it'll keep happening for a while, until she's a fair bit bigger than this, anyway.

What did you do? How Mandy could speak was a mystery.

Not a lot. I blew on her face, that's all. You only need to do it gently. Doesn't take much to remind them.

Sweet relief, collapsing like a fucked tent, again.

christ youre up and down like a brides drawers this is the kind of shit no one tells you about when you said you had a kid on the way it was all knowing looks cracks about sleepless nights and shit under your fingernails like everyone was in on some fucking side-splitting joke and only you dont know the punchline no fucker said anything about hospitals and tubes and wires and **dont fucking think it cunt** *well that fucking thing you* **know** *what it is why wont you think the word its all the same whether you name it or not present every second of every day how the fuck does anyone cope with that look youre fucking demented and its the first day of the rest of forever after and fuck this shit fuck it fuck it fuck it this is all your fault cunt all of it youre being punished for saying yes to mand when every sensible part of you was screaming nonononononono you didnt want to never wanted to ever what else could you do could have said fucking no then what you had to do it yes you said yes and now look what youve done*

■

215

When his turn came after dinner he was so worked up he could barely hold it together. Christ, he'd never held a normal baby, never mind one that weighed as much as a bag of flour. He was bound to drop her. It was inevitable as rain on holiday and Man Utd winning the league. He tried to tell them but he'd lost the power of speech again and once Samara opened the incubator he had to go through with it.

remember that time driving back from liverpool you and the captain with two ounces of uncut coke straight off the boat a digiscale a load of baggies in the boot of the motor wired off your fucking chops with the pigs following behind you for twenty miles after you came off the motorway three years at least if you got busted intent to supply court clink life ruined thought you could live to be a hundred and never be that scared again didnt you but ah guess that was just the warm up act a different blag altogether to this stupid to think you were so scared then when you look at where you are now fucking christ stick me in room 101 with a box of spiders on my dome ah dont give a fuck itd be a cakewalk hows this for an image cunt you know how clumsy you are fucking useless always dropping shit on the site when you worked for that fat fuck marl howabout seeing yourself drop the baby you know you will this is exactly how it will happen watch this samara will pass her over her body slick like a wet fish daisy pops out of your hands look just like that you can see her head bursting like a pomegranate on the floor mandys screaming so hard all the windows shatter and youre running over to slit your wrists on the shards this is the future cunt dont say ah didnt warn—

Strapped to his chest she was warm as a pie, but weightless. He could feel her heart beating against him, the rise and fall of her ribcage. She was such a clever girl to be breathing on her own, it made him so proud he could have popped. Ecstasy had nothing on this; the feeling was the same but so much more intense it was like comparing the heat from the sun to putting a hand on a fucked pilot light. No wonder the Mother Mary had that look of joy, deep in the throes of God's greatest orgasm. It was rapturous, transcendent, and the dam was surely about to burst.

Fuck that.

His tongue screwdrivered the wound in his cheek until it bled. Mandy needed him. Even if he was going crazy she couldn't know. He wouldn't let her. Or anyone else.

get it together cunt you're the man now your job to look after mand and the baby what would they think back home a big lad like yer bawling like a fucking bairn can't have them thinking you're some kind of pussy who can't even look after his own family can you

All day long they went up and down, up and down in the lift. He pushed Mandy in a squeaky wheelchair with what little strength he had; she kept saying she was sorry for not being able to walk. Man, she was girders talking like that when it was obvious even speaking was an effort. On the ward she ate like was never gonna see food again while he made small-talk with words he couldn't understand. Later he watched her sleep, chasing thoughtless thoughts in ever-decreasing circles of baffled incomprehension.

Upstairs they were glued to the incubator. Babies in ICU had one-to-one care twenty-four seven but that didn't stop him eyeballing the monitors, alert for the slightest change, awaiting disaster regardless of what Samara had said about the SATS. Hours after the alarm had stopped ringing his heart hadn't slowed; he wanted to go to the nearest church and boot a hole in a stained-glass window.

From the outside, he was impassive.

*shove it down you spineless cunt youre stone rock granite diamond the shatterproof man **do not** show a fucking thing*

Mandy must have been the only person in the hospital who loved the food, but the portions were meagre compared to what they made at home so she was permanently famished, craved chocolate. The sweetness of her tooth was a standing joke but now she could justify it, needed the extra calories to get her strength up and help with milk production. It cost him a fortune in Snickers from the Tesco Express by the refectory but he could grab a crafty fag to go with his coffee while he was down there, which helped steady him, but not a lot.

They gave him the boot again at eight. He promised he'd try to get some kip and a proper hot meal but he had fuck all intention of doing either, and didn't. His mam and dad were waiting at home and ordered a curry but looking at it made him feel gippy so he set about working through the eight cans of Becks he'd bought on the way home instead, nibbled the edges of poppadoms to keep his mam happy while she probed him with questions and he tried to explain everything that had happened that day.

Again she wanted to stay; again he said no. He told them to take the leftovers with them but she said they'd be back tomorrow and they'd eat it then. The thought of the hand-sized spider upstairs nearly sent him over the hills with the little people when he remembered the cunt, and that was any plans of going to bed royally fucked. He spent the night sweating through his clothes and pretending to kip half-upright, wedged into the corner of the sofa with the raggedy rug from in front of the fire as a blanket.

In the morning he was cryogenically frozen, aching like he'd had a proper kicking. Mandy's texts were lighter, at least. She was tired, hadn't slept much because her boobs were sore :-(but a nurse had helped her express some more and that had eased it. Daisy was fine; she'd had another good night and the doctors were pleased. She couldn't wait to see him, hoped he was okay and that he was looking after himself, and could he PLEASE bring some chocolate 8D 8D 8D?

Up in ICU, the other incubator was gone.

Mandy was so focused on Daisy that she hadn't noticed, thank Christ, but the supermassive black hole that gaped in its absence swallowed Sean whole. While Mand was doing some skin-to-skin, safely out of earshot, he asked Samara where the family had gone. Not that he needed telling. But some fucked-up part of him wanted to hear it, to ram it home that the same could happen to Daisy, there but for the grace of, and would before too long, so he'd best get fucking ready to deal with it.

It was the first time he'd seen Samara's face do anything but smile. That baby was a twenty-three-weeker. She was very, very poorly, and sometimes there's not a lot we can do. It's always a sad day when it happens but it's just how it goes in here sometimes.

shes so accepting of it so young to be talking like that soft brown eyes wise in her childs face the woman by the cot could have been her mam were they there the parents when it happened or did they have to call them in who told them cant have been samara can it how the fuck do you tell someone something like that when you know the next words you speak are going to—

He nodded in earnest agreement. Yes. Yes. It's sad, god, really, really fucking sad. He breathed it like Paddy incanting a rosary, unsure if he'd said it aloud or thought it to himself.

there you have it cunt as you are so they once were as they are so you shall be happens like that you might not even be in the fucking building no getting over it ever the happy future unwritten overnight the poor poor bastards thats gotta be it for them now life over no coming back the baby tiny mite barely half cooked couldve grown up to be anything a whole life unlived god ahd do anything to help them what can anyone do nothing nothing nothing but whats that you say cunt you cant be about to think what Ah think youre going to think surely but here it is thank jesus fucking christ and all his angels that whatever it was that came in here last night took that couples baby and not mine and thats it cunt you fucking thought it as if you didnt have enough guilt on your plate a drop in the ocean a grain of sand on blackpool beach youre glad that baby died cos she wasnt yours dont bullshit me thats not what you meant it fucking was you might as well have killed her yourself snuck in here unplugged something sneezed in the cot whatever same fucking thing your fault shes gone your fault those two people have had their lives wrecked forever your fault your fault your fault but thank fuck thank fuck thank fuck its not its not its not not yet cunt not yet but soon and youll have killed that kid for nothing mark of cain cunt mark of fucking cain youll never get this blood off your hands as long as you—

■

A week came and went.

Daisy was doing well; Mandy was mending, slowly.

Sean was a mess, still kipping downstairs with a gutful of ale for fear of the spider. He knew the cunt would be long gone and he'd probably never see it again, but rational thought had fucked off days ago and didn't look like making the return trip any time soon.

Slowly a routine developed, dictated by visiting hours and Mandy's mealtimes. The spaces in between were spent upstairs admiring Daisy, a cyborg sleeping beauty in her magic robot box. There was daily skin to skin, but he was paralysed with dread after the first time and let Mandy take his turns.

If it'll help with feeding it's best you do it.

double dealing again arent you cunt dont think you can hide it from me making out youre some unselfish fucking hero doing whats right for mandy and the kid when really its because youre terrified to hold your own baby in case—

Mandy was weak but the chocolate was building her up. She could walk to the lift unaided most of the time, but she trod with

220

ginger steps, the tension in her jaw betraying that her teeth were pressed together but she never complained of the pain. When he suggested using a wheelchair if she was tired she looked so wrathful he didn't dare risk it again. The odd time if she was resting he'd go up by himself. Sometimes he'd talk to the nurses, especially when Samara was there. He was more comfortable with her purely because her name was the only one he could remember. She was the first nurse they'd met too; bonds formed quickly in the crucible of ICU. Once when Mand was asleep Samara asked if he'd like to get Daisy out for a cuddle but he flat-out refused, almost offended, as if doing it without her would be an act of betrayal, never mind he was still tormented by thoughts of the littl'uns brains smeared all over the floor.

The consultant, Mr Johnson – Sean had finally remembered his name after reading it from his lanyard and making a proper effort – came daily with words of wisdom and hope, so relaxed they're like social calls. At the end of the first week he said he had some news; it was time for Daisy to move on to the High Dependency Unit at Jimmy's.

Was does that mean? Mandy looked frightened. Sean was worried too. Fuck, everything was cause for concern in the early days.

There's nothing to fret about. ICU is for babies that are at the most serious levels of risk. Daisy doesn't fall into that category anymore. She's done amazingly well considering the circumstances of her birth. You must have done a very good job of growing her.

Mandy's whole being glowed, the pink rose of a blush colouring her pallid face. For the first time in forever her mouth cracked into what might nearly have been something like the start of a smile; her eyes were liquid black.

Now, just because she's moving doesn't mean that everything is *guaranteed* to be okay – that gentle emphasis again, fucking hell he was good at that – but to be born at twenty-nine weeks and be going to HDU after such a short time is a very positive step. It's a bit different to how it is here, but the nurses will explain when you get there. It's much more relaxed and hopefully you'll both feel calmer once you're settled. If everything's okay, we'll see how she goes, and then later on you *might* be able to start thinking about what happens when you get her home.

It was the first time the h-bomb had been dropped, and there were more tears then. It felt at times like she cried constantly, but she was so fucking strong with it. She couldn't fake it like Sean. He could drown his feelings like kittens in a bucket, waxwork face hiding the carnage inside. If he wanted to know how Mandy was doing he could tell it in a glance. He marvelled at her steel; he'd never loved her more.

Now don't get *too* excited – the same trick, the shit in the feed-back sandwich like on those awful management courses at work – usually we wouldn't send a pre-term baby home until sometime around the actual due date and we're a long way off that yet. The good news though, is that *you* can go home. There'll be a bed for you at Jimmy's tonight, but tomorrow you can go back with Sean and he can look after you there.

She looked so relieved it nearly set Sean off, but he bossed it. He hugged her tight and whispered how great it would be to have her back, how lonely the nights had been without her. He was freaking the fuck out though, shattered at the thought of them both being away from Daisy, boggled as to how Mandy would cope without being able to see her whenever she wanted.

I'll leave you two to have a chat about it. It's nearly lunchtime, so let's get Mandy fed. There won't be many who enjoy the food here as much as you do so we can't have you missing out, can we? After that you can get dressed and someone will come and tell you what's going to happen when we move her later on. It's a big day for all of you. Like I said, we're not out of the woods yet, but this is as good an outcome as possible at this point in time. I'll be at Jimmy's later in the week to see how Daisy's doing, and we can all have a good catch-up then.

13

7 a.m.: Time to wake up, although he'd like as not have had another sleepless one. With Mandy home he'd braved the bedroom but his nerves were shot, his vision fucked; he'd developed a nervous twitch from cringing at things that crept and crawled in his peripheral. He was fixated on the fucking spider, imagined it everywhere, more afraid of the fear he'd feel if it actually appeared than the thing itself. Then he blagged his head that if he kept thinking about it he'd project it into being, which made everything ten times worse. Luke Stoppard's scruffy old fleabag had a lot to answer for. Settling was impossible.

Mandy slept well in fits and starts but she had to get up in the night to express breastmilk into sterilised bottles to take to the hospital. Often he'd keep her company, but neither of them said much. She'd get the job done with a hand pump she must have squeezed a thousand times a night, then trudge back up for a couple of hours until the pain in her boobs roused her for the next repeat.

At least my supply is good, that's the main thing. And all this will be good practice for when she comes home and we're doing night feeds, was her corpse-faced mantra.

look at the way she gets on with it never complains not like you moaning to yourself all the time about how tired you are you're sitting here now feeling like you've run a hundred marathons worrying about how you're going to deal with it when you've got a fucking baby in the house an all you'll never manage it can't ask for help bet your old man never

224

did or any of his before him never mind that they did fuck all around
the house they'll still have been knackered breaking their backs all day
schlepping and carrying and digging and shit all you'll have to do when
you go back is sit on your arse at your desk all day and you probably
won't even be able to cope with that bite your tongue get the fuck on
with it you're on your—

At home, he made himself useful. While Mandy sat in front of the gas fire for her morning milking he'd bumble round the kitchen, killing the after-taste of yesterday's anaesthetics with coffee so strong it was like chonging a speedbomb for breakfast. He craved a smoke with it but Mandy would have gone fucking nuclear if he had one. He was her personal servant, knocked up sweet tea with toast and jam or bacon sarnies with mushrooms and hash browns, whatever she wanted. She was ravenous, always, so the endless rounds of cooking and washing up gave him something to do to keep from sitting still and thinking.

8.00: HDU was on-call twenty-four seven, but Mand liked to leave it until eight before she called. There was mostly nothing to report; Daisy had slept, been fed, was happy and content. They might say that her SATs had dropped once or twice and she'd righted herself, but that was generally it. Mand would greet the news like a lottery win as she related every word while he cleaned up between glugs on a brew that had gone cold while he sorted everything else out. The post-call forensics would kill at least half an hour, thank fuck.

9.00: Showered, wearing whatever he found on the floor, teeth cleaned, pacing the carpets bare. They could drive to Jimmy's in fifteen minutes once rush hour was over, but Mandy would want to leave as soon as they were ready.

There's no point going now. It doesn't matter what time we show up, they won't let us in until visiting starts.

Yes but at least we'll be *there*. You can go to Costa. I'll grab some chocolate from the shop while we're waiting. Come on, get your shoes on. Car key's over there.

9.20: Drinking shit coffee and eating thirty milligram codeine tablets four at a time to take the edge off his nerves, watching the porters and patients smoking outside the double doors, the lucky bastards. He'd half-listen while Mandy scoffed a Snickers or Twirl and went on and on, again, about how amazing it was that she could eat as much chocolate as she wanted and no one could tell her not to. One morning he clocked an old lass, top seventies no bother, shuffle across the foyer in a dressing gown and slippers dragging a four-foot oxygen cylinder on wheels behind her, gasping with every step until she got through the doors to freedom, took off her mask and sparked up a Superking-sized fag. Her willpower was astonishing; she was a fucking hero.

With waiting he'd get twitchy; panic could lurch in unannounced. He'd have to run to the bogs to swallow a couple more pills to keep it down, sit on the crapper scratching his arm with a broken fingernail. It was never enough to draw blood, which was probably for the best, but he wished he could see some all the same, the pathetic claw marks pitifully inadequate for the release he needed.

9:50: They might let us in early *today*. Each morning the same, but they never did. Ten more minutes of hanging around as she repeated the same things she'd been saying since breakfast while he fantasised about running headlong into the wall and sparking himself right out of the whole fucking shitshow.

10.00: Straight through the doors, scrubbed and sanitised. They washed their hands every time they came in, every time they left, every time they touched Daisy, every time after. Like checking the mirrors in a moving car, they couldn't do a fucking thing without. After a fortnight their skin had aged twenty years, so cracked and wizened their hands would never be the same again.

10.05: Hello, my precious darling, how are you today? Don't you look gorgeous this morning? Oh Sean, look, she opened her eyes when she heard my voice isn't she the most wonderful thing…

They'd say hi to the nurses, Mandy eager for a blow-by-blow rundown of everything that had happened in the two hours since she'd phoned. They'd say their good mornings to the other parents too. The room was low-lit and quiet, but with less pressure on people were happier to chat. Mand nailed the local small-talk straight off the bat – what a *beautiful* baby, what were they called, how many weeks early were they, how long have you been here, all that. Sean was the quiet man, the sidekick, King Cunt, trying to hold back the tides of anxiety that threatened to sweep him away.

10:10: They called it the kitchen. A sterile room with a couple of massive stainless steel sinks and an enormous fridge freezer full of breastmilk from the mams on the ward. Here they'd deposit the spoils of the night, labelled and dated, on the shelf they'd been allocated, for use in the weeks ahead, and take out to defrost the milk they'd feed to Daisy that day. Despite such a difficult birth, she had nothing but breastmilk from day one, which was a huge source of pride for Mandy.

10:15–11:00: Daily cares, starting with a clean nappy. They'd stand on opposite sides of the incubator, put their hands through flaps that opened like fairy doors and somehow remove the old one without getting shit all over the wires. There was the SATS monitor, the ECG, the canula giving her a cocktail that included, weirdly, caffeine to keep up her heart rate – all these had to be avoided, and that wasn't even the hardest part. They'd swab her arse with cotton buds and water from miniature bottles kept in a cupboard on the side of the ward, distilled and sterilised to minimise the risk of infection; then came the task of putting on the new nappy amidst the gordian knot of cables, which would have been a task and a half even if they'd had Harry Houdini's sleight of hand. The nurses who taught them the tricks of the trade soaked up Mandy's frustrated tears on their saintly shoulders with assurances that it was like this for everyone at first and one day it'd be the easiest thing in the world.

One morning there was a wet squelch as they got the nappy off and a jet of liquid shit shot out with incredible force, decorated the Perspex with a faecal Pollock pattern the colour of Colman's mustard. Mand laughed so much she pissed in her knickers and had to grab some spares from one of the nurses.

We've got to be prepared for everything here, chuck. Could probably fit two of you in these with a little bum like yours but they're all we've got for now. A bit of a damp patch is nowt on what happens to some lasses if their pelvic floor's gone. I'll give you some exercises to do later.

The other parents cracked up too, glad of something to break the tedium. It was a memorable moment of reprieve in those difficult early days.

Next was an Octenesin wash, a sponge bath with industrial strength anti-bacterial baby wipes that could kill most bugs stone dead, weapons of mass destruction in the fight against pathogens which could be catastrophic for babies with under-developed immune systems. It was tricky to do around the wires, but a piece of cake compared to the nappy change and at least it only had to be done once.

They gave her miniscule drops of liquid supplements to help build her up. Abidec for her vitamin levels, Sitron to help with iron production and increase the flow of oxygen round her blood. HDU was like taking a crash course in pre-term neo-natal paediatrics; Sean would've found it fascinating if it was a documentary he was watching half-cut from safety of the sofa, but stuck in the middle of it he was at the end of his rope.

11:00: Feeding time. Babies as early as Daisy were too young to breastfeed, so they had to feed her through a tube. Like the nappy, it was tricky to learn but they sussed it soon enough. The tube went up her nose and down into her tummy, so before feeding they had to check that it was still in the right place. Flashbacks to Mr Taylor and his shithouse chemistry lessons as they used a syringe to suck some aspirate from the tube and drop it on a piece of litmus, hoping for a splash of blood-red to indicate stomach acid. The defrosted milk was fed into the tube via a second syringe that they'd hold in the air until gravity took over and pulled it down into Daisy's tummy.

They were bricking it when they were given a leaflet about how to tube-feed at home within a couple of days of arriving. It had instructions on how to fit an NGT – or naso-gastric tube -, warnings about the dangers of doing it incorrectly, what could happen if they stuck it in her lung by mistake. Mandy was adamant she'd never fit one; she *would* breastfeed Daisy and that was all there was to it

The nurses were savvy enough not to push her but Sean had a demo one day. One of them had to, just in case, and it sure as shit wasn't going to be Mandy, who did a runner in tears. It was a lot to take in. You had to take the fresh tube and stretch it from the tip of the nose to the earlobe, then from the earlobe to the middle of the belly, halfway between the sternum and the navel; then you marked the tube there to tell you how far to insert it. When you'd done measuring and marking you lubed it and basically shoved up the baby's hooter until you reached the bit you'd marked. She made it look like nothing but jesus fucking wept, it was complicated.

Don't worry if she starts retching, the nurse said. It doesn't hurt a bit, but imagine how you'd feel it someone were doing it to you? That's why we try to do it while they're asleep.

Having seen it in action Sean wasn't shit hot keen to tube feed at home either, especially knowing he'd be the poor cunt doing it. One day there was scary moment for another mam as a feed went wrong and her baby's face turned blue. It was heart-in-mouth time for everyone bar the nurses, who sorted it in no time, but not exactly an encouraging sign.

thatll be you if youve got to do it at home blue baby choking and no nurse to help what do you think youll do then another fucking thing to worry about as if youve not enough on your plate already feel it crushing you day on day pressed between two rocks slow style youre still on easy street in here with all these people around cant even cope with this and youre hardly doing fuck all just mincing around the gaff pretending to help mandy out doing what youre told more like the nurses can see right through you and your fucking mister nice guy act cunt youre fooling no one

After about three weeks they offered Daisy the tit and she took to it first go. The nursery nurse said that medically Daisy was too young to have developed the suckling reflex and she'd never seen a baby able to do it at her age. It was more proof of how forward she was, everyone said so. Best of all if she kept it up she'd be on the breast full-time when she came out and there'd be no need for the dreaded NGT.

dont get suckered by the good news cunt no news is good news its bad news in disguise she could take a step back anytime and youll end up with the fucking tube anyway or worse Ah know youre trying to forget that she might—

12:00–13:00: Mealtimes were one of Mandy's highlights. Because she was expressing and planning to breastfeed, she was given vouchers to get scran from the refectory, two hot feeds a day for nothing. It looked and smelled like school dinners – limp pizza, burned Shepherd's pies, pots of goop with beans, baked potatoes an that, but she scoffed it down just the same.

You not having anything? You should try some. Oh god, it's *delicious*. It didn't matter what she was eating, the conversation never altered. But the sight of food made him sick, plus the codeine and coffee he necked all day gave him excruciating stomach cramps. I'm not right hungry, he'd say. I'll get something later.

He'd text Rob and Pops while she chowed down, or send updates to his mam and dad on the days they weren't coming to visit. He was a one-man telegraph, getting the news out so Mandy didn't have to, another task taken care of so she could focus on herself and Daisy. Sometimes he'd say he needed some fresh air and stand outside with the smokers for a bit of passive and occasionally he'd blag one if he was proper struggling, but if he did he'd call at the shop for her next chocolate fix to ease his guilty conscience once he was sure the smell had gone.

13:00–17:00: The afternoon shift could be a real drag, alternating between feeding Daisy and sitting in one of the family rooms, if there was one free, while Mandy expressed. The family rooms were kinda like bedsits with wall-mounted TV's, a kitchen area with a cooker, microwave and kettle, sofas that could be turned into beds. If they wanted to, parents could spend a night on their own with their baby in them before going home, but in the daytime they were welcome respite from the clinical ambience of the unit.

There, in the cloying heat from the ancient radiators, on full blast to keep the babies warm, Mandy could express with Sean's help. They used an electric pump to drain one side, then the other, the automatic motor pumping away like the machine he remembered Harry having fitted in the big shippon to speed up milking time on the farm. Her engorged boobs were at risk of developing mastitis so a breastfeeding co-ordinator gave him a crash course in tit massage one afternoon as a dusting of snow fell the Mosque that dominated the skyline outside. She showed him the best way to fit the cup, where to press first to get the milk flowing, how to find the pockets that were the hardest to empty – down the sides, mostly, and tucked all the way underneath at the back. It could take an hour to get it all out, Sean with the pump in one hand and a boob in the other, milking her like he used to do with Harry's goat, although this was more about rolling and pressing than the gentle twist and squeeze of the animals teat. It was a right grumpy cunt, the goat, a little white thing, always after picking a scrap, but a few folk liked the sweeter taste of the milk so Harry kept it on. He told her about the time it butted him up the arse when he was tiny and left a bruise on each cheek where the horns had pronged him, which gave them something to laugh about at least.

Afternoon was also cuddle time, the lone pleasure of the day. When Daisy had put on enough weight they were given some clothes – smaller than a doll's – so they could dress her. Clothed she looked more like a normal baby, only in miniature, and a lot less vulnerable, which calmed them no end. Once she was dressed, the lid came off the incubator; she proved quickly that she could maintain a steady body temperature, so off came the hat too, showing her thick mop of dark brown hair, another source of wonder when both of them were fair. This in turn meant she could spend longer out of the cot and her SATS didn't drop as often so there was more skin-to-skin contact, the miracle of a half-hour holding her, the indescribable feeling of bonding. Each small achievement was hailed as a huge triumph, celebrated by staff and other parents alike. They shared each other's victories, comforted each other in their pain. Weepy mams swapped tissues and hugs on bad days; masculine hands patted stiff shoulders while trying not to actually touch them, quiet promises that tomorrow would be better. There were bound to be days like this, mate, but as long as there were more good than bad they were keeping on the right side of things, yeah? Chin up, lad, chest out. We'll get there.

17:00–18:00: Back to the refectory for more of the same. Tepid coffee with six sugars and a handful of pills while Mandy wolfed her bait and they raked over the afternoon, no talk of anything outside the four walls of HDU. The wider world had ceased to be.

18:00–19:55: Upstairs for the final laps. More milking, more feeding. The evening slot was when the grandparents came. His mam and dad would be over most nights Monday to Thursday, hers on weekends when they caught the train up straight after work. Only two people were allowed by the cot at once, so they'd take it in turns to escort their folks one at a time while the other sat in the waiting room outside and got the full SP on everything that had gone down since they were last there. Pre-recorded conversations, a rolling news channel screaming the same headlines till the end of days.

20:00: Kicking out time. Fond farewells that got harder with every passing day.

20:15: Saturdays they'd go for a meal with Mandy's folks or chip back to theirs for a takeaway. During the week there might be a cheap pub tea or two with his mam and dad and a chance to smash four or five quick ones while they ate.

Thirsty again tonight, lad, eh?

Fucking parched. It's boiling in there. I'm off for another. Mam, you after a top-up? We can share a bottle if it's cheaper.

When it was just the two of them they'd find the car in the multi-storey, then, I'm just gonna call at the shop for a couple of things on the way back.

20:30: Milking Mandy in front of the TV if they'd been lucky enough to borrow an automatic pump from the ward, helping her do it manually if not. They hung on every minor detail from the day that showed for certain she was going to be alright, made molehills into mountains if she'd been a bit off-colour.

21:30: Halfway through an eight pack. Mandy's eyes rolling. I think I'll give the hospital a quick ring before the night shift starts, then I'm off to bed.

Okay, let me know what they say.

Two more pills while she was on the blower, three, four, another can, and another. Not even tasting it. Swig swig swig.

21:45–22:15: A half-hour conversation to relay a five-minute phone call, then, are you coming up with me? You look so tired.

I'm okay. I won't be able to switch off anyway. I'm gonna stay down here for a bit. I won't be late.

Don't be. You need to keep your strength up. Love you.

You too. Gnight.

????: Creeping upstairs in the dark trying to be quiet, holding onto the walls. The codeine and alcohol snuck up slowly then overpowered him in a rush like warm wire in his veins that left him barely able to stand, but it helped him black out for patches in the night so at least he wasn't conscious the *whole* time. Small mercies an that.

youre not having any tomorrow no definitely not and no booze either this is no way to deal with it how long do you think you can keep this up but its done the job till now if its not broke why fix it but youre losing your shit every fucking day exhausted headfucked but its for mandy all for mandy you need the time at night to let it hang out blow off steam slow you down to a level you can try to think straight shut down these negative thoughts youre fucking doing me in with them haha yeah right tomorrow will be a good day it has to be cant cope with anything else fucking good days are bad enough a hard one might be the end of you please no no no no no please no more fucking do something this has got to—

■

Examinations.

Assessments.

Observations.

Weigh-ins.

Test after test after motherfucking test, often repeated two or three times to confirm the previous results.

One shit-shaking ordeal after another.

They checked her ears to make sure they were developing right and see how she responded to sound. The ocular examinations were done with a machine that looked like a medieval torture device or something from *A Clockwork Orange* – another one that had Mandy pezzing from the room in sobbing hysterics – but he had to stay so Daisy wouldn't be alone while they did it, ground his teeth to powder trying to block out her whimpering as the ophthalmologists did the business. He told himself that NHS staff were heroes, they knew what they were doing, they'd make it as quick and comfortable for Daisy as they could; but god help him he wanted to kill those fuckers for making his baby cry.

When they first mentioned brain scans it nearly finished him. What the fuck did they mean, brain scans? No one had said anything about that before.

Mr Johnson, ever patient, explained that sometimes premature babies can have bleeds on the brain. These could be small, so the brain develops around them and swallow them up without any ill effects; but sometimes they could be bigger – like a stroke in an adult – and the brain could be damaged, leading to problems with motor functions, cognition, speech and so on. He must have clocked that Sean was on the verge of his own apoplexy and was quick to say that seeing as though the other tests had been clear there was little to worry about, that these were more a matter of routine than cause for alarm in Daisy's case, but it did fuck all to help.

wanna see into the future walk this way ahll show you check out daisy in that wheelchair probably the age you are now fucking head lolling like her necks broken tongue hanging out like the ligaments been cut eyes rolling in opposite directions like a pair of dropped marbles the mind of a newborn in the body of a woman theres mandy next to her look grey haggard you an all withered away bald shaking spoonfeeding her brown mush thatll look no different when you have to clean it up out the other end shes slobbering all over mucus dripping sucking and slurping it down snot and grub together thirty years of that no wonder you look like youve a foot and a half in the grave be better if shed no not that but whats worse talking to her in the same baby voice you were using earlier she wont understand any more of it then than she does now whats the value in keeping her ali—gonna drive yourself insane with this cunt well down that road already speeding up all the time hows this for a home video get your ball peen hammer from the shed when you get back tonight and cave your fucking face in with it—

The test results were fine but it was an agonizing three weeks waiting for the final one, and still the shocks kept coming. The jolt on hearing she had jaundice

that means her livers fucked cunt like yours soon will be

was tempered by the cure, the sight of Daisy under a UV lamp like a mini sunbed with bumblebee goggles and everything, which sorted it sharpish. Later she developed anaemia so her SATs kept dropping again and she was given a transfusion. Mandy exited stage left, put Sean on sentry duty for another operation she couldn't stand to witness.

They'd been told as usual not to worry, that lots of pre-termers– most in fact – have to have a transfusion at some point, sometimes two or three. Daisy'd had one on the day she was born, according to her records, but no one could blame them for forgetting.

It gives them a little boost, that's all, Mr Johnson said. She'll be a different baby after this. If that man was ever wrong, Sean wasn't there to see it. By the end of the same day she was livelier, much more alert, and from there she started to visibly develop a personality, although she should have been safe in the womb for a good while yet.

Not everyone was so lucky.

News filtered through one morning that a thirty-one weeker called Kai from the cubicle next door had a blood infection. They watched in sombre silence as he was put into a transportation incubator like the one Daisy had arrived in and wheeled away with his ashen parents, to be taken in an emergency ambulance back to the ICU. The nurses said he needed some extra care until the infection was clear, but he never came back.

Another memory to bury forever.

When Mandy was in transitional care – the final rung on the ladder – getting ready for Daisy coming home, they heard that the baby further down the ward that had been screaming like a wounded animal for days had been born to a young woman who it was implied was addicted to something – alcohol or heroin, they guessed, but the nurses couldn't say – and was going through withdrawal. But the child's howls of distress were a chorus of angels compared to the banshee shrieks when social services came for its mam. Sean caught sight of her as two women with lanyards and grim faces, one on each side, dragged her down the corridor and off the ward, fighting them all the way with hands and feet and teeth and nails, spitting and snarling like a rabid dog. She couldn't have been a day past sixteen.

That night Mandy said the girl knew what was coming; she'd seen the women from the social talking to her in the afternoon while Sean was on a chocolate mission. As soon as they'd left she'd made a phone call and gone out, came back after an hour slack-jawed and dead-eyed; but whatever she'd taken was never going to be enough. There wasn't much to say after that and Mandy went to bed, left him alone with his thoughts and his wine and the pills in his pocket, the tortured cries of both children – the baby and its mam – reverberating around his skull, an echo that only amplified the more he drank to quell it.

He could still hear them when Mandy came to express, blotting out whatever conversation passed between them. When she next appeared for her pre-breakfast brew and biscuits he hadn't moved; he was petrified, transfixed by the reciprocal gaze of an abyss he couldn't tear his eyes from.

14

Six weeks.

Forty two days.

One thousand and eight hours.

Sixty thousand four hundred and eighty minutes that felt like decades apiece and sometimes longer. But today it was their turn.

Mr Johnson had been full of apologies that he wasn't able to see them off, but he was going to be in theatre doing a bit of operating, he said, as if he was talking about some everyday mundanity like rewiring a plug or washing his car. He made a point of visiting them the day before and Mandy had hugged him like she never wanted to stop, washed-out with tears. Ever the oracle, he patted her on the back and waited for her to cry herself out, his bodhisattva smile making clear this was the natural order of things, that he'd seen it all before, would do so many times again.

Now, he said, once she'd calmed herself. Tomorrow is a special day, but I *do* need to give you a few words of advice to take home with Daisy.

Here we fucking go, the shit in the sandwich. Sean didn't want to hear any more scare stories, forced himself to focus while his mind was trying to race out of the door ahead of him.

You *have* to remember that Daisy is a pre-term baby. She's five weeks off her due date yet – some babies are *born* at this gestation and have to stay in hospital for a while, so you're very lucky she's coming home now. But the risk of infection is still high, so you need to keep visitors to a minimum. And you can't go out with

Daisy at first. It's not unlike being under house arrest, I'm afraid, but it'll pass sooner than you think. And the outreach team will be there to make sure everyone's doing okay. You'll be in very good hands.

What about my parents? Can they come?

Yes, of course. They've been coming in here for weeks so there's no reason for that to change. But the same rules apply at home as they do in HDU. Hand washing, sanitising frequently, and under no circumstances let them come in if they've been showing any symptoms of illness, you have to be absolutely clear about that.

Of course, Mr Johnson. They wouldn't dream of it.

I'm sure. I suppose what I'm saying is, don't be like the couple who got home from here after two months with a thirty-four-week-pre-termer and put photographs of themselves all over Facebook. You can guess what happened there.

What happened, Mr Johnson? She was looking at him like the class swot asking a question they knew was so smart the rest of the kids wouldn't even understand it.

Well, their friends descended *en masse*, someone brought an infection in and—

Oh god. She was crestfallen now, looked like she wished she'd never asked.

The baby was fine *in the end*. But she was back here for a couple of extra weeks, and she was very fortunate that's all it was.

Thank you, Mr Johnson, we'll bear it in mind.

And the tears came again.

It was a day for bittersweet goodbyes, hugs of a kind that can only be shared by those who *knew*, numbers swapped, plans made to meet up when everyone had settled back into normal life, whatever the hell that was. Sean couldn't remember most of the other parent's names and didn't give a shit if he ever set eyes on them again but he played his part well. All he wanted was to get home, lock this whole binfire in a box and inter it with the other ash heaps of trash and tragedy he refused to remember or acknowledge ever existed.

There were hugs for the doctors, the nurses, the consultants, the nursery nurses; even the cleaners didn't escape. Mandy was gushing in her thanks and so was Sean in his understated way, although his hugs came with the stiff limbs of one who shies from touch, as warm and pliant as a high street mannequin.

They were cheered from the ward with applause and wolf-whistles like newlyweds; the only thing missing was the confetti. Daisy was strapped into a car seat-cum-carry cot that needed special padding to secure a baby so small, and still she was dwarfed like a pea on the centre spot at Elland Road. The seat was heavy in Sean's hands, but the weight was in his mind. Last count Daisy had tipped the scales at a tad over four pounds and the carrier was mostly plastic. A guy who'd worked shifting bags of compo for a living should have been able to juggle with it, but it felt like it could have pulled him over.

It was breastfeeding that sealed the deal. Once Daisy took to it, she never stopped. Every three hours on the dot she'd wake up and start rooting, sucking her fist like a tiny crone slobbering on a sherbet lemon. With no need for tube-feeding and the risk of any other complications ruled out, once she'd put on enough weight there was no reason to stay. Mandy spent a few peaceful days in the transitional care ward – a place at the far end of HDU where babies were left with their mams but the staff were hands-off unless something went drastically wrong – breastfeeding in bed and kipping whenever Daisy did; once that acid test was passed there was nowhere to go but home.

Before she went in trans care Mand spent the evenings after visiting getting the house ready, dusting and vacuuming and tidying till all hours while Sean drank his medicine and did his best to help out, but she made him sit down. She wanted to do everything herself, so he left her to get on with it.

It's great you're doing this, but I'm not sure Daisy will notice.

Oh shush. A touch of her old sparkle flashed through the white-wash of exhaustion. I want everything to be *perfect* for her. She deserves it.

He was apprehensive at best, not that he could tell anyone. He was Mandy's anchor, projected it for all to see; he was every bit the devoted, dedicated partner and daddy who'd be there for his family come hell or high water and there the discussion ended.

good front youre putting on it cunt but you wont be able to keep it up how can you youre so fucking freaked you keep thinking your hearts going to stop which it is you cant ignore me I know your game you want to step outside disassociate pretend youre not you so you can watch this truckload of shit dumped on some other poor cunts head but you cant fool me Im still here even if youre blagging yourself that emaciated wreck of a pathetic excuse of a human is anyone else youre nothing but a shitscared little boy playing at being a man like youve done since you were a kid you cant fool everyone forever so why bother trying youll fail at it like youve failed at every other fucking thing youve ever attempted mental disintegration cunt stand in the corner then Ill come with you we can watch together while you—

■

April Fools.

Late morning.

They walked through the double doors for the last time with Mandy eyeing death rays at the smokers and pointedly waving the pall away, into an unfamiliar world with a frostblue sky that suddenly seemed so big and so wide it gave Sean vertigo. Eyes

242

forward, he swore he'd never set foot in the fucking place again. He'd be grateful forever for what everyone in there had done, but part of him wanted to see the bastard razed to the ground. There was a chill in the wind, the sun a dead white pinprick, but a few trees showed the first green shoots of spring. The rest of their lives started here, so the story went.

His hands were numb, quivering with nerves and hunger and a touch of something else. It took him a while to fasten the seatbelt around the carriage while Mandy chuckled behind her hand. He was appalled at himself for struggling with such a simple task, could have ripped out his teeth with his fingers, but he forced a smile and laughed along.

He was tired of this already and they'd not got off the grounds. The relief at knowing tomorrow would dawn without a call to Jimmy's and no need to leave the house was immense, but he felt like a boxer battered senseless for twelve rounds when his corner should have chucked in the towel after two. He wanted to go to sleep and never wake up.

Daisy had had a big feed before they left and was out for the count when they got home. They set her down on the living room floor and eyed her like a telly, not knowing what to do, or say. But they didn't need words when the centre of their world was right there in front of them. Mandy had set the heating to full bollocks so the house would be warm for Daisy; the room was as cloyingly hot as the ward. He closed his eyes for a minute, just one, to rest them while Daisy was quiet, and here they were, safe at last in their own place with their child, alone; no nurses and no noise, the pure silence of a warm house on a cold spring morning and fleetingly all was well, and all was well, and all manner of things were well.

■

Now she was home, he was harried by the prospect of work.

After the psychological violence of being institutionalised in Jimmy's the housing office should have been like Eden before the Fall, but it was a fresh kind of hell with Denise to deal with. The day after Daisy was born his mam had called Denise and explained what had happened, said Sean would phone when he could.

Technically, Denise had said, it's an unauthorised absence, but I suppose under the circumstances I'll have to turn a blind eye.

Frigging snotty-nosed cow. His mam was raging when she told him. Is she like that all the time? If she'd said that to my face I'd've took her bloody head off.

Sounds like you caught her on one of her better days, he'd replied, and the funny thing was, he wasn't joking.

He rang in himself a few days after. Daisy was in ICU, that much he was sure of, because he was on his own; he did it from home before visiting and was that fucking radged after that he nearly pranged the Polo into the back of a bus going down Clarendon Road, so he must've been en route to LGI. He told Denise that he wasn't going to be in work for a few days at least, that everything was unclear at the moment but he'd try to let her know what was going on once it had settled. I'll see about coming in when I can, he remembered saying. He must have been having a brainstorm to even think it.

She interrupted without letting him finish. I don't think that *you* can dictate to *me* when you can and can't work, regardless of what's happening in your personal life. Anyway, do you *have* to go to the hospital every day?

The handset shattered into a thousand pieces when it hit the living room wall.

Later Mr Johnson said he should ask his GP for a sicknote. They'll write you one on the spot, he told him. Dr Bell, saint that she was, did just that. He hadn't spoken to work since; he sent the notes as and when, and that was all he needed to do, thank fuck. Denise would be a dickhead about him going back whatever though. He couldn't trust himself to face her without losing his shit, and most likely his job, so he gave it the ostrich treatment instead. Simple.

For the first week he didn't bother to tell her they were home; he was onto a winner and clean forgot about the bastard place until his sicknote ran out, then the voicemails started arriving, so many in such short order it was like he was being stalked.

Did he know his medical certificate had expired?

Was he aware that he was in breach of the employee code of conduct by being off work without a valid certificate?

How long did he propose to be away from blah blah blah blah fucking blah.

He booked an appointment at the surgery to ask for another extension but she said she couldn't write another one unless he was physically ill now Daisy was home.

He fucking well looked it and felt even worse, but he didn't say so.

But, she said, it'd be worth checking if he had any holidays left to use and to remember that he could take his two weeks paternity leave concurrently if he wanted to. She shook his hand before he left. You've had a hell of a time, but you're going to be a great daddy. Best of luck.

He called Denise from the car. He didn't want Daisy's delicate ears being sullied by the sound of him going nuclear, didn't want Mandy to hear either. The last thing she needed was to be earwigging while he went off on one and be worrying about him getting the sack. He knew this though; he'd never forget the way Denise had spoken to him and his mam, and he wasn't gonna take the slightest bit of shit from her ever again. It only rang once.

Sean, how nice of you to call. She was such a prick. Always had to get the first dig in.

Y'alright Denise? Channelling his inner teen, brimming with unrepentant swagger.

When are you coming back? You've an awful backlog to get through. Your medical certificate expired over a week ago, are you aware of that?

I won't be in for a while yet. She hadn't even asked about Daisy, the heartless twat. No way she was winning this one.

I think I'll be the judge of that.

Well, let me tell you how I see it…

In his head he punctuated it with a big draw on a fag, made a mental note to buy a pack of Luckies or Reds at the first available op. Aside from the odd one he crashed outside the hospital, he'd not had one since Mandy came home and he was gasping.

She barely heard him out before she started to argue. This was her style, like a fucking Pitbull. She said he couldn't take his holidays – she *needed* him back at work *now*. If she didn't sign the paperwork to approve them, he'd *have* to come in or it would go down as another unauthorised absence and there was nothing he could do about it. And anyway, he'd lost what he had left over – he knew full well it had to be taken by the end of March.

She spoke in her usual tone – supercilious, icy, a voice used to commanding and being obeyed, although she'd shifted up a pitch and become strident, her first warning signal. Most folk at work were cowed enough by it to stop arguing but he didn't give a flying flatulent fuck. On another day he'd've gone ballistic, told her to give her head a wobble and fuck all the way off while she was at it, but not this time. He pointed out with codeine calmness that paternity leave was a *legal* right, and so was his annual leave, which he would lose if the remainder wasn't carried over from last year.

He'd been under an inordinate amount of stress and needed to come back to a calm working environment which he wouldn't be able to do if he couldn't take the holiday he was entitled to, and how could he have taken his leave when he'd been in hospital with a pre-term baby? He was aware the policy said he couldn't carry it over, but allowances could surely be made in light of that.

She tried to butt in, but this time he was the one talking over her.

He could always get signed off with stress and speak to his union rep about how to get back his lost holiday entitlement, but they'd probably take a dim view of any manager, particularly a senior one at her pay grade, denying an employee something they were legally entitled to as an apparent punishment for being away from work during the traumatic and potentially fatal birth of their first child, wouldn't she agree?

That shut her fucking cakehole.

He'd seen her on occasions when she'd proper blown her stack and her face went so red it was almost black. That was probably how she looked then, temple veins throbbing, eyes bugging like she'd been strung up on Tyburn Tree.

Tell you what, he broke the silence himself when it became clear her rage had left her speechless. I'll check my paperwork when I get in and see how much holiday I've got left, start that from today, and then add my paternity on at the end. Once I've sussed it, I'll email you a date for me to come back. Oh, and am I right in thinking if I've been off over a month it's got to be a phased return? Best have a think about that an all, and we'll figure it out at the Friday before I come back, alright, but I reckon it'll be a couple of half days the first week, *under the circumstances*. So I'll be in touch in a month or so. See ya. He hung up.

Have that, you fucking pustulating wanker.

BLOOD AND GUTS
IN HIGH SCHOOL

The first punch came from behind out of nowhere, smacked into the back of your head and knocked you off balance. You stumbled forward, nearly tripped and went full-length but caught yourself in time and turned around, teetering on jelly legs.

There were three of them.

You were in deep shit.

Fuck—

You didn't get time to say off before one of them lamped you again, a proper clean one right in the kisser. Your lip mashed into your front teeth, popped like a sausage brayed with a mallet. Blood in your mouth, dripping down your chin, seeing fucking stars; you reeled, tried to stay up. You swayed out of the arc of the next one more by accident than design and threw the biggest left you had, but lads like that ate kids like you for breakfast. Nearly every day someone got battered on the way home by cunts from the comp who said everyone at your school was posh and stuck up and a bunch of soft-arse fucking bender boys who deserved everything they got. You'd been lucky so far, but everyone got their turn in the end.

He wasn't much bigger than you and but you never stood a chance with his mates there an all. He stepped to the side, grinning like the Joker as the weight of your punch carried you forward, then stuck out a foot and legged you up, sent you crashing to the deck. You'd just about pushed yourself up onto your hands and knees when one of the others booted you in the stomach; you puked, bile and spit, blood from your mangled mouth and the regurgitated syrup of the Diet Coke you'd just finished drinking. You looked up in time to see one of them raising his rucksack high in the air then he hammered it down on top of your head and fuck knows what happened after that.

It doesn't hurt much when you're getting a right proper kicking, and you should know; this might have been the first time but it sure as shit wasn't the last. It's soft and dull. You feel the fists connecting and the trainers banging into your body but the pain doesn't hit home till the adrenaline's worn off a good while after. All you can do is cover your face and your nuts and hope they get bored or disturbed before the damage gets serious.

Ah hope you gorra few good shots in, your old man said when you went home late, looking like you'd been chucked out of a window and broken your fall with your face. Your mam was fussing around you with a warm flannel, scraping bits of grit from the grazes on your cheek where you'd smacked it on the pavement.

Don't worry, love, it looks worse than it is, she said as you winced at the sting of the TCP she'd tortured you with in the name of cleanliness for every minor injury you'd had since you were a littl'un. It'll be better once I get it cleaned up. You might be a bit sore in the morning though.

You'd clocked yourself in the hallway mirror and knew she was lying. With your swollen cheeks, eyes purpling and a bloody hole where your gob used to be, you made John Merrick look like River Phoenix.

Ah don't care how many of em there were, the big fella carried on in between mouthfuls of egg and chips, red sauce smeared round his stubbly chops. If it happens again, make sure you fuckin hurt someone, right? When Ah were your age some little bastards jumped me one night, called us a thick Mick and a spudshagger and a bogtrotter cos of me dad an that. There were no way I could take em all, but Ah gave as good as Ah got and Ah had to pull one o' their teeth out me knuckle after. There were as much blood o' theirs on me as there was mine on them an they never dared come near us after that Ah can tell you. You don't want any cunt thinking yer soft or you won't last five fuckin minutes round here. You need to learn to use your fists as well as that brain of yours, boy.

1994 was a rough year.

You were thirteen; life had taken you by surprise. Part of you was trying to hang on to what was left of the child you'd never be again while the rest was ravaged by hormones and turmoil reigned inside, your little boy body betraying you as it sprouted hair, spots erupted, and you stank like a pan of frying onions no matter how often you showered. That spring your first love Kurt Cobain blew his head off with a shotgun after jacking up more black tar smack than most people could fit in their pockets because he couldn't stand himself or his pain any longer. It's better to burn out that fade away, said the note. You thought you knew how he felt and wished you could do the same thing, only without the smack. Or the gun.

The same day the news about Kurt broke, your dog Honey started pissing and shitting blood all over the living room floor while you were eating your tea. Before the day was out she was dead too, poisoned by sepsis after the vets had scwn a wad of gauze inside her when she'd been spayed the week before; she'd rotted from the inside out, breeding death in the space vacated by organs that were there to create life.

Your old man was a proper Northern powerhouse. He was brought up on the estate and left school at the same age you were then to start work, sick of being caned by the nuns from the convent at St Stephen's every time they caught him running away.

Nay point worrying about Hell with them bitches on the loose, he used to say. They had the devil in em, no messin. Ah wanted to burn that fuckin convent to ashes wi' all them cunts in it an warm me feet up on t'flames.

He'd never read a book in his life and was proud of it, but he could take apart an engine and put it back together as easily as if it were a toddler's jigsaw. He could lay a patio, plumb in a washing machine, fix a broken toaster. The kind of guy who could drink ten pints of an evening, drive home without a thought and be up for work at six, raring to go. Though you never saw him have a fight, folk said he'd finished a lot more than he'd started and tales were told after a few too many scoops about times of old when all-comers were taken on, arguments settled with a single blow, or two if he'd not supped enough to have his eye in. Your family was full of blokes like that – him, Tez, those mad bastards in Essex who made the Wild Bunch look like the Care Bears; the kind of man you were meant to become but everyone knew you never could, with your books and your quizbook brain, your panda eyes, coloured hair and all your other nancy boy ways. You were the turd in the gene pool, an outcast in a family where black sheep were sources of pride on the quiet – as long as they were of the drinking fucking or fighting breeds – destined to be a permanent disappointment

You'd never seen him rattled but you could tell from the wet film on his eyes he was struggling when he said there was nothing the vets could do. He kept it tight though so you did too, desperate to be a man although you wanted to fall into your mam's lap and bawl like the little boy you were. The idea of him crying was so out there it verged on impossible; until the day they found Hayley, that was the closest you ever came to seeing it.

Moving to high school had knocked you sideways, and you were in your second year then. You were the smartest kid in primary by a country mile and passed an exam like the old eleven plus to go to the local grammar school, a single-sex shithole with delusions of old-Etonian grandeur. Most of the pupils were cunts; the staff were ten times worse.

Like the rest of the town, Steadman's was stuck in a time warp where the Sixties had never happened; the shit they got away with was eye-watering. One of the design and technology masters, a short-arse fascist from New Zealand, loved to pull boys' ties tight and trap them in a vise, only cutting them loose with a craft knife at the end of the class unless they started choking first, which more often than not they did, then he'd put them in detention for not wearing full uniform. The games teacher carried on like that loud-mouth bald bastard from the film about the miner's boy and his hunting bird you watched in English Lit, made kids he didn't like hang by their fingers from the wall-bars till you could hear their shoulders cracking in their sockets. There was a tiny pool where each class was made to swim once a week, even in winter when the ice on top had to be broken with a pole and was so thick and sharp it could break the skin if you bumped into it. Anyone who couldn't swim was forced to wear a pink girl's cossie with a rubber ring sewn around the middle, then pushed in at the deep end.

Your first week there they made you have a medical, a humiliation you never got over. They inspected your eyes and ears, tapped your knees with a hammer, made you strip to your kecks so they could weight you, measured your height like you were a cow getting ready for market. If they'd lifted your lips to check your teeth you'd've bitten their fucking fingers off.

Tall lad like you'll soon fill out, they said approvingly. Get three stone on and we'll have you in the front row of the scrum before the second year's out. Fuck that, you thought, and started spending your lunch money on fags instead of food.

Legend had it that in the Seventies there was a kid at Steadman's who couldn't hack it and brained the headteacher with a crowbar, but that might have been a myth. More tangible was the one about the sixth former who was bullied so badly by the staff and the other kids that he strung himself with a bike chain in the common room one night when everyone else had left. That one you knew was true – it happened the year before you started and caused such a shitstorm it made the national news.

The pressure to succeed was immense. High achievers were exalted, sanctified; the kids in the middle were tolerated as an inconvenience but never persecuted like the scum at the bottom of the class, who were left in no doubt they'd've been beaten black and blue to knock some good old-fashioned English discipline into them if only the government weren't so bloody soft. It was there, with the dregs, the dropouts and the just-don't-give-a-fucks that you spent the first year.

They told us you were smart when you came here, Mr Dalston, one of the Geography teachers once said during Friday night detention. You don't seem so bloody smart to me. Quite the opposite. I think there's more brains in a pork pie than a thicko like you. You don't belong here, and everyone knows it. Look at the bloody state of you, you don't even have a blazer that fits right. You should be up the road at the comp with all the other scratters.

Yeah well you can fuck right off. I don't give two sloppy shits what you think, you stuck-up prick.

So that was you in detention again the next week, and the one after. Your mam wasn't best pleased, but the big fella was. Good effort, lad, he said. Tha's learning.

You'd never think the biggest bully in school would be one of the masters but that fucker Dalston was and even the other teachers knew it. He never let up for a second, picking and poking at you every time you crossed his path, which he made sure happened daily. Your shirt was untucked, your tie wasn't straight, your shoes weren't shiny enough; he'd bawl you out in his classes in front of everyone when you'd done nothing wrong, and the kids around you would have a free pass to fuck about cos they knew you'd cop for the blame whatever they did. Why should I fear hell, you wrote on your pencil case in a moment of angsty inspiration, when I am already there?

You never clicked with the other lads. They had parents who were doctors and lawyers, accountants, bank managers, lived in houses with garages the size of your living room. They were from a different world. So were the lasses from the girls' grammar next door with their bare legs and pleated skirts, the bumps in the front of their blouses and hair you wanted to wrap around your neck till you choked. They were the forbidden fruit you craved till it drove you insane, so remote they may as well have lived on Mars.

No one else had any bother. They were mini-men already, strong, muscular, could grow beards in year two while you had nothing but bumfluff and bare bones in the sixth form. They went to weekend discos, house parties, came in Mondays with loud stories about French kissing and sticky fingers and how Sally Hanson slapped Sam Roberts' face when he tried to feel her tits playing spin the bottle. Terminally uncool, you were never invited to anything so you seethed, yet secretly you were relieved, knowing if you went you'd have no idea what to do or say and no fucker would talk to you anyway.

Mostly you were alone. But over time the freaks united and you found a few allies, other kids who liked punk rock and shoplifting cider, lads who'd duck out halfway through a cross-country run to smoke a spliff behind a wall in a roofless barn. One of them,

Luke Stoppard, went through a phase of saying he was a vampire. He was a seriously weird cunt and even the freaks gave him a wide berth but you and him got on alright and managed to fight through it together, when you weren't brawling with each other. His folks were minted and lived over the road from school in a three-storey townhouse that was like a castle compared to yours. His older sister had moved out and they'd knocked the two attic rooms together, so he had free run of the place. Here you hid when you bunked off, getting stoned on squidgy black and nicking what booze you could from his mam and dad's stash, giggling your balls off like Beavis and Butthead, which you watched on VHS till the tapes wore out. Sometimes you'd walk to the park and dab speed out of wraps you bought off his sister's mate, a biker who hung out in the rockers' pub opposite the Club, gibber on a bench for hours then do one back to Luke's to smoke yourself straight before home time.

Fuck, you were so bored.

For most of the first five years you spent more time there than you did at home, or at school. The teachers turned a blind-eye to you and Luke skiving, happy that they didn't have to deal with Cheech and Chong for a second longer than they had to. Anyway, after the shock of adjusting in the first year had ebbed away your marks rocketed – so much for that cunt Dalston and his fucking pie – not through any effort, just because your brain was always ahead of the game and remembered everything it saw or heard, so the work was a piece of piss and you could ping through most of it with your eyes shut. You were canonised with the swots then and had carte blanche to do as you pleased; even Dalston backed off a bit. Top grades and never in bother even though you got up to more shit than the rest of the class put together. The other lads hated it.

In the sixth form the weekend was pub time. The comp kids and the flash lads from your school went to the big pubs on the High Street but you, Luke and the other misfits kept well clear of those cos you'd've been asking for a twatting just by walking in. The Rose and Crown was a rough old hole that no fucker wanted to go anywhere near, apart from a few old alkies who knocked about with Paddy in the Club, so that was where your lot congregated. The landlady was a dragonhided Glaswegian called Morag, who ran the gaff with her vertically challenged husband Wee Malky. She knew you were underage but didn't give a fuck as long as you spent plenty of coin and didn't give her any grief. Once a flood they'd get a tip-off that the coppers were raiding places so she'd ring the bell and announce in a voice so smoky her breath could give you lymphoma.

Alreet youse lawt, the pegs are awn thir way, so if y'aint gawt ID fuck awf oot ae et for half an 'oor an come back whin thiv gawn.

One time she heard you hurling in the bogs when you'd had more double Jacks than your mates had had pints and she was waiting when you came out. Away wi' youse till ye've sobered up ye fuckin radge cunt, she cackled as she smacked you upside the head and shoved you out through fire exit. She was great.

The Crown and Luke's place were slivers of light in the immense darkness of the seven miserable bastard years you endured at Steadman's. The whole time you were there, only two happy memories stand out. The first was the day you left to start study leave for your A-levels, the happiest day of your life at that point, which you celebrated by necking three double-dipped strawberries and a couple of Mitsubishis during morning register. You lasted till about half ten before you were escorted down the drive by four members of staff, tripping your bollocks off and gurning while they lectured you about wasting your life and all the rest of it and you laughed in their faces like they were carting you away to the madhouse. It was fucking epic.

The other time was when a rumour started going round that there was something up with Mr Dalston, some mystery illness or something, but it was proper hush-hush and no one could get the right end of the stick. When it came out he had malignant growths all over his kidneys and liver and the prognosis was terminal you punched the air and imagined it was his face. He died – slowly, painfully, you hoped – in the summer holidays between the lower and upper sixth. You were at Luke's when you heard the good news. You rolled up a walking stick with an eighth in four king size skins and swore one day you'd find the cunt's grave so you could piss on it. What a shitter when it turned out he'd been cremated.

■

You can't remember the first time but you're sure it was sometime that year. That was when the rage took a hold of you bad-style, more powerful even than the hormones that left you so confused and sad you knew you were insane. Your overactive brain went into hyperspeed when puberty kicked in. You'd never been good at winding down, restless and unsettled at night as a nipper but now you couldn't sleep at all, even if you wanted to, and fuck knows you tried. It didn't matter how tired you were, as soon as the lights went off you were wide awake – ding! – wired, mainlined into some colossal power source you couldn't switch off, thoughts like a pinball machine with fifty silver spheres pinging and clanging all over the shop, and not a single one of them happy.

When childhood's bubble burst and you became aware of the wider world, something changed. Your old man was glued to the news every night, and now you were too. War in Bosnia, war in Somalia, Russian soldiers terrorising Chechnya, Rwandan tribes massacring each other to extinction; AIDS as a weapon of war, Fred fucking West and his mad wife inventing new ways to torture raped women for shits and giggles.

The horror; the horror; the horror.

Up all night, you ate books like air. Doorstoppers about Hitler and Stalin, Pol Pot, the Crusades, the African slave trade, the Belgian Congo, the Holocaust – the pornography of genocide and other crimes of war, Hiroshima, Dresden, Nagasaki. You must have read an entire library's worth of stuff about serial killers. Hindley and Brady, Son of Sam, John Wayne Gacy, Jeffrey Dahmer, Ted Bundy, Peter Sutcliffe from just up the road, the Manson Family, the two Ed's, Gein and Kemper. All of human history reduced to ashes and misery in the dustbin of your sleepless psyche, a bad trip lasting millennia that only reinforced what you already knew, that people were shit, always had been, modern life a cesspit beyond redemption. And something buried in your blood said you were one of the worst, culpable by the very fact of your existence, therefore complicit in every atrocity ever committed. The knowledge of your guilt was a cross of lead to bear forever, a reminder that you needed to atone for the crime of your birth and shouldn't continue to live for a second longer than you had to.

You started with scratches. A blunt compass that tore the skin of your arms in ragged flecks, but never enough to draw blood. Where the urge came from, fuck knows, but it felt soooooooo good, the pain of your tormented mind traded off for pain of another kind; the fix was instant. For a while you used a rusty blade you'd screwed out of a pencil sharpener, then you fucked that off and swiped one of your old man's Stanleys from the shed and it was serious tackle then, the type of wounds that couldn't be explained away, deep cuts bordered with pock marked craters from septic fag burns that oozed pus the colour of infected phlegm.

Summer 95 was one of the hottest on record. It was Britpop year, the radio airwaves awash with songs about pigeons and chip shops, Mockney arseholes belting out jaunty tunes about how laaarverley it was to talk about the wevvah. Union Jacks, ticker tape, bunting, street parties to mark the 50th anniversary of VE Day in May and again in September to commemorate victory over Japan, as if Harry Truman and that despicable cunt Churchill vaporizing a couple of hundred thousand civilians to put the frighteners on Uncle Joe after the peace was made was something worth celebrating. Endless sun, merciless heat, stand pipes, talk of the army being called in. A reservoir up the Dale baked so dry people could walk around the village at the bottom that had been evacuated in the Sixties and flooded. You sweltered for weeks in your customary uniform of long-sleeved shirts and combats when everyone else was stripping off, so many girls in the shortest skirts, the tiniest tops, hotpants, boob tubes, practically naked to your goggling eyes, so much bare skin heaping pain upon pain upon pain, rubbing your face in the fact you were alone, always would be, never to be understood by anyone, especially your stupid fucking family, but even more so especially your stupid fucking self.

Clock Mister Misery over there wearing that in t'summer, eh? Black an all. Just like him. Allus has to be different to normal folk.

To think when you were little you'd want to wear shorts and t-shirts if the sun came out in December, and sometimes Ah'd let you just to keep the peace. People must've thought Ah were mad letting you go out like that, but it were easier than arguing t'toss for hours. Your mam lacked the big man's disdain, but still sounded boggled as to how her loins could have spawned such a creature.

It went tits-up sometime in the sixth form when your folks came home at the end of their Saturday night sesh round town and found you bollock naked on your bed, cunted on a cocktail of spirits nicked from their booze cupboard and half a case of your old man's Worthies. You were puking into a bucket, or trying to, but for every bit that hit the target there was more that went on the floor. It was all over your legs an all, and your feet.

But that wasn't what made your mam scream like she'd walked in on Fred and Rose.

No.

It was the blood.

Fucking everywhere.

Your arms were scarlet with it, your chest, drops spattered all over your naked thighs, so much red they couldn't tell where it had come from. Carrie on prom night, without the white dress, and a shrivelled cock and balls; they were dripping too.

The four-inch letterbox in your left bicep needed twenty-three stitches and made such a mess your folks had to put in for a new carpet on the house insurance. When they pulled it up, you'd stained the underlay, and the floorboards too. Fuck knows what they put on the claim form, but they got paid out. Blood money, the big man said, but he wasn't smiling.

It was him drove you to A&E that night, fifteen pints to the good and three sheets to the wind, but he'll never talk about it and neither will your mam. Sometimes when she's maudlin drunk she starts on about how bad things were then, as if they ever got better, and you know it's in the post. As soon as she says, the state you were in when we came home and found you that night, it's a sure sign she needs to get on the water wagon, pronto, but it never goes any further than that cos before she's finished the sentence she's up and on her way to the bog, reckoning to blow her nose while she's blubbing into a tissue.

You'd've thought it'd be a wakeup call for everyone; until then no one at home had any idea how dark things had got for you.

They'd say that you were quiet, you should eat more, it wasn't healthy for a strapping young lad like you to be walking round looking like the Belsen Horror, but you'd tell them you were fine, tired, stressed about exams, whatever bullshit came to mind that would shut them up, and they were eager to be fobbed off.

You never talked about how you felt and they weren't the kind to either. They'd been brought up poor and hard and that was fucking life. Emotions were a luxury, especially for men, who should only express their feelings with their fists. Your mam suggested once or twice that maybe you should see the doctor, but you wouldn't have it. You were just pissed, you said, you didn't know what had happened, but you'd never do anything like that again.

They must have seen the old scars and other half-healed wounds when they were watching you get cleaned you up at the infirmary – the surface of the little remaining flesh you had was a contour map of pain – or maybe they were in so much shock they didn't notice. Either way they took you at your word and buried it.

If it was a shock for them, it was even worse for you.

You'd have to be more careful in future.

15

The novelty of being home didn't last long; it was same shit, different location.

Sleep.

Change.

Feed.

Change.

Sleep.

A three-hourly cycle, rinsed and repeated eight times a day.

Mandy grabbed snatches of rest while she could, in armchairs, on the sofa, sometimes in bed, exhausted from feeding while Sean tried to do pretty much everything else, the fumes he'd been running on long-since spent.

Cooking. Cleaning. The shitting cunting bastard Everest of washing up he conquered fuck knows how many times each day, willing the lot to tumble down and bury him for good. He'd've done anything for his little miracle but when he looked in the mirror, he saw a stranger. A thirty-something with crow's feet and pensioner's hands, a skag-chic skeleton with a beer gut stuck to the front whose home life wasn't much more than stuffing piles of baby gros, muslins and nursing bras stiff with yellowed milk, and untold pairs of Mandy's bloodstained knickers into the washing machine's gob, sterilising the tit pump so she could ease the pressure when there was more milk than Daisy could handle, home-cooking her three hot meals a day and snacks in between. Who the fuck was this guy? But he took it all on, played the family man like

De Niro on *Raging Bull* form, waiting for the day when he tripped himself up and the charade would disintegrate around him.

Mandy was tired and over-anxious, but that was to be expected, his mam said; when it came to maternal matters she bowed to no one. Regular visits from the neo-natal outreach team helped ease her mind when she was worried Daisy wasn't feeding enough, or putting on enough weight, if she was too hot at night, would she catch a chill if they left the window open a crack, all that. Sean was the voice of reason, the placid reassurer. She's doing great, Mand, look at her. A proper happy little chicken. There's nothing to worry about. All the while panicking about exactly the same things and a thousand others on top.

The mams that do the most worrying are never the ones that need to, Debbie, their keyworker from the ORT told her. Daisy's doing fine. Listen to your fella. He's the most sensible man I've ever met, and there aren't too many about, love, trust me. Try and enjoy her like this, they don't stay small for long.

There was a huge panic a couple of weeks in when Daisy didn't get up for one of her night feeds and they couldn't wake her themselves. Mandy, doing one, on the phone in tears to HDU who were still on call while they were under the ORT, asking what she should do, the full disaster of hospital kicking off afresh in the comfort of their living room until the nurses said that if Daisy was sleeping well it could only be a good thing, she'd feed as much as she wanted when she woke up. One day you'll laugh about it, one of the nurses said, but it wasn't fucking funny for Sean, on his knees with a make-up mirror under the wean's nose to check she was breathing, shaking like fuck, blood in his mouth again.

Days without end; weeks that vanished. Daisy changed with each rise and fall of the sun, full of life; her eyes sparkled like her mam's did before eight feeds a day and everything else that came before it took the shine right out. When she'd been home for a few days they put a touch and feel book in the Moses basket, watched in wonder as she reached over, tried to stroke the synthetic lamb's fur on the cardboard cover.

She can't be doing that on purpose?

She's a clever girl. Course she can. Watch.

Mandy moved the book ever so slowly to the opposite side of the crib, and as if by magic, she turned to follow, sossing and slurping and grasping with her other hand.

A few days later:

Mandy! Mand! Come quick, she's smiling at me!

She's too young to smile. It's probably just wind.

But then she clocked Daisy's face. What a *clever* girl. Tickling her under her chin as she slobbered and gurgled. Who loves her daddy? I think *you* do, don't you? You love your daddy, yes you do. Can you smile for *me*? *There* she goes, isn't she *clever*?

When she was stronger they put her on the floor, on her back to start, then on her front surrounded by toys, more touch and feel books. She loved her tummy time. She was fascinated with everything, scrabbled around to reach the toys so she could stick them in her mouth and give them a good gumming. Everything she did was amazing. Sean was bewitched by this micro-enchantress whose sorcery made the drudgery worthwhile, but he was breaking into tiny pieces and every one ground to dust.

Full spring, she was strong enough to go out. He loved taking her for long walks with the pram, proud to be seen as a doting dad, looking after the little one so mummy could rest. He never came back without a Kit Kat or something, all part of the performance. She'd pretend to protest, you shouldn't keep buying me these; then she'd shrug and grin. But seeing as though you have, I suppose I'll *have* to eat them.

264

They never mentioned the hospital.

That part is all done now, was all Mandy would say if it cropped up.

It was tough with visitors. They wanted to know about the birth, the ICU, the weeks in High Dependency, gasped at the photos of the skinned rabbit in the incubator with only Sean's finger for scale, gawking ghouls at a two-bob freakshow.

What was it like? It must have been awful.

there's no fucking way you should be driving sliding the car round corners like you're playing mario kart mandy's horrorstruck in the passenger seat sobbing this is going to keep track of your heart rate it might feel cold at first but don't worry it'll soon warm up ready good girl shit shit it's blood it's blood it's fucking blood

It was grim, she'd sigh. That's all there is to say. We got through it. What else can you do? She's fine now, that's all that matters.

so fucking determined furious possessed the sharp metal tang of the blood that hasn't stopped oozing out of her since you got here soaking through the thick cotton pads they keep stuffing under her arse between her thighs the darkest maroon trickling out so stickythick it looks like engine oil—

If you can change a nappy on something that weighs less than a bag of sugar and has more wires than a super-computer while it's stuck inside a plastic box it's no great shakes to do it on a changing mat in your own living room. That was Sean's favourite line, casual as you like, flashing an A-list smile for good measure.

youre doing a great job here for your wife love youll be an expert at this by the time youre done beeeeeeeeeeeeeeeeeeeeeeeeeeeeeeeeeeeeeeeeeeeeeeeeeeeeeeeee eeeeeeeeeeeeeeeep

shes screaming properly properly fucking screaming like shes fighting for her life or someone elses—

They'd laugh at his wit, applaud their stoicism, marvel at how strong they must've been to get through all that unscathed, and just look how well they were doing now.

legs stuck up in the air fucking black blood all over her arse her thighs what a fucking mess shes not moving glass eyes like a stuffed cat you love her so so so much right at this second it makes you want to—

■

He was a right state on the bus on his first day back at work, dreading having to deal with Denise and find out what mountain of shit she'd have piled up for him. He was fucked if he could handle telling the story to all the staff either, but he'd have to at some point, more than once when there were different people in on different days.

The first two hours were spent in Her Majesty's office, a meeting in which he barely spoke; he sipped his coffee without hearing a word of her shite, nodded when he was supposed to and looked forward to the fags he was going to smoke as soon as she let him out. When he escaped and sparked up, the baccy rush nearly knocked him over.

He started slowly on drastically reduced hours, a nine till two on day one. He hadn't planned a liquid lunch but decided he'd earned one and had a couple of pints in a pub most people would cross the street to avoid, savoured over three quarters of an hour with a bag of Walkers salt n vinegar. Later that week when he was in for the next short shift he did the same, and again on the third day. By the time he was back on full hours it was as much part of the routine as his ten o' clock fag.

The job did his box in more than ever. The complaints from angry folk whose building repairs had been delayed, again; the guilt of asking stressed-out frontliners to chase rent from people who said they had no means of paying when he was actually on the tenants' side and wouldn't want to take their money even if they had it. The form-filling, box-ticking, data-entering, bureaucratic nightmare of local authority work.

Meetings.

Meetings.

Meetings.

Meetings to arrange meetings to talk about other meetings; followed by more fucking meetings. Almost as bad as the office politics.

Someone's been drinking out of my cup again. Urgh, it's not been washed up properly either. Look, there's lipstick on it.

Whose turn is it to buy the milk?

Not me, I got it yesterday.

No you didn't, I did.

You fucking well did *not*. *I* went when I got off the train. Sheila saw me, didn't you, Sheila?

Alright, who's been messing with my paper clips? I've told you, if I catch anyone touching the stuff on my desk again, I'm telling Denise.

For God's sake, is it too much to ask that people put more paper in the printer when they use the last piece? How hard can it be?

Futile, facile, terminal tedium. He wanted to blow the whole fucking place sky high with Denise and all the other doylems inside. He missed Daisy, resented every precious second of her life that was stolen from him by this arsehole of a place.

Mornings he'd roll in black-eyed and bewildered, reckoning to work while watching the clock crawl backwards and counting down the minutes until dinnertime. Afternoons were better, when the hands moved faster. Sometimes if he'd had a chaser or a couple of extra codeines he dozed off at his desk, but apart from Denise, no one gave a monkeys.

He's had a rough time, he heard someone tell her as he half-slept on his swivel chair. You're always on his case. The poor lad needs all the kip he can get.

You're too soft. He's been back for a month now, he needs to get his bloody finger out. And so do the rest of you. Don't think it's passed me by how slack things have been getting round here since he came back. Call *that* a manager – he's meant to keep you lot in line but he does the exact opposite. Terrible influence, he is, terrible.

He'd have loved the chance to be a bad influence just to wind Denise up, but he was stupefied. He'd find himself in a room with no idea what he'd gone in for, or come to his senses next to the photocopier with a sheaf of papers in hand and look at the machine like it had come down from space and asked to be taken to his leader. He made daft mistakes, sent late replies to urgent emails, misread new policies, passed on incorrect information, or sent the right information to the wrong people. Little things that didn't matter much but pissed him off just the same because it was all ammunition for Denise. If someone asked what day of the week it was he was stumped, unless it was a weekend; but he only knew that because he wasn't at work.

He lived for the evenings. He'd eat a couple of codeine on the bus to kill the headache from lunch, arrive home at six and rush straight in to see Daisy. He was elated when she was awake so he could pick her up and give her a cuddle, heartbroken if she was sleeping and he had to wait. Playtime, bathtime, reading her stories – he loved it.

Fuck he was lonely though.

Every phone call, every visit, every chance meeting on the street, the chat was the same. Hey, Sean. How's the little one doing? And how's Mandy? Brilliant, yeah, we'll have to call round and see you sometime. You take care of those two, yeah?

Never a word about him.

Right from the days of the place he wouldn't name, no one wondered how he was feeling. All eyes were on mam and child;

and rightly so. But it would have been nice if someone at least acknowledged that he might not have been okay either; even his mam rarely asked. He'd've only bullshitted her if she had, mind.

I'm looking after Mandy and the baby, what else am I gonna do? I'm fine. I'm *fine*.

And that would have been it.

youre not fine though are you pretty fucking far from fine quite the fucking opposite actually you know where this is going dont you dont tell me youve not noticed that crippling fucking dread when you wake up fucking hell not this again cursing the fact youre still alive its only the start cunt you know it is the endless slide slow spiralling free fall like an aeroplane thats screaming from the sky waiting for the explosion at the bottom that never comes going down down down down down the crash not even the worst part is knowing where youll be how many times is it now how long this time weeks months could be fucking years cunt has been before no reason why not again you dont have it in you to do it not with the kid the shit at work fucking denise shes an even bigger cunt than you are so fucking dull this crushing grind of everyday living in a box cant move see think hear breathe fuck all time to call it quits cunt youve put it off long enough you know fucking well you cant do it again so save yourself the fucking bother checkout time sayonara son end of the fucking line but but but but daisymandy they dont need you no one does better without you if you really stop and think about it games over might as well do everyone a favour get the fuck on with it cunt Im waiting

FERN HILL

The farm was your Uncle Harry's place, him and Aunty Jean. They were your godparents, really, your mam and dad's best mates since their schooldays and none of you were related by blood, but they never felt like anything other than family.

Ah were born in a barn, me, an Ah came out wi' cowshit under me nails. Ah could milk a Friesian by hand afore most kids learned to walk, Harry used to say. So straight you couldn't tell if he was joking but knowing him he probably wasn't.

It was a couple of miles out of town, past the old cemetery where the road mirrors the river's meanders until it cuts away onto a village high street that homes the kind of post office/general store that became extinct after Cameron, a couple of pubs and not much else. On the other side of the village it trickles out towards the A59, which mainlines traffic day and night towards Colne and Burnley, darkest Lancashire, where the gothic monolith of Pendle Hill looms implacably in the distance. The turnoff was almost hidden by low-hanging tree branches and it'd've been easy to miss if you didn't know it was there, but you'd hang a left onto a winding shingle lane that wended its way through a couple of fields choked with crab grass, sheep shit and thistles as thick as a man's finger; these belonged to John Willey, who farmed the lower slopes and whose name you couldn't hear without sniggering.

After that you forded a permanent puddle six feet across and five inches deep that babbled out of the beck at the bottom of the hill, then went through a sturdy wicket gate and up, up, up for about half a mile, always taken in first or second gear in your old man's bangers but no bother for Uncle Harry's Land Rover. Once you'd crested the hill you could glimpse it as a speck on the horizon before the lane dipped down a ways to hide it from view, then up again, gently this time, arrowing across a cattle grid before the last push towards the farm buildings.

There was an ancient blue Massey Ferguson with tyres taller than Harry parked on the left next to the dairy opposite a midden the size of a small swimming pool where twice a day your uncle would tip barrow after barrow of piss and shite mucked out from the cattle in the big shippon next door. You were always careful there, frightened out of your wits by scare stories of silly little boys who walked too close to the edge of shitpits on other farms and fell in and drowned, although you couldn't resist getting up close sometimes to see the methane bubbles burping on the surface, the stinking steam rising like it was a hot bath.

Stacked against the wall of this weathered outhouse were giant round bales of house-high hay, wrapped in black cellophane to keep them dry for winter. They made a brilliant climbing frame and were always good for a laugh, especially when you'd slip and fall into the mud that caked the pathway beside it.

Next to that was the little shippon and the hayloft where rats the size of cats would scurry around your feet as you played, moving targets for your Mega-78 catapult and later the air rifle that belonged to Neil, Jean and Harry's son, who you always called your cousin though you weren't properly kin. There was another barn opposite, filled with straw and rusting machinery, bits of string, pop bottles full of used motor oil or red diesel, a couple of old mountain bikes that hadn't turned a wheel in years. Mindy lived in there; she was a yappy Jack Russel that Harry had bought off his mate as a champion ratter, and so she was, until she started worrying the hens and Harry took her down to the beck for a lead earring. There was a horse for a while an all, named Blaze for the long white stripe down her nose. You rode her bareback, clinging to her wispy mane as she cantered around the Croft and snorted like she owned the place, which she kind of did.

The house was a century old and then some, a tumbledown picture from a book of fairytales. The front door went into the kitchen where there was always something cooking, then you'd go from there into a living room with a deep pine dining table and a Rayburn in it, a telly and a couple of armchairs, a dark, cool pantry at the back where mousetraps lay baited with chocolate buttons and scraps of mouldy cheese. There was a smaller sitting room with a stone hearth and a sheepskin rug in front of the fireplace, but it was rarely used unless it was Christmas or someone's birthday, or when the grown-ups wanted you and Neil to fuck off out the way when it was too wet even for you two mucky buggers to go outside and play. A splintered door at the back led to the steep narrow stairs that creaked and groaned up to the top floor where the bedrooms and the crapper were.

It was freezing in winter; the sash windows did shag all to keep out the cold. Often when you stayed over there was ice on the inside of the glass, as hard and white as the hoarfrost that coated the fields in a layer so thick it looked like snow and your wellies left deep crisp prints when you walked on it.

The coal shed was round the back. One of your favourite games was to climb out the landing window and jump down onto the sloping roof four or five feet below. It jarred when your feet hit and you had to be careful not to slip on the slate when it was wet or you'd come a right cropper, but even into your teens you never tired of doing it. It was dark as pitch when you were sent out there at night to fetch another scuttle for the fire. You'd need a lamp to see and even then it was tough, especially when the moon was waning or strait-jacketed with clouds and the only lights you could see were those that flickered dimly from behind the net curtains.

All the fields had names, starting with the Croft where the coal shed was and spreading out from there; there was the Top Field, the Thistle Field, the Long Meadow filled with daisies and buttercups so numerous you could barely see the grass. That was Blaze's preferred spot to chew away a lazy day. Your favourite was the Front Field, directly opposite the house on the other side of the stream that cut through the bottom of the garden near the hen hut. It was an immense hill of staggering gradient where the sheep used to graze, awesome for sledging when it snowed. You and Neil would bomb down it headfirst, sometimes backwards too, playing chicken to see how close you could get to the bottom before you had to bail out. Your mam and Aunty Jean used to have a go an all, jammed into your plastic sleds, cracking jokes about getting their arses stuck till one year Jean lost control. She set off too quick and never got a hold of it, zigzagged for the first few meters and nearly rolled out but gravity took over before she got time and shot her gun barrel straight down the steepest bit of the hill. She was a big lass and her weight only made things worse – she was going like shit off a stick when she pranged through the fence and crash-landed in the frozen beck. She couldn't work out whether to laugh or cry and settled for cursing a streak so blue it'd've embarrassed a navvy while you and Neil pissed yourselves and your mam nearly measured her length trying to fish her out. It turned out she'd fractured her coccyx, which meant spending three months taking a blow-up rubber ring everywhere she went so she could sit down without pain.

Who'da thought you could break you bloody arse bone, eh? She'd say, puffing on a Rothmans as her flabby cheeks squashed the inflatable flat. Ah never knew there were such a thing as one of them. Ah must be frigging daft. Tell you one thing, that's last time you'll see me in one o' them buggers. She was true to her word, but you and Neil still nailed it down there every chance you got.

The winters were harsher then, snow drifted so high against the drystone walls it was deeper than you were tall. You'd dig networks of tunnels, make full-sized snowmen, lob the biggest stones you could lift to try to crack the ice on the pond. There were so many games to invent, until you realised you were frozen to the marrow and your fingers had gone the colour of blueberries. Then you'd go inside to warm your bones and fill up on a beef stew or lamb hotpot that had been cooking all day, made with tender cuts but loads of fat for flavour, proper grub that stuck to your ribs and warmed your insides like you had a paraffin stove in your belly. A couple of dishes of that and half an hour with the fire steaming the cold from your clothes and you'd be ready for off again, forgetting that not so long ago your balls were so close to freezing off you could have wept with the pain of it.

With spring would come the thaw, and all was mud. You and Neil, partners in grime, terminally caked from arsehole to elbow in a crusted agglomeration of dirt and animal shit that it was futile trying to scrub off. It was also lambing season. Poor Harry was a zombie, crawling in at all hours, scarfing whatever food Jean heaped in front of him, a couple of giant coffees with fresh cream and two tablespoons of sugar, four or five fags smoked to the cork for pudding before he shuffled back out again to tend to the flock.

The first time you watched a lamb being born was wild. Your childish surprise at the sight of the woolly bag of bones sluicing into the world and the mother licking off the gunk, the wonder of being in the presence of life where it hadn't been before. Sometimes Harry would take the lamb of a mother that hadn't made it and slather it quick-style in the warmth and stink of another sheep's afterbirth, a false scent to trick the prospective foster parent into believing the lamb was hers. You told the kids at school about this but they stuck their tongues out and laughed, urgh, gross, and made puking noises until they were bored of embarrassing you and moved onto something else while you were left exasperated and alone, again.

When this folk magic failed the orphans were reared by hand, kept in shoeboxes full of straw next to the Rayburn, sucking your fingers like teats with sandpaper tongues while Jean warmed milk fresh from the dairy for you to bottle feed them like newborn babies, which they were. You could live to be a hundred and still gag at the memory of the stench of a dead ewe, but it was a price worth paying for the time you spent ensuring the survival of the ones they died to give life to, even if they were destined to end up blathered in mint sauce on someone's Sunday roast.

The sweet summer holidays. Six weeks of unfettered freedom.

You can't have been at the farm all the time and there are photos of Pontins holidays in Skeggie and Yarmouth to prove it, but your memory says you were never anywhere else. You'd awake on the camp bed in Neil's room as soon as the sun was up. The decrepit wire frame with the springs and cogs of its folding mechanism looked like something hauled from York Dungeon, but it gave you the kind of flat-out, peaceful kip you've never had anywhere since. There were no nightmares there. You'd spring to life and pez down to the kitchen where Aunty Jean was making her second breakfast of the day – Harry having gone on his morning rounds hours ago – frying sausages and bacon in a skillet the size of a car tyre, the whole lot swimming in lard. Neil was always one step ahead, barefoot on the mudbrown lino in his Superman pyjamas going, mam, mam, is it ready yet, is it ready yet? Hopping from one leg to the other like he was desperate for a piss but worried if he went to the bog there'd be no scran left when he got back.

Best get down the henhouse if you want some eggs, she'd say, but you didn't need to be told. The chickens clucked in umbrage as soon as they clocked you, nipping and pinching as you picked them up like feathered hot water bottles and set them on the floor so you could raid their roosts, grabbing half a dozen so fresh they were warm and Jean had to scrape shit and straw from the shells before she could crack them. She'd chuck a couple of tins of beans in with the meat and the eggs to finish it off, a butty for her and a plate each for you and Neil to scoff with brown sauce while she fried you a slice of bread half an inch thick to mop up the bean juice and egg yolks at the end. She'd stand there with a Royal half-burned in the ashpan next to her, smoke from the fag mixed with smoke from the skillet, pushing the bread around with the wooden spoon in one hand while taking prodigious bites of the breakfast barmcake she held in the other. She wielded the spoon like a wand when she was cooking, but god help anyone brave enough to cross her when she had it in hand. She could crack it across your arse like a bullwhip and leave your cheeks red and stinging before you saw her move, and if she caught you a good'un round the back of the napper you'd still be seeing stars when you sat down for your tea. It made the best breakfast though.

Belly stuffed and lubricated with a pint of milk straight from the cow, the days were yours to do as you pleased. You'd roam the fields, wade in the becks and brooks till the water got too deep and slopped over the tops of your wellies and soaked your socks for the rest of the day; you'd chuck stones at the geese by the duck pond and get them to chase you, the thrill of the pursuit made all the more intense by the knowledge that the spitting, hissing gaggle would peck the living fuck out of you if they ever caught up.

There were trees to climb, spent shotgun cartridges to collect, shards of clay pigeons shattered by blasts from your old man and Harry's twelve bores to piece together, desiccated, yellowed cowpats bound with old straw that could be used as frisbees until you tired of that game and looked for fresh, ripe, squishy ones to boot at each other instead. Sometimes Jean would give you bags of rubbish from the pantry to get rid of so you'd make a fire near the beck under the crab apple tree across from the Front Field, poking it with sticks to stoke the flames as you piled on more plastic bags, crisp packets, biscuit wrappers that sizzled and melted in seconds as a cloud of acrid smoke billowed all around. It scorched your eyes, blackened your face and whipped the breath from your lungs, but it was all part of the fun and no one knew, or cared, that it was toxic as all hell.

You spent whole weeks buzzing around on Neil's scrambler; the engine can't have been bigger than a petrol mower's but it was fucking rapid from where you were sitting and there were no health and safety maniacs on at you about not wearing a helmet. You laughed it away when you came off and burned your bare legs on the hot exhaust; if you banged your head on the grass the worst you got was a bruise or two and some pisstaking from Neil, which hurt way more than the fall itself.

You didn't think it could get any better than that, until Harry's sheepdog Trim, which was about seventeen, he thought, but he'd had it so long he couldn't remember exactly, got too old to work. Harry said he didn't have time to train another Collie so he replaced him with a brand new red quad bike that looked like something off The A-Team. Harry needed it twice a day when he was rounding up the sheep, Clem perched on the back like a wise old owl, tongue lolling in the breeze as he eyeballed the stock, letting them know he was still in charge while he contemplated his retirement; but for the rest of the day, it was yours.

You had a blast on that thing. Compared to the trials bike it was a fucking monster and the first time you rode it the power took you completely by surprise. You were only about ten so you'd no idea what you were doing, and no one bothered to show you. You opened the throttle a touch too wide and nigh-on shit yourself as it shot off, roaring and spewing smoke from the arse end. It sped into a grassy hillock and you caught some serious air before you let go of the handlebars, crashed to the floor and rolled clear, hoping you looked as cool as Colt Sievers in The Fall Guy when he did stunts like that. The quad landed tits-up in a ditch, engine still running, while Neil threw himself on the floor laughing fit to crap in his kecks.

The start of haymaking season was a sure sign that summer's end was at hand, sad in that with it came the prospect of returning to the grey of the classroom, but a time of year you looked forward to because you got to proper join in with the work. Grass that had been mown, dried, made into square bales – way smaller than the round ones stacked outside – and left in the fields had to be thrown onto the back of a trailer then hoofed into the loft for the winter before the autumn rains could soak and spoilt them.

The dry grass could be sharp enough to cut; they're called blades for a reason, Harry said. They scratched the skin on your bare chest till it was bloody and raw, and the pollen brought you out in hives all over. It made your nose glow red like Rudolph's and run like a tap as your eyes streamed along in sympathy, but you didn't care. Your old man and Harry, powerful fellas who'd known manual work as a way of life since childhood, were godlike as they handballed bales up the ladder like they were made of matchwood. They gave you and Neil some kid-sized ones to lift and your puny arms even struggled with those, but they left you to it and you were stoked to be involved, putting your hands on their bales as if you were actually making a difference. You swept the floor, took pot shots at rats with the air rifle, anything you could do to help. This was man's work; for one fortnight a year as you sweated and strained, grunted and groaned, scratched your balls and sniffed your hand and spat the dust from your arid mouth, you were a man too.

Autumn brought welcome relief, the mercury plunging as the nights pulled in. The first frost would coat the fields like icing sugar, a tantalising prelude to the snow that would surely come later. Every year there was a bonfire piled so high it looked like a rickety wooden mountain, the guy you and Neil spent weeks fashioning laid on the top with straw bulging out of his strides awaiting his fiery demise. There were scores of people, your mam and Aunty chained to the cooker dishing out pie and peas, jacket spuds with curls of freshly churned butter, sausages straight from the skillet caked with the grease of the ages. Later there was bonfire toffee so black and hard you could have broken your teeth on it and Aunty Jean's fudge which makes you feel hyperglycaemic just remembering it. There'd be country kids you only met once a year walking around with sparklers and eyes alight, women flapping around them pulling down hats, tightening scarves, zipping up coats that would be taken off and dumped on the floor as soon as she wasn't looking.

The men stood apart, taciturn, supping bitter from cases stacked up by the coal shed, the star-scattered November night keeping them colder than any fridge. Their only task was to fill their bellies, smoke their tabs, warm their arses on the flames and make sure the bairns didn't fall in the fire. They had the best seats in the house; one day, you'd join them.

There were fireworks too – traffic lights, mount Vesuvius, Catherine wheels nailed to fencing posts, rockets that shimmered and sparkled with the splendour of daybreak and none of the noise that comes as standard with the heavy ordinance detonated in the name of Guy Fawkes nowadays. It took you ages to come down from plot night; your hands and face recalled the warmth of the blaze for weeks, until December approached and Father Christmas crashed your thoughts.

The last time you remember visiting was New Year's Day, the year before you went to uni, you think. You'd been at a party the night before and hadn't been to bed. Your old man picked you up outside the Esso near the edge of town wired to fuck on pink champagne, sipping on a half-bottle of Vladivar. There's are no lasting impressions of the day, only that you were there, but that's good enough. You don't always know when you're leaving a place for the last time and maybe that's for the best. You've always missed it though, and you've visited it in your dreams ever since.

In these visions you remember it all. Every nook and cranny of the winding old house, the cobwebby corners, the mousehole in the kitchen beside the oven, the toy cupboard near the pantry where Neil kept the spacehopper and his plastic farm animals, the translucent rolls of amber flypaper speckled with carcasses that dangled like streamers above the table you ate at, the stink of the bathroom when you and Neil used to shit together after tea and use up a whole roll of arsewipe between you, how it would suddenly start to smell sweet when you opened the window to air it out. You can walk through the fields and name them in turn, see the stiles and the gates and the holes in the drystone you could crawl through before you grew too big to fit; the bogs and the becks and the puddles, the pop bottle hanging from the apple tree you used to shoot at with the air gun; the whole fucking world of it.

This, not the old mill terrace on the cobbled street that existed half a century too late even to your child's eyes in the grim

Northern days of Thatcher's 1980s, feels like your real childhood home. If you've ever dreamed of that house you've forgotten; but not a week goes by without your second self visiting the farm. Maybe it's an alchemical reaction in your brain, some warp in the fabric of space and time, or maybe you've just spent too much fucking time tripping and your capacity for visualisation is way more advanced than most, but in these dreams you're not just thinking about it, or imagining it, you're actually, physically, one hundred percent fucking there, and you feel it down to your body's last atom.

But then some rational impulse rips away the veil, reminds you that Jean and Harry were forced out when the foot and mouth outbreak of 2001 ravaged the land. You were at uni, but when you went home for the summer the countryside was a charnel house heaped with stinking pyres of culled cattle infected and healthy alike, defiant hooves sticking up like flicked V's from the roaring flames and palls of blackest smoke. You couldn't believe the state of Harry when him and Jean bobbed in for a brew. The poor cunt had lost about four stone since you saw him at Easter; half his hair had gone grey, the rest had fallen out. Twenty five years banged on his clock just like that, his life incinerated before his disbelieving eyes.

Your brain starts to wake at the memory but you fight it, determined to stay, knowing if you open your eyes you might never come back because what if you never dreamed of it again? The idea of that kills you. Sometimes then when the battle's been lost and accursed consciousness returns you'll find your salty face sticking to a sodden pillow and Mandy will ask if you're alright, but you turn away and tell her it's nothing, a bad dream that died at dawn's approach, and you don't remember a thing.

16

Sean, have you been drinking?

Mandy was standing over the kitchen sink with suds up to her elbows, frowning at whatever she was scrubbing. Her face was puffy and flushed, a mess of damp hair plastered to her forehead. He looked at the floor and shrugged.

I bloody knew it. I can smell you from here. You stink of fags too.

I only had a quick one. It's been a shitty day.

Is that why you're late home? I was wondering where you'd got to. It's after seven, look, I was expecting you back an hour ago. I made us some tea. Not that it's any good now. I burnt it while I was feeding Daisy. Her tired eyes threatened tears.

On the worktop by the kettle was a dish containing the remains of a dried-out sauce, some ragged spaghetti, peppered with burned black flakes like peeling paint. He smelled cremated garlic, something like melted plastic; the walls and windows wet with steam.

Cheers. I'll have it in a bit. Is Daisy awake?

No she's not, and I wouldn't let you near her in that state if she was. You're propping yourself up against the door frame. And you're slurring so much I can barely tell what you're saying.

Mand—

Don't you dare think about bullshitting me. How much have you had? You look wrecked. Do you think I'm blind? You're a fucking idiot.

Just a couple.

You said one a minute ago. Make your mind up.

282

She had him bang to rights, but it wasn't his fault. The day had been a shitshow. Daisy had kept them up all night, again, crying and crying for no reason they could fathom. It had been going on for weeks. Dr Bell said she was fine; maybe she was getting ready to cut another tooth or something, but she certainly wasn't ill. He was late for his bus, which meant he'd missed the first part of a meeting with Denise and a few top brass about some bollocks or other, but fuck it, he'd remember what it was once he got into the swing and blag it as usual.

He'd faked some apologies, put on his best listening face, but he was so unfocused he might as well have not been there. When the time came for the presentation he'd forgotten he was doing he had no notes, and the USB stick with the PowerPoint on had disappeared. He feigned another dose of remorse and the senior lot were sympathetic, a couple of the older ones dishing out anecdotes about how hellish life could be when they had young kids of their own, and doesn't not sleeping do funny things to your mind? How brilliant it was now they were grandparents so they had the fun of little ones to spoil but could give them back at the end of the day, all that shit.

He smiled and nodded, consummate pro. He didn't give a fuck whether they were annoyed or not, but behind the smile his teeth were grinding. Since he'd been back, by some fucking miracle, he'd avoided having a serious row with Denise, but there'd be no ducking it this time.

What the hell do you think you're playing at? She'd screeched when the Management had gone; this, while he was at his desk, in full view of everyone. That was bloody embarrassing, turning up late and then not having anything to deliver. Who do you think you are, exactly? We've had to reschedule this meeting once already because you had to go to the doctors for the baby to get a jab. I don't see why your wife couldn't have gone on her own anyway but that's beside the point now. Have you actually *done* the presentation?

Course I've done it. Deep breath in, slow exhale. A cloud of imaginary smoke enshrouding her head; choking her, slowly.

Well, *I* don't think you have. Where is it, then? Show me. I want to see it. Now.

If I had it for you to see I'd have done the fucking presentation, wouldn't I? It's on a pen drive. It must be at home somewhere. I needed to take some files off my laptop—

You think I'm going to fall for that? And you know you shouldn't keep work files on a personal device, or have you forgotten your information governance training? The dog ate my homework, miss. Sing-song voice, pulling a face.

All eyes were on him. Face flushed scarlet, knuckles white. He looked at her in a way that said she was a dog turd squashed into the treads of a new pair of boots; a disgusting irritation, an inconvenient ballache. Nothing more.

Well? Hands on hips, the full double-teapot. Christ, she was ridiculous. Aren't you even going to apologise? I think that's the least you could do for making me look stupid in front of Strategic, don't you?

You don't need me to make you look stupid.

What did you say? WHAT—

I said, you don't need *me* to make *you* look stupid, Denise. You're a genius at doing it yourself.

Her face was puce. A few laughcoughs in the background, some sniggering. Denise wasn't much liked but it was rare to see her openly challenged and the office was getting ready to enjoy the fireworks. They'd've set up deckchairs, cracked some cans and opened bags of popcorn if they could.

You can't talk to *me* like that.

I'll talk to you however I fucking well want. His voice was steady but he was volcanic. It was bound to happen eventually, now it was showtime. Click, click, boom. Both fucking barrels. You prance around here all high and mighty like you've got a broom handle stuck up your arse, barking out orders and thinking you're the dog's dangling ballsack but let me tell you something—

That's *enough*. I want to talk to you in my office. Now.

Well I don't want to talk to you, right? I've had enough of your shit. Bollocks to you and your poxy cunting office. You can get fucked. I'm off for me dinner.

He swept out to an imaginary ovation through an electric silence, an instant superhero. That'd give the boring bastards something to gossip about. He went straight in the Templar and slammed a few quick ones without pausing for breath. After a couple of double Jameson's he realised he'd overshot his lunchbreak, decided he might as well be hung for a sheep as for a lamb and went round to the Three Legs where a shitfaced seventy-something in painted lady slap was on the karaoke stage butchering a Dusty Springfield tune, more flats than a tower block. The regulars were even more tragically fucked than he was – one of the main reasons he liked the place; some of them were so hammered they were cheering the tone deaf old bat on as if she had a voice like Amy Winehouse. It would have been pathetic if it wasn't so fucking funny.

He couldn't remember much after that, but he was shitfaced enough to be confident he'd get away with faking sobriety, right up to the point when he walked in and Mandy clocked him stumble over the mat, only avoiding a full-on faceplant by twatting his shoulder on the wall and springing back like a jack-in-a-box.

I'm not fucking having this, Sean. I won't put up with it. I just won't. I had enough of you drinking before and you *promised* me you'd stop when we had the baby.

I've stopped, haven't I?

you get her fucking told youve not been pissed for ages youre entitled to this one whatever she fucking says shes not the boss of you any more than that arsehole at work stick to your guns you cant be rolling over now

Yeah. Looks like it.

Denise—

Always someone else's fault, isn't it? I know Denise is a cow but you can't blame her for you coming home ratarsed on a Tuesday teatime.

Don't you want me to tell you what happened?

No. I don't want to know, and to be honest, I don't care.

But—

But nothing. Get yourself in the shower and sober up. I can't stand to look at you like this. She turned her back, shaking her head.

fucking denise its all her fucking fault giving you grief at work and now youre copping shit at home for it too what the fuck mandys meant to be on your side why wont she let you explain at least then she might under-stand fuck it no point trying to talk her round when shes like this you need another drink nothing in the fridge house is dryer than a nuns cunt these days if this is how its gonna be get yourself back to the fucking kings and finish what you started if you werent such a fucking pussy youdve gone there in the first place and not bothered coming here at—

So off he went, a righteous man lost in an unjust world that existed purely to torment him.

N

The forbidden door.

Forever shut.

Keeps *them* in.

Him out.

The pain behind it.

Infinite.

Once white, now grey. Streaked with brown. Chunks hacked out. Unblemished wood inside. Clean wounds.

Well into the first bottle. No pleasure. Hates the stuff. Drinks it anyway. Tastes like turps. Sears his throat. Raw from puking.

Steady enough to stand. No need to lean.

Yet.

Stares at it.

Door stares back.

Dares him.

Never goes in.

But.

It's calling.

Siren's song. Never one for willpower. Pull of the dark.

Fag's burned down. Drops it. Grinds into carpet. Can't tell where pattern stops, dirt starts. Shades of greyblackbrown. Silver fuzz. Underneath, oxblood. She loved that. When they first came to look. Never changed it.

Goes for the handle. Like grasping a Cobra. Nearly gets there. Shies away. Another try. Copper effect. Burns like frostbite. Jerks down. Hand slides off. Timber creaks. Cracks.

Bad idea.

Fucking worst idea.

Run downstairs.

Into the street.

The road.

In front of a fucking bus.

Anywhere but here.

Anything but this.

Dull thud. Sole on wood.

At the threshold.

A portal.

Hesitates.

Suddenly inside

what the fuck what the fuck what the FUCK
what the FUCK

Big pulls

ONE

TWO

THREE

FOUR

FIVE

SIX

SEVEN

This can't be it.

Remembers pink walls. Ceiling shone white. Moonbright.
Silverblue carpet. Bed plush. Pillows. Cuddly toys. Polka dots.
Hello Kittys braindead smile. Sees it all. Net curtains. Dragonflies.
Fairies enmeshed in the pattern. Wicker clothes hamper. Turned
her into a witch. A nurse. The girl from that snow film. Knew
every word. Coloured lights round the mirror. Twinkling. Wooden
dressing table. Everything a rightful place. Nothing where it

should be. Clutter. Games half-finished. Forgotten. Lure of imagination. Led her away. Another yellow brick road.

Waiting. Waiting. Waiting.

His princess. Back to reclaim her kingdom.

Blissful nights. Rare. Holding her. Breathing her smell. Strawberry shampoo. The food on her face. Her heartbeat. His. As one. Molten tears. Swears it. Never let her stray again. Never leave his sight. Never let her go.

Never. Never. Never. Never. Never.

No more make-believe. Spell breaks. Heart. Illusions. Like glass. Like him. His life. Hers. Theirs. The desolate hell in which he wakes. Shivering. Shaking. Puking. Prisoner. Shitting brown water. Spitting blood. Wrench of the vision ended.

Stands, dumb.

Drinks
drinks
drinks
drinks
drinks
until
it's

Has to look

No

Eyes tight shut

Pull them out. Finger flick Could squash them in his hands. Pop pop.

Too late cant unsee it. Even blind

Break the glass

Sharp shard swift slash

Under the chin left to right

Done

Bottles dropped lazy grip long way down

Looks again
Has to
Murder scene
Rustybrownred

E V E R Y F U C K I N G W H E R E

handprints on wall smeared arc splashed in claret wide thick
bed stabbed up to fuck spilling foam and feathers stains on mattress blood stains on duvet blood chucked aside like a dishcloth
hello kittys not smiling now soft toy slaughter mutilated missing
heads arms holes in faces legs feet matted fleece encrusted blood
lipstick kisses blood scattered round in bits like no mans land
doll with lifelike eyes trancelike calm screwdriver in her chest
fist shaped holes in plasterboard gangrenous blood pine wardrobe kicked to death footprints all over blood curtains tattered
port-stained rags windows dark smeared shit blood blood blood
blood blood cant roll straights thank fuck sparks three huge drags
vacuum lungs glows white hot crushes on forearm twists till it
dies sparks repeats redgreen raw charred black meat third on bed
who did this sees them could be twins if she wasnt so small dark
blonde their hair party dress pink white yellow bows lace her mam
tight jeans old t-shirt stardust unicorn stir of echoes looks at them
looking at each other so much love somethings missing theyre
having a tea party with the animals fingers jamsticky bourbons
dipped in milk happy smiles here comes daddy stubble spiked
hair holes in denim long-sleeves knackered beaten worn the mam
too so so tired tired to death daddys familiar sits on floor reads
while they eat pip and posy says the cover oh dear hears her say it
like the rabbit in the book three of them laughing daddy opens his
mouth she feeds him a biscuit crocodile bite gives the rest to mam
dissolve and fade morning shes waking up daddy again eyes open

slowly big grin pearly whites holds up her arms theyre talking laughing cuddles kisses happy happy families her face big brown eyes hazel like mams gazing up up up at daddy he makes the sun rise holds up the sky fade to black gone alone all all all alone three lives wrecked gone so so wrong wants a drink this ones dead like him have to get the other stands to leave it hits at once half the bottle like water stumbles head hits wall curses blames hates it cursesblameshates himself you fucking cunt you fucking cunt you fucking cunt steadies with one hand head back bangs again proper style you fucking cunt you fucking *cunt* harder again fucking *cunt* fucking *cunt cunt cunt CUNT* again again more space between each one something warm thick eyes sting wet slap another wetter harder BANG BANG have that you fucking CUNT you fucking CUNT you fucking CUNT CUNT CUNT CUNT CU—

TH

EN

17

I can't leave her, Sean. I can't. Mandy's eyes were swimming.

Maternity leave had fled the nest; it was time to go back to work. She'd cut down to three days including alternate Saturdays, leaving Daisy at nursery for two days a week and one when she worked weekends. Those would be Daisy's Daddy Days.

She'll be fine. Won't you, love? Sean was driving, checked the mirror to see his pride and joy grinning like Shane MacGowan, a couple of her new peggies on show. She was fourteen months old, not far off walking and talking; so advanced despite it all. She was small for her age, still lost in the seat, but she was perfect. Are you looking forward to going to nursery with all the other big girls?

Yeh. She jammed her cuddly Friesian, Molly Moo, headfirst into her mouth.

See? But Mandy looked like a woman who's had an urgent callback after a smear test.

It had taken ages to find a nursery they liked, seriously hard graft. The first they visited was way too formal, made the older children wear a uniform, which even Mandy agreed was a fucking pisstake.

It's bad enough having to wear one of those at primary school, never mind before they've even started, he'd fumed afterwards. It's fucking bullshit. They're trying to condition them to conform before they're old enough to learn to think for themselves. It's capitalist brainwashing. Fuck that.

It's definitely a bit OTT.

A bit?! People must be mental putting their kids through that. It's proper sinister.

Others looked nice enough but Mandy said she didn't click with the manager, or thought that the rooms looked too small; they were too hot, or too cold, or there weren't enough staff. Her reasons for rejecting them were many and varied; sometimes they appeared to depend on the direction of the wind or what colour socks she was wearing.

The food looked gross and I could smell shit, she'd said about one he thought was spot on.

There were fifteen babies in the room, Mand, what do you expect it to smell of, Chanel Number Five? His patience was paper thin.

There were a couple of places where she didn't like the vibe and that was that. You know how much I believe in intuition, was all she'd say. One had a lovely playground with swings and a slide and a seesaw, but she was worried that the equipment looked old and might have been dangerous so that was a no-go too.

He was frustrated to the point of insanity. They were small places and they should have been able to put each recce to bed in ten or fifteen minutes, but they could be there for a couple of hours at a time and they went to so *many*. It was a battle trying to keep his mind on the job while Mandy sought reassurances about the kind of details he wouldn't have thought of if you'd offered him a million quid. Did they use organic milk? Was the food Fair Trade? Stuff like that. What the fuck. He wanted the best for the kid, but after the ninth or tenth place he was done. When Mandy regurgitated the forensics of each option for the twentieth time he couldn't remember one from another and his opinions were guesswork at best. He tried to be as supportive as he could while subtly prodding her to make up her fucking mind and stick to it, but it was like pulling teeth.

One evening Pops came over to help give Daisy a bath and get her ready for bed. Once she'd left Mandy doing the bedtime feed and Sean had poured the wine, he said they were struggling to find a nursery and she mentioned a mate of her mam's used to work at one.

It's called Little Acorns. You guys will *totally* love it. You should have asked me. I can't think why it didn't occur to me before. It was set up by hippies in the Seventies and it's not for profit, definitely your kinda spot. Diane worked there for years. It's got its own garden and there's a wall outside for them to paint on. There's a disco ball in the baby room and everything, apparently, you should check it out.

Mandy loved it on sight.

Oh Sean it's lush, isn't it? They'd barely arrived when she said that, more positive than she'd been about all the others combined. It's so relaxed and homely, can you feel it? Don't the babies look happy?

He nodded and smiled, distracted by the mirror ball twinkling above, zoning in and out of the chat and thanking fuck it looked like mission accomplished. Mandy and the staff were bosom buddies from the get-go and they stayed the whole afternoon, scoffing biscuits and drinking tea in the office like they were old mates round for a catch-up. Daisy had a blast playing with the other tinies; she didn't even cry when they handed her over to one of the nursery nurses and went for a skeg without her.

Such a good omen, Mandy said later when the manager, Caroline, had gone to put another brew on. Did you pick up on it?

Sure. Definitely. So, is this the one, do you think?

When she said she wouldn't consider sending Daisy anywhere else, his relief was that of a fella fished from a lake at the instant his life started flashing before his eyes.

■

Shall I come in with you?

She nodded furiously. You'll have to. She looked like a little girl herself, clinging to mam's legs on her first day of big school

Come on then. He killed the engine and got out. Are you ready, little missus?

Yeh yeh yeh. She sounded like Muttley. So cute.

Right then. She held out her arms while he unfastened the harness. Her dark hair had faded to almost-blonde in her first year, just like Mandy's. When she looked up at him like that she was the spit of her mam, same eyes, mouth, right down to the dimples on her cheeks. He was crushed by love.

He hefted her on one arm, took Mandy's hand with the other, led her through the gate and up the access ramp to the front door, past the flowerbed where wooden signs said there were strawberries, carrots, spuds.

Look at that. They're growing fruit and veg with them and everything.

Mmmmmm.

Daisy's keyworker Angie let them in when they buzzed. She was in her fifties, she'd said when they'd first met, but I know, love, you'd never tell, eh? I don't look a day over forty-nine. She had raven hair down to her waist, a pierced nose, a well-worn face with a smoker's sandpaper skin. She'd make a brilliant friendly witch at Halloween.

Hello Daisy! She smiled with her whole face, opened her arms as the bairn reached for her.

E yo.

She looks pleased to see you. Sean handed her over.

Course she is. We made friends when you came to visit, didn't we darling? Yes we did. Now you come with me and let your mam and dad get to work.

Can I give her a kiss?

You don't my need permission, love. Angie laughed. Here. She gave her to Mandy and she clasped her tight, properly crying now. Bye bye my sweet little baby, mummy will be back soon. Kissing her like she'd never see her again.

Don't worry, love, Angie prised the child back. She'll be *fine*. We're going to have some breakfast now and then we're going to do some potato painting. Yes we are. She tickled Daisy's tummy and she chuckled, dribbled down her chin.

If you're sure. Mandy wasn't moving.

Course I'm sure. I was doing this job when you were in nappies yourself with the looks of you, or not far off it anyroad. I've seen a few come and go in my time, don't you worry about that. Even the ones that cry are alright in the end.

Come on, Mand. Let's go.

He had to escort her out, like a copper with his coat round a suspect as they hustle them to the car. She kept turning her head but Angie and Daisy were gone. She was inconsolable in the motor; for once, his voice of reason schtick didn't cut it.

I can't believe we're just leaving her like this. I'll miss her. She'll miss me too, I know she will. Tears, tears, tears. Scrunched-up Kleenex filling the footwell.

They left the car at the multi-storey on Woodhouse Lane and parted on the street outside the gallery.

Hey. You did great today. First time's always gonna be the hardest, you know? It was bound to be tough when you think about everything you've been through. But Daisy wasn't fussed, was she? She was dead happy to see Angie.

What if she's upset when she realises I've been gone for hours?

She doesn't know what an hour is. They don't experience time like we do. And anyway, you heard what she said – she's worked there forever and they're always alright. Remember how happy you said the other babies were the first time we went? I couldn't hear any crying today, could you?

You're right. I know you are. But I can't help the way I feel. I'm… I'm her mum. Off she went again, snot pouring, black streaked cheeks.

Course you can't. It's a big thing leaving her for the first time, but it'll be great for you both. She can make some friends and learn some independence, and you'll be happy to have your life back once you get settled in at work, won't you? Look, good job I brought these extra tissues – blow your nose, that's it. Better get yourself inside. I'm gonna be late as it is but they're used to that. No one gives a toss apart from you know who and she can fuck right off. No point you picking up my bad habits though, is there?

Oh Sean, I love you so much. You always know the right thing to say.

Come here.

A real hug, pressing into each other. Fuck, it had been so long. A kiss on the lips like they'd remembered how to do it right, then he walked slowly to work, already looking forward to his dinner and thinking about where he was going to drink it.

■

Being back at work did Mandy in. She was way too conscientious to take it easy, and she couldn't phone it in like he could. Every day she came home more tired than ever and then there was the evening shift with Daisy. They did bathtime and the bedtime story together, but the nights were still broken by feeding and he couldn't help with that as long as she was on the tit. She was happy to see her mates again and have some chat that wasn't *all* about babies, but physically it knocked her for six. Sean aced it playing superdad and picked up the slack, but there was so much more of it now and he was on his chinstrap to begin with.

Financially it was the pits. Even with Mand going part-time they were on the wrong side of the line for Child Tax Credits so they had to pay the nursery fees themselves. At nearly four ton a month it was barely worth Mand working but she needed to do it for herself and he wanted to encourage her. His own wage was adequate at best. Every week the shopping bill got bigger as inflation kept rising, and there were all the extras to buy for Daisy on top. The cost of keeping her in nappies alone was eye-watering. Mandy had wanted to go old-school with reusable ones because disposables were so bad for the environment, but there was too much washing to do as it was and it was minging having a pot of crap-plastered terrycloth bleaching in the bathroom twenty-four seven.

Anyway, it's six and two threes innit, he'd said after less than a week when the pong of shite, ammonia and chlorine had conquered every room in the house. These might be reusable, but how many chemicals are we putting in the tub to keep them white? And how much extra power do we use running the washer and the dryer?

It was a good point, so old-school got fucked off in pretty short order. The disposables were so much easier, another necessary evil. There was more washing liquid to buy, baby food now she was weaning. As soon as she moved onto solids she outgrew clothes nearly every bloody week, and the price of children's shoes once she was toddling? He bought cheaper ones for himself, and his didn't need replacing every three months. It was fucking scandalous but what could he do? The mam's group mafia Mandy got a lot of her intel from said cheap shoes would deform a child's feet for life, and there was no arguing with that lot.

His bank balance was his mortal enemy. He'd eyeball it daily, especially from the middle of the month when it plummeted in freefall towards zero, flipping him the bird as it went with a shit-eating grin that said, don't say I didn't warn you.

Unexpected bills were a disaster. A hundred quid for a pair of car tyres. A hundred and fifty for a new vacuum when the old one blew up. Two and a half ton when the telly, an old-school cathode that was as heavy as a small car and took up a whole corner of the living room, finally carked so they had to bite the bullet and shell out for a flat-screen, years after everyone they knew had bought one. Dull, commonplace things that were a pain in the arse but no big deal before now took months to sort out. The temptation of the overdraft. Payments spread between wages with a credit card; a juggling act that did his tits in. The idea of having anything leftover by payday was laughable. A couple of years ago, half-cut on the beach in the melanomic blaze of the Cypriot summer, he'd never imagined having to live like this again.

So. This was family life. Slave to the wage, slave to the grind till their twilight years and death did them part. Poxy shithead cunting bastard reality had him beaten all ends up. Too tired to function at home, too bored to care at work, too fucked to put up a fight about anything anywhere anymore.

Do you know, he said one night when they were too tired to bother turning on the box and neither of them had spoken for what felt like hours, that the word mortgage has the French word for death in it?

Fuckin' A she'd know. Back in the day when they watched a lot of foreign films he was astonished by her understanding of it. Her family had friends who'd moved there when she was in reception so they'd made regular trips across the Channel all the way up to her finishing high school. She said that was when she fell in love with the language so she studied it at A-level and did a module in her first year at uni as a free choice. When they first got together it was still fresh and she kept her hand in reading the odd book in the original when she had the time. He'd test her as a joke, play a scene on a DVD without the subtitles and get her to write down what they were saying; usually she was spot on. It was magic, like reading music. She could do that too, when there was a piano around. He'd done well in German at school but it wasn't a place he wanted to go and he'd never been abroad so he didn't bother with it after his GCSEs and it was all gone now. He'd wanted to learn an instrument so he could start a punk band but no chance of that when his folks couldn't afford to buy him one or pay for lessons. So many things her childhood took for granted were nowhere to be seen in his. That night she replied with a snore so he had to wake her and help her to bed, again. Yet another Thing To Do at the end of Yet Another Day filled with nothing but more and more Things To Fucking Do.

The housing office was shedding staff left right and centre as the next round of funding cuts hit. Year on year since Cameron – I said we were all fucked, didn't I? he said after work when they'd seen the email from the council Chief Exec about the savings running to hundreds of millions that needed to be made across the authority – there were less staff doing more work under increased pressure, punters getting fighty when benefit cuts and sky-high prices put further strain on purses that were already empty. The poor bastards on the front-line who copped nothing but abuse for thirty seven hours a week as tensions spiralled out of control were paid fuck all for the privilege, and he didn't blame them for doing one. He'd've been out of there like a shot in their shoes, Daisy or no Daisy. Panic buttons were pressed daily; folk being carted off in handcuffs scrapping with the filth became such a regular thing it was barely worthy of conversation. Staff turnover had been high before; now it was in overdrive. There were more on long-term sick than there were in work, and those that still came had checked out mentally. They put up with it however they could till they either lucked out and found another job – which wasn't easy with the labour market on its arse – or went off for months on end with stress, depression, anxiety.

Permanent recruitment. Ten, twelve, sometimes twenty vacancies at a time to fill, hundreds of dogshit applications from bastards who could barely spell their own names and didn't give a fuck whether they got the job or not, going through the motions to keep the vicious cunts at the DWP off their case. He had to admire them, so brazen in their contempt they'd submit a form that was more or less blank, just so's they could say they'd done it and tick another box on some stuffed shirt's computer screen. Once of a day, he'd done it himself.

He spent whole weeks sitting on interview panels with Denise and A.N Other manager depending on who was well enough to work, asking the same questions for six hours a day, barely bothering look interested. Every second of every minute of every hour of every day was the sound of nails on a blackboard, a scrubbing brush on flagstones, the echo of tap-dancing heels on an empty stage. The kind of noises that made him want to do himself physical harm. His arse was numb from sitting, swollen and raw with piles every time he reckoned to have a shit just to get out of there for a couple of minutes before he lost it entirely and brained someone, ideally Denise, or maybe himself if it was a really bad day.

They'd subsided into an uneasy truce, of sorts. She could still be an utter cunt when she was in the mood but her heart wasn't in it anymore. She was too stressed to pursue her vendetta, and besides, he'd won. The morning after the day he'd blown his stack and gone on a bender she summoned him in, closed the door and told him in a voice like an assassins blade that she was going get him fired if it was the last thing she did.

Deep in the throes of a wonderful hangover, reeking of Guinness and the bile he'd heaved up two minutes before the meeting began, he waited for her to shut her yap then demanded an immediate referral to occupational health and a stress risk assessment, said that if she didn't sort it out ASAP – he actually said it, ay sap, just like she did when she was trying to sound officious – he'd be lodging a formal grievance with UNISON about how she'd mishandled his return to work.

I'll have a word about the way you've been victimising me for all this time an all, see what they have to say about that. He was calm as you like, trying to decide whether to puke on the floor to make his point or leg it to the khazi after. Call my bluff if you want, like. Wouldn't fancy my chances with your previous though. You think no one here knows but I've seen your rap sheet and it's not pretty reading. Anyone'd think you only get away with it cos you're best mates with the head of the service… Since then she'd been, not exactly *nice*, but about as reasonable as a dictatorial gobshite like her was going to get.

Thank fuck for dinnertimes.

And thank fuck for the days when Mandy had nursery pick-up after work, so she'd come home to find him washed and refreshed and cooking the tea, smelling of Lynx Africa and Colgate and frying onions instead of Amber Leaf, Newkie Brown and Three Barrels. One night he got a real thirst on and bought a four pack on his way back from the King's for when Daisy had gone to sleep. He'd barely drunk in the house since they'd had her home, unless someone was round in the evening which was pretty much never. He had his arguments prepared for the inevitable row, but she was out on her feet when she came in, too tired to care.

Just a couple, he said, when he did it again the following week. This time eyebrows *were* raised.

I've heard that one before.

I only bought four. Look.

Well, alright then. I know it's not been an easy time. But don't make it a regular thing, alright? We've enough on as it is without you falling back into your old ways.

I won't, I promise.

Make sure you don't. I'm going upstairs. It's been a hell of a week.

He did three cans while she was pottering around getting ready for bed. The fourth he supped as slowly as he could, bitterly regretting the fact that the worst of his itch would have to remain unscratched.

18

He was Daisy's first word, something he'd treasure forever.

Mandy was in bed, shattered. Sean had been too fucked to function for far too long, but her need was greater so he had to get on with it. The day his name first passed her lips, they were in the park. He had the pram buggy-style so she could sit up and look around, chatted away to her the whole time they were out.

Look, Daisy, can you see the tree? Can you see the sky? The sky is *blue* today. Can you see the doggies over there? That doggy is black. *That* one is brown. Look at the grass. The grass is *green*. He felt like such a prick; he couldn't help it. It sounded so wrong coming out of his mouth, so right from everyone else's.

He lived for spending time with Daisy. She was such a happy sausage, so much fun to hang out with. He loved the way she looked at him like he was the most important thing in the world; she could melt him with a smile in the same way Mand used to. He desperately wanted to be a good daddy but he'd never measure up.

look at everyone looking judging everyone in this park laughing at the way you speak to her any fucker with eyes in their sockets can see youre a fraud but keep pretending if it makes you feel better its clear you dont know what the fuck youre doing though youre fucking useless always was still are always will be imagine the poor little thing growing up with a cunt like you as a dad talk about unlucky better if—

They'd just done lap two round the duck pond – the water is *dirty* today – when she began to cry.

What's the matter, little missus?

He scooped her out of the pram, spun her round, wheeeeeeeee, raised her like a trophy and sniffed her arse. He used to gip when he saw mams and grandmas do it, but now it was an instinctive response. There was shite in there alright, but like the fully competent and on-the-ball daddy he was reckoning to be, he had all the kit with him.

He spread the mat out on the grass, bathed in sunshine and changed her with the verve of a street magician. He could have done it blindfolded with all the practice he'd had but he was petrified of fucking it up in public.

focus cunt youre putting on a good show so far but youll balls it up in a minute drop the shitty nappy on her head or put the new one on backwards or something in front of all these people can you feel them watching you course you can waiting for you to get it wrong prove them right look at that fucking loser over there thinking hes so clever changing his little babys bum not so clever now is he what a fucking joke

He carried on nattering about the tweety birds and the grey squirrels and cawcawcaw, that's the noise the crow makes, yes it is, that big black bird is a *crow*, hands shaking with the pressure of doing it in front of an audience. He was tying a knot in the nappy bag when a change in her babbling spun him all the way out. She couldn't be saying what he thought she was. Could she?

Dadadadadadadadadadadadadada.

Are you saying my name? A Kundalini rush like he was off his head. Can you say it again? Dadadadadada.

Da. Da. Da. Da.

She was happy with her whole body, wriggling in the purest joy. She only stopped when he put her back in the pram and even then she was cackling. As soon as she was fastened in she started again and carried on all the way home, da da da da da da, waving her mitts like she was conducting an orchestra. It was the sweetest sound. He couldn't wait to tell Mandy, but she was out for the count. By the time she got up, Daisy was zonked on her play mat, suckling on Molly Moos ears.

Once she started, she never stopped, moved onto full words in no time. Soon, he couldn't remember a time when she didn't talk. She was speaking in sentences when some kids at nursery were struggling with single words. She was so bright, so advanced. Everyone said so, but he didn't need telling. It was obvious. Only an idiot could fail to see it.

Every morning they were dragged awake after a night splintered by feeds and disturbed by static from the monitor, sometimes so early that the dark hour before dawn was yet to materialise.

Muuuuuuuuummymuuuuuuuummymuuuuuuuuummy daaaaaaaaaddydaaaaaaaaaddydaaaaaaaaaaddy. Her not-yet-little-girl voice would pierce the wall in a ghostly loop until one of them hauled their corpse out of bed and went in. Most days it was Sean, trying to let Mandy get some extra kip.

He'd been a restless baby himself. Cried and cried and no amount of tit or cuddles could settle him, his mam said, screamed the place down if she tried to leave him. You must've woken up the whole frigging street carrying on like that, raising merry hell like you were being murdered. It's a wonder no one called the social. Things were different then, mind. Folk didn't interfere like they do now.

Allus wanted a few sprogs, me an your mam, but all your fuckin noise put us off, like. We could barely cope wi' one o' you, so we decided enough were enough and never bothered n'more. They were down the Club when his old man dropped that one. He tried to pass it off as a joke but Sean wasn't buying it. It fucking hurt to hear the old fella say that, but he understood him right enough now.

Eyo daddy.

Hey little missus. How are you today? Like relearning to talk, his gob clagged with the gack of the restless; rheumy boulders crusted on craggy tear ducts.

Good.

Did you have some nice dreams?

Cows. COWS, daddy. Daddy, COWS.

You dreamed about cows?

Yeh.

Was Molly there?

Yehyehyeh.

And what were they doing?

MOOOOOOOOOOO.

She'd talk all day and still be at it when they put her down at night. They could hear her from the living room over the monitor, chattering and chuntering and singing in the dark. When she fell quiet, they knew she'd gone off. She talked while she was eating, wittering with a mouthful of mush, half-chewed paste oozing out of her grinning hole, spraying them with spit and sauce when she tried to make a plosive and blew a raspberry instead. It was fucking gross. Even the thought of it put him off his own scran, not that he ever had time to eat, or the desire to do it.

She'd babble while she played, talking herself through whatever latest game she'd invented. She'd do different voices for each teddy or doll, pretend to read aloud to them from books when she was so little she could barely pick them up.

Life was one big noise.

Every. Fucking. Toy. Made a sound. They buzzed; they squelched; they whizzed and whirred, clanged and banged, boinged and burped and farted and fuck knows what else. It was unbearable. Some of them even talked. Plummy women crackling in Watch With Mother tones; monotone men drenched in reverb who sounded like Robocop with the monk on.

I am number three. Can you point to me?

My name is Bobo. Will you be my friend?

Triangle. Square. Square. Circle. Square. Squaresquaresquare-squaresquare.

They were bad enough when they were new, worse when the batteries went and the voices became the ravings of a drunk on the edge of blackout, recorded and played back on a cassette that was mangled beyond repair. When her toys were silent the house was cacophonous with the wheeze of a spit-clogged mouth organ, the broken bottle tinkling of the glockenspiel, the hammering of wooden spoons on a saucepan drumkit.

He wasn't gonna let Daisy miss out on music like he had, just like he planned to take her to art galleries and museums as soon as he could, however hard it was for him; but the racket drove him crackers and he'd imagine adding to the beat by twatting his head on the walls. Once, desperate for a break, he suggested sticking the telly on, but Mandy was aghast.

There's *way* too much reliance on screens these days. I went for a coffee with Toni after Stay and Play the other day – did I tell you about her? I met her there a few weeks ago, she'd dead nice. Anyway, we went to Costa, and some of the mums in there gave their kids their *phones* to play with to keep them quiet. Can you believe that? I mean, think about how bad it must be for their eyes, never mind anything else. I don't know what they're *thinking*.

So that was him told.

Again.

He was wrong about everything, always. The tried and tested methods his mam and grandmas had used for generations were potentially lethal to twenty first century babies, apparently. When he suggested using warm milk to bathe a sore eye, she snapped that it could be an irritant – what if Daisy was allergic? That'd only make it worse. She could go blind. A cold flannel for a fever was even worse. Why would he even think that would be a good idea? What if she cooled down too quickly and caught a chill? That could be *really* dangerous. The biggest shock was learning Calpol was no longer the go-to frontline solution to snots and sniffles and general poorliness. Using it was ridiculous when it might mask the symptoms of something much more serious, she preached, how could he be so irresponsible? The way she kept shooting him down it was a wonder she trusted him with Daisy at all.

One night he cracked and stuck CBeebies on. Mandy and Daisy hadn't even come home, but he'd had a cunt of a day and wanted something to chill to after the King's. *In the Night Garden* was starting. He'd never heard of it, but it ticked every box. Psychedelic fuzzy aliens in a make-believe world; polyphonic infantile babbling; Derek Jacobi – what the fuck? Did he read that right on the credits?! – freely flying his freak flag, parroting gnomic nonsense like he was coming up on mescaline and about to flip his wig. Five minutes of that was better than a lobotomy, like when him and Luke used to get mashed in front of *Teletubbies*. It was the greatest show he'd ever seen.

He was almost away with it when they got back. Mandy dumped her work bag on the floor, sat in the armchair with Daisy reclining on her knee, and without thinking, they all watched it together. There was a character called Upsy Daisy – my name, daddy, my name! – the little missus loved so much that she wobbled over to the telly and tried to hug the screen. Sean thought it was cute and tried to snap a pic on his phone, but Mand was horrified.

We shouldn't encourage her to get so close, she'll ruin her eyes. Fuck's sake. Maybe he should pack in talking altogether.

In time Daisy came to love *Peppa Pig* too, another oasis of chill that Sean could happily slide into for an hour at a time; she was bang into *Paw Patrol* for a bit, but that saccharine shite did his box in so he tried to keep that to a minimum. These snatches of screen time were the only quiet intervals when she was up and about. As soon as the telly went off her monologue would start all over again. Watching her learn to talk was one of life's great miracles, but by Christ it was nice to have a rest from it sometimes.

From wake-up to bedtime, all eyes were on Daisy. After lights out it could take an hour or more to get the house – not even tidy, but at least not looking like it had been burgled and vandalised. It didn't matter how knackered he was, he was restless if the room was totalled, couldn't settle until he'd at least had a go. It wasn't even really about the mess; he just wanted the space to feel like it belonged to him for a couple of hours so he could relax in peace, not feel like he was a stranger in his own home, forever tiptoeing around someone else's junk. He'd do his best to get somewhere near straight and Mandy would help if it wasn't a day she'd been working, but there was always more to do, no task ever finished. By nine they were spent, the shattered survivors of a trauma doomed to repeat forever like your man pushing his rock up the hill.

There was only ever one topic of conversation.

Did Daisy have a good day at nursery?

I think she was sick on the carpet earlier but now I can't find it. I think it was near the TV somewhere but there are so many old stains it's hard to tell.

You'll *never* guess what she learned to do today.

Did you see what she was doing earlier with that pan on her head? She looked like a little Dalek.

Onandonandonandonandonandonandfuckingon.

■

He could never get his head around how serious Mandy was about work. He was made up for her that she loved her job and respected her dedication to it but she took things to heart way too readily. So often she'd come home with a minor gripe that'd quickly turn into tears.

Christ sake, Mand, what is it this time? It's only work. Fuck it. Who cares?

He spent all day dealing with other people's shit and had no headspace or patience for it at home. He was too blasted to search for the words she needed, the placid reassurer's silken tone locked in a brain vault he'd lost the access code for.

you're letting it slip cunt don't think I've not seen it it's gonna be glorious watching you fuck this up you've had a good run but I've said from the start this would happen one day you've done well to keep it up as long as you have and I salute you for it but victory's gonna be mine soon you wait and—

They'd sit like bookends at opposite sides of the sofa while he tried not to down his cider and forget about craving his fags, drumming his fingers on the can, right foot tapping a tattoo that shook the whole settee, never still in body or mind. Mandy would be glued to her phone, Googling symptoms of deadly childhood illnesses and convincing herself that Daisy had them all.

Oh my God, Sean, listen to this. A slight redness in the cheeks could indicate…

Give it a rest. Whatever you think she's got, she hasn't. You'll make yourself ill reading shit like that every night. It's like you *want* it to happen.

What if she *does* have it though?

Where would she catch TB? You need to give your head a shake.

Her anxiety drove him spare. Daisy was a happy, healthy little girl, why couldn't she see that? She was obsessed with finding things wrong with her, worried that she wasn't eating enough, or was eating too much, or that she wasn't putting on enough weight. Had she started walking too early? Was it normal for her to want to breastfeed when she'd been eating solid food for months? Did all babies get the shits when they were teething? Was nappy rash *supposed* to look like that? Oh God, maybe it was meningitis?

It was another storm of noise when his senses were so far in the red zone it's a wonder the gauge hadn't popped. Every time he thought there was nowhere else to go, something would dial it up another couple of notches. It was new mam nerves, that was all, but it jarred. Back home there was none of this agonising over when weaning should start, and is it gonna fuck up my child's development if I do it a week too early? When he was a baby his mam said he was on the tit so damn much she couldn't get any housework done so at six weeks the doctor told her to give him a rusk, something that Mandy and her middle-class mates saw as not far off being a child protection issue.

He tried to dampen her down but there was something masochistic about it, like she didn't want to be comforted and that's what did him in. There was a crazy competitive edge, like they were vying for top spot in a contest to decide whose child could get the strangest illness or something. He'd overhear car park conversations at nursery:

Those blisters the doctor said were thrush? I think it's hand, foot and mouth. I'm taking her back tomorrow.

Ouch. Oh, did I tell you – I'm worried that Caleb might be autistic.

Really? I thought that about Kaya, but now I think it might be something genetic. I was reading an article the other day that says…

What pissed him off most of all was the fear that – while it was statically unlikely verging on impossible that Daisy would have contracted bowel cancer, or Hodgkinson's Lymphoma – she *could* have been right.

theres no fucking way you should be driving sliding the car round corners like youre playing mario kart mandys horrorstruck in the passenger seat sobbing this is going to keep track of your heart rate it might feel cold at first but dont worry itll soon warm up ready good girl Im sorry nurse i think Ive wet myself shit shit its blood its blood its fucking blood you guys need to understand that this baby is definitely coming out and theres nothing we can do to stop it

He had his own worries.

Big ones.

He'd lay awake at night creating footage of Daisy being hit by a car, ragdoll body cartwheeling through the air, a broken bag of bones skidding across the grey tarmac of the road near the park, hair matted with blood and brains; or being torn to pieces by dogs, worried like a rat, her skin shredded like paper, her beautiful, beautiful face gnawed to a bloody pulp. Worse, he'd be back In There, a cancer ward this time, his pride and joy wasted to a skeleton with a bald lollipop head, all tubes and wires again, gently pressing her hand as the familiar monitor sounds filled the room, waiting for the moment when she stopped squeezing back and faded out forever.

No fucking wonder he was going crazy.

Maybe if he could have said, look, Mand, it's natural to be worried after what we've been through. I'm worried as well, it would have helped; but he'd said all that till his face was blue and he didn't have the energy to think about what came next.

One day he realised they'd stopped talking about Daisy too. They'd put her to bed and all would be silent. The peace was bliss, the absence of sound now an opulent luxury. It wasn't awkward, not at first. By the time he realised they hadn't had a proper conversation for weeks, it was too late. The silence had become a physical presence, like the BBC documentary he'd watched about the invisible dark energy pushing the universe further and further apart, still accelerating billions of years after the Big Bang.

A tangible, vast, impenetrable nothingness that paltry things like words could never hope to fill.

19

Sean Molloy? I'm sorry to have kept you waiting. You can come in now.

He eased himself up and followed, glad to be out of the waiting room. On a local radio station playing at uncomfortable volume from a speaker on the wall, two presenters who obviously hated each other were faking laughs and pretending they didn't; he was tense enough without the cringe of listening to them squabbling on air and could've done without it. Blood spotted every finger on his right hand where he'd been picking at the cuticles, peeling away flaps of loose skin to distract himself from the dread.

need to watch what you say in here cunt you start on with everything about how youve never felt anything but shit how youre so sad some days youd blow up the world and everything in it out of pure disgust theyd section you on the spot straight down the psych ward where you belong with the other fucking nutjobs lunatics mental defectives might not be such a bad thing better than

Fuck it was warm. He'd been in cooler saunas. Wet heat, sweat, sick breath. Billions of airborne microbes sneezed and spluttered by the other patients, invisible pathogens gleefully moving from host to host. The thought made him want to hurl.

Dr Bell held open the door and showed him to a chair. He sat down. Waited.

So. She leaned forward with her hands clasped on the chipped wooden desk. What can I help you with today?

Fuck. He shook his head. It's hard to know where to start.

go on then cunt tell her there is no fucking start youre a humpty dumpty job is all fucked well beyond repair theres no putting you back together again dunno why you even think its worth trying

Well, why don't you start at the beginning? That's usually the best place. She was warm, gently encouraging. He'd never forgotten her kindness when Daisy was born and had specifically asked to see her, even though she worked part-time and it meant waiting an extra couple of weeks for the appointment.

Well…

He wanted to leap up and flee but with the door closed he was trapped. His nerves were shredded raw, dipped in salt, every sense screaming danger, danger, danger.

Basically, I'm very, very depressed. It sounded strange coming out of his mouth. Had he even said it before? Probably not since he first talked to that fat useless fuck back home.

Okay. And how long have you been feeling like this?

Forever. No. Well, I mean. Yeah. It feels like forever, anyway. Look, I don't remember a time when I didn't, how's that? Fuck's sake. I'm no good at this.

How would you describe your mood right now?

Fucking *low*, that's the word docs use now isn't it? My mood's always low. Low is normal. This is worse than that, but it's not as bad as it can be, nowhere fucking near, and that's the thing. I know how this goes. It's gonna get worse and worse until. God, I'm so fucking *tired* of it. I can't do it anymore. It's been too long. I can't. I can't.

golden rule broken there cunt youll never hear the last of this one what the fuck do you think youre doing bawling like a fucking fanny thats not how shit rolls where we come from son we dont show weakness we dont feel pain and we never ever cry especially not at the fucking doctors sort it out like when you were a kid get up dont be so soft theres nowt up

323

with you its only a scratch imagine a big boy like carrying on over a bit of blood like that stop that bastard bawling or Ill give you summat to properly cry about—

He wiped his nose on his arm, waved away the Kleenex she pushed across the desk. Sorry. Sorry. Sorry. I'm alright now. I'm alright. I'm fine. I'm fine… I'm fine.

Okay, Mr Molloy, let's take it steady. When was the first time you remember feeling like this?

He laid it out then. All of it. A torrent of shit. Once the gate opened there was no stopping. He told her about the nightmares so vivid he'd wake up screaming the house down, the hundred TV's tuned to different channels playing at the same time all the time in his brain so he couldn't hold a thought for longer than a few seconds even though somehow he could follow them all in detail while thinking he was focused on none. He talked about bath towels ruined soaking up the mess from wounds that bled so much he could have puked, hiding them in the bottom of the bin when his folks were at work; sweltering long-sleeved summers hiding his blind butcher's work, a six foot boy with an eight stone body, too sad too eat, too scared to talk, who hated the whole shitcunt world and it's granny almost as much as he hated himself.

He found words where they'd never been before, words to describe it all. How even before Daisy every day was like running back-to-back marathons when he barely had the energy to get out of bed; the impossibility of the most basic human interactions, the terror he had to overcome just to get out of the house. The way he could be so disconnected he felt like he was watching his life on film, like he was now, part of him standing in a corner of the room, separate, a sardonic observer, judging him, sickened at the spectacle he was making of himself. Mocking him with the same voice that raked over all his happy memories looking for, and never failing to find, evidence confirming that he was shit, upset folk every time he opened his mouth. Multitudes of lives ruined by the misfortune of being related to him, or being his friend, or just having a random ten-minute chat outside the pub. How he was so numb he could hurt himself and not feel the pain for days after. His mind as a cell. A life in solitary confinement, no matter how many friends and family he had. The lifelong loneliness that language was laughably unfit to describe. The miracle of surviving this for even a single day, then another, again and again, for weeks and months, years, and now here he was, two whole fucking decades later and nothing had changed. The hopelessness of it all, knowing this was just how it was, had been, would be forever.

youre doing it again cunt ahve warned you about this once fucking spineless you are weak pathetic fucking scum choke it fucking down she must think youre a right fucking arsehole dont think Ill ever let you forget about this one oh fuck no you might feel embarrassed now fucking nothing on how youll feel later remembering it ahll make sure of that cunt fucking count on it

Mr Molloy, thank you. I know that can't have been easy for you. Her voice came from a million miles away. His second self watched his physical body register that she'd spoken.

Do you ever think about harming yourself?

I've just told you—

I mean, thoughts about ending your own life.

I can't, can I? I've got a kid to think about.

Have you thought about it before?

He nodded.

And now?

Some days he thought about little else. The compulsive urge to dive headlong into traffic. Visions of his limp body in a red hot bath, razor blades, a bottle of gin, a gutful of pills. The time they walked with Daisy half the way from Whitby Abbey to Saltwick Bay along the winding clifftop path, peering down at the boiling sea, imagining himself in free-fall, his shattered body on the rocks, bent and mangled like a spider hit with a shoe.

If I could die tomorrow without fucking up my family for the rest of their lives, I'd do it in a heartbeat. Fuck it, I don't want to *die*. But I'm done with this.

So it's your responsibilities to your family that are keeping you in check, so to speak?

S'pose.

And have you been cutting yourself at all?

No. Fucking wish I could. I'd never stop though. Wife'd go spare if she saw.

Is there any history of mental illness in the family?

Hayley's moods. His old man's mam with her smelling salts and fainting fits, weeks bedridden with her nerves. The car crash of the young Tez. And the rest. Stories of long-gone relatives whispered behind closed doors away from prying ears. But mental illness? No one ever called it that. Even after Hayley the most explicit his mam ever got, when she could bring herself to speak her name, was, she was a very unhappy girl.

Not that I know of. No one's ever talked about it, anyway. Where I come from you'd think this stuff doesn't exist.

Have you tried to get any help before?

A couple of times.

Were you given any medication?

He reeled off a list.

Flupentixol, are you sure? We use that in whacking great doses to treat schizophrenia. I don't know why it would be prescribed as a frontline anti-depressant. Are you sure you don't mean fluoxetine?

I've had that an all, but flupentixol was the first.

She shook her head, tappety tapped her fingers on the keyboard, checked the screen.

Yes, 2005, it says here. What else have we got? She mumbled a few under her breath, then trailed off. Well, you've certainly had quite the variety, haven't you? How do you feel about medication now?

I don't think it'll work. It never has before. All it does is make me shake like fuck and stops me shitting for weeks at a time. Makes me gip just thinking about it.

His quivering hand counting out pills at bedtime. Six Dosulepin, three Lithium. The dry scrape of them in his cracked throat, no matter how much water he took them with. The prick of a needle every other week as they took his bloods at the clinic to make sure the lithium wasn't wrecking his liver, the smell of shit from the colostomy bags of coffin-dodgers queuing to get theirs tested for the Warfarin clinic. He felt like a junkie, might as well have been one. The shrink had said Dosulepin would help him sleep, couldn't believe it when he told him he was as wide awake as ever. There's enough there to knock out an elephant, he'd said, while Sean seethed in the silence of despair, not thinking of the pint he was going to drink after the appointment, but maybe the fifth, sixth, seventh.

Hmmmmm. Well, I can certainly understand that. The thing is, whatever long-term treatment we decide on, medication is usually the starting point. It can be a bit of scaffolding, you know? To boost you up a little before we can start trying to get to the bottom of what's going on here. What do you think about that? It's going to take some sorting, though, and it won't be an easy process, no two ways about that. It won't be quick either, I'm afraid to say, although I suspect you know that already. But how about we try this while we look into what else we can do?

I'm fucking desperate.

last chance saloon cunt double or quits russian roulette with one chamber empty spin and pull fucker make my day

Were you ever prescribed Citalopram?

Not that I remember.

Right, let's try you on these then. We'll start with a low dose and see how it goes. They'll take a while to build up in your system but you should start to feel something after a few weeks. See how you get on, and if you don't think they agree with you, come straight back. If not, come and see me in a month and we'll see how you're getting on; that'll give me time to see what else is out there for you. There may be some places we can try to refer you to, but the waiting lists are quite long. We'll need to make sure we pick the right ones so we're not wasting any more time than absolutely necessary. But in the meantime, if things get worse, book another appointment with me right away and tell them it's urgent.

His grandma used to say a problem shared was a problem halved; but he went home like a guy who'd gone in for a check-up and been told he'd be dead in a month.

■

Mandy greeted him with a filthy look.

Where the hell have you been? Daisy's waiting. She's worn out but she won't go to bed without seeing you first and she's getting really arsey. She'll be over-tired now, I'm gonna have a nightmare getting her to sleep. You'd better not have been to the bloody pub.

Sorry. I was at the doctors after work. They didn't have any appointments until half five. I thought I'd still have been home before you but they were running late. You know what Dr Bell's like. She's got so much time for everyone.

You should have called. Her voice had softened. What did you go to the doctor for?

I'll fill you in after. Now, where's my favourite little girl?

Later he told her all about it. He was lead-limbed, glazed, slumped on the sofa with a can of Kronenberg, five empties on the floor. For once, Mandy didn't complain. She just wanted to know what was wrong.

He didn't go deep into detail. Once had been enough and he hated himself for spilling his guts like he had. But she was visibly perked up that he'd gone and was trying to talk instead of giving it the usual bullshit about stress and tiredness. She was even more pleased when he showed her the pills he'd picked up from the chemist on the way back.

Have you had those ones before?

Not these, no. They won't fucking work anyway so don't get too excited.

You need to be positive, Sean. You don't know what they're going to do if you've never had them.

I can probably guess.

Don't be like that. This could be the start of something new for you.

Mmmmmm.

You'll have to give up your beer though.

Doctor never said.

Don't be silly, Sean. You shouldn't drink with *any* medication. She probably thought you were smart enough that she didn't need to say. Did she ask you about drinking?

He tensed up. No. For once, he wasn't lying; she hadn't, and he wasn't going to be the one to bring it up.

Maybe you should mention it next time?

Mmmmmm. Let's see what happens, anyway. I'll start taking these in the morning.

I'm so proud of you asking for help. She shuffled up the sofa and gave him a hug, eyes moist. I know how tough it is for you to talk about how you feel. This is a big step, Sean.

Maybe.

You've done the hard part now. Hopefully the pills will help and you can start getting better, and maybe we can be happy again then. Like we used to be, remember?

He almost could, if he really tried.

Almost.

20

He wasn't conscious of the hot coffee swishing over the side of the mug and scalding his hand. The sting of the burn was nothing compared to the pyroclastic rage exploding from his spleen.

For fuck's *sake.*

He swung a foot at the doll that had tripped him up and booted it across the room. It flopped uselessly on the sofa with its chin on its chest, eyes scarily lifelike beneath its wiry blonde curls. It looked like it had been alive until seconds ago when the impact broke its neck.

Stupid fucking bastard thing. I'm *sick* of this shit all over the floor, all this crap everywhere *all* the *fucking* time. Can we not just tidy the fucking house for a change? How hard can it be?

Sean...

What? What? Fucking *what?*

I think you need to calm down, Sean. Her voice was shaking.

I *am* fucking calm.

You shouldn't be swearing like this in front of Daisy, Sean. You're scaring her.

What's wrong with daddy, mummy?

She was three, standing next to her mam by the door. She looked puzzled, waiting for a cue, ready to smile as soon as someone told her silly daddy was playing a joke like always, pretending to be a big cross monkey bashing up the place.

Daddy's tired, sweetie. He's been working very hard.

Daddy, do you need a nap?

No I fucking don't. I just—

Sean—

Fuck off. I'm tired of this. Look at it.

His arms flailed over the mass of toys, games, clothes, crayons, scattered like a bomb had gone off.

Every fucking day the same. I spent an hour and a half clearing this shit yesterday and now look. More coffee spilled. Blisters he wouldn't notice till later. More deferred pain.

What's the fucking point? He watched the arc of his arm launch the brew, the coffee splattering a shit-coloured Rorschach onto the magnolia as the mug disintegrated. Mostly he was horrified. If he'd clocked someone carrying on like this in front of their kid he'd have waded in and panelled the cunt. But breaking something was such a release that he carried on, kicking whatever was closest in indiscriminate frenzy until he went arse over tit and sprawled full-length on his side. A short, sharp hit of real, unmistakeable pain as his ribcage took the impact. The dull thud of his head bouncing off the carpet.

Daisy's lip was wobbling, fat tears brimming. Mandy had taken a couple of steps back, shuffled her daughter with her. The shock of the fall stunned him into silence. The calm after the storm; or maybe the eye of a hurricane.

Sean, I think—

Don't fucking talk to me. I'm done with all this, fucking done with it. Off he went again, hoarse and ragged like he'd been gargling powdered glass. I can't do it anymore, right? I fucking can't. I'm going mental. *Mental*. Don't you get it? He lifted his head and let it fall back, hard.

Daddy, are you hurt? Her voice was muddied, like he was hearing it through ear defenders.

I'm fine, sweetie, I'm fine. Daddy needs to lay down for a while. Do you want a cuddle?

NO. No. I mean, you can cuddle me later, okay? Daddy has to rest now. He has to. He. So tired he couldn't finish.

His veins were full of molten metal, vision blurred, the room spinning more now than it had been when he staggered to bed at fuck knows what time, full of the cider he'd started pouring down as soon as he got in from work. He shut his eyes, slayed by the effort. He was dimly conscious of Mandy's voice but her words washed over him with the softness of a shroud on a face after the final breath.

Two cinema screens played out what could happen next. On one, he stayed where he was. The peace of the grave, the house a suburban mausoleum as he embraced the unthinking unending darkness of everlasting sleep. The second was a montage of choppy shots, patchwork editing like a music video.

A close up of his hand sweeping the ornaments from the top of the fireplace.

A slow-mo tracking shot as they tumbled to the ground.

Zooming in on shattering porcelain and glass as they hit the floor, slow-mo again when they started to break, cutting to normal speed as they flew apart.

A long shot of him wrestling with the pine bookcase, muscles straining as he rocked it back and forth until the momentum tipped it. Panning back as he jumped out of the way and the unit toppled over, books and records everywhere.

A close-up of his bare feet as he kicked fuck out of the wooden frame, blood shimmering, droplets misting like spritzed perfume as the skin was torn open by vicious splinters, screws laid bare as the thing collapsed. Shards of vinyl like jagged dorsal fins as he trampled the wax.

At the climax he ripped out a shelf like a tooth from a diseased gum and hurled it at the window, spiderwebbing the glass, then another full speed shot as two more shelves followed and the whole window was destroyed. He'd have loved to have done it but he was finished.

When he opened his eyes they were gone. The mirrored clock by the record player said half past eight. The weekend was off to a flying start. He'd've cried if he could.

Guilt. Fear. Shame. Vicious self-hate.

Fuck feelings. Fuck them forever.

It was lunchtime when they came back. They'd been to the park to feed the ducks and Daisy was full of it, the morning forgotten. He'd had a go at wiping down the paintwork and it didn't look *too* bad but there was no hiding the stain. Other than that he'd left things as they were; the place was such a fucking state that his tantrum had done nothing but move bits of shit from one place to another. The faecal abstract expressionist piece aside, the room looked the same.

Daddy, daddy! She flew through the front door and leapt into his arms. Did you have a rest on the floor, daddy? We fed the ducks. We took them bread. I was hungry so I ate it too. Can I have a sandwich?

I'll make one, sweetie. Mandy was taking her shoes off. Do you want cheese or ham?

Both.

In the same sandwich, or one cheese and one ham?

The same one. I'm starving, mummy. Is it ready yet?

Five minutes. Maternal smile, worried eyes. Why don't you and daddy go read a book and I'll bring you it in when it's done.

Yay. Daddy, I want to read *Pip and Posy*. The balloon one.

You go get it then, Upsy Daisy. I'll wait here and keep your seat warm. He patted the cushion next to him. He was so hungover he could hardly see but he'd have to get on with it. If he was lucky she'd have a nap later and he could get his head down, but she'd been cutting them out recently and he couldn't count on it.

Sean, do you want a sarnie? Amazing how she could make her voice sound normal when Daisy was around. Flawless every time.

I'll get something later. You sort you two, I'm alright for now. Hey, that was quick. This to Daisy, who'd come bounding back with her book. Are you ready? Okay, let's go…

■

What was all that about, then?

They were staring at an old film on Freeview, some black and white Edwardian psychodrama but the sound was so low they couldn't hear and they weren't watching it anyway. Daisy was in bed, and for now there was peace.

Mmmmmm? He sipped his wine.

You know exactly what I'm talking about. That was fucking scary this morning, Sean. What the hell is wrong with you? And don't tell me you're tired. *I'm* tired too, but you don't see me launching cups at the wall.

I dunno.

What do you mean, I don't know? *How* can you not know? No one behaves like that without a reason.

you think you're going to tell her don't you but you're not I won't let you I know how much you'd love it to let it go and bawl like a bairn and spew it all out soft as shite but you can't you can't you can't

I'm proper struggling, Mand. I don't know what else to say.

I *know* you're struggling. Her patience was infinite. She touched his arm.

He'd been on eggshells all day waiting for a bollocking that never arrived, but in some ways this was worse.

But you've been so much better the last few months. I thought the pills—

The pills? Fucking useless. Surprise surprise.

335

That's not what you said when you started taking them.

I know.

So what's changed?

Nothing. Shit, I don't fucking know, alright? They were fine for a little while but now they don't do a thing. It's pointless. I told you they never work when I got them.

You *have* been taking them though, right?

Sure.

I was reading the other day that mixing them with alcohol can lessen the effects.

He emptied most of the rest of the bottle into his glass. Down it went.

Can't see it makes much difference. My brain's just fucked. I've had more meds in my life than you've had chocolate bars, Mand. It'll take more than that to fix me.

You weren't drinking at the start. You were loads better then.

Well, shit happens.

Is that all you can say?

What the fuck do you want me to say?

just cant help it can you cunt always on the aggro be easier if you could try to explain it but youre straight out with it every time like that cunt at work so fucking bad hate hate hate look at her face shes done so much for you this is how you talk to her fucking disgrace cunt why cant you just fucking die daisys young shell get over it wont even remember having a fucking dad better that than grow up in your shadow with all this fucking baggage hanging over her little head youre a fucking disease infecting everything you—

We can't carry on like this, Sean. It's not good for you, it's not good for me and it's terrible for Daisy. She's tiny, Sean, it must be so weird for her. When we were in the park she kept asking why is daddy so sad, why does he get so cross. She doesn't know from one day to the next which daddy she's going to have to deal with. It's not fair to her. Your moods are all over the fucking place.

What's new?

and again cunt thousand and one answers you could have given there but you had to go with that one didnt you

Sean, you need to stop drinking.

He necked the dregs straight from the bottle, winced. Council pay had been frozen, again, so he was on the cheap stuff and had been for ages.

Well?

Well what?

You *know* what, Sean. You're killing yourself with that stuff.

That'd solve a lot of my problems.

You selfish bastard. Suddenly she was shouting. You don't give a shit about me, do you, or Daisy? You don't care what happens to anyone as long as you can sit there getting pissed every night, turning your lips blue with that fucking slop and waking up so hungover you can barely get a sentence out.

What the fuck do you know about it? People where you're from haven't got a fucking scooby. Look at your mam, she gets a bloody headache and takes to her bed for a week. If my mam had done that when I was a kid she'd've had her wages docked and we'd've struggled to eat. Your lot are so fucking soft their kids have their own therapists for fuck's sake. You've no bastard clue what it's like in the real world. None.

Oh piss off with your hard luck stories, and don't you dare start on my mum. She works bloody hard for her money and it's a stressful job.

What—

You think dying would make things better? *How?* What about Daisy, Sean, your *daughter?* How's it going to be for her growing up

337

without a daddy? She idolises you. And what about *me*? You think that would be alright, making a widow out of me and an orphan of your own child? Dying might be the answer for you, but it's a cop-out, Sean, a total fucking cop-out.

A greyscale snapshot, like a film still. Hayley, cold and alone in the darkness of the woods. A fragile body and a butcher's knife. A lake of stickyblack blood.

You don't know fuck all about that either. You think it's fucking easy? How the fuck would you know how it feels?

How could I when you never fucking *talk* to me. *Why* won't you talk to me? All I want to do is help but you make out like I'm the problem and I'm fucking not, Sean, it's *you* and I'm so fed up of it now. I *know* you're unhappy. I *know* you're depressed, and I'm sorry I've never been able to help. But guess what, Sean? So am I. So am I.

I'm going for a smoke.

why can't you cuddle her cunt let her cry it out you know full fucking well that's what she needs you're fucking useless course it's all your fucking fault she be better off well shut

There's a surprise. Fuck off out then, you don't give a shit about me. I don't care anymore. I'm past it. Do what you want – you always do anyway. I'm going to bed.

She stayed seated though, eyes down, wracked with guttural sobs that made him want to smash his face into the fireplace. He'd made her so unhappy for so long.

He kept his fags padlocked in the garden shed, stashed on a high shelf behind a row of plant pots with a litre of Gordons wrapped in a towel.

Neither lasted the night.

21

Work was a bitch.

So was Denise.

The ceasefire was never gonna last. She'd finally got him a written warning, citing his atrocious timekeeping and gross lack of professionalism. He took his union rep to the meeting when she called him in, but he couldn't bullshit his way out of this one. He was late more days that not, snuck off early every chance he got; he took fag breaks that lasted twenty minutes, spent more time in the khazi than at his desk – sometimes shitting stale ale or vomming his breakfast brew, often just sitting there staring into the crotch of his kecks to drag himself closer to home time. He didn't give a three ton toss about the warning, but he was fucking radged she'd stolen back the advantage. She'd only got him because he didn't have the energy to pretend to care but it pissed him off all the same.

He never told Mandy. She'd've flipped her lid and started blethering on about needing to knuckle down and be responsible, you've got a family to think of, we can't have you getting sacked just because you can't get organised enough to get work on time. Things are different now we have Daisy, in case you hadn't realised.

More ballache he didn't need. She did enough moaning as it was.

You didn't put fabric softener in the machine when you washed Daisy's clothes, did you? You *know* that sometimes makes her itch. God, I can't believe you've done it *again*. How many times do I have to tell you?

I don't think you brushed her teeth for long enough then, Sean. I mean, that definitely wasn't two minutes. It's really bad for them if you don't do it properly. Why don't you use the timer like I keep telling you?

I don't think Daisy enjoyed that dinner as much as when you made it last time. Couldn't you have made the broccoli any softer?

He couldn't do anything right. Do it your fucking self then, he wanted to scream. He was so used to biting his tongue it was a wonder he'd not snipped the end off. When Mandy wasn't complaining about things like that, it was all, Have you made an appointment with the doctor yet? Cos this is getting silly now, Sean, you're getting worse and worse. Your clothes are falling off you. I can't remember the last time I saw you eat.

Sean, if you don't phone the GP I swear to god I will. I can't take much more of this.

Here's the phone, Sean. You call them, right now, or I'm taking Daisy and I don't know when we'll be back, I'm not even kidding.

The rest was silence.

■

This time the appointment was easier. Dr Bell knew the story so there was no need to tear open old wounds by repeating it. He'd checked in with her once or twice after she'd prescribed him the pills, but there wasn't a lot more she could do. Demand was through the roof and funding cuts were crippling what few services were left so there was no room at the inn. Even the Council mental health support wouldn't see him because he'd already spoken to a GP. No fucking wonder the suicide rate in men his age was so high.

How have things been? It looks like we've not seen each other for a couple of months. She checked her notes. Last time we met

340

you said that the Citalopram was starting to help. How do you feel about that now? Are you still feeling some positive effects?

Not exactly. They were alright for a bit, apart from making me shake and block my arse, but I said they'd do that, didn't I?

When you say they were alright…

Kinda felt like my brain was bubble wrapped, you know? I still felt rough as fuck but it softened it. Then that faded so it's pretty much back to square one. But at least we've tried.

Let's look at the positives. You're saying that the Citalopram *did* work for a while?

Yeah.

For how long?

I dunno. How long have I been taking them?

She squinted at the screen, tapped the mouse a couple of times. According to this, nearly six months, she said.

So, they probably worked for about half of that time.

Three months, then?

If that.

Okay. Well it's a good sign that they at least did *something*. You said before that none of the other medications you've been pre-scribed have done anything at all?

Yeah.

So let's look at this as a step in the right direction, shall we? The question is, what do we do next? Now, you can agree or disagree with me here and that's entirely up to you, but I think it'd be a good idea if we keep you on these tablets, but at a higher dosage. How would that be?

He was ambivalent at best, but with no other options on the table he shrugged and said, sure, whatever you think.

It's always good to start with a low dose. You were obviously responding to them initially, so let's try you on twenty milligrams instead of ten and see how you get on. She tapped the mouse again and the printer whirred into life. How have you been in general? Is your mood still low?

You could say that.

Do you want to expand on that?

Not really. I mean. Nothing's changed. I feel like shit. I'm here, aren't I?

Mmhmmmm. Do you feel safe, though? Have you had any urges to harm yourself? I don't mean when we talked about it before. I mean recently.

Thoughts of kitchen knives on scarred skin, blood blooming in open wounds. The smack of fist on concrete, throb of bruises that lasted for weeks, the crack of fractured bones.

Sometimes.

Ok. And hurt yourself in what way?

Any way. The usual. You know about all that, I don't need to tell you again.

Any thoughts of going further?

I can't, can I? We talked about that before an all.

Have we ever made a crisis plan together?

What?

A crisis plan. It's what to do and who to speak to if you ever get to the point where you don't feel safe. It won't take long, but we definitely need one of those. Hopefully you'll never need to use it but it's a good thing to have just in case.

The ten-minute appointment stretched to half an hour. He'd been hoping to get in and out rapid-style but she was unbelievably thorough, he had to give her that even if he was going through the motions. His crisis plan was a printed sheet listing the phone numbers of people he'd call if he lost his shit entirely. Top of the list was Pops, then Rob, then the Samaritans, a couple of local mental health helplines. At the bottom were strict instructions that if he had nowhere else to turn he had to report to A&E and ask to speak to the registered mental health nurse in charge. He crumpled it like an unwanted receipt, chucked it in the bin while he was waiting for his script having a fag outside the chemists.

■

I'm so proud of you, mister.

Fuck, he couldn't remember the last time she'd called him that. It used to turn him inside out. It had been so long it crashed into him all over again, coursing through blood and guts and brain like in the early days when he'd not seen her for a day or two, his heart a hummingbird desperate to escape the cage of his ribs.

They really loved each other, once.

Make sure you ask the doctor about mixing them with alcohol, she'd said as he was leaving that morning – one last nag for the road. There was no chance of him doing it, but she was right. She'd been right all along.

He was tired of being hungover. Every night sunk deep in his cups he swore that tomorrow would be a new beginning. Every sickened morning he steeled his resolve that this was the last time he'd spew at work, that he'd actually eat something at dinnertime; but by half ten he'd be shaking, and one wouldn't hurt if it got him through the day and he made sure he left it at that. He *had* to stop. But how else to deal with the impossibility of life? He was forever caught between the devil and the deep blue, and the cunt with horns and hooves was a real sweet talker.

He didn't tell her he was laying off. He'd made so many big announcements about fresh starts, lives reinvented. She'd never have believed him. Why would she? He could wax lyrical about how much he meant it this time and he might have even bullshitted himself on a good night, but his good intentions only ever led where the old wives' tale said.

The sun was shining so I was celebrating.

It was raining so I needed cheering up.

I can't watch the snooker without a beer.

Shit like that. Excuses so transparent they weren't fucking there.

But this time *would* be different. He'd do it on the quiet so he wouldn't get bollocked if – when, if he was gonna be perfectly fucking honest – he toppled off the wagon. She couldn't give him grief for breaking a promise he'd never made. And he might get a few brownie points when she realised he'd been laying off. Win/win.

Aren't you going to come sit next to me, mister? You're always so far away.

That word again, a key to another world. He wanted to gather their past in his hands and reshape it like clay, mould it into the life they could have had if things had been different and he hadn't fucked everything up. But the past was a wasteland. Nothing could fix that.

Mmmmmmmm. He shuffled up but the intimacy that saw them pissing together on the first star-crossed morning had fallen through the cracks into someone else's life; it was embarrassing how awkward they'd become.

Daisy had been on the tit for two and a half years. Morning feeds, feeds before nursery, after nursery, the night feeds that took so long to wean her off. He'd rock her for hours in the dark singing hushed lullabies, whispering words of comfort with intoxicating breath while she cried and cried for mummy. There was no time for a morning cuddle with Daisy as their wake-up call; the few nights they went to bed at the same time, they were so shattered they'd be out for the count before they thought to snuggle up.

Time was if they tried to get through a door at the same time they'd pull together for a smooch, a squeezed arse, maybe a hand up her dress if she was wearing one. If it was a weekend they might end up in bed, or at it on the floor. Now it was, sorry, you go first, no, you, okay, right, there you go, sorry, thanks, sorry, sorry, sorry. The kisses that could stop time were dusty memories and fading even from there. They were a pair of ghosts, weary of haunting themselves.

Aren't you gonna give me a cuddle?

Mmmmm? Back in the present his cheeks reddened like in the old times when he'd colour up every time a woman so much as looked at him sober. He was as flustered now as he was when he first met Pops and she'd sit opposite him in her open robe, playing with her knicker elastic and talking about the size of some guy's dick.

A cuddle. You *do* remember what one of those is?

He scanned for signs she was flirting, or annoyed, or both. She was a cipher now, nothing but glyphs. Gone were the days when could read her like a book, so open that she shone.

We cuddled up on here all the time when we first moved in. It was always nice, wasn't it? Her hand brushed the hem of her work skirt and shifted it up a few inches; a deliberate accident his eyes couldn't avoid. He tried to smile. God, he was tired.

be lovely if there was some cider in the fridge but there isnt and therell be fucking hell on if you say youre off to buy some now unless what do you mean unless you cant not today no fucking way its the first day if you cant even do this you might as well admit youre fucked forever but you know that already so it doesnt matter anyway and its only a quick walk youll be there and back in five minutes and

Images spooled before him. The chillers in the shop full to the doors, so much choice. The emerald lure of green glass bottles, cans sweating condensation. The shiver of the first sip, Dracula licking blood from a blade. He was about to tell her that he was on his way when she leaned and sort of fell into him so he was pushed onto his back with his head on the sofa arm and her on top, her tongue writhing in his mouth like that lass Cassie's or whatever the fuck she was called all those years ago. A duet of nasal, shallow breaths, hands all over as she fought her way out of her clothes, he gulped in air as she stopped kissing him for long enough to close the curtains, snatched them together, still a gap but closed enough that no one could see her leaning down in her mismatched under-wear, unfastening his belt, zipping down his jeans, brushing the dark hair of his concave stomach with ravenous lips.

They fucked more times than they had in all the years since Daisy combined. On the sofa, against the door, from behind over the dining room table, then again underneath it, once more in the bubble bath they shared when they went upstairs to get cleaned up, giggling like pre-schoolers as the water sluiced over the side. When they got into bed, skin glowing and perfumed with blue Radox, she carried on grabbing at him, but his response was half-hearted and for once in his life on a sober night he went off without a struggle.

The next morning was blessed. For the first time in fuck knows how long, Daisy slept in. He awoke just before seven, way past the time she normally got up, thanked his luckies and shut his eyes again. He'd not get back to sleep now his brain had fired but waking up without Daisy calling was decadence itself, and he had nothing else to get him out of bed.

Hey. Mandy whispered, so close that her lips tickled his ear. I've been waiting for you to come round. He scrunched his eyes, reckoned he hadn't heard. That's not going to work, mister. Don't you *dare* pretend to be asleep. She reached under the duvet, squeezed.

I want *this*, in *me*. *Now*. And if you don't do as I say there's going to be trouble.

They were clumsy, rushed, like one shag too many at the end of a mad one when the comedown's hitting hard and it's time to get gone. He had an ear and a half open for Daisy and couldn't focus, expecting to be disturbed any minute, but Mand was content to do the work. You look tired, mister. Just lay there and relax, I'll take care of *everything*.

She'd come three times and was in the shower by the time Daisy started calling. Sean was downstairs making breakfast. She'd be grumpy as hell if he didn't have something ready when she'd slept so late.

I'm in the kitchen, Upsy Daisy, he called up the stairs. I've got your brekkie ready for you. He was spooning a dish of steaming spaghetti hoops onto a couple of chopped up waffles when she came in.

Daddy, she said, waving a scrap of neon pink fabric at him. Why are mummy's pants on the floor?

They must have fallen out of the washing basket, sweetie. Pass me them here, I'll put them away. A fucking great answer. His face straight, didn't miss a beat.

He took the knickers from her outstretched hand and was shoving them in his pocket when he clocked Mandy in the hall, damp-haired and flushed with the faintest of smirks, signs of the dimples he thought he'd never see again. An invisible wall crumbled as their eyes met and they creased up.

Mummy, daddy, what's funny?

Neither of them could stop for long enough to invent something.

Why are you laughing? Why, mummy? Daddy, why are you laughing? What's funny? Tell me. TELL ME!

347

They carried on for way longer than they needed to, like if they stopped it'd be the end of something they'd never get back again. Mandy was bent double, hands covering her face, sounding like a Z-list list actress fucking up a screen test where she'd been asked to pretend her dog had just died. Sean was no better, laughed like it was the last chance he'd get, beyond recall of what had set him off but still he went on, laughing and laughing and laughing until his sides ached, his eyes streamed and his cheeks were slick with tears.

BAGGAGE HANDLING

There's a suitcase in the loft at your mam's house that she loves to get out when she's pissed and sentimental. It's a big old seventies thing, brown leather, scuffed all to fuck from being dragged up and down the ladder over the years. It's full of old photos, so many of the fuckers that it's bursting open and the zip bit the dust a long while since. You tend to bugger off out the way when she starts with that game, take a bottle of port back to the dining room with the big man and keep your heads down till she's done, but the first time you took Mandy round for Sunday dinner she got the full treatment and there wasn't a lot you could do about it.

Sean, love, go on up into t'loft and fetch t'suitcase down, will you?

Mam, not today—

Ah'm sure Mandy'd love to see some old photos of you, wouldn't you love?

Old photos of Sean? Have you got some?

Mebbe the odd one or two, like. Off you go, Sean, and no arguing or ah'll stick me foot up your jacksie and boot you through t'hatch meself.

■

Your old man on top of the moors. The print's faded so it's hard to get a feel for the light but it looks like it's a mad hot day. He's never been one for flashing his legs so he's wearing jeans but he's got his shirt off and you can see how fit he used to be. He's fucking stacked, actually, not exactly a six pack but his stomach's wash-board flat compared to the dwarf planet he ended up with and there's proper definition to the muscles in his arms. His hair's kinda shaggy, not proper long but well past his ears, bit of a pis-stake when you think how much stick he gave you for growing yours like Kurt's in the Nineties. He's got shades on and with his permanent five o'clock shadow he looks fully serious, but that's his thing when he's made to pose, never has any bother not smiling for his passport. You're sitting on his shoulders, probably about seven or eight. You're a skinny thing, all spidery arms and legs, your short back and sides so blonde it's white. You've no shirt on either and you're flexing your biceps – or would be if you had any – like a bodybuilder, proper beaming. High in the hills with the big man's back as your throne, you're King of the World.

You used to go walking up there on Sundays when you wer-en't eating dinner in the pub. Your old man loved a wander and your mam did an all, country people on both sides, village folk on hers. Between there and those treasured days on Jean and Harry's farm you spent half your childhood outside and it's the one thing you remember fondly about growing up where you did. The place where the photo was shot is at the pinnacle, the highest point of the moor you can reach from your mam's house. Only takes twenty minutes and it's uphill all the way, but it feels like the middle of nowhere. You can see the whole town from up there, Bronte country all burnt bracken purple and red across the valley behind you, the green hills, scars and limestone scree of the lower Dales directly in front. On a clear day you can see over to Pendle an all, the hill glowering like a bad omen however nice the sky is. After uni you used to go up there to hide when you'd been on a binge too many and wanted to get away from yourself, as if that's fucking possible, or when you'd smashed a load of your old man's booze and had the paras the day after, keeping out the way to avoid the arsing you knew you'd have to face when he clocked you'd cleaned out his ale fridge again.

You've been up there that much, sitting on the rocks by the cairn to your old man's left as he's facing you, you can time-lapse the view in your memory, watch the town shift and grow as it digests the surrounding fields. It'd be wild to wind it back in time and see it shrink back to how it was when it was entered in the Domesday book, before the Castle was built. You bet the moors wouldn't be much different, mind. There are new estates going up on the outskirts all the time now, encircling the place like cancer cells swarming a healthy organ. It's all outside money, rich bastards from down South buying second homes or for Air BnB rentals an that. It's fucked the house prices right up so local folk can't afford to move; there's no extra schools, doctors, dentists, whatever, and the roads can't cope either but the developers don't give a fuck about that and neither do the council once enough dirty money's greased the right sweaty palms.

Your old man says when he snuffs it he wants cremating and scattering up there. Maybe you'd like your dust chucked around to join his when the time comes, but some cunt will probably have levelled it for flats by then, concrete and tarmac stretching beyond every horizon, from the lowest valley bottom to the crest of the highest peak.

■

Looks like your grandma's wedding, this. After her first husband died she said she was too young to be a widow for the rest of her life and she got married again in nineteen eighty five, you think it was, so that'll've made you about four. Check out your get-up in this one. Pressed black strides, white shirt, mini-penguin jacket and black dickie bow. You were so proud of that tie, kept fiddling with the elastic band that held it on when you showed it to folk. You've got a white rose in your buttonhole, which you were more excited about than the tie. Where's my flower, where's my flower? You remember asking all morning, when your poor fucking mam must have been torn in half watching hers get wed to someone that wasn't her dad, although she got on great with Jim for the twenty odd years they were hitched and no one cried more than she did when he carked.

She's standing next to you, must weigh half what she does now, got a tidy dress on, carnation pink, nothing fancy but nicely fitted, unfussy. She looks pretty good it has to be said, but the fright-wig perm and those stupid square red-framed specs she has on in every pic from the Eighties don't do her any favours. They make her look like a cross between Dennis Taylor and Su Pollard.

Apart from the dickie bow and the flower you don't remember much of the day, but you remember the hangover alright. You were doing that thing little kids do where you go round asking the grown-ups If you can try their drink. Everyone was humouring you, as they do, probably letting you wet your lips at a push if they were feeling indulgent or their hand slipped cos they'd had one too many themselves, but not your great uncle Alf. He was a proper lad, loved his ale, had a wooden leg from where he collided with a German shell on D-day. Jim was on Sword Beach that day an all. He was a boy soldier who signed up at 16 – come back tomorrow when you've had a couple of birthdays, the recruiting sergeant said when he gave them his real date of birth the first time he tried to enlist – but he'd never talk about it. You heard so many war stories as a kid, but none from any of the fellas that did the actual fighting, and there were still a lot of them about back then. There's a lesson in that.

Great uncle Alf weren't quite the full shilling, as your gran used to say. A bit soft in the head, like, cos of the war an that, and the silly old twat gave you the second half of the pint of Guinness he was on with. You were paralytic, obviously, and sick as a fucking dog later, fell down the attic stairs at home and everything. You've known some bed-spins in your time when you're so sick and dizzy your brain feels like it's been put in a dustbin and rolled down a hill but never again have they been as bad as they were then. All night and all the next day you spewed and spewed and spewed and your little loaf throbbed so much you thought it was gonna burst.

You'd've thought it'd put you off for life.

■

You can see Jim in this one. Seems funny calling him that. He was first introduced as an uncle, but once they were married he was always grandad. No one told you to call him that, you just did. He was a good bloke, from Burnage originally but you'd never tell to hear him talk, always sounded more Yorkie than anything else. He'd had a win on the horses in the seventies – a proper big one – and packed in work by the time he met your gran, but he was a landlord for most of his life. He ran one of the big pubs on the High Street once of a day, had a couple round and about the Dales at different times an all. He loved making people laugh and he was great at it, a joke for every occasion. Came from being in the pub, you reckon, always had a tale to tell, riddles to box your brain, tricks that made you think he was a magician, like the way he could pull coins out of your ears or make a playing card disappear from under his hand when it was flat on the table with yours pressing down on top. He was like an old school variety guy without the song and dance shit, although he could waltz like a motherfucker when he was in the mood and taught you how to do it too, standing on his shoes so shiny you could see your face in them while he talked you through the steps.

He did his own cooking in the pubs so he was a whizz in the kitchen and he's in his element here, white pinny wrapped round his gut, comedy chef's hat on, bending over the barbie with a pair of tongs. He used to do this wicked chicken tandoori stuff that he marinaded himself, made your mouth explode the first time you had it. You'd never heard of Indian food till he came along.

Bloody wog jock, your old man said when he smelled it. Ah'm not eating that. Wake us up when he's put t'sirloins on. Meat and two veg all the way, the big fella, never wanted owt else. When you told Mand you didn't know what pasta was until you clocked Luke's mam and dad eating it – the twisty stuff, you distinctly remember it being that – around the time of your SATs while you were making a mushie brew in the kitchen, she laughed her tits off. You are funny, Mister, she said, wiping away the tears. Don't ever change. It took you so long to explain you weren't joking you wished you'd kept it shut.

In the photo you're sitting on the grass a little way away from where your grandad's cooking. You've got shades on, jeans too, like your old man in the first one, but you're not at the stage where you needed to cover your arms, so if you add that to the pasty face and spots you're thirteenish. Look at the state of your fucking hair. Curtains, shit the bed; must've been taken just before you started growing it. You're drinking some piss coloured stuff out of a half-pint glass but you know what it is alright.

Woodpecker. You can taste it just from looking.

You'd never heard of cider either, till you met Jim. Those barbies were always boozy dos – often one or both of your folks got shitfaced and you had to walk home with them staggering and singing in the cool of the late evening – and that was where you got your first proper taste. He'd fill a two-gallon drum with ice and chuck everything in there, tinnies of Smiths, Boddies, Worthies, whatever him and your old man were supping that month, and a few bottles of the Liebfraumilch and Hock your mam and gran used to quaff, so no matter how high the mercury rose the bevs would be chilled to the nuts.

Go grab us a can, will you love, he said one day while he was burger-flipping. If you have a look there's a couple for you an all.

I don't like beer. You were twelve and had a lot to learn.

Not beer, love, it's cider. It's made from apples. Look for the red ones.

Fuck's sake but didn't it taste like green Tango? Soon as you got the first glug in your gob you knew you'd made a friend for life. You went off Woodpecker sharpish when you found the stronger stuff, mind – Olde English, Blackthorne, Stowford Press too – but it was lush for the couple of years you drank it.

Sunday dinners round there were the same, always tipping you bits of wine, sweet liqueurs an that after pudding if everyone else was having one with their cheese.

Good to let you try these things when you're younger, he'd say. Means you get used to it, like. So when you're old enough to do it legally you don't go mad on it, see what I mean?

■

A bunch of lads of late primary age in full footy kit. White shorts, red socks, red and white vertical stripes on the shirt like Sheffield United. They're in two rows, one in front of the other, with the taller lads at the back and the ones in front down on their haunches. In front of them on the muddy grass is a crappy looking silver cup, maybe about ten inches high, so cheap it's in danger of falling off its wooden mount. A couple of fellas, players' dads who ran training, are hanging round the back with a football apiece looking so uncomfortable you can't tell whether they're know they're in the shot and trying to get out of it or the other way round.

You used to love your footy. Never much good at it, mind, but you tried. Every dinnertime at school there'd be a proper game on in the playground. All the sporty kids would be buzzing about nutmegging each other, reckoning to be John Barnes and Peter Beardsley an that, and you'd be like a headless fucking chicken charging all over the shop, never getting anywhere near the ball. No one would pass to you cos they knew you were shit, and if you did manage to get a touch you usually panicked and hoofed it out of play. You thought joining a local team might help you get better, but did it fuck. It was worse than being at school, cos at training everyone was super-serious and it was proper hard graft. They had you doing circuit training and running laps of a full-sized pitch down the sports centre when you were nine, ten, and sure, it got you fit but it didn't help your skills cos in the practice matches the same lads would boss it and you'd still never get a look in. They were all tougher, stronger, faster than you, full of mesmerising tricks and flicks they pulled off like it was no big thing. When you tried to copy them you'd fall flat on your arse while they stood in a circle jeering, pointing their fingers and laughing, calling you a spacker and a spazz while you closed your eyes as tightly as you could to keep the tears in and wished instant death on every last one of them.

You stuck it out, god knows why, till they got a new coach instead of the dads, some fucking doylem that used to play for Halifax who called you a lazy no-mark tosspot for having your hands in your pockets when the pitch was frozen so hard your studs were like ice skates. The same cunt who laughed his knackers off during a diving header drill and said with your limp wrists and dying swan impersonation maybe you'd be better having a go at ballet. You told him to piss off with as much contempt as an eleven year old could manage and never went back.

They must've played sixty matches in the three years you were there. You made one appearance, for six minutes, as a sub one night in the pissing rain somewhere over the border, Barrowford or some shithole like that, in the season they won the cup at the front of the photo. You didn't get a touch.

Where are you? Probably standing up. You were always tallish for your age. Scanning, scanning, scanning. There. There you are. Back row, far left, about six inches between you and the lad next door, that obnoxious ginger twat Paul Somethingorother who thought he was the hottest shit in town and would rather take a shot from forty yards out than demean himself by actually passing the fucking ball. The whole team have got their arms around each other but no one's touching you.

You count twenty two lads on the picture.

Twenty one of them are smiling.

■

Christmas at the Working Men's Club. This is the function room upstairs, you can clock it a mile off. The tatty imitation leather seats around the edge, the faux gas-lamp lights on the walls covered with nicotine-sticky patterned paper that looks like it's been around since Queen Victoria was a lass. You're onstage with your dad's mate Mick, but you think he's Father Christmas. You're wearing beige chinos and a white shirt cos your mam always made you look smart for the Christmas do even though you hated dressing up. You're nine in this one, you know you are, because it was the year you got your first proper football, one with stitches and panelling and not just

357

some cheap shite from a funfair that blows away if you fart too close to it. You're taking it from his hand, eyes agog. It was an amazing thing – all the lads at school had them but you knew how much they cost and thought you'd never have one of your own. You played with it for years, kicking it around in the street commentating on yourself like a junior Barry Davis before it dropped in bits – full-on holes in the sides and the rubber orange bladder sticking out like a haemorrhoid – and you never got another.

You adored the Club. Your grandad Paddy was on the committee so he was in most nights; your old man spent a fair bit of time in there too. You used to go together, you and your folks, Paddy and your grandma, sometimes your old man's brother Brendan and his missus an all, on Saturday afternoons when your old man finished his morning overtime. It was always warmth and babble and chat, smoke so thick you could have sliced the air like your mam's chocolate cake. You loved the stale ale smell too, the stink of human bodies, the old records on the jukebox, the sound of the coins clanging from the bandit, the cheering when someone dropped the jackpot or knocked a pint glass off the bar and broke it, the click click click of snooker balls in the games room where a wall-mounted telly showed sports programmes presented by a man with a bushy moustache and wild white hair who reminded you of a badger.

You were fascinated with Paddy's mates, grizzled men of the industrial north with perpetual fags and pints of black and tan never far away, men with names like Bopper, Capper, Coggy, Old Jock McTavish, Tealeaf, Barmy Arthur, Sidevalve. You couldn't wait to be just like them, a fully-grown man with whiskers and beer breath and a funny name of your own. By the time you were old enough to buy them a pint half of them were dead, the ones that hadn't been carried off by liver disease or kidney failure slain by strokes, heart attacks, lung cancer. The one's that were still around were always chuffed to see you, like, but you never got the name you wanted. All they ever called you was Pat's Lad, but it came with a smile and a nod that said you were one of them, and always had been, and that was all you really wanted to know.

■

You, your mam and Paddy in the living room at your grandparents' house. Your grandma Dorothy hated cameras so she's nowhere to be seen, but she must be out of shot somewhere, probably behind whoever's taking the photo, with her B&H and a brew. You're wearing your new school uniform – grey strides, white shirt, green and blue striped tie and a blazer that drowns you, sleeves so long you can't see your hands, the bottom of it hanging nearly to your knees. It looks like it'd've been big on a kid at least a couple of years older. On the floor next to Paddy's ashtray there's a couple of carrier bags with the logo of the shop where the clothes came from. It must've been the day you bought them or somewhere near. Bloody hell, you remember your mam saying when she clocked the price tag. We'll have to get one wi' some growing room. When Ah met you dad he drove a car that cost less than this.

When you started in September you had the piss ripped out of you from the off because your uniform, not just the jacket, all of it, was so big everyone said you looked like a tramp who shopped at Oxfam. Worse, the school logo on the breast pocket of the blazer was a patch sewn on by your mam instead of being properly embroidered at the place that made them. That marked you out for kids and staff alike as one of the paupers who couldn't afford a proper jacket, so you copped a ton of shit for that an all.

Your mam and Paddy are looking right into the lens, smiling like they've won the pools, raising glasses in celebration that you'd been picked to go to the grammar. He's on whiskey and lemonade, your mam's on the wine as per. You're on the cusp here. The little kid in you is made up with his new togs and loving showing them off to the old folk; the teenager you're about to become is having a word in your shell-like, telling you that under no circumstances are you to smile. You're desperate to do as he says, but little boy blue's still got the upper hand and you can see it all over your face.

■

A couple of proper old ones, almost identical when you put them side by side. They're smaller than standard, sepia-tinted, curled round the edges like they've been on fire. In the centre of the frame is the wooden front door at the church your mam and gran used to go to, less than a hundred yards up the main road from the terrace you spent your early childhood in, a carpet of confetti scattered like blossom in late spring.

Standing in front of it is your mam in her wedding dress. It's yellow on the pic but it was a fully traditional wedding she says, so it must have been dazzling white on the day. She looks happy to the point of tears. It's scary how young she is, lithe and thin with a schoolgirl face. She was barely out of her teens when she got up the stick with you but she was a lass of her time and she'd already been wed for a couple of years, scratching a living behind the checkouts in Hillards while your old man worked for peanuts as a grease monkey in a backstreet garage, counting every penny to keep on top of the mortgage they could barely afford. As the clusters of cells that would turn into you grew safe and warm, oblivious inside her, a tumour the size of a football was swelling in her own dad's guts. The docs said the poor bugger, still a couple of years shy of his half-century, wouldn't live to see it, and he'd be lucky if he even made one short. His sole desire before he died was to hold his first grandchild even if only once and your grandma said later that's what kept him hanging on for as long as he did, while the flesh fell from his bones and his eyes sank like pebbles into his skull. But cancer doesn't give a fuck for dying men's wishes and it carried him off in in triumph in your mam's seventh month.

He's standing next to her in the doorway, stocky, paunchy, balding, very dapper in his waistcoat and tie. He's every bit the typical Yorkshireman – you can imagine him at the cricket with a pint of best and a flat cap, eating cheese and pickle sarnies and reading his paper whenever there's a lull in play, supping a bottle of Bass. He's looks bashful, like he's embarrassed to be in front a camera but he radiates pride. He's on the wrong side of his forties and sliding into middle age but he looks content with it, healthy too. It's unreal to think that within three years he'd be dead.

His passing hit your mam so hard that even decades later she struggled to talk about it; better by far to treasure him inside than raise his ghost by invoking his memory out loud. She was on anti-depressants for years and swore that the crippling grief on losing him so young was passed on to you in the womb, the damage done before you'd made your way out into the world. That's what was responsible for everything that happened to you later, she said, like you were born under a gypsy's curse. She's always been a super-stitious old moo and you laughed the first time she said it, but sometimes in the coalblack hell of your darkest days it's crossed your mind that maybe she was right.

Next one. Same shot, different bloke. Your old fella's next to her this time, mop-haired, sideburns, looks like a proper Jack the lad. If the stories are true, there's a fucking good reason for that. If you didn't already know the picture was taken in the early seventies you could date it just looking at him. Even the strides of his wedding suit are flared. They're hand in hand facing the door, turning their heads behind them to look at the photographer. Your mam's wearing the same joyful smile; the big man's doing his best impersonation of one, mouth pointed upwards ever so slightly in the corners, but it's more a smirk than anything else. You've never wanted to admit it but there's not getting away from it when you see him with his barnet like that – the same as yours once was before you slashed and shaved and went for the spikes – the shape of his eyes, the high cheekbones, jutting chin and the famous Molloy conk.

You could be twins.

■

Jesus fucking arsewipe Christ. You hate this picture but it always finds its way to the top of the pile, like a turd that won't flush. Inside the student union on Oxford Road in Manchester, 2002, wearing your rented gown and mortar board. The date, incredibly, July 4th, Independence Day. You're sat next to your mam, holding your degree certificate like it's a dead animal someone else's cat's left on your doorstep and you can't wait to drop it in the wheelie bin. Your mam's eyes are brimming with tears, not helped by the fact that she's put away three quarters of the bottle of SU plonk that's half-in the shot on the right hand side of the frame. She's got her arm around your shoulders but not in a way either of you look comfortable with. It's like you're someone famous she admires who she's randomly clocked and blagged into having a quick snap taken so she can boast about it to her mates. You look like a smack-head. Your phizzog's all bone, crooked yellow teeth, black bags under your eyes like you've walked into a Lennox Lewis special. You're trying to smile for your mam's sake but it's looks like a proper sneer. If looks could kill, your old man behind the camera is in big fucking trouble.

22

Two beers, that was a bonus. He assumed they'd all gone; they usually had.

They were tucked away at the back of the fridge on the top shelf that froze every bit of food they put there so they were deadly cold. Peronis too, even better.

They hadn't had company for way too long. There wasn't the time, and they were so tired it wasn't worth the effort trying to entertain; but Pops had been over last night and they'd got carried away as per. The showreel had a lot of scenes missing and Christ knew what time she'd left, but he *did* remember having to help her into the taxi, slaloming a sibilant line down the drive, stumbling out of her sandals. Mandy was long gone, out for the count on the sofa. The two drinks she had went straight to her head, prompting a rush of giddy, girly giggles that slurred into a drowsy slump then crashed into the kind of kip that would outlast a nuclear war. He was pretty pissed himself but he was wearing it well.

You text me when you get back, alright? It's been so great to see you.

You're the boss, babe. She was arseholed, yanking her skirt down as she got into the back of the car but she wasn't covering anything he'd not seen before; scraps of delicate satin and lace that probably cost more than he earned in a week.

It's been such a good night. Like how it was when we lived together.

Yeah, can't believe it's been so long.

I really miss those days, you know.

Me too. I always loved having you around, Blondie.

You ready to go? The driver tapped the meter.

Just a minute. I need a squeeze first. She put out her arms, looking like a five foot four Daisy in twenty-something clothes. Time hadn't caught up with her yet. She was free and easy, rabbiting about her recent conquests, fit guys – but none as fit as you, blonde boy – girls too these days, she said with a twinkle, if someone really caught her eye. Hers was a reckless life of daytime binges and all-night parties, not a care in the world with all her family money to fall back on. Jealous wasn't the word.

The ravages of parenthood were etched on Sean and Mandy, four hard years that had aged them by double that number and more. He'd never been much of a looker, all haggard cheeks and ragbag clothes, but Mandy, so fresh and bright, had dimmed like a guttering candle, the fashion-hunting trips of old like pictures from a book about a time before they were born. Poppy's style hadn't changed. Grungy chic with hippy hints, bare flesh and bangles, everything just the right side of indecent but making a good job of pretending it wasn't. He leaned down to hug her and she turned her cheek for a kiss, but their snaking heads met in the middle, lips on lips, warm, soft, pliant. She tasted of vodka and orange and raspberry lip-gloss, tobacco from the joint they'd smoked on the step while they were waiting. She giggled through her nose and so did he Talk about fucking awkward; but at least they were mates, it was a pissed-up misunderstanding, no drama. Maybe it lingered a *tiny* bit, and when he moved back she followed, or did she, surely not, but she might have done and it could have felt worse, but then he was shocked big time like when they were kids and Neil had dared him to piss on an electric fence. He pulled away, cracked his head.

Fuck's sake.

Oh babe, you've hurt yourself. Here, let me kiss it for you. She started trying to undo the seatbelt.

It's fine, I'm alright. Come back soon, yeah? He swung the door shut, cutting off her reply and waved as the taxi drove away, awash with booze and confusion, telling himself nothing had happened. Which it hadn't.

Everything black after that.

Christ, he was rough as arseholes. Pissed, actually. He could hear *Ben and Holly's Little Kingdom* through the front room door. So that was why Daisy hadn't disturbed him. She was old enough to have sussed the remote, and if Mandy didn't hide it she'd put it on as soon as she came downstairs. His tongue was matted and furred, his breath probably flammable. A skullfucked headache. Nausea of the kind that mocked from the inside and said this was another day he wouldn't get through without spending some time talking on the porcelain phone.

There wasn't much to eat in the fridge. Half an avocado, browning around the stone; a block of cheese, a packet of ham that had been open for a good week and smelled like it was on the turn. He'd promised to go to Morrisons today, but fuck that. There were chicken dippers in the freezer that Daisy never said no to, and he could maybe treat him and Mand to a curry later to kill the last of the hangover.

He pulled out a Peroni, pressed the cold glass to his forehead. The sensation was heavenly so he rolled it around, squishing it against his burning cheeks before resting it on his head again. Maybe he should just drink it.

He almost gagged at the thought.

But.

If he could get it down it'd stave off the sickness before the hangover had the chance to kick in proper-style and it'd be early afternoon by then so he might get away with it, especially if he snuck to the shop for a few more.

Hair of the dog an that.

No.

Fucking.

Way.

The clock on the cooker said it was half ten. The dim red glow of the LEDs hurt his eyes. Half *ten*. He liked a few on a Saturday afternoon if they had nothing else on, but it was way too early.

Wasn't it.

Over by the sink was the damage from last night. More dead Peronis than he could count, some wine bottles too. If he nailed this one rapid-style he could stick the bottle with the empties and Mandy would never know.

Fuck it.

He started to prise off the cap with a lighter, got halfway then thought better of it when a whiff of the foam made him dizzy.

He stood up and closed the fridge but left the bottle on the counter next to the kettle while he stuck his head into the living room. Daisy was sitting on the carpet with Maisie, glued to the screen; Mandy was on the sofa, face white beneath a pile of hair. She'd started dyeing it again but couldn't keep on top of it so instead of bright red it was a washed-out kind of pink. She was wearing her pyjamas so she must have made it to bed, but he had no idea when. Maybe he'd left her on the sofa after Poppy went; or maybe he'd helped her up when he'd gone. It was a mystery. He barely remembered getting up this morning, never mind when he went to bed. He didn't even know how long he'd been in the kitchen.

Good morning, my darling. He put on his best Daddy voice.

She looked round at him with her soft brown eyes and pressed a finger to her lips. Shhhh, daddy. Mummy's asleep.

Okay sweetie. Have you had breakfast? He dropped his voice to a whisper, gave her an exaggerated wink to let her know he didn't want to wake mummy up either.

She nodded. I had Coco Pops, daddy. Mummy let me eat down here. Ben and Holly's on.

I can see. Are you okay if I go do some cleaning up in the kitchen? Mummy and daddy and Aunty Pops made a big mess last night.

Yes, daddy.

Alright then. Can I get you anything?

Shhhhhhh. She shook her head, turned back to the TV, and with that he was dismissed.

He had the bottle open in no time and nailed it, wholesale, but his guts didn't want it and his mouth filled up with suds. Gross. He wanted to swallow but his body said no, so he spat the foam into the sink and swilled it down with cold water, stuck the empty with the others. He spotted about an inch of liquid left in one of the wine bottles, a smooth Pinot Noir he couldn't afford that he'd bought to go with the griddled lamb steaks. It'd've been a shame to waste it, so he caned that too.

It was disorientating feeling pissed so early in the day and he didn't want to deal with Daisy until he'd got a hold of himself, so he distracted himself tidying up, took the empties outside and put them in the garage with the others. Fuck, he needed to go to the tip. Yet Another Fucking Thing To Do. There was enough glass to fill the boot of the car twice over. He wanted a smoke now and there was a pack of Luckies stashed in there somewhere, but that'd be too much; he'd fucking stink, and he couldn't have Daisy smelling it, not that she'd know what it was. He'd have to find a way to sneak one later. He'd just got the top off the second Peroni when Mandy walked in. She looked like death warmed up.

What are you doing?

He looked from her thunderstruck face to the bottle in his hand and back again.

Are you going to *drink* that?

Yeah. Yeah I was, actually.

You're a fucking idiot.

He was in the wrong but that fucking patronising tone, like she was talking to a stupid child, never failed to bring out the worst out in him and usually made him act like one. He necked half, burped like he was making an important announcement, wiped his trap on his forearm. A delicious sting as his stubble rubbed the scab off a deep scratch from where he told Mand he'd caught his arm on a nail in the garage. He should try to calm things down but he was pissed enough to be feeling self-righteous.

So I'm having a beer. So fucking what? I'm a fully grown man, aren't I?

It's not even dinnertime.

Come on, it's Saturday. Aren't I allowed some fun on a weekend?

You call this fun? You're slurring for fuck's sake. Again. And you're shaking.

Mummy, I can't hear Ben and Holly.

Sorry sweety, mummy will just close the door. She reached behind her and pulled it to, turned back to him, whiplash fast. He wanted to get the next word in, but she didn't give him chance.

So this is your idea of fun, is it? Her voice had dropped to a whisper. Getting pissed in the kitchen first thing in a morning while your four-year-old daughter's in the living room.

It's hardly first—

Fuck off, Sean, just fuck off. I didn't think you'd be wanting to drink ever again after last night.

here we go cunt what have you done this time you might well fucking
panic boy cos youve not a single clue have you this is gonna be fun

Flashback to the taxi. A clumsy goodbye. A kiss that definitely wasn't a kiss. Surely she'd not seen that? She'd been kaffled for hours. Anyway, there was nothing in it. Was there. It lasted a couple of seconds, if that, and it not like there were any tongues, maybe a hint but that's all and he'd kept his mouth shut, mostly. It wouldn't have looked great if she'd spied it through the window, mind, whatever he said.

What's that supposed to mean? He wasn't so sure of himself now.

What do you mean, what's that supposed to mean? You were shitfaced before Daisy went to bed. Downing beers in the kitchen while you were cooking and thinking I wouldn't notice. You were halfway down a bottle of wine by the time Poppy arrived. Do you think I'm blind or something? What happened to not drinking on medication? You said you'd have a couple cos it was a special occasion. Couple of gallons, more like. *And* you were all over Pops.

No I fu—

You fucking *were*. Oh Poppy, I love what you've done with your hair. Is that a new top, Pops? The colour matches your eyes perfectly. Those are great sandals too, where did you get them? Disgusting. The scorn was enough to strip the skin from his face.

What the fuck? I was trying to be nice. She's your fucking friend, you know she likes compliments. She'd have been in a right mood if one of us hadn't said something.

Her dismissive snort stung like a slap.

Jesus, Sean, is that the best you can do? You were being nice? Is that it? You're pathetic.

Wait a min—

Then what was it you said? You'd better cross your legs, Pops, or you'll be showing me your breakfast. You can't fucking remember, can you?

shes got you there fucker you mustve been really trashed to be coming out with something like that in front of Mand what the fuck were you thinking oh yeah right you werent were you go on then say something lets see what youve got

God. We're *mates*, how long have we known each other? We can have a laugh, can't we?

A laugh, is that what you call it? If you'd said that to me I'd've thrown my drink at you.

Pops thought it was funny.

He was bluffing, but sure as shit he was right. It was Poppy's line, blurted in some bar or other lifetimes ago when they used to go out more weekends than not and drink themselves silly while Mandy paced herself with a couple of rum and diet cokes.

God, check out the state of her, she'd dug an elbow in his ribs and pointed her cocktail at a drunk girl half-sprawled across a booth a few seats away, legs akimbo. I've got belts that are longer than that dress. *Hey,* I think I can see what she had for her dinner. Pot Noodles, I reckon. Then she'd punched his arm and laughed so hard she fell off her chair.

That's besides the point. *I* didn't think it was funny. Don't you care what I think? Actually, don't answer that. You obviously don't, otherwise you wouldn't have sat there staring at her legs all night. You were practically drooling.

What the fuck? She was sitting right opposite me. Where am I supposed to look when I'm talking to her, at the ceiling? Shit, Mand, when we lived together she was only ever half-dressed the whole bastard time. And now you're flying off—

Yeah and you couldn't stop looking then either, could you?

What? It was *years* ago. How can you—

Well you're the one that brought it up.

Only because you're losing your shit over nothing.

You think being pissed and ogling my friend is nothing, do you?

For fuck's sake. No one was ogling anyone. She's my friend too. And you can't talk about anyone being pissed. You invited her round and you fucking passed out as soon as we'd finished eating.

You must have been loving it. Having me out of the equation so you could look up her skirt in peace. Incandescent hate flaming in her eyes; in that moment, he hated her right back.

He drained the bottle and saw himself throw it at her, panicked for a second and thought he'd actually done it before he clocked it was still in his hand, gripping the neck so tight it's a wonder it didn't snap. He turned slowly, deliberately away and put it on the counter where the others had been. He imagined his fist going through the window, his foot panning in the glass of the back door, his hand picking the bottle back up and smashing it into his own face, blood and glass and shredded skin, the pair of them screaming like someone was being murdered.

Motionless now, trying to slow his breathing to a standstill. So, here it was. He'd been expecting it, but not today, not like this. Her eyes drilled holes in his back, but he couldn't turn round. His bravado was gone, the will to fight. He was finished. They were. It was over. Kaput. Done.

Mummy, the postman's here. Daisy's helium chime came through the door.

Thanks darling. Mandy slid back to her mummy voice but it was a pale imitation. The stand-off continued, seconds like decades in an intense, violent silence. When it was broken by the sound of the letterbox flapping, he jumped so hard he bit his tongue.

Forget it, Sean. Forget it. I'm gonna get the post. She turned and stamped off down the hall. He used the diversion to duck into the living room.

How's my little girl? He crouched down for a kiss.

Pooh, daddy, you're smelly.

You shouldn't be rude to daddy like that. He ruffled her hair with a hand that was shaking more than ever.

Why are you and mummy shouting? It's not nice to shout.

We weren't shouting, sweetie.

I heard you. Why is mummy annoyed?

Mummy's very tired.

He bombed into an armchair. Another couple of beers would put him out for the day, if he had some, and what a fucking relief that would be.

We both are. He rubbed his eyes, dug his knuckles in till he saw stars.

Well you still shouldn't shout. Self-righteous in a way only the young can be.

Whatever you say, sweetie. Mummy will calm down soon.

You said lots of bad words, daddy. Naughty mummy did too.

Sometimes grown-ups have to, sweetie. You'll understand one day.

Shhhhhh. Peppa's on now.

Sean, what's this? Enter Mandy, waving a letter.

Dunno. You tell me. Here we go, straight back into it. He could have said anything but that. So much for the conflict management training he'd done at work.

I didn't know you had a credit card.

I don't.

Oh yeah? Well this Visa bill's got your name on it. There's nearly three hundred quid owing on here, and nearly every one is from

Booze Buster or… what's this? The Admiral Duncan. The Regent. The Three fucking *Legs*. There's a whole bloody list of them. What the hell have you been doing in the Three Legs at – she studied the paper – half past bloody twelve. Have you been going to the pub at work?

You shouldn't be opening my mail.

Yeah, well you've got me so fucking mad I didn't realise it was yours. Good job I did though. You keep telling me we're skint.

We are.

Yeah, and no fucking wonder with you pissing all our money away on this. Three hundred quid. Three fucking *hundred*. Is this just for a month?

Mand—

Is this why Denise is always on your case? Cos they've caught you getting pissed on their time?

No. This, at least, was true.

I don't believe you. I don't believe a word you say any more. What's happened to you? You used to be such a nice guy. Now it's like I don't know you at all. You're such a… Such a… *Cunt*.

She'd always hated it when he used that word so it was the last thing he ever expected to hear her say. For once, he was stuck for a reply.

Daisy, come on sweetie, we're going out. Mummy voice hanging by a thread.

But I'm watching Peppa.

You've seen enough telly for today. Come on, you're coming with me.

Where to?

Never mind that. Go into the hall and get your shoes on, there's a good chicken.

Where are you going?

373

That's for me to know. We're going out. Away from you, and your lies and your mood swings and your fucking beer breath. I've had enough. I'm going. That's it.

Bye, daddy. Daisy scampered past, waving. He tried to catch her for a cuddle but she'd gone.

Bye, Upsy Daisy. I'll see you later.

I wouldn't bet on it.

What—

You need to fucking sort yourself out and I'm not coming back until you do. And don't bother calling. I won't want to talk to you.

The slam of the living room door was echoed by the front one, which banged so hard the walls shook. He got up and stumbled to the window but the car was halfway down the road.

Ah well, fuck it.

She'd be back.

He shut the door and went to the garage, choked his way down a fag and another straight after. The nicotine made his head spin and the buzz hit the sweet spot on top of the Peroni.

might as well get some in cunt what else is there to do youve fucked it good and proper doesnt sound like shell be back any time soon bang some tunes on smash a few and you can be showered and fed by the time she comes back then see about sorting it out might take some doing its partly her fucking fault though opening the post all that shit about poppy christ youve seen that girl in her knickers more times than youve seen her dressed the way she walked about with that fucking robe wide open you even fucking told mand how embarrassed it made you not that she fucking remembers fuck her anyway youre wasting time come on come on lets go shops not far

The rest of the day melted into a bad edit. The street; the offie, the street again. Fumbling with the turntable, knocking off the anti-skate weight and losing it behind the unit, fucking it off for an iTunes playlist. Lots of punk, lots of metal. Loud, fast, filthy.

the thing with mand fuck that fuck her wheres that can get it down boy get it down you can think about that shit later you need to get on with the job how long since you had a day to yourself to sit and do this gotta make the most of it dont give me that shit about feeling sick and being rough youre made of sterner stuff than that lets get this eight pack down sharpish and if youre still standing well fucking well go get some mo—

BANG. BANG. BANG. BANG.

He was **woken** slooooooooowly by a rhythmic thumping.

It took him a few seconds to come round and realise where he was. Where was it coming from? Maybe the stupid old woman next door was braying on the walls because of the noise. The maungy old bag was always mithering on about something. He wasn't in the mood today; she could get properly fucked and he wasn't gonna be shy about telling her.

He was halfway to his feet when he heard a tap on the window.

Alright alright you miserable cow, I'm coming.

Then he clocked the cop car outside, blue lights casting an eerie neon glow as they spun silently on top. He moistened his mouth with the dregs of a can from the floor, went to the door.

Mr Molloy, is it? Sean Molloy?

Yeah. Who's asking? He never had it in him to talk nicely to the pigs.

West Yorkshire Police. We're looking for the registered owner of a 2005 Volkswagen Polo, registration PB55 DNR and our records show it belongs to you. Can we come in?

23

Two caskets at the front of the chapel.

A body apiece.

You killed them.

You killed.

You.

The large one, light oak, the same colour as her hair. Copper handles flaming red like it was before she had Daisy. The second child-sized, made of wicker like the Moses basket she slept in that first year she came out of hospital. Flowers on top spelled out her name in yellow and white. Mandy's mam and dad had made the arrangements. They wanted to bring their little girl home where she belonged; it was only right her own child should be with her. You walked in to her favourite song, Just Like Heaven. She used to play it when she was feeling sad because she couldn't listen to it without smiling. A perfect song about finding the perfect love, she used to say, and it lasting forever.

You were in the middle of the front row, Kevin and Veronica on your left, your mam and dad on the right, all dressed in full-on formal funeral wear. You'd managed some black jeans and a plain black shirt, a thin black tie you wanted to string yourself up with. Your mam looked like she'd shrunk, timewarped into her eighties, older than her own mam ever was. She'd cried so much it was a wonder she had any tears left, but they kept on coming. Kevin was doing his best to be stoic, murmuring in Veronica's ear the whole time, patting her knee as she dabbed her eyes with a black silk handkerchief behind the dark veil hanging down from the brim of her hat. Your old man looked ready to go on a killing spree.

That morning you got a taxi from the tiny B&B to Mandy's parents' house to be greeted with drip-white faces streaked with salt-lines. Shattered embraces all round, then you stood in the silent kitchen while Kevin offered tea in delicate china cups with saucers, a matching plate with a few biscuits on. Bourbons and Jammy Dodgers, Daisy's favourite. Your mam said yes to tea but didn't touch it; your old man shook his head, said nothing.

You'd steadied yourself with half a bottle of brandy before you went down to meet your folks for the cab ride and poured the rest into a hipflask. The first time you opened your mouth was to excuse yourself for a smoke. You gave your old man the side-eye, the slightest tilt of the head. Yes, yes, of course, help yourself to the garden. Kevin, so polite and fussy, a proper old woman, your gran would've said. He ushered you to the back door like you were the guest of honour at a party he'd thrown and your wish was his command. Your old man had clocked the signal. He followed you out.

The cars will be here soon but I'm sure you'll have come in by then, Kev said before he went back in. But do let me know if you chaps need anything, alright?

You were straight into your pocket, your old man the same. You knew he'd've come prepared. You belted down half the flask, smoked, put away some more. You thought about saving some for later but you wouldn't be able to drink it at the church so you necked the rest as your old man was tipping the last drops of his onto his tongue, head at ninety degrees to the sky. You lit two more, passed one over.

Couple of minutes, gents. We're getting our shoes on so we're ready when you are. It's almost time. Kevin's voice like an announcer from the early days of the Beeb.

Set? The big man, monotone.

No.

You dropped your tab end into the flowerbed and hugged him. You had permission to cry that day, how the fuck could you not, but it was too soon for that. He wrapped his arms round you like the fucking bear of a man he was and hugged you back and it was the first time in your adult life he'd done that, and you clung and clung and clung as the brandy fuzzed your eyes out of focus and you were back to being a little boy when one cuddle from the chief made everything alright and you never wanted it to end, ever, wanted to stay like that, cocooned, warm, where it was safe and secure and none of this fucking shitshow you'd caused by murdering your own woman and kid had ever happened. You were still holding each other, both of you shaking like fuck with the effort of holding it all in, when Kevin came to get you.

■

You don't remember a lot.

After that stupid fucking row with Mandy there's nothing until the two coppers showed up and there's not much of that either to be fair, only the handful of words that blasted your world to pieces.

Head-on Collision.

Driver and passenger.

Dead at the scene.

And after of the post-mortem:

Blunt force trauma.

Killed on impact.

When you saw the bodies laid out in the hospital you dropped like you'd been plugged by a sniper and puked all over the floor. They were so still, so peaceful, so much the same but so very clearly undeniably fucking dead, the skin on Daisy's little face grey and

379

cold and felt like candlewax under your lips, her own mouth tinged with blue. Mandy's hand stiff and hard in yours. Your fingers remembered how it was before, surprisingly strong when she squeezed back but you pressed as hard as you could and it didn't give a millimetre.

The chapel was full. Outside you'd seen Jean and Harry, your old man's brother Uncle Liam and his wife Christine, faces the colour of wetted ashes. They tried to catch your eye but you couldn't look at them. A few more of your mam and dad's mates who'd missioned down to support them, and you, you suppose, but you couldn't put names on them. The lasses from the caff were there and a lot of your own friends too, but you struggled to remember who they were when you'd not seen so many of them since Daisy was born and you weren't really there anyway; nor have you been anywhere since.

Lost, lost, lost.

There were tons of people Kev and Veronica knew, a lot of folk Mandy must've gone to school with an all. Pops was behind you, kept her hand on your shoulder all the way through, so tense you could feel her nails draw blood through your shirt as she hung on for dear life but it was a bit fucking late for that. Someone at the front, a celebrant, you think they called it, not a religious thing, but someone to talk about the deceased, and how strange that word sounded, you couldn't make the connection, spoke about the light they brought into the world, how much joy they gave to everyone they met. You couldn't focus to listen, didn't fucking want to anyway, and you couldn't have made much out cos Pops was crying in your ear, not sobbing, nothing elegant or demure like the silver spoons on the other side of the church, none of that discreet stiff-upper-lip shit, full-on, full-blast heartbroken, keening like it was the end of the fucking world, which it was.

Rob was next to her, looking like a bouncer in his suit, sniffing and kind of half-coughing like he had something caught in his throat; clouds of hot vodka breath making you wish you'd brought some with you.

There were two readings, one by one of Mandy's childhood mates and another from a friend of the family. Poems, you think, but none of it went in. Loads of crying then from all around, not just Pops. Everyone giving into it, letting it go. All you could think about was your sweet beautiful little girl laid there in that fucking box with her favourite blanket, her Peppa Pig hot water bottle and Maisy Moo, the black satin lining decorated with yellow stars because she loved gazing at them, gasped in wonder when you told her their names and tried to say how far away they are, and what they are, and how really everything and everyone in the world is made of dust from stars that lived so long ago but even most grown-ups can't understand it, and she'd nod her little head and go, wow, daddy, wow, how come you know everything, daddy, tell me something else.

And then it was over.

It was set up so everyone had to walk past the caskets to get out and you had to wait until they'd finished. Mourners pausing to say their last goodbyes or whisper a prayer. Some of them didn't stop, just let their fingers brush the wood on the way. Poppy's knees buckled when she got there and Rob had to stoop to stop her from falling. He held her up until she'd finished saying whatever it was she had to say and then more or less carried her away. She was there longer than the rest put together.

The five of you went up together and it was awkward, like no one could suss what order you were meant to go in, after you, no, after you, like you were queueing for a fucking taxi or something and as if it made any fucking difference. Your mam and dad went first in the end, then Kevin and Veronica, all of them properly in fucking bits except the big man but he wasn't gonna be able to keep it together much longer. They hung around by the door waiting as you stood there with a hand on each box, rattling, and all you could think of to say was sorry, because it was your fault they were there, you'd killed them, your own partner and child, murdered for the sake of a poxy fucking cunting bastard beer cos if you'd never opened that Peroni you'd never have had the second and Mandy wouldn't have caught you drinking it and you'd never have had that row and if you'd never had it she wouldn't have got in the fucking car that morning and they'd both be alive, the other guy too, driving the car that hit them when Mand went through the red light, three of them dead because of you and all the guilt you'd carried all your life, maybe this was why, was it always pointing here, pre-ordained and everything that came before was building up to it, and you stood there with all that running through your head whispering I'm sorry I'm sorry I'm so so sorry over and over as if they could hear you and as if that would ever be enough and your legs folded good and proper then and down you went, banged your arm on the bigger casket and you'd've fallen into the little one but for the big man hoiking you up with his hands under your armpits and you cried then, Jesus Christ how you fucking cried, all those years of holding it back, and you cried for them both, for your mam and dad, Kev and Veronica, the wife and kids of the other poor cunt you'd killed and you cried for Tez and Hayley, poor, poor fucked up Hayley and you were sorry to her too, for missing her funeral being such a selfish cunt so no one could see you do this, and what did it matter, and you cried and cried, couldn't stop, your old man at it too, the fucking state of the pair of you, all the way outside where everyone was massed round the family plot, waiting, and you listened without hearing as someone else spoke and people put in handfuls of earth, soil on the flowers, the most wretched, desolate thing, the worst that could ever happen to anyone, happening to you right there and then and you couldn't believe it, never will, and you knew, and know, an eternity of penance wouldn't begin to atone, forgive me father for I have… what? sinned? what kind of a fucking word was that to describe what you'd done and then it must have been finished, like their lives, yours, everyone's, people filtering away in dribs and drabs, hands on your shoulderbackarms as they went, maybe a few soft words but none that you heard and none that would have made two shits of difference, no platitudes to trot out, well, she had a good innings or, none of that, no, what could they say, what could anyone say, nothing nothing nothing like the endless black nothing where your reasons to live had gone—

■

A posh country pub. Dark wood, polished brasses, real ale. A stag's head mounted on a plinth above the fireplace. Packed with mourners you didn't speak to. A lavish spread of food you didn't eat. You sat at a table within easy reach of the bar with your old man and your mam, and you drank, and you drank, and you drank. Hours later when the bell rang to call time you were still there, the three of you, destroyed, drinking. Pops and Rob paralytic at the table next door, doing the same.

■

Thank fuck for your mam.

So much to do in the days and weeks after. Bank accounts, phone contracts, bills in Mandy's name, life insurance claims. She sorted it all while you surveyed the wreck of the rest of your life and drank.

■

They couldn't keep coming over every night but they did it for as long as they thought was right until you told them to stop. You spoke to your mam on the phone most days, if you could call ten minutes of silence talking. The rest of the time you sat at home, alone, and drank.

■

Pops phoned often. Talking to you kept Mandy's memory alive for her, she said. Daisy's too. Your own life ever after, a ceaseless struggle to forget. On the phone with her, there was only ever one voice.

She came to visit once. The first time you'd seen her since—

She was wrecked when she arrived.

So were you.

The food she brought was left untouched. Weeks later it was still there on the table, rotting like the bodies of those you'd buried.

You drank; she drank.

She talked. And talked. And talked.

She drank, she talked.

You drank.

She drank and talked, talked and drank, you drank and drank and drank and drank to drown your guilt, unvoiced forever. No one could ever know. You killed them.

Later she lay in your bed in the vacant space where the faint scent of vanilla essence and coconut lingered on the unwashed pillow. You cuddled under the covers like kids cowering in a storm, ruined beyond comprehension, eyes blurred by so many tears you could barely see her face although it was only inches from yours. Finally, you'd learned to cry. When it no longer had a use.

You held each other so hard it hurt, beside yourselves beside each other, bawling gasping tighter, closer, palms on wet cheeks, fingertips stroking soothing whispering nothings to hear another voice, nose to nose, stung by the stink of neat Smirnoff, taste of raw vodka and raspberry lip gloss, tobacco tongues twisting, starving mouths, frantic hands, her jeans pooled at her feet, two bodies bags of bare bones, and you might have thought about it once or twice, maybe, or more, how she'd feel in your hands inside her robe, her breath and yours one, wanted it even, both of you, but you didn't then, not really, and you didn't start it, did you, or did you, what did it matter, you let it happen, her too, but if anyone came no one noticed, and in the infernal light of a devil's red dawn you were cold and dying alone and it might not have happened at all but for the pink and white knickers you found by the bed and a text that read: I can't see you again. I'm sorry. Goodbye.

∎

A call from Denise.

Your sicknote had run out. Were you getting another one? She sounded contrite, like she was sorry to have bothered you. You told her, go fuck yourself you sour-faced cunt, then went right back to your new job, working all the hours under the sun and the moon and the cold dead stars; drinking and drinking and drinking and drinking and drinking.

∎

The last time you saw your mam she was the shadow of a ghost. In the remains of your family home, as you drank and drank and drank, she pleaded with you to get in the car, leave it behind. Next to her the big man, not so big now, shrunk by half and shrinking still, a carcass searching for a soul, staring down,

385

down, down, trembling like a leaf a heartbeat since the bird has fled the branch.

Please, Sean. Ah'm begging you now, love. You can't stay here. You've got to come home. You need someone to look after you. Won't you come with us? Do it for me, love. Please. Do it for you mam. You can't go on living like this.

She was right. You couldn't.

Hoped it would be soon.

NO

on the floor struggling to right himself like a beetle on its back half-blinded by blood, gashed wide open too fucked to feel he's fallen apart, rolling to push himself up like a baby learning to crawl, arms so weak they can't, he's down, bangs chin, carpet burn, bottle in reach empty, fucking empty, ghosts in here, she's back, hair like a horses mane, big brown eyes, what's she doing, dressing up, rooting through the hamper that long blue dress the cape the gloves, blonde wig plaits down to the floor she's got it all on sing-ing croaky little kid voice let it go let it go blood and tears pissing like a fucked tap, whole face washed, needs a drink, she's dancing, spinning around cow in hand singing to it, hugging it tight, bundle of black and white, moo, moo, she used to say, one of first sounds she learned to make, what do the cows say, moo, moo, moo, over and over, radiated joy when he gave her it wouldn't be parted from it after, fucking thing was minging, took it everywhere, slept with it, ate with it, shoved it in her mouth, covered in fucking food, caked in it, jesus fucking christ how it stank when he tried to wash it she cried and cried till he gave her it back, tried to blag her, bought another the old switcheroo, she was smart, couldn't even talk, barely walking but knew the difference, clutched the other wouldn't let go, so strong, always so strong, had to be, everything she had to go through just to be born, six minutes it took to get her started and was she, was she, no, they just need a little bit of help sometimes but always the thought what if the baby what if the what if what couldn't say the word bad luck worst luck, hex, didn't want to bring it down on them, on her, cursed them even in his silence, she looks so happy, a happy little chicken, always was, a smile for everyone, isn't she beautiful they used to say who

391

was he to argue the most beautiful thing the world ever did see and how he loved her, what a fucking word, pitiful, language can't describe it, felt like that about her mam once god, it was him, all him, all along, all afucking long, mea culpa, mea culpa, pushing her away and she could have helped, wanted to, they really loved each other once, grabbing the bottle shaking the fucker tipping it up his old man with the hip flask, hoping for drops dregs nothing, nothing, empty like the house, like life, haunted here, kneeling reeling half-upright swings the bottle at the wall, clonk, swings again, and again that's more like it neck snaps off and straight to his arm, right one, always started there, stabs left-handed rips like wrapping paper red red red beneath red on his face, standing, hand on wall bottle other sticks it chest gives that a fucking good twist, no meat there, jars his hand when it hits his ribs sticky and wet and sticking to his skin and he needs to drink, the little girl and her mam's here now dancing together singing the song to the cow, the mam picks her up lifts her high wheeeeeee like he used to do, whirl of love she'd laugh and laugh and laugh, the sweetness, taunting him, he killed them he killed them he fucking killed them and no one will ever know, vow of silence, some monk, pure and clean in this shit-stained blood splattered charnel house halfway out now, bangs doorframe, bounces one side to the other stumbles out where did he leave it in the bag its down the stairs got to get it got to got to got to shatterproof man so much for that made himself an icicle look where it got him, revenant smeared in gore, trailing behind him polka dots carpet like the cover and curtains, tears and blood awash and half blind loose carpet stumbles trips and falling flip stomach rollercoaster hand slick wet red slips off wooden rail half-spins tangled feet, tangled web lies half-truths, mea culpa, mea culpa, masks and masks and masks all slipped ugly monstrous truth getting what he deserves misses mea culpa,

mea culpa, mea maxima culpa, too late now plummets back bump
bump bump red whirl blurred colour sound lead limbs bump bump
down down down snap of bone scrape of skin faster and faster
down down down down down top to bottom headfirst backwards
like sledging down the front field smashcrackcrack and just like
that everything

ACKNOWLEDGEMENTS

Thanks and maximum respect to Henry at Ortac for taking a chance on such a gnarly and fucked-up bit of work when others may have fled in terror; a great lad and a great publisher. Big up editor Tom Witcomb who came in to tidy the last bits, grasped instantly what the fuck it was all about and properly put the tin hat on it. Much gratitude to Sue Smith at Brook Smith Funeral Directors in Skipton for her invaluable assistance early on with some seriously grim research; and to Rachel Haines-Clarke for providing critical medical information that had evaded me during a nine month wild goose chase round various luminary institutions. Thank also to Federica Marino-Francis, whose role will be explained At Some Point Elsewhere.

Cheers to comrades Naomi Booth, Wayne Holloway, Dan Jenkins, Sean McKiernan and Pete Keeley for casting their astute critical eyes over the MS at various stages, and to Angharad Hampshire for convincing me to change the title despite my initial misgivings; to James Scudamore whose microscopic observation changed the novel seismically without him even knowing it after he read the first chapter of the very first draft; and to my dark soul sisters Rose Ruane and Terri White, without whom this ride would be a totally different blag.

Props to the gaffer Lee Brackstone, Andrew Gallix at *3:AM* and Jo Murray at *Prospect* for numerous opportunities put my way; to Steve Kirby at Industrial Coast Records for giving me the freedom to road test some of the weirder bits of this in front of incredibly generous live audiences; and to Andy Leach, who was the first person to ever publish my fiction in physical form.

Shout out to my awesome bandmates in Kamień – Emma, Mike, Matty, and my beloved big brother Gav Musto – for putting up with me being a flaky bastard and missing tons of rehearsals when literary life has to take precedence over filthy riffing.

To the real Captain Trips – the prophecy is fulfilled. *Now* who's fucking baffled, eh?!

Thanks to me mam, dad and sister, who shouldn't be anywhere *near* this; if you've ignored us and read it this far, don't say you weren't warned. And, of course, to my wife Ania, Luka and Kita.

Special thanks, again and always, to Jenn Ashworth.

Dedicated to the memory of Brian Whitaker and Our Gary.